IMPOSSIBLY ALIEN

IMPOSSIBLY ALIEN

FREEMAN UNIVERSE
BOOK 5

PATRICK O'SULLIVAN

dunkerron press

A Dunkerron Press™ Book.

BOOKS IN THIS SERIES

Novels:

Quite Possibly Alien

Quite Possibly Allies

Quite Possibly Heroes

Quite Possibly Final

Impossibly Alien

Novellas, Novelettes, and Short Story Collections:

Quite Possibly True

Quite Possibly False

Singularity Sun

1

The Aison Corporation departure lounge swam with flesh. Word had come down from on high that all minor children and adult dependents were being evacuated. The compartment hadn't been designed for crowds, and in particular, crowds of kids. Running, shouting, playing kids. Kids that, since the lockdown, had been storing up energy, and were now releasing it all at once.

Tang could have been on any commercial moon in the League and the compartment would have looked the same: bolted-down seats in groups of five spanning nearly bulkhead to bulkhead, upholstered in a bright orange to deter lingering, carpeted in a threadbare mottled orange that hid stains. All reeking of industrial disinfectant. The overhead lighting was bright and shadowless. The annunciators were brassy and constantly bleating, which seemed like overkill as there was only the one shuttle. The same shuttle everyone in the lounge had originally arrived on. They knew the drill.

Layer a hundred screaming kids on top of that expert-system generated roar and it was hard to hear yourself think, not that he needed to do any thinking. He was done with that. Today Tang was engaged in *doing*.

He watched a dozen games of uthali. Of hide-and-go-seek. Of hana ichi monme. Even before the emergency, there weren't a lot of places for kids to play on an airless moon. The way Tang saw it, you had to be a monster to bring your kid to a place like this. He could see bringing the aged grandparents in their mobility frames or the adult child with motor skills problems, sure. But kids? They belonged on planets where they could grow up strong and straight.

He'd had a kid once. Later he'd had two more. Thought he had, anyway. Now he wasn't sure, and he didn't want to think about it. He sat in the crowded canteen, elbow to elbow with the smarter among his neighbors. He'd been there for more than an hour, watching. Got there early to get a seat. The food wasn't much but at least it didn't come out of a tube. He finished his drink.

When Tang saw faces he recognized in the crowd, he shoved his plate away and pocketed the silverware.

The boarding announcement began. The crowd aimed itself at the shuttle gate. An orderly withdrawal. No panic. No fear. They were shutting down operations in the system. All the top brass and their dependents had already transited to the station—and from there to Sizemore. It was a restructuring. A reordering. It was no longer profitable to keep doing things the old way. Tang had written the press release himself. He was in public relations. He related to the public on behalf of the Jackson Combine Corporation, Aison's principal software subcontractor.

He wasn't part of the evacuation. He'd been summoned to the station by his superiors. As had the faces he'd recognized in the crowd. Fellow Combine employees.

Lamb, a skinny woman, was a workaholic and senior research and development engineer who headed up the

Reformer project. She had the final prototype in her handbag. He knew her but they'd never met. *Reformer* wasn't the sort of project that benefited from public relations. And Lamb wouldn't be the face of the project, even if it was. For that Tang would need someone glossy and sleek. Sallow-skinned fanatics need not apply.

He waded into the crowd, jostling Lamb as they were boarding. She didn't notice. With so many kids and mobility assists, it was just one more bump on the road.

Once aboard, Lamb glanced about. Her gaze washed over Tang and carried on. She was looking for someone. Someone special. Someone like her. She smiled when she spotted him, the shortest flash of a smile. She shuffled through the crowd toward her golden idol.

Tang couldn't do anything about the kids. He liked kids. And he sympathized with the aged. He just couldn't help them. It was too big a task. It had always been too big a task. His boy, his first boy, despised him. He'd made sure of that. He could do that with one kid. Set their feet on a path. He couldn't do that with hundreds. He couldn't even do that with the twins. Maybe if he'd started earlier. By then he was very nearly aged himself, and tired. All his life he'd pushed the boulder up hill. All his life he'd poured energy into the machine.

Hugh, that's how Tang thought of him, leaned casually against the bulkhead between the shuttle's flight deck and the passenger compartment.

All of the seats had been stripped out of the compartment. They were cramming people in, and the shuttle was automated, everything in the system was automated, easy out, glide to the station, easy in, not so much as a hair out of place. There was no traffic to contend with. This was the last shuttle out.

Lamb elbowed in beside Hugh. She gazed up at him, adoringly, Tang recognized, though he doubted others would identify the signs. But he knew them. Knew them like a hover-drone parent. Knew them like a stalker.

Tang waded through the sea of flesh and carry-on luggage toward Hugh and Lamb. His progress wasn't obvious because it wasn't direct. It couldn't be with all the movement in the compartment.

Hugh appeared the opposite of Lamb. Tall, relaxed, languid even, the self-confident face of the *Regulator* project. Hugh hadn't written a line of code or worked an hour of overtime. He was placed atop *Regulator* by a hand from above. One that knew if it ever went public it would need a public face, and a public neck. And that revolutionary passions were most rapidly sated when the blood flowed blue. Hugh had, in his pocket, a data crystal containing the final version of the *Regulator* code. The final and *only* copy.

The purging of all Jackson Combine records in this star system was a planned and scheduled event. Tang had the honor of writing that press release as well. The withdrawal was proceeding, not just on time, but ahead of schedule. He'd met with countless department heads and *pushed* so that he could trumpet that public relations coup. Of course, it would be the legal department, and not public relations, called in later. When it was discovered that all backups shipped off world were lost or corrupted. That there *was* no Jackson Combine Corporation anymore. Every last bit of *Regulator* and *Reformer* code existed nowhere else in the world but on this shuttle.

Tang stepped on Hugh's toe.

Hugh lurched forward, cursing, "Watch your feet, old man!"

Tang gripped Hugh's sleeve, steadying himself. "A thousand pardons," Tang said, and moved slightly apart.

If only that were true. If only he had a thousand pardons. He glanced about the crowded shuttle. The young, the aged, the infirm. He had been all of these at one time or another. He had experienced the ups and downs of a carnival life. And now the fun ride was nearing its end.

Tang vectored toward a viewport, wading through the crowd. A small boy blocked his way. Ten, twelve years standard. A glorious age. Old enough his promise showed, yet young enough to remain blind to a parent's failings. *The age of hopeful delusion.* "What do you see out there?" Tang asked.

"One ship," the boy said. "A superluminal."

"No other shuttles?"

"None."

"No warships?"

"None."

"Perhaps they are hidden by the ring."

"No. We are below the plane of the station. See for yourself."

"I believe you," Tang said.

All commercial traffic had dried up. The system picket remained on patrol. And his greatest concern, that the heavy cruiser, LRN *Vigilant*, might not have departed as scheduled, was no longer a concern.

The shuttle docked, glassy-eyed parents met their charges, and led them away, along the docking ring. Tang did not search the crowd, looking for the boy. He did not let his anger control him. His anger, or his compassion. He'd discovered, as he'd grown older, that emotions were rarely a reliable guide to correct action.

Hugh and Lamb stood together on the ring, gazing at Hugh's handheld computer. They were searching the station's schematic for the compartment where the meeting was to be held.

They would not find it. That compartment did not exist. It seemed, from the description, and from common knowledge, that there *should be* an Aison Corporation reception lounge on the station. There had been at one time, but it had recently been determined to be superfluous to requirements.

He walked up to them and waited for them to notice him. He did not glance at their employee badges. He did not want to be reminded of their names. It was best to continue to think of them by the descriptors he'd invented.

"Go away," Hugh said.

"Wait," Lamb said. She had recognized the Combine employee ID on the lanyard around Tang's neck.

"*You* work for us?" Hugh said. "In software?"

"I work *with* you," Tang said. "In marketing."

"Do you know—" Lamb began.

"You are here for the examination," Tang said. "I know the way."

It was a short walk to what had, until recently, been the reception lounge. It presently resembled unclaimed luggage storage. Mountains of luggage, luggage haphazardly piled, surrounded them.

"Huh," Hugh said. "What sort of person *checks* their carry-on?" There were dozens, perhaps hundreds of backpacks and handbags heaped in amongst the larger bags.

Lamb had begun to slow. She was the smarter of the two. Not clever, or observant, but smart. Very smart and very motivated. He thought it fitting that she observed, firsthand, the inevitable byproduct of her handiwork.

"No," Lamb said. "No."

"We will tidy it up for the brochure," Tang said. "It will appear... organized." An orderly clearance was much more palatable than a pogrom.

"What is this?" Lamb glanced about the compartment, not uncomprehendingly, but unwilling to believe her own eyes. She hadn't imagined there would be *evidence*. That there would be residue left to clean up.

"What did you imagine you were making?" Tang said. "A toy?"

"Where is everyone?" Hugh said.

"Ahead. Follow me," Tang said.

The compartment had a sweaty odor, underlaid with the faint scent of charred meat. It was a large compartment, one designed for entertaining large parties. The deckhead was high, the space expansive, the air handlers oversized.

He led them around the largest pile of luggage, to where the single pile of bodies lay. He did not bother to introduce them to the two men and one woman that stood over the bodies. The head of Aison and her deputy were well known to all. And the security guard, holding an adaptive-pulse-width frequency-modulated handheld beam projector, while relatively anonymous, seemed to monopolize their attention. Tang knew all their names, but again, he preferred to think of them in the abstract. Madam Big, Deputy Hatchet, Officer Stutterer.

Tang glanced from face to face. It was too much for Hugh and Lamb to take in all at once. They were each told to report for an examination. To bring their work product. The obvious and erroneous conclusion was that it was the work product to be examined. That they were possibly up for a promotion if the bosses liked what they saw.

Once the shock of the stutterer aimed at them wore off, Lamb and Hugh glanced at the bodies. These were recognizable as well. Perhaps the pair didn't enjoy the irony of the situation. Tang recognized the elegant bracelet on one of the arms jutting from the pile. It seemed Tang was no longer the most ancient scribe toiling in the scriptorium. He appeared to be the only monk left standing. *Department head, meet department noose.* By his count every last senior executive of the Jackson Combine Corporation littered the deck in front of him.

He watched Hugh's face as the idea sank in. They'd run out

of executives to murder. Now they were coming for middle managers.

Lamb's mouth gaped open, her hand pressed to her lips, her fingers fluttering.

She turned on her heel and ran.

The guard put her down. Center of mass, Tang noted. It would have been a tragedy if she'd had what they were looking for in a breast pocket.

A rivulet of dark smoke rose from her corpse, the odor more of roasted clothing than charred flesh. The guard had the stutterer locked on full power. It didn't make a mess that way. *Searing and sealing.* That was what the sales brochure called the high-power effect.

"Search her," Madam Big said.

"We paid the ransom," Mr. Hatchet said, "And now we want our money and our property back. We won't be cheated twice."

The guard holstered his weapon. He searched Lamb's pockets and found nothing. He grabbed her by the arms and dragged her across the deck. He hoisted her by both arms and heaved her onto the pile of corpses.

The guard retrieved her handbag and dumped it onto a nearby table. He pawed through the contents. The only two items that seemed out of place were a *Reformer* prototype and a spoon from the departure lounge canteen.

"Finally," Madam Big said. "Find the data crystal."

"It's not here," the guard said.

Tang retrieved a data crystal from his pocket and tossed it to the guard. The guard nearly fumbled it. He was right-handed, Tang noted.

"Scan it," Tang said. "It's full of press releases for trivial rubbish. You said to bring my work." He pointed at the top corpse on the heap. "I don't know that woman."

Madam Big stared at Tang.

"Maybe they were in it together." Tang jerked his chin

toward Hugh. "They were standing together on the shuttle. And later, I found them together on the dock."

"I don't know what any of this is about," Hugh said. "Whatever it is, I didn't do it."

"There's been a ransomware attack," Tang said. "Both *Reformer* and *Regulator*. It was covered up. No one at Aison was told. The ransom was paid with money owed Aison. Now they want the products they funded and the money they're owed. They've been squeezing stones, trying to strike blood. Working their way down the corporate ladder."

"You're well informed," Madam Big said.

"I'm in marketing. Who do you think covers these things up? We're the waving hand. Look over here. Not over there."

"None of your superiors knew," Mr. Hatchet said.

"Neither did you," Tang said. "Your inexperience shows." He glanced at the pile. "You started looking in the wrong place. First you kill all the lawyers."

"I'm unconvinced," Madam Big said.

"Then look at the data crystal," Tang said. "I wrote press releases for when we rolled out new user's manuals. For when the customer support desk went ten days without anyone calling in sick. Press releases for every trivial, idiotic event. I was all waving hand, all the time. And we each know when that started, and why. Look at my face and tell me it doesn't show. I've been around."

Something silver and blue crawled out from under the pile of bodies. A cranial implant.

Tang crushed it beneath his heel.

"Search him," Madam Big said.

The guard moved toward Tang.

"Not him." Mr. Hatchet said. "Him."

Hugh was big, and he had a wild-eyed look.

The guard had figured it out. *First, I lead him to the table. Then I tell him to empty his pockets.* That way he didn't have to holster his weapon. A wrestling contest with Hugh would prove sweaty work.

"Empty your pockets.," the guard said.

Hugh emptied his pockets. A handheld. A data crystal. A fork from the departure lounge canteen.

A wave of incomprehension washed over Hugh's face. He stared at the fork in his hand wondering how that had ended up in his pocket. How it had ended up in his hand. Why it had to be a fork, instead of a knife. If it was a knife he could fight back. He was being set up. He was being set up and these people weren't messing around.

The guard noticed the fork.

People holding guns underestimate the fork.

Desperate people staring down a gun barrel don't.

Hugh twisted suddenly.

He stabbed the fork into the guard's eye.

He ran.

Tang much preferred the knife to the fork. It wasn't perfect but it worked best when the enemy didn't see it coming.

He jabbed the butter knife into the guard's kidney. It didn't penetrate as far as Tang liked but when the guard lurched and screamed Tang gripped the guard's neck from behind, kicked his feet out from under him, hammering the fork handle against the table, driving it in.

The guard went down like a sack of gears, his stutterer firing briefly, burning a track across the bulkhead behind the table. Tang had the stutterer in his fist, he scooped up the data crystal he'd tossed to the guard, slamming it into the stutterer's service port. He waited for the upgrade to kick in.

Hugh had disappeared behind Luggage Mountain, but he would be back, and until then Tang had a little speech he wanted to make.

Madam Big and Mr. Hatchet stared at him, stone-faced. It wasn't their faces that he watched, but whatever it was that lurked behind their eyes. Whatever it was that *controlled* them.

"I'm going to walk away," Tang said. "This is not my fight."

"It was you," Madam Big said.

Tang pointed at the table. "There's your *Reformer* prototype. There's your final *Regulator* code. That was the deal. Now where's my ride?"

"On the Ring," Mr. Hatchet said. "Though you won't make it that far."

"He'll be coming down the mountain when he comes," Tang said.

Hugh's lifeless body slammed to the deck a meter from Tang.

When Tang turned, the second security guard was there, atop the pile of luggage. It was perilous footing, and thus the last place someone like Tang would look. The guard was wearing an exo. Exoskeletal armor. The mechanized war-suit's servo-actuated muscles and gyro-stabilizers made him sure-footed. It also made him a big target.

And that was the problem with overthinking things. Tang had been at this so long that the last place he'd expect was the first place he'd look. And whatever it was that had taken over Aison Corporation and its people absolutely knew it was cleverer than Ruleth Tang.

Hubris was his hamartia. If he had a pingin for every time he'd heard that, and over his own grave, no less.

The data crystal popped out of the stutterer and Tang turned the weapon on the exo, not center of mass but on the face shield. He held the trigger firm and counted down from ten. He stopped at two and tossed the handgun away as the exo slammed to the deck beside Hugh.

He gripped Human Shield, and, groaning, tossed 'Hugh' onto the pile atop Lamb to the Slaughter. He didn't need to do that, but it would feel symbolic. Like it was over.

He turned toward Madam Big, Mr. Hatchet, and the starship captain that had joined them.

"Brain," Tang said.

The expat Alexandrian captain had agreed to supply Tang's getaway ride.

"Tang." Brain aimed the hacked stutterer at Tang.

"Bang," Brain said.

He pulled the trigger.

"One," Tang said.

The hacked stutterer exploded in Brain's fist.

Brain wasn't quite dead, but he decided to stay down as Tang planted a foot on his chest. Tang took the command wand from Brain's belt. He glanced at Madam Big and Mr. Hatchet. "This is not my fight. And I won't make it my fight unless you come after me. Understood?"

He didn't wait for an answer. He figured he didn't need to.

He made it to the docking ring.

He made it to the ship.

When he strode on board the crew asked where Emperor Dmitry was. Tang showed them the command rod and they decided they didn't care about Braindead Loser any more than Tang did. As long as Emperor Tang kept the lights on and the grog flowing, they were good to go. They showed him the menu of destinations within the Alexandrine.

Garrison Station.

Kinsey-Severn.

Eliph's Star.

Tang leaned back in the captain's throne and considered the navigational plot. Something was jabbing him in the side, so he emptied his pockets onto the throne's sidecar. He took a short inventory.

A starship command key.

The *Reformer* prototype he'd boosted from Lamb and replaced with a *somewhat* copy.

And a data crystal containing the only fully functional instance of *Regulator* code.

The copy he'd pawned off on Hugh along with the fork was, like Tang himself, *almost* what it seemed.

It wasn't Tang's fight, but he knew a guy. A *buttinski*, who needed all the help he could get. Tang wasn't going soft. It's just that kids were off limits. Whoever, or *whatever*, now controlling Aison had gone too far.

Tang was just one bent shaft. He didn't belong in a war machine. He'd shake it apart.

He could never go straight. It was too late for that.

But it was never too late to do the wrong thing for the right reason.

"Eliph's Star," Tang said. "It sounds... fanciful."

2

A Merchant Captain's great coat was designed for use on a space station's docking ring. Draping to his ankles, it contained active heating and cooling technology that Ciarán mac Diarmuid neither understood nor needed to understand. Every fortnight the coat, like the Overseer's rod tucked beneath the belt of his navy-blue Thin Star Line utilities, indicated its need for recharging.

Both coat and rod were freshly charged, and Ciarán was working on refueling himself. Breakfast in the Freeman sector docking ring canteen with Gilpatrick Moore, Ruairí Kavanagh, and Aoife nic Cartaí was a rare treat. For once Ciarán was able to get a good feed on while the three space-born Freemen jawed. Last time he'd dined with Moore and Kavanagh, he'd nearly starved. All he had to do today was listen and chew.

A fair number of cargo handlers were seasonal workers up from Trinity Surface. The food the ringside canteen dispensed was the best anyone could expect on the station at any price, and also the most civilized. The canteen catered not just to family ship spacers, who thrived on juice bulbs and nutrient pastes, but to normal people as well, who'd grown up eating normal foods—foods that looked and tasted like they were made out of naturally occurring components of a meal, like meat, vegetables, and fruit of the non-juice-bulb variety. Juice bulbs had about as much in common with juice as Ciarán mac Diarmuid did with family-ship spacers.

He'd grown up on Trinity Surface and could live to be a thousand without having the slightest desire for another tube-and-bulb meal. He tucked in one more slice of streaky bacon and what appeared to be a fried egg, over easy, with granulated salt and pepper—condiments that were necessary for a true meal under any star's light. He sipped his *tae* not just because he preferred it, but also because it was likely the last cup he would taste for two years standard. He was outbound and knew it, though that fact was news for Moore and Kavanagh. Aoife nic Cartaí was his boss and could handle the talking. The others poured down shipboard caife and argued per usual.

"You're an idiot to trust Lionel Aster," Ruairí Kavanagh said, stating the obvious. He'd aimed that statement at Aoife, who was only then extruding the nutrient dregs from a tube of something pasty brown and vilely odiferous.

Lionel Aster was the private citizen's name of the Leagueman who was, in his official capacity, Lord Aster, First Space Lord of the Earth Restoration League, or what Freemen called the ERL, when disparagingly speaking, or the League, when informally speaking—or in general. Even the League didn't call itself the Earth Restoration League anymore except on formal contracts; Ciarán believed this a consequence of having thousands of years to restore Earth if they had really wanted to. In all that time they had accomplished no more than he had toward that goal, i.e., absolutely nothing.

Ciarán hadn't even been aware that the ERL could locate Earth, let alone restore it, but it now seemed clear they knew all along where Earth was, and he could have known as well, if he had the slightest interest in Earth.

He didn't. He wasn't *from* Earth, nor were his parents, or grandparents, or great grandparents, and so on. Earth was a place where old stories came from and where people like Lionel Aster and his ancestors had screwed over Ciarán's ancestors so totally they still taught the history of that betrayal beginning in primary school. No one needed to be *reminded* not to trust a Leagueman.

Due to some unfortunate luck, the mechanics of slowship travel, and the later development of superluminal technology, it had been only four hundred years of waking memory since Ciarán's ancestors had left Earth. They had been cryo-ed, packed in with the farm animals, and forgotten about. When the Huangxu Eng stumbled upon them by accident, they decanted one hundred and twenty pregnant women. Those that had survived the process were declared "free men" in the terraforming vessel's log.

The handle had stuck. That they were all women, and they and their children listed as property, and subsequently treated as such, wasn't worth noting. And the less said about the slave revolt that cost the Huangxu Eng a fleet of starships the better. Defrosting Saoirse nic Cartaí and her lot had turned out to be the most expensive mistake in Huangxu Eng history. A Freeman merchant vessel or ten unloading cargo at every port in the wider world was reminder enough.

The departure from Earth had been over six thousand years ago for the League and their neighbors, the Ojin, Huangxu, and Alexandrian Eng. They were all very different people, but they were all related. They each shared a common... something. Not a belief. Opinion, maybe. Conclusion, more likely. And that conclusion?

No one cared about Earth. It wasn't even *yesterday*. In *prehistory* Earth had been destroyed by an asteroid strike. They were all the survivors of that strike. Every sentient being in the universe was a survivor of that asteroid strike. And sentient beings licked their wounds and moved on.

"Ciarán is going to Earth," Aoife said. "It's a done deal."

He rarely corrected his boss in public. But this seemed like one of those times when clarity seemed necessary. He pointed his fork toward Aoife. "Ciarán is fleeing *in the direction* of Earth." And Lionel Aster was paying for him to do so.

Ciarán glanced toward the deckhead and the vast array of sensors dangling there. *From my lips to the stationmaster's ears.* "Ciarán mac Diarmuid promises to depart on the morning tide."

"Metaphorically speaking," Ruairí Kavanagh said. He was a recently minted merchant captain, and Maura Kavanagh's brother. Maura was navigator aboard *Quite Possibly Alien*. Which meant she would soon be, like Ciarán, fleeing in the direction of Earth.

"Is there some other way of speaking?" Gilpatrick Moore said. Moore, like Ciarán, was a merchant captain without a merchant's license. The only way either of them could step inside a Guild Hall was as an employee of another merchant.

Moore was also Truxton's matchmaker. If Ciarán followed the traditional career arc he'd end up as Aoife's matchmaker. And if Aoife followed the traditional career arc she'd end up as The nic Cartaí, should they both live that long, which wasn't likely.

As it was, all of the Big Three Freeman merchant empires were represented here: Truxton, nic Cartaí, and Kavanagh. It wasn't principals, but that was the way it was done. The sharing of information. And the stationmaster, Lucan mac Tír, and his little electronic eyes and ears made a fortunate four.

"We might speak plainly," Aoife said. "It is my thought that Ciarán and Maura and the ship will be safer in the Alexandrine." By 'the ship' she meant *Quite Possibly Alien*, the second-epoch survey vessel Aoife and Maura had excavated from beneath a glacier on Murrisk.

"Safer than what?" Ruairí asked. The Alexandrine was that vast volume of space beyond the League. Demesne of the Alexandrian Eng, it lay across the League from the Federation. Federation traders no longer went there, preferring local trade and the retention of their skin. The Alexandrians had a foul reputation among foreigners.

"Safer than remaining here," Aoife said. "There is only so much one may do."

Moore glanced toward the deckhead sensors. "May do without complications." He meant complications from the stationmaster, who served three masters; the Federation, the League, and the Ojinate. Trinity Station was so named because it hosted the trade hub of Freeman space, leasing space to the Federation's closest trading partners and fiercest competitors. If Aoife's problems arose from the League or the Ojinate, Moore implied, she would be concerned about fallout from above. Fallout Truxton might be able to make go away.

"This is Thin Star Line business," Aoife said. "The end."

"It doesn't need to be," Moore said. "Truxton could make it their business."

"And Kavanagh has an interest," Ruairí said. "Maura is, after all, an heir."

"A disinherited heir," Aoife said.

"Things change," Ruairí said. "They could change, I mean."

Aoife glanced at Moore. "Do things also change with Truxton?"

"Don't be such a hard ass," Moore said. "We're extending a hand. Take it."

"What for?" Aoife said.

"Because you look like you need it," Ruairí said. "The League has tried to abduct my sister three times now. Three times you've barely managed to protect her. One of those rescues seems largely accidental from the evidence I've seen."

"Four times," Ciarán said. There'd been another attempt late the previous night. And it wasn't the League trying to abduct them according to Lord Aster, but a specific faction within the League. One not explicitly linked to the government, whatever that meant.

"Lovely," Aoife said. "Was it the same cabal this time?"

"Seems like it," Ciarán said.

"They want what Maura Kavanagh knows about that ship of yours," Moore said. "And what the lad knows as well."

Ciarán was the lad, according to Mr. Moore. Ciarán liked Gilpatrick Moore; liked him far more than he'd expected he would when Moore had been some distant and deadly rival's fist, and Ciarán had been a merchant apprentice out of his depth and in need of a hand. That Moore had unclenched to help him had been both welcome and surprising. As mentors went Ciarán could do worse. With both Aoife and Moore showing him the ropes, he might not find himself hanged by accident—but on purpose.

"They want the ship," Ciarán said. "Maura and I are just the means to an end."

"Who wouldn't want that ship?" Moore said. "It's unique."

"And disruptive," Ruairí Kavanagh said.

"And sentient," Aoife said. "So it doesn't matter what anyone but the ship wants. It isn't something anyone can own. It's *someone* decent people strive to accommodate. It's as antisocial as Gil, though," she said, nodding at Moore, "and it tolerates fools not at all." She glanced at Ciarán. "It does have its favorites, however. And it desires association."

"With worthies," Moore said.

"By its own lights," Aoife said. "It is as particular as a mong hu."

"It should associate with us," Ruairí said. "The Federation, I mean."

Moore chuckled. "Or maybe just that part of the Federation that gets things done."

"The ship believes it should depart Freeman space and distance itself from the League for a time," Aoife said. "Taking along endangered friends and allies. This disruption in the League can't last forever."

"It can last as long as the League lasts," Moore said. "The Alexandrine's not the place for the job. In order to distance itself from the League in the Alexandrine the ship would first need to cross the League."

"We have a contract in the Alexandrine," Aoife said. "It's a done deal."

Moore nodded. "That being the case you'll want all hands pulling."

"In return for what?" Aoife said.

"What Maura and the lad know," Moore said. "And what the ship cares to share regarding its drive technology and theory of operation. Truxton's has better engineering talent than nic Cartaí."

"And Kavanagh has the mathematicians and research scientists capable of turning theory into something the Federation can replicate. If the ship wasn't unique and Maura and Ciarán not so valuable as assets, the threat would simply disappear."

"You make it sound like the Federation is a thing," Aoife said.

Ciarán understood exactly what she meant. The Freeman Federation was more idea than entity. A mental placeholder for a government.

"He'd like it to be a thing," Moore said. "So he could play with it."

As the smallest of the Big Three, Kavanagh was always trying to rope in partners. And Ruairí was the youngest of the

Kavanagh heirs. He had a modern sensibility regarding custom and contract.

"I wouldn't," Ruairí said. "But if the League splinters we're going to need some structure to grip simply to hang together."

"Bad choice of words," Aoife said.

"Hold together, then," Ruairí said.

"The empty hand grips best," Moore said.

"We are born with two hands for a reason," Ciarán said, quoting from the first page of the *Freeman Manual of Trade. One hand for the ship and one hand for ourselves.*

"Word of a merchant," Moore said. "Grow a third hand, Red, and we'll talk. Until then," Moore said, glancing at Aoife, "There's custom and contract, and that's the offer. We'll stand up a combine, sharing resources, collaborating like we did during the Outsiders war, and whatever comes of it gets shared out equally. A dozen of these second-epoch vessels and your *Quite Possibly Alien* isn't such a target anymore. And your man here, and Red's sister, don't have bullseyes painted on their utilities for all to see."

"Or we go it alone," Aoife said. "Per usual."

"With our best wishes," Ruairí said.

"That," Moore said, which sounded like agreement, but on the lips of an old-school Freeman meant, "I'm not publicly disagreeing, but speak for yourself".

"We're going to—" Aoife began before her gaze veered away from the conversation toward the canteen serving counter. Ciarán followed her gaze with his own.

Lorelei Ellis stood chatting with a nicely turned-out woman grown, who was gesturing for the gray-haired canteen server to come over and meet someone. The three of them might have been daughter, mother, and grandmother, so alike were their gestures and expressions. *Island-born,* he caught himself thinking, which explained the decent food, but which didn't explain the way Aoife had gone all stiff in her seat, or the way Ruairí

Kavanagh had jerked out of his chair and now stood at attention; and, if he owned one, would be holding a cap in his empty fidgeting hands. Ciarán glanced at Gilpatrick Moore who shrugged, and mouthed, "The nic Cartaí with your wan."

"Oh." He meant that the woman with Lorelei was Saoirse nic Cartaí, head of the nic Cartaí family. "She looks spry for four hundred."

"Or six thousand, depending," Moore said.

Saoirse nic Cartaí had been born on Earth and subsequently lost in the cold sleep. Now she still spent most of her time in cold sleep, only being awakened when there were decisions of import to be made. She was Fionnuala nic Cartaí's mother and Aoife nic Cartaí's grandmother. Fionnuala ran the day-to-day operations of the nic Cartaí trading empire. Ciarán glanced about for her.

"Give it up," Moore said. "One nic Cartaí is more than enough woman for the job."

"What job?"

"Any job imaginable," Aoife said. "She shouldn't be awake."

"Should I stand?" Ciarán asked.

"Do you generally stand when you meet a woman?" Moore said.

"I do."

"Then do that and no more, if you want to get on her good side."

"Suppose I wanted to get on her bad side?"

"Then do what young Red there is doing, and act like you've been granted an audience with god almighty."

"Nic Cartaí does own the station we're sitting in and the air we're breathing," Ciarán said.

"She doesn't need us to remind her of that. But it might raise her spirits to know someone has used her blood investment to grow men worthy of the effort."

"I don't think my father has ever met her," Ruairí said. "This is a rare occasion."

"Well, by all means, make her regret it, lad. Do you not have a scraper or two in your own crew?"

"A couple," Ruairí admitted.

"And you steer clear of them," Moore said.

"As often as I can."

"Look her in the eye like a captain. She has no use for servants. Only peers and granddaughters."

Aoife chuckled. "And scant use for those. I wonder who it was that did wake her?"

They were headed toward the table. It seemed that Lorelei had graduated from Nuala nic Cartaí's assistant to that of Saoirse nic Cartaí's attendant. Ciarán waited for Mr. Moore to stand before standing himself to greet the pair.

"You I know," Saoirse said to Moore, before turning her attention to Ciarán, "And you I've heard about," and when she turned to Ruairí said, "Don't you just look all Kavanagh," as she shoved him aside and took his seat.

Ciarán brushed fingertips with Lorelei as she took his seat.

"Sit," Saoirse said to Aoife, who sat. "Spill the cargo girl, and be brief."

Moore took his own seat while motioning for Ruairí and Ciarán to appropriate a pair of chairs from an adjacent table.

"Not you," Saoirse said to Ciarán. "You're to stand behind your wan and remain silent."

Aoife glanced at him. As did Lorelei. This was the sort of no-win situation heroes in ancient stories found themselves in. It was a test, everything in life was a test, and there was no avoiding it. Saoirse nic Cartaí was asking him to choose between the woman he loved and the captain he served. He couldn't stand behind them both.

But she wasn't watching his face for the answer, but Aoife's, and Lorelei's, who weren't looking at him either, but at each other, like rivals.

For him there was no choosing between them. They each held separate places in his heart. He wished they could both see that. And there was only one way they could. He stepped past Mr. Moore to stand behind Saoirse nic Cartaí. Where he could keep an eye on them both, and they on him.

Saoirse nic Cartaí chuckled. "More Ulysses than Solomon, your man."

"He is a native son," Moore said.

"More native than you imagine," Saoirse said.

"Huh." Moore eyeballed Ciarán with one eyebrow raised. "I am informed."

Ruairí scraped a chair across the deck and elbowed in between Lorelei and Aoife.

Saoirse glanced at Ruairí as he settled, and shook her head, and said, "Sliced off the same wheel as the father, I swear it." She glanced at Moore. "Is this the best you can scrape up?"

"His sister's the navigator," Moore said.

"She has to have more than one sibling."

"Red's her champion."

"Did I miss something here?" Ruairí said.

"Undoubtedly you did, and you will," Saoirse said. "We have about two minutes until someone from the League shows up here to arrest a nic Cartaí hand or two. Now talk, granddaughter. What have you done this time?"

3

Aoife explained simply and without preamble that she had accepted a contract with Adderly Bosditch, Stationmaster of Freeport Station in the Contract system. She had agreed to place memorial beacons in the void between Prix Canada and Sizemore, commemorating the death of Bosditch's *Last Stand* and the loss of all hands and passengers.

"Passengers?" Saoirse said.

"Sixty Contract system natives in cryogenic stasis."

Technically they weren't lost in the void but abducted, and murdered later, in Gallarus system. But the crime that led to their deaths occurred in the void, not that Saoirse needed to know that. Adderly wanted to witness the beacon placement and perform a brief memorial service herself. As Aoife intended to do business in Contract system, the agreement represented both good business and a wise investment in amity between future allies.

"Go on," Saoirse said.

"In addition Ciarán has executed a contract as agent of the Thin Star Line. He has contracted with Lionel Aster, in Aster's capacity as Lord Aster, to send a vessel to Earth, and to investigate the loss of League diplomatic and exploratory missions in the Alexandrine. As Earth lies across the Alexandrine from us, these two contracts may be executed by a single vessel."

"Is that your intent?" Saoirse said. "To send a single vessel?"

Aoife nodded. "It is."

"Across the League and *then* the Alexandrine," Saoirse said. "Obviously."

"The ship and merchant?"

"*Quite Possibly Alien.* And Merchant Captain Ciarán mac Diarmuid."

"Who is as much a Merchant as Gilpatrick Moore."

"At least as much," Aoife said. "It's only the Guild Master's enmity standing between Ciarán and a merchant license."

"And in the meantime you will be?"

"Merchant Captaining *Thin Star* and standing up a new mercantile enterprise. It's not easy building a business without help."

"Meaning I could offer you help."

"Meaning you might ask Mother to offer me some help."

"She doesn't want the competition. And she thinks you're a hothead and a do-gooder."

"Is that what you think?"

"I don't need to think. She's said as much to my face."

"You know what I mean."

"I barely know you. But I know your mother, and she's a good judge of character."

"Fine. In that case—"

"She has a lower opinion of hotheads and do-gooders than I do."

"Oh."

"She also said you're an interrupter and neither of us like that."

"I am informed."

"Where were you planning to set up this mercantile enterprise?"

"I *am* setting it up in Contract system. Flagged under the Eight Banners Empire."

"Not anymore. You're hanging your shingle here, and Penelope is going to help you."

"Who?"

"She means Lorelei," Ciarán said, and immediately regretted it.

"I think not," Lorelei said. "I already have a job."

"Think what you want, but your man has the right of it. And you need all the friends you can get, the pair of you."

"He's not *my* man," Lorelei said. "He's outbound, and on a years-long cruise for *her*."

"For *us*," Saoirse said. "You're just the woman footing the bill." Saoirse winked. "Focus on the homecoming."

Lorelei blushed.

"The Ellis of Oileán Chléire is not a hothead, or a do-gooder," Saoirse said. "Your mother approves of her."

Lorelei had been The Ellis since her father's recent murder. Before that she was Laura Ellis to everyone that knew her.

"Lorelei Ellis, the daughter she's never had," Aoife said.

"More like the calculator she's dreamed of." Saoirse grinned. "No offense, Laura."

"None taken, Saoirse."

"That's grand," Aoife said. "A pet name. And I'm still 'the granddaughter.'"

"You have a sister," Saoirse said. "So that makes you 'one of the granddaughters.'"

"The troublesome one," Aoife said.

"The one I can deal with," Saoirse said. "The one who doesn't despise me entirely."

"The ship—" Aoife began.

"Has a mind of its own," Saoirse said. "So I've been told. And it wants to go to Earth."

"Ciarán can explain," Aoife said.

"Speak," Saoirse said.

"The ship wishes to go somewhere distant," Ciarán said. "It isn't particular about where. But with Lord Aster's support we've been able to outfit for the journey far more competently than if we'd been resource constrained."

"How much is he paying?"

Ciarán glanced at Aoife.

"Cost plus," Aoife said. "No set limit."

"Then he expects your man to die in the attempt. And for the ship to be lost."

"That was our conclusion," Aoife said. "Unless he also expects Ciarán to embroil the Federation in a war with the Alexandrians first. Lord Aster believes that if the ship is lost it should be lost in the Alexandrine, where its passing would not... involve the League."

Ciarán glanced at Lorelei. He hadn't told her. There hadn't been a good time.

"Then Lord Aster is a fool," Lorelei said. "To bet against the People."

"He is anything but," Saoirse said. "He is a gambler, and a survivor. One who is right more often than he is wrong. And it isn't the People he's betting against. It's the People's *children*."

"I don't understand," Ruairí said.

"Said the red-headed stepchild." Saoirse eyed Aoife. "Your mother would not have entered into such a contract. Nor would Tom Truxton, or Michaél Kavanagh."

"Aster wouldn't have offered them such a contract," Aoife said. "Not without coming to you first."

"Maybe he did," Saoirse said. "And maybe I told him what I'm telling you. Only a fool or a child would agree to such terms."

"He is acting with incomplete facts," Lorelei said.

"He is if the two of you pitch in together," Saoirse said.

"Together with you," Aoife said.

"It is true, I am in possession of certain information Lord Aster is unaware of," Saoirse said. "Details I am willing to share under those circumstances."

"Details such as?" Moore said.

"A complete itinerary and route for Devin Vale's journey across the Alexandrine. As well as a comprehensive set of charts known to be accurate sixty years ago. A list of known parties active in the region at the time and amenable to commerce with the People and their agents."

"That would be handy," Moore said.

"Talk it up, why don't you, Gil?" Saoirse said. "No merchant sense, at all, at all. It's more than *handy*. It's *indispensable* for the traveler looking for a way home. It changes the odds tenfold, at least."

"You wish," Lorelei said.

"We're supposed to be on the same side," Saoirse said.

"We are," Laura said. "But tenfold is an exaggeration. I've seen the documents."

"And?" Moore said.

"I won't begin entertaining suitors, you eejits. Not for two years and one day, anyway."

Laura crossed her arms and scowled, but Ciarán could tell. It was a good deal. She'd been weepy for the last two weeks and unwilling to say why.

She gazed up at Ciarán and a shadow of a smile crossed her lips. "Come home and bend the bow for me, will you?"

"I swear it," Ciarán said. "If it can be done I will so do."

"It can be done," Saoirse said. "If done smartly. Here come your Leaguemen now, and let me do the talking. Aoife?"

"I'll do it," Aoife said, eying Lorelei. "If she has the guts for it."

"I'm all in," Lorelei said.

"As am I," Saoirse said. "Now not a word, and no killing unless I say so, Gil Moore."

"Am I free to do some killing?" Ruairí said. "Or do I need permission?"

"That is the first intelligent thought I've ever heard from a Kavanagh," Saoirse said.

"It wasn't a thought," Ruairí said. "It was a sarcastic comment."

"A mouth on him, and a spine," Saoirse said. "And it only took four hundred years of evolution."

Ruairí grinned. "Inbreeding, you wanted to say."

"I did," Saoirse said. "But I was feeling charitable. Now shut your gob. And you there, watching my back?"

"No killing," Ciarán said.

"No killing unless I say so."

4

There were five of them, four in military police armbands, the fifth in a Lieutenant Commander's utilities—all sinister as a storm cloud in their blues blacker than a bruise. The four enlisted men carried pulse rifles of recent manufacture. The lieutenant commander sported a sidearm—not a needler, but a directed-energy weapon that had recently become fashionable in the League. It fired in rapid short pulses that could make a mess of flesh but lacked the sustained power to penetrate a hull.

Ciarán wasn't sure what the League called the weapon, but Maris Solon and the Legion of Heroes called it a "stutterer" and no one would touch one, preferring the old-fashioned needlers and razor guns that had been in use for centuries.

Supposedly there was a hack that converted a stutterer into a constant-fire weapon almost as powerful as a pulse rifle. It would work for ten full seconds before it blew the operator's hand off. The hack wasn't field-detectable. Irregular mercenaries like the Legion of Heroes, where promotion was often just one dead or disabled superior officer away, were understandably wary of such modern innovations.

Plus, you couldn't get spares for them anyway. Not without paying a licensed manufacturer an extortionist's fee.

Without the hack they were useless against anyone in exoskeletal armor, what the League called 'exos'. With the hack? A strong temptation existed to count down from nine and take your chances. A needler or razor gun was useless against an exo under any circumstances.

The lieutenant commander's stutterer appeared to have gem-encrusted grips, a fact not lost on Gilpatrick Moore, who chuckled and muttered to himself about guns and gunners going off half-peacocked.

None of the Leaguemen looked happy to be there on a Freeman deck in their shirtsleeves. The League Navy preferred the feel of an exo boot on a Freeman's neck before stating their purpose. Powered armor wasn't banned on Trinity Station, but you needed to post a peace bond with the Stationmaster before togging up. The fee was high and only seventy percent refundable. They could have shown up in hardsuits, but that would be an odd thing to do. And noted down as craven and laughed about by observers later—regardless of the outcome of the confrontation.

Ciarán wished he had a hardsuit. He didn't mind a good laugh at his expense so long as he was alive to hear it. Likewise, all of his friends and comrades could use some protection. He had his Overseer's rod, which could project a force bubble, one that would encompass him and Saoirse nic Cartaí, but leave Lorelei and Aoife on their own. Of course Aoife and Mr. Moore each had rods, and when he glanced at Aoife she tapped the rod beneath her belt and scooted closer to Ruairí. Which left everyone potentially covered except Lorelei, who seemed oblivious to the subtle shifting of positions.

Ciarán tried to imagine some way to keep her safe without leaving Saoirse uncovered.

"Move over behind her," Saoirse said. "I have my own rod."

Ciarán did just that, placing his hands on the back of Lorelei's chair.

"Don't get up and move away," Ciarán said. "No matter what they say."

"I am informed," Lorelei said.

And then they were there, pulse rifles at port arms, two on either side of the lieutenant commander who didn't bother to introduce himself but just launched into his speech.

"Aoife nic Cartaí and Ciarán mac Diarmuid you are under arrest for crimes against the League. Step forward and present yourselves."

"Or what?" Saoirse said.

"I beg your pardon?"

"Beg all you want, but we both know what I asked. They're to come with you or what?"

"The Stationmaster assured us there wouldn't be trouble."

"Did he now?"

"Not precisely," Ruairí Kavanagh said. "I was present with the Stationmaster during his conversation with the captain of LRN *Vigilant*."

"Did I tell you to talk?" Saoirse said.

"You *instructed* me not to talk," Ruairí said. "But I feel I have important information to add."

"The only information I'm interested in is the answer to my question. They're to come with you or *what*?"

The lieutenant commander was only too happy to ignore Saoirse. "Then you, sir, understand I have proper authority to arrest these people and escort them to the League sector."

"The stationmaster said, 'I can't stop you'," Ruairí said. "And that's all he said."

"There, you see? Now—"

"That statement doesn't imply permission," Ruairí said. "It's nothing more than a comment about the Stationmaster's perception of the extent of his authority."

"Ruairí, you should shut up now," Moore said.

"Normally I would agree," Ruairí said, "But I promised the stationmaster I'd straighten this out. You see, he couldn't stop you because I'd withdrawn Kavanagh support of his appointment as stationmaster. It's rather like I'd ordered him not to stop you. It's a more complicated procedure than that, of course, because we don't have the formal mechanisms of government. Only contracts and customs that need to be massaged into shape before every job.

"What could be accomplished in the League with a simple authoritative command requires hours or even days of inefficient wrangling and manipulation. It's tedious, and time consuming, so you'll have to forgive me if I cut to the chase. You see," Ruairí said, placing an instantly recognizable, small silver box on the table. He pressed the single button on the device and four of the five Leaguemen began to writhe and scream on the deck. He had to shout over the effects of the implant reprogrammer. "We've detected emissions of a very disturbing nature from the League sector!" He placed another instantly recognizable device on the table. An implant extractor. "Separating one of you from the herd required some doing!"

The lieutenant commander drew his handgun.

Ruairí Kavanagh shot him in the eye with a stutterer. As the man fell, Ruairí shot him in the other eye.

"What part of no talking and no killing did I not make clear?" Saoirse shouted.

Kavanagh stood, and crossed to the lieutenant commander, shooting him in one ear, then the other. "The weapon is set on low power. I've only blinded him and rendered him deaf."

Ruairí shut the implant reprogrammer off, and the screaming instantly stopped.

"Pile your guns up over there," Kavanagh said, pointing. "Then proceed to the League sector. You may inform your captain that Lieutenant Commander..." Ruairí toed the man over to read his name patch. "Steyr. Will not be returning to duty."

When the Leaguemen had retreated Ruairí glanced at the deckhead. "Are the communications channels still active?"

The stationmaster's voice roared from the nearest overhead annunciator. "They are."

"Good," Ruairí said. "I'm going to extract the implant now, and we'll see what it does."

"It's a bomb," Ciarán and Aoife both said at the same time.

Aoife continued. "If it's an Ixatl-Nine-Go implant then it has a bomb in it."

"A surprisingly explosive bomb for its size," Ciarán said.

"This design is similar but different," Ruairí said.

"Who is this *we* that will take it and see?" Saoirse said.

"Kavanagh, obviously. We're not all accountants and moneylenders. Some of us have to actively manage our portfolio companies. And on occasion?" He locked gazes with Saoirse. "We need to liquidate them."

"You're saying you made an Ixatl-Nine-Go clone?" Aoife said.

"As I said, a portfolio company exceeded its research-only mandate. It appears they entered into a joint development agreement with the League without approval."

"An agreement with the League government?" Aoife said.

"With some shell organization based in the League. It could be the government or not. We're attempting to determine precisely who is providing funding. Not to fear, we are on top of it."

Ruairí dragged the man away a distance before plunging the extractor in.

"Disconnected," the overhead annunciator said.

"Right, well, it was worth a chance. Tell Michaél to get a crash cart down here."

"And the Kavanagh support?"

"Restored in its entirety, Mr. mac Tír, and many thanks to you."

"Never darken my hatch again, Ruairí Kavanagh," the stationmaster said.

"Not unless I need to." Ruairí took his seat as if nothing had happened. He popped the implant out of the extractor and worked the power-down sequence one-handed.

It looked like an Ixatl-Nine-Go although the power-down routine was slightly different.

"Who was it communicating with?" Ciarán asked.

"Who or what," Ruairí said. "We're working on that."

"That's grand," Aoife said. "I'm glad for you."

"You're an accountant?" Lorelei said.

"I... could be," Ruairí said. "Do you fancy accounting?"

"Very much so," Lorelei said. "Numbers show us the shape of the world, stripped of all the lies."

"Exactly," Ruairí said. He glanced at Ciarán as he scooted his chair closer to Lorelei's. "How long are you off for now, Mr. mac Diarmuid?"

"Two years," Lorelei said. "Maybe forever."

"That is unfortunate," Ruairí said. "I predict there will be no end to the action here, once we get this device back to the lab and under test."

"I'd like to see that," Lorelei said.

"Then so you shall."

"I can't wait," Lorelei said.

"Excellent," Ruairí said.

"You'd think so, wouldn't you?" Saoirse glanced at Ciarán and winked.

Lorelei fancied accounting and hated Freeman accountants. She thought that people ought to use numbers to tell the truth and not to obscure it. Clearly she had shared that opinion with Saoirse nic Cartaí, or Fionnuala nic Cartaí had. It's why Nuala had hired Lorelei in the first place. She had a way with numbers and a purity of purpose when it came to them. It made her seem simple and easy to manipulate. It also made her extraordinarily difficult to deceive. If it seemed like Lorelei was being used it was because she had chosen to permit it.

Saoirse wound down the meeting while they waited for the crash cart. She ordered Ruairí to disperse the crowd his antics had precipitated. While he was gone Saoirse and Lorelei had a rapid-fire discussion in nic Cartaí family hand cant, most of which Ciarán could follow because he and Aoife used the nic Cartaí dialect for their silent discussions. He glanced at Gilpatrick Moore who seemed to have no problem following along, either.

The net was that Ruairí Kavanagh now had a spy in his camp, at least until after this upcoming lab visit. The idea of an Ixatl-Nine-Go variant was chilling for any number of reasons. That it might be loose in Freeman space unnerving. He would have to tell the ship's minder, of course, but that was for another day.

"You will be careful," Ciarán whispered in Lorelei's ear.

"I will take precautions, if that is what you mean."

Ciarán chuckled. "It isn't."

"Good. Because he's not even remotely my type."

"You mean because he's clever, and attractive, and wealthy."

"Exactly," she whispered, imitating Ruairí. "You're everything he's not."

5

Ciarán cycled the airlock and rested his chin on the crown of Lorelei's head. She could have rested her chin on Aoife's or Saoirse nic Cartaí's crown, and Lorelei was short for an island woman. When the lock opened, he followed them through and into the bog-standard longboat. Saoirse nic Cartaí said she wanted to tour Aoife's flagship. Ciarán figured what she really wanted was a private conversation the stationmaster couldn't overhear. A longboat was as good a spot as any.

"Take us out," Aoife said to the pilot.

"Will do," the pilot said. "Belt in ladies."

Ciarán cringed. He'd forgotten Janie Byrne was Aoife's new pilot. He belted in beside Lorelei.

"You can come ride up front with your auntie," Janie said.

"Thanks," Ciarán said. "I'm good here."

"Auntie?" Aoife said.

"Janie is Ciarán's aunt," Lorelei said. "Her mother is Ciarán's grandfather's youngest sister."

"She seems so..."

"Reckless and irresponsible?" Ciarán said.

"Youthful," Aoife said.

"She's two years younger than Ciarán," Lorelei said. "They don't get on."

"Shocking," Aoife said, and laughed.

"Punch it," Saoirse said.

"Waiting for clearance from the stationmaster, ma'am," Janie said.

"Why?" Saoirse said.

"Regs say I'm supposed to."

"Why?"

"So I don't run into anyone, and no one runs into me."

"Is there anyone around for you to run into?"

"There isn't."

"You're sure?"

"She isn't," Ciarán said.

"Dead cert, ma'am."

"Then punch it."

Janie glanced at Aoife. "Merchant Captain?"

"Don't encourage her," Ciarán said.

Aoife chuckled. "When it is safe to take us out—"

"On it," Janie said, and punched it.

6

"That was some rivet-popping acceleration," Saoirse said.

Janie grinned. "Thank you, ma'am." They'd gone ballistic on a course toward *Thin Star*. Aoife didn't believe in paying for dockage at the station. She much preferred a parking orbit slot. They'd barely missed an inbound longboat when they'd broken seal with the docking ring and Janie boosted outbound.

Saoirse smiled. "Why don't you suit up and go out and check the hull integrity?"

"Ma'am?"

"While you're out there I'll handle any incoming messages from the stationmaster. And Aoife can keep an eye on the scanners."

"We call them sensors nowadays," Aoife said.

Saoirse nodded. "Good you do, and they need an eye just the same, don't they?"

Aoife chuckled. "They do. You know there hasn't been a riveted longboat in service for three hundred years, Grandmother."

Saoirse patted Aoife's sleeve. "I'm glad to know it. They were rubbish. Nonetheless, I'm concerned about the hull integrity, and I'd like your pilot to go check it."

"The hull's fine," Janie said. "You're just trying to get rid of me."

Saoirse frowned. "Are you a mind reader?"

"I'm not," Janie said.

"You're a pilot. In charge of a vessel, its passengers, and crew."

"I am."

"I've expressed a concern. Is there no regulation that states your responsibilities under such circumstances?"

"There isn't."

"Would you like there to be one?"

"I wouldn't," Janie said.

"Neither would I," Saoirse said, as Janie unbelted and began to suit up.

"Will you talk about me while I'm out there?" Janie asked.

"Will you do a thorough and professional job? Taking your time and doing it right?"

"I will."

"How long will that take?"

"Twenty minutes."

"Then we won't have time to talk about you. Any less than that, though, and we will."

"I am informed," Janie said.

"Finally," Ciarán muttered.

Janie elbowed him in the temple on the way toward the airlock.

Saoirse frowned. "Would you like go out on the hull and help her, Merchant Captain mac Diarmuid?"

"I would, very much so," Ciarán said.

"Tough," Saoirse said as the airlock cycled. "Now let's get down to it."

7

Saoirse held out her hand, a data crystal on her palm. "All I've offered and more. We'll do this in the old style, our word alone our bond. I don't want Truxton or Kavanagh involved. Or anyone else. This remains a deal between nic Cartaí and the Willow Bride Folk."

Ciarán rubbed the corner of his eye. "The who?"

"When we arrived here almost four hundred years ago," Saoirse said, "There were people already resident. They called themselves the Willow Bride Folk, and they looked exactly like your wan." She nodded in Lorelei's direction. "They helped us and we helped them, and some of our people, tired of life on the run, chose to live amongst them. Many of my own crew were numbered in that lot. Powers. Murtagh. Names you'd recognize.

"We were a rough and tumble bunch after years of fighting the Huangxu Eng. And there were resentments and feuds brought with us. The Willow Bride Folk didn't want much to do with us after those ancient disagreements surfaced. If you look at the old charts, you'll see your Oileán Chléire listed as 'Keep Clear Island'. That's the arrangement we had for most of our history together, until the Outsiders war. Then we needed all the help we could get, and Nuala and I negotiated a deal with the islanders. They could work nic Cartaí vessels for hard currency, one-year standard contracts, and we'd continue to leave them as alone as they wanted us to. There'd been a population explosion on the island and people were starving."

"But we've been going back and forth to the mainland for centuries," Ciarán said.

"But not up to the station, or onto the family ships. That was our arrangement with the mac Manus. No islanders to go off world. Ever."

Ciarán glanced at Lorelei. "The only mac Manus I know is the Gant's herdsman."

"He's the one," Saoirse said. "King Manus mac Manus of the Willow Bride Folk, he called himself."

"And that's who you dealt with earlier." Ciarán said. "When you made first contact with the Willow Bride Folk."

"The same man," Saoirse said. "That's how I knew who to talk to the second time. I went to his croft and met with his dog. And the dog went and fetched him."

Ciarán laughed out loud. "That's ridiculous."

"Molly," Lorelei said.

"That was the dog's name," Saoirse said. "It could understand what I wanted but don't ask me how."

"He's dead," Lorelei said. "Mac Manus."

"I'm sorry to hear that," Saoirse said. "He was an interesting fellow. And a good neighbor."

"He was ancient," Ciarán said. "Even when I was a boy. But he wasn't any king. And he didn't look four hundred years old."

Saoirse chuckled. "I hope I don't either."

"I doubt he had a cryo chamber," Ciarán said.

"I'm certain he did," Lorelei said. "I believe we've played ignorant long enough."

"What do you mean?" Ciarán said. "I'm not pretending. I've never heard *any* of this before."

"You didn't have a need to know," Lorelei said.

"And you did."

"I am his daughter, after all," Lorelei said. "Have you forgotten I was adopted by The Ellis?"

"You are old man mac Manus's daughter." Ciarán said.

"In part," Lorelei said. "Enough that I can speak for the Willow Bride Folk."

Ciarán shook his head. "Unbelievable. This is waking the dead."

"I agree," Aoife said. "I fail to see the point—"

"Seamus Reynard," Saoirse said. "He informs me he sent you a missive."

"The Indecent Proposal," Lorelei said.

"Indeed," Saoirse said. "I very much wish for Nevin Green to take the Oath. I wish Green to understand that, while this might seem like a risky proposition for him, it is nothing new to us. That we are good neighbors and people of our word. That he and his kind would be better served in alliance with the People of the Mong Hu than with the League. Twice now we have proven the strength of our bond. No fancy League title can match the hand of friendship."

"You wish the Willow Bride Folk to reveal themselves to this Green," Lorelei said. "And to vouch for the Federation."

"Vouch for nic Cartaí and the People of the Mong Hu. The Federation is a topic for another day."

"There is nothing to reveal," Ciarán said. "And nothing to vouch for but your unsubstantiated claim."

"Ciarán," Aoife said. "Moderate your tone."

"That is my moderate tone. We live the Oath. We do not wake the dead."

Saoirse closed her fingers around the data crystal. "Then I suggest the pair of you islanders have a teary goodbye. Because it's the last you'll see of each other for all time. You need what I have to offer to make it home."

"Grandmother—"

"Silence," Saoirse said.

Lorelei leaned forward in her seat. "They said you were hard. Cruel, even. That I would be unwise to treat with you."

"I don't know who *they* are," Saoirse said.

"I'm certain you do," Lorelei said. "For I doubt you could name one person who would say otherwise."

"I can name one," Aoife said.

"We will see," Lorelei said. "I will do as you ask. And for that you will give me three things I want. And if you betray me, it will be the ruin of you and of your kind."

"Lorelei," Ciarán said. "Stop."

"Let's hear your terms," Saoirse said.

"I demand that data crystal and access to all nic Cartaí data in perpetuity."

"Agreed."

"I demand Fionnuala nic Cartaí name me apprentice and extend nic Cartaí protection to me and mine for seven years and one day."

"Nuala doesn't take apprentices," Aoife said. "She wouldn't take her own children—"

"Agreed."

"You can't speak for—"

"I said silence, girl. I can and I will, so zip it."

"I demand that Saoirse nic Cartaí name me heir to all that is hers, such payment due in full upon her death."

"That's absurd," Aoife said.

Saoirse nodded. "You are certain mac Manus is dead?"

"Kirill Olek murdered him," Lorelei said. "His remains were discovered not long ago."

"I see."

"This is madness," Aoife said. "You can't—"

"She can," Lorelei said. "That was the deal she made with mac Manus."

"It was, and again, agreed," Saoirse said. "Pending verification of mac Manus's death."

"And so the wheel turns," Lorelei said. "You may ask me three questions."

Saoirse licked her lips. "Was mac Manus human?"

"He was," Lorelei said.

She glanced at Ciarán. "Is he?"

"In part," Lorelei said.

"Are you?"

"Stop," Ciarán said. "You must not—"

"Don't you see?" Lorelei said. "It was the deal. Whichever survived the longest inherited from the other. All that mac Manus owned is now Saoirse nic Cartaí's. And when it ceases being hers it will be mine, and all she owns with it."

"You can't do this," Aoife said.

"I have done it," Saoirse said. "You'll thank me later."

"I doubt that," Aoife said.

Ciarán wasn't sure. "What did mac Manus own?"

"An aisling," Lorelei said. "And a dog."

An aisling was a very specific type of dream or vision. It wasn't anything tangible, and it wasn't even *intangible* without the dreamer. It could be written down, like a poem, but Ciarán didn't think that was what Lorelei meant. She meant he had a vision of the future. A dream for his people.

"And what does Saoirse nic Cartaí own?"

"Obligation," Saoirse said. "And a cryo chamber. Now tell me about this aisling. And be quick about it."

"Is that your third question?" Lorelei said. "Or the other."

Saoirse looked Lorelei up and down. "This. Anything I need to know about you I can learn by watching you."

"That is the way of the People," Lorelei said.

"And of the Folk," Saoirse said.

"It is," Lorelei said.

The airlock cycled and Janie Byrne stormed through, tossed her helmet into the crash webbing of an empty seat, and slid behind the piloting controls.

"It's only been seventeen minutes," Saoirse said.

"Janie sniffled and wiped her nose. "And you said you'd watch the sensors and monitor the comms. But you didn't and now there's a honking-big League shuttle bearing down on us and, see here, the stationmaster has priority hailed us two score times."

"There were no alarms," Saoirse said.

"I keep them turned off. If I didn't, I wouldn't get a wink of sleep." She sniffled again and wiped her nose on her sleeve. "He was my uncle you know," Janie said. "And Molly was a beauty. Rigel's going to be crushed when he hears."

"You were listening in," Ciarán said. "From the airlock."

"It's a double hull," Janie said. "You can't listen in from anywhere else. It's been my experience, whatever people say, they always end up talking about me."

Aoife eased into the first officer's seat. She glanced at the sensors display. "Put the stationmaster on the comm."

"That tears it," Lucan mac Tír said. "I've a station to run and no time to be wasting on you and your spoiled brats. Now answer this hail, Saoirse nic Cartaí, or I'm done with you and yours."

"Mr. mac Tír. This is Aoife nic Cartaí. How can this spoiled brat help you?"

"You could drop dead, the lot of you, and a third of my headache gone. Is your granny there?"

"She is," Saoirse said.

"I've got a riot here, in the League sector, a fight between the Navy and the Consulate staff. The captain of that over-sized cruiser lashed to the ring is demanding I cut off the environmentals to flush the diplomats and spies out. He has crew crouched outside the exits and they're togged up in exos."

"Did you fine him?" Saoirse said.

"Very funny. The Kavanagh handed over the captain's executive officer to the Consular staff an hour ago, alive and walking. According to this captain he got his man back in a body bag. For now he's blaming his own lot. But it's just a matter of time until Aster's Army cobbles together a plausible lie and ends the siege with a finger pointed at Kavanagh. I'm not having Leaguemen armored up in the Freeman sector. I'll flush them out the airlocks before that happens."

"Fine," Saoirse said. "Do what you need to."

"I'd prefer it if you'd talk them down."

"I'm done talking to those people. What's this vessel bearing down on us?"

"Shuttle from the same hull. They've an ironlanger to see that mac Diarmuid eejit and your pampered princess in their grip."

"For?"

"Her, for tax evasion and violating salvage laws on Murrisk. Him for a long list of crimes. They're saying he robbed some museum on Pandora. They found some hardhands of his at the scene."

"There are no salvage laws on Murrisk, and no tax," Aoife said. "And Ciarán didn't rob any museum."

"It's a retroactive law just passed," mac Tír said. "They're claiming the vessel you dug up as League property to settle the lien. And only an idiot would imagine that plowboy oaf could find a museum, let alone rob one. It's more likely someone clever stole his gloves and framed him. But so long as they have a head that meets specifications for the noose, they'll be happy."

"They want to hang a Freeman," Saoirse said.

"They want to make an example of one and aim their

people's ire outward, and away from their own fumbling. And they want that vessel, don't ask me why."

"We're going to need maneuvering room. Route local traffic away from us and keep it clear."

"Already done. You can't have a mind to fight them."

"I don't intend to fight them."

"Good. If you hand them the plowboy that should hold them. I'll keep the lights on in the consulate while Nuala gets an injunction against extradition pending a judgement regarding this law."

"Is she there with you?" Saoirse said.

A woman's voice replied, Fionnuala nic Cartaí's, it seemed. "Mother—"

"Listen," Saoirse said. "I want you to name The Ellis as your apprentice."

"I don't take apprentices. Everyone knows that."

"You didn't take apprentices. And now you do."

"I will," Nuala said. "Is Aoife with you?"

"She's fine. It will all be fine. Do you recall, when you were a wee girl, and I told you about Junh and the River, and how when the men had chased him and the bear to the river they found a single set of tracks?"

"Bear tracks. Because the bear had followed Junh, and had walked in his footsteps."

"That's what a mother tells a child," Saoirse said.

"Because the bear ate Junh," Nuala said. "I figured it out later."

"That's what I thought. Junh was human, and weak, and the bear was a beast, and powerful, and could never eat its fill. We were Junh, and when we fought the bear it wasn't to win but to survive."

"And we did survive," Nuala said.

"We did. By becoming tigers. Because a bear is no match for a tiger."

"Why are you telling me this now?"

"Because you asked why I woke." Saoirse licked her lips. "I received a message. From The mac Manus, I thought."

"He's dead," Nuala said. "I meant to tell you next time you woke."

"I know that now. Anyway, this message said, 'The bear carried Junh' and that was it."

"Why would the bear do that?" Nuala said.

"That's what I wondered," Saoirse said.

"Because the bear was strong, and sensible, and Junh was clever and quick," Janie said. "Everyone knows that."

Saoirse stared at Janie. "That idea hadn't occurred to me."

"How else was Junh going to survive?" Janie said. "He was just a man. One without a single friend in the world. And the bear was hated and feared. But it wasn't the bear chasing Junh. It was other men. Men who would kill both Junh and the bear if they could. Together they were strong. Separately they were prey. Do you people lack wise mothers to explain this to you?" Janie glanced at Lorelei. "Tell her."

"She did," Saoirse said. "When I awakened."

"The Ellis woke you?" Nuala said.

"It was the question that woke me," Saoirse said. "But it was the girl that raised it. Why would a bear do such a thing?"

"Because Junh asked," Janie said.

"Politely," Lorelei said. "And at the appropriate time."

"Ciarán hates Junh," Janie said.

"I don't hate Junh. They're foreign stories and needlessly opaque. Our own seanscéalta are better. Now if I'm to be handed over for a hanging I'd like to know it. That shuttle is braking to match vectors."

"In seanscéalta it's people fighting people," Janie said. "In The Book of Junh it's Junh fighting the darkness."

"It's Junh fighting Junh," Lorelei said. "The darkness is *part* of Junh."

Ciaran glanced about the compartment. There was an armed League shuttle inbound and Lorelei and Janie and the entire nic Cartaí hierarchy were arguing about a religious book from the Ojinate. A text, or lack thereof, that scholars in the Ojinate didn't even agree on. There were two competing Books of Junh, and one was just an empty cover, and a couple blank pages. The rest of the pages were supposedly torn out and burned by Junh himself.

If he ever told anyone about this, they wouldn't believe him. Not even Junh would believe him. In the stories Junh was accounted a sensible man. Junh would be on the comms, deescalating the situation. Either that or boosting outbound for the tripwire.

"Mother?" Nuala said.

"I'm going to be up for a while this time. Have them air up my apartment. And Nuala?"

"Anything a bear can do a tiger can do better."

"That's my girl. Lucan, I want space between the League sector and the Ojin and our own people. Get those nearby vessels off the ring and evacuate any compartment within the drive failure radius of that hull."

"I'll have to notify the League," mac Tír said.

"Whatever's in your contract," Saoirse said. "There's no need to tiptoe or whisper."

"Welcome back to the living."

"Same to you. Nic Cartaí out." Saoirse unbelted. "Get up girl and give me the controls."

"I don't work for you," Janie said, "And this isn't your longboat."

"Aoife," Saoirse said.

"She's right. Belt in, Grandmother. If you want something done say the word."

"There will be blood," Saoirse said.

"There always is with Janie at the yoke," Ciarán said. "Even on the station to surface shuttle."

"Belt in means belt in," Janie said. "Now what's the flight plan?"

"Are they hailing us?"

"Threatening us is more like it. Nonstop."

"Let them. They'll want to lock up with us. Let them do that too."

"They'll come aboard in exos," Aoife said.

"I certainly hope so," Saoirse said.

Ciarán glanced at Lorelei. She smiled when she noticed him watching. "She's rather fierce for her age."

"She's not that much older than me," Ciarán said.

"I meant Saoirse."

Ciarán glanced at Saoirse. She was a fierce talker, no doubt. But he'd seen Aoife in action.

"Is there anything we're not going to let them do to us?" Janie said.

"They won't be taking our Ulysses. But we'll give them a look up our skirts before we tell them."

"What does that mean?" Lorelei said.

"It means hang on," Ciarán said.

8

Locking up with a longboat in free space was a lot different than at a station. A longboat had two airlocks, one forward and one aft, and docks built to accommodate them allowed the simultaneous use of both. One was traditionally called the egress lock and the other the ingress lock because that was how cargo was loaded and unloaded. One lock for outgoing cargo and one for incoming. An experienced crew could load and unload a longboat in minutes using fast pallets. The hatches were oversized—and the weak points on the hull. A standard League access tube wouldn't mate up. There was always a gap, so the work was done in hardsuits or, as now, in exos.

"They don't have the tube extended," Janie said.

Aoife had visual on the shuttle. "It's a planetary occupation shuttle. The stern opens into a ramp."

"I'd use the tube," Janie said.

"Is it armed?" Saoirse said.

"Heavily," Aoife said.

"Good. Call out when you see the ramp open and the exos beginning to emerge.

"Jamie," Saoirse said, leaning forward to eyeball the pilot. "When Aoife calls out hail them and tell them to stand off. We're experiencing flight control issues."

"It's Janie," she said.

"Good to know. Suppose I just call you Ace."

"I'd like that."

"I see them," Aoife said.

"Hailing," Janie said.

"Swing us around on thrusters, Ace. Aim the torch up the ramp."

"They're scrambling," Aoife said.

"Punch it, Ace."

"Captain?" Janie said.

"Belay that," Aoife said.

"I asked for the controls, Granddaughter. Next time you'll obey me."

"There won't be a next time." Aoife toggled the main drive active—

And punched it.

9

"That was something," Janie said. "I knew they should have gone with the tube."

"It wouldn't have mattered," Saoirse said. "Their impact shielding would have been down either way. Scan the debris field. See if any of those exos are still intact."

"There are no survivors," Aoife said.

"I know that," Saoirse said. "What I want is a trophy I can dump on the League consulate steps. Burning up a League shuttle might be an act of war, but attempting to board a Freeman longboat in powered armor surely is. I don't want them claiming they were rendering aid unless I agree they were."

"They won't," Aoife said.

"They will," Saoirse said. "That's why I had Ace send the hail. There has to be an exit with honor. That vessel's captain's career is over. But it can end there."

"It won't end there," Lorelei said.

"I've got one on the sensors," Janie said. "An exo."

"How crispy is it?"

"Hard to say."

"Mac Diarmuid. Go out and get it or I will."

Ciarán glanced at Aoife. She seemed as appalled as he felt. "I will," he said, and unbelted.

"Make sure it's dead before you drag it inside. Unless you want to watch me kill it."

"I'm not murdering a prisoner," Ciarán said. "And I'm not letting anyone murder prisoners."

"You let me burn down a shuttle full of Leaguemen."

"To my shame."

"Is this your argument? It would be better if they'd taken and hung you. If they'd taken my granddaughter. Claimed her vessel. Stripped it to the cross frames to plumb its secrets. Murdered or enslaved its sentience. Used what they learned to come after you and yours. Me and mine. After all Freemen. After the Ojin. The Huangxu, much as I detest them for what they did to us.

"Do you know, I hate Junh as well because your wan is right. The book of Junh is about Junh. The darkness Junh fights is inside Junh. He's a navel-gazer of the first order. Our people's stories aren't about us. They are about our debts and our mistakes out here, in the world. I will not make the same mistake twice. Once a tiger always a tiger. If you wish to dismount I suggest you do it now. Because henceforth there is no getting off until we reach the farthest shore."

"We do not wish to dismount," Lorelei said. "We wish to write a new saga together. One that is not about our debts or regrets. One that is not about us at all, but about our children, and their shared future."

"I tried that once," Saoirse said.

"Try again," Lorelei said. "Go get the body, Ciarán. If there's a human yet in it, we will try to save it."

"Hail the station, Ace," Saoirse said. "Tell Lucan mac Tír to pinion that League warship to the dock. Have him tell Nuala to file a formal complaint with the Consulate. Piracy, I think. Armed men, attempting to board without permission."

"On it," Janie said.

Ciarán began to suit up.

"No quitting," Saoirse said.

"None," Lorelei said.

"Good. Then here is the plan. I'll tell the Consul that we will hand over Ciarán mac Diarmuid for a fair trial but not for some lynching of convenience. And Aoife will dispute these salvage and tax claims, as will nic Cartaí and the Federation as a whole. We can't have retroactive laws apply to us. Else we might as well not do business in the League at all.

"Until such time as a court can rule on the legality of the law, however, we are willing to impound the vessel *Quite Possibly Alien*. We'll even deliver it to Brasil Yards for safe-keeping by a neutral party. That should suffice to restore the appearance of peace. We'll forward mac Diarmuid to the regional administration center in Sizemore on the way to Brasil."

"You know that will never happen," Aoife said.

"I don't *know* that, else it would be a lie," Saoirse said. "I do, however suspect the ship would prove an unwilling participant, and would say as much. As it is a sentience, I can't compel it to do my will. And while I think my granddaughter is a good judge of character, and Mr. mac Diarmuid appears honorable from a distance, there is this ongoing business with the Guild Master. It wouldn't be surprising to anyone if he turned out to be the sort to hare off with the fugitive ship in some misguided attempt to prove his worthiness to the Merchant Guild. He is, after all, on the hook for the execution of a contract with Lord Aster. It seems perfectly consistent with his character that he would wish to see that through. If the League wanted him and the vessel bad enough, they would know precisely where to find them."

"I like it." Ciarán pulled on his second hardsuit gauntlet. "It does exactly what we need it to do."

"You'll look like a criminal," Janie said.

"The ship and I will look like fugitives. See if you can get a bounty put on us, dead or alive."

"You're joking," Aoife said.

"He isn't," Saoirse said. "And it's a good idea. Don't kid yourself there isn't a bounty on them already. This way it would be public, and there might be competition to contend with. We want every eye in the League focused on that pair and that pair alone. Unless they're staring at one another through targeting reticules. What we don't want them doing is watching us here. In fact, I think I'm going to kick the League off the station. Maybe the Ojin as well, but then maybe not. Are they still all Ojin or Eight Banners Empire now?"

"I'm not sure," Lorelei said.

"You and Nuala talk it over. We'll come up with some pretext if required."

"To what end?" Aoife said. "And what am I supposed to do during all of this?"

"Carry out your contracts and stand up your mercantile house. Nuala's new apprentice will help you." Saoirse glanced at Lorelei. "Do you trust Ace?"

"Janie? We're not close, if that's what you mean."

"Trust her to keep a secret," Saoirse said.

"We're going to have to," Lorelei said. "Either that or kill her."

"Let up, Laura," Janie said. "You know I'm like a vault. And it's not a time to be funny. Look out the viewport if you don't believe me."

"I trust her," Lorelei said.

"Good. Would people believe it if she crashed a longboat into a lake?"

"They wouldn't believe it," Ciarán said. "They'd expect it."

"Outside with you," Janie said. "You can leave the helmet here."

"It's true," Lorelei said. "Janie has a rep."

"I said it's not a time for joking," Janie said.

"Good. Then a crash landing is what she'll do," Saoirse said. "The pair of you need to be aboard so when Nuala overreacts and sends a massive recovery team it won't look contrived."

"Why would she want to do that?" Aoife said.

"Did I not say? Lorelei here says there's a second-epoch starship down there. One that isn't occupied."

"Initialized," Ciarán said. "'It isn't initialized' is the proper phrase for a vessel absent an active sentience."

"Either that or terminated," Lorelei said.

"Oh," Ciarán said. "That's right. Let's think cheerier thoughts."

"You may if you like," Lorelei said.

"Are they always like this when together?" Saoirse asked.

"He's a know-it-all," Janie said. "And she's a downer. It's why they don't have any friends but each other."

"And all this time I thought it was body odor," Ciarán said.

Lorelei smiled. "Of course, I couldn't smell you with my snout stuck in a book."

"I was ten years old when I said those things," Janie said. "Give it a rest."

"There's a second epoch starship on Trinity Surface?" Aoife seemed ready to eject from her seat. Her eyes blazed. "And yet *my apprentice* didn't think to mention this?"

"I thought about it," Ciarán said. "But that would have been waking the dead."

"You might have asked," Lorelei said. "As your apprentice he'd have been bound to answer truthfully or refuse to answer. That's an answer, by the way, refusing to answer. No chemical interrogation needed."

He had no idea how Lorelei had learned about his chemical

interrogation at Aoife's hands. That was ancient history... and waking the dead.

"I didn't know back then," Ciarán said. "It's only recently I learned."

"That's true," Lorelei said. "As a Merchant Captain you'd be under no such obligation. It's quite handy how that all worked out." She smiled at Aoife.

The smile bounced off. "Is there anything else down there on the planet I'd want to know about?" Aoife glanced from face to face. "Anything at all?"

Ciarán glanced at Lorelei.

"No comment," Lorelei said.

"There's a good sandwich shop in the shuttle terminal," Janie said. "That's a rarity."

"You know what I mean, Pilot," Aoife said.

"I do, and give it up," Janie said. "Island folk are like a diamond made of moonlight. You can't pin them down and you won't wear them down. We're drifting clear of the debris field. If someone spiteful toward his auntie is going to wrangle an exo? They'd better get out on the hull right now."

10

The nic Cartaí shipyard was running at capacity, three full shifts. Every now and then sweeping beams of light slashed across the ceiling of the guest apartment, the viewport in the outer hull practically as large as the bulkhead itself. They'd returned to the station and had dinner on the Spindle, because Lorelei wanted to say she'd seen it, and then a shuttle to the nic Cartaí Yards where Aoife was staying and where guests were put up. Saoirse had abandoned them for a meeting with the stationmaster.

Ciarán stared at the ceiling and ran through a mental inventory of all the balls in the air. He'd tossed a fair number of them skyward himself, but Ruairí Kavanagh and his subterfuge and ambush had priority-interrupted some of what Ciarán had set in motion.

The idea that an Ixatl-Nine-Go variant might be loose on the station made all his concerns seem trivial in comparison. He'd thought that threat behind them, and then to find out it was *here*, and him unaware. If he wasn't aware of that what else was he ignorant of?

Nic Cartaí had done the apartment up like a planetary

home. It had an actual bed, not a bunk, interior doors instead of hatches, frescoed ceiling instead of ceramic composite deckhead, a big pressure-sealed picture window that any spacer knew made the compartment a deathtrap. The luxury furnishings were a gilded frame for the big show, the view the main attraction. Look how busy and powerful we are. Look at all we're doing. Ants in hullwalkers crawled across hulls, and the husks of hulls, clambering up and down scaffolding, the spark and glow of fusing metal. No, we don't buck rivets anymore, and you couldn't hear the gun or feel the impact in your chest. There's no air out there, nothing to transmit sound, and scent, and touch, and taste.

We've become a people of a single sense. If it couldn't be seen it didn't exist. *Look at me. Look at me. Look at me.*

The mattress shook, Lorelei's feet touching the carpet silently as she sat up, stood, and donned a dressing gown—one embroidered with the nic Cartaí crest, a leaping stag. On loan, like the compartment and everything in it.

He hoped they'd done the right thing. It bothered him, not being alone. He could confront anything alone. Face any fear. It was easier, simpler, when he'd had no hope of ever being with Lorelei. When he hadn't needed to don armor every day, not against *his* foes, but against the enemies of whatever *this* was. The unity they presented to the world expanded his threat surface—and hers.

Lorelei gazed out the broad viewport, her face alternately in light and shadow. "I had to tell her."

"You might have warned me. We'd agreed. Deny everything. Admit nothing. And then you tell Saoirse nic Cartaí about the starship. Did you tell her everything?"

"I told her what we needed her to know."

"What you and House needed her to know."

"And you. And all the Willow Bride Folk."

"House decided for us."

"She is the Willow Bride. But it wasn't her. It was mac Manus. House only told me of the agreement upon our discovering he was dead."

"And when was that?"

"While you were in Contract system loading up for the Journey."

Lorelei always said it like that. *The Journey.* As if this contract with Lord Aster were somehow different than any other contract. It wasn't different in any significant way. It only felt that way because he wasn't ignorant of the dangers anymore.

If anything, it should be safer than his apprentice cruise, when he didn't know the landscape of the wider world and remained blind to the machinations of those who strode between the stars. He'd had a storybook image of the world, of good and evil, imagining one could tell friend from foe by the color of their armor and the banners that they carried. He didn't believe that evil existed because he'd never truly experienced it. He imagined good and evil as a false duality. That the extent of evil's supposed grip on the world was entirely a result of an absence of sufficient good.

His mother had warned him. She said in the olden days they'd thought of gravity in much the same way. But now we had fast pallets and all sorts of tech that relied, not on a masking of gravity's effects, but upon a negation of its essence. That was the tip of the oar one felt against one's breast. Not the rough oak of the oar itself, but the hands wielding it and pinning one's face below the tide line. We live and die in the depths and never see the sky. Is it no wonder we choke and sputter and cry when first we taste clean air?

There is a hidden world above us, raging with a dozen hidden wars, and where good and evil, truth and lie shift like black sand. If you stand still, this world will swallow you. If you run, this world will pull you under. The harder you struggle the harder and faster the world will pull. This dark world cannot be fought. Not in any way you imagine. It can only be masked from sight. From time to time the mask will slip and you will glimpse an eye. An ear. A talon. A fang.

This masking itself requires a great and constant effort. That is why the dark world hates mirrors. Why it hates sunlight on water. Why it offers every class of mindless distraction. Every shiver of sensual delight. You are constructed atop animals. Never forget this, the dark world says.

And so distracted, the dark world works its will unseen. It needs no longer wear the mask. It has followers. Worshipers. Minions who have willingly blinded themselves to it. Can you hear its whisper, son? *Close your eyes. Close your eyes. Close your eyes and behold your master.*

Now wipe the sleep away and rise.

There is only one way to fight the dark world.

Say it now.

I said say it now.

Say it now, curse you boy!

Hands were shaking him.

"Ciarán? What's wrong?"

His heart raced.

It took him an instant to realize where he was.

In a bed on a space station.

Not on a straw tick in the cabin at home.

He scrubbed his palm across his face.

"Sorry. I must have fallen back asleep."

"You were having a nightmare."

"I wouldn't call it that. Let me get some clothes on. We need to talk."

Lorelei's voice had gone instantly cold. "About us?"

"What is there to say about us? We're a singularity. The end."

"I figured maybe you were having second thoughts. That the reality of us didn't match the idea of us."

"Suppose it did? We'd have no room to improve. What would we do with all our spare time together? Talk about how awesome we are?"

"But we won't be together."

"It might feel that way to you. But I can hear you now, like I can hear the ship's minder in my head when we speak. And since I can tell the difference between you speaking and House speaking *through you*, I imagine distance won't be an issue."

"You can tell that?"

"I've known Laura Ellis all my life. Lorelei Ellis is new to me, but she's just Laura Ellis upgraded. And then there's this other you. The girl that's mouthing mommy's words and executing her commands. The Laura I know never followed an order in her life."

"They're not orders. They're advice."

"But she's here with you now. House. The Willow Bride."

"I don't know. But if I asked her a question, she'd hear me and answer."

"It's the same for the ship's minder and me. I only know it's with me when it speaks. But when it speaks it does so with full knowledge of my past actions taken in its presence. I can't hear it at any distance, though. I have to be on the ship or with one of its spiders."

"It's like that. Except I can be anywhere and House will answer."

"The difference, as I see it," Ciarán said, "is that your relationship with House is like the kinship relationships between synthetic intelligences. I think that's the main reason the League Navy has them on their warships. Not as navigation or fire control computers, but as—"

"Portable superluminal nodes," Lorelei said.

"Right. Ones that can survive a Templeman drive translation."

Ordinary superluminal nodes needed to be deployed and positioned using slowships. Their connectivity didn't survive the transition into and out of a bubble universe. But the faster-than-light links between synthetic intelligences did. Having superluminal nodes on their capital vessels gave the League huge strategic and tactical advantages.

"What about *our* relationship? When I speak to you at a distance why don't you respond?"

"When you whisper my name, I hear it."

"What about when I don't?"

"You mean like when you moan it, or cry it out in ecstasy?"

"I mean when I'm not thinking about you."

"When is that?"

"Get serious."

"I don't hear you, just like I don't hear the ship's minder's thoughts unless they're specifically directed at me."

"But I can't hear you."

"I blame my mother."

"I said stop joking."

"I am serious. She was onboard the *Willow Bride* as a delivery pilot. She wasn't one of the *Willow Bride* crew."

"Neither was your father."

"But his family has been on the island for four centuries. My mother awakened from cryo less than four decades ago."

"So, you're only half the man you ought to be," Lorelei said.

"I'm the strong silent type. I hear a lot of women find that appealing."

"I'll ask Janie Byrne if that's true, Stinky."

"You do that, Bookworm."

"Can you believe it? We're lashed to her in this affair."

"It's not ideal," Ciarán said. "But she is tight-lipped. That whole Byrne lot is."

"So even if she tells her mother?"

"She won't. They're estranged at the moment. She told me that after she helped me haul the exo to the aft end of the hull." The person inside the exoskeletal armor was dead, and the suit itself had a chary reek that they could only keep at bay with the air handlers on full and the suit strapped down aft.

Ciarán glanced at Lorelei. "What we need to talk about is how we do business with these people without *becoming* like them."

"I thought you *wanted* to become like them."

"I thought I did too. But what I really wanted was to become like I thought they were."

"What was that?"

"Heroes. Champions. Better people than those I met every day at home."

"And they're not?"

"Some are."

"But not Saoirse nic Cartaí, you mean."

"She burned down a shuttle full of people to make a *statement*."

"And to keep them from hanging you."

"No one wants to hang me. That's just an excuse for them to take me. They want to interrogate me and learn all I know and then they want to stuff me out an airlock. Unless they can use me as bait to catch a second-epoch starship."

"She stopped them from doing that."

"She postponed them from doing that. And I don't need her help to stop them. I don't mind defending myself, and I'm a good bit better at talking than I am at shooting. We didn't even try to talk to them."

"We exchanged words."

"Like gunfire we did. It's playground stuff, and while I don't imagine talking was much good during a slave revolt, we are not going to shoot our way to safety and prosperity. She's the wrong woman for the job."

"Who is the right woman then? Your precious Aoife?"

"Do you know why I love Aoife?"

"You love her."

"I said that."

"Tell me then."

"Because she *isn't* a hero."

"And you love that about her."

"I love that she knows she isn't yet *aspires* to be. That she does the work. Nonstop."

"Therefore, you want me to do what? Defer to her judgement?"

"That would be insane. She's just like Saoirse to a degree. She sometimes equates ruthlessness with strength. These spaceborn people are proud, prickly, and arrogant."

"I'm proud, prickly, and arrogant," Lorelei said.

"Would you wash a longboat's main drive output over an enemy?"

"I might."

"Would you do it in anger? Would you brag about it later? Would your friends look up to you because you had? Would you look for some excuse to do it again?"

"That's sickening."

"Suppose I told you I'd burned men down with a main drive."

"Then I'd think you had good reason to."

"I know I did. And later I decided that I'd have rather died myself. Except I was standing between something *fine* and the dark world."

"Ciarán—"

"There must remain something *fine* to fight for. If there isn't then we've already lost."

"I don't know what you want me to do. You'll need to say it."

"I want you to *fix* these people while I'm gone. Start with Aoife."

"Fix them how?"

"Ruairí Kavanagh is a good man. But this luring of Leaguemen to the Freeman sector and making a spectacle of them. Did you not find that appalling?"

"I hadn't thought about it."

"Do you imagine I'd do something like that?"

"Not in a million years."

"Why not?"

"First, because if it had gone wrong, it would have gone wrong publicly. Second, because it could have gotten bystanders hurt. And third, and probably the most important reason, the Ixatl-Nine-Go I encountered were outlandishly clever, brutal, vindictive, deadly, and practically unstoppable. And you've had more truck with them than I did. You wouldn't have treated it like a child's rattle, but like a rattlesnake."

"That wasn't an Ixatl-Nine-Go," Ciarán said. "Or anything close. I've thought about it, replaying the scenario in my mind, and if it had been we'd have all been dead. Because it wouldn't have come alone. One of those guards would have been an ally. One that would have hosed us down with carbine rounds."

"Ruairí was showing off. And playing with fire."

"They all do that. That's what makes Aoife different from all the rest. Something terrible happened on Murrisk that altered the course of her life. It stripped away the need for a public facade. One can see her bones."

"What happened?"

"I don't know. It was before I met her. I didn't realize at the time she was still recovering from that loss. She is a very strong person, and a hider. I doubt you'll get along."

"But you love her."

"I would die for her."

"But not for me."

"Not unless I have to. I prefer to live for you."

"Do you ever turn it off?"

"The merchant gab? I turned it off when we entered this compartment. And you know it."

Ciarán crossed to her, and put his arms around her, and together they gazed out at the nic Cartaí shipyards.

"Here is my advice. Trust Aoife's judgement except when she is angry. Trust Gilpatrick Moore's judgement so long as Truxton's interests and yours align. Trust Kavanagh as you would an expert system. Do not rely on their judgement. And test their facts."

"But we're not to involve Truxton or Kavanagh."

"Saoirse said she didn't *want* them involved. Them or anyone else. The first rule of merchanting? Customers don't know what they want. But they have a solid understanding of what they need once they see it. And right now Saoirse nic Cartaí needs what we have."

"A second-epoch starship. That, and for me to endorse her in front of some League sentience."

"That's what she says she wants. But we're people, and they're people. Deep down we all want the same thing."

"A cause worth fighting for."

"A future worth living for. Don't let her escape into cold sleep. Keep Saoirse nic Cartaí awake and engaged. And don't meet with any synthetic intelligence under any circumstances. We admit nothing. We deny everything. We make counteraccusations. We do not wake the dead. I'm sending you help to keep Saoirse in the fight. And to distract her from this Nevin Green business."

"An ally?"

"Maris Solon is more like a universal irritant. She's purchased the Gant property and title. You'll be neighbors. She's also Academy Commandant for the Legion of Heroes. She'll be shifting the surface combat training from Contact system to Oileán Chléire. She will be personally supervising the move."

"That's extreme."

"Everything gets extreme from here on out. One of the reasons Aoife decided to locate the Thin Star Line headquarters in Contract space is cost. She can't afford space on Trinity Station. And we don't want her under Saoirse or Nuala's wing and beholden to them for a handout. You should lease her space at Ellis House. It's just you there alone, and even with an army next door you'd be safer with her people coming and going."

"I don't like that idea. Doesn't she need orbital docking space?"

"She doesn't like using the ring for docking. She thinks it's unsanitary."

"Is it?"

"Rats big as hedgehogs," Ciarán said. "So it's no hardship not being on the station, other than the up and down. You'll want a glassfield long term, but you can use the Gant's for now. If you decide you don't want her in your house, she can set up with the Legion. But I want her nearby."

"I'm not fragile as all that."

"I'm not worried about you. I'm worried about her. She leaned on me. I didn't realize it at first, but we are better as a team than either of us working alone. And now I won't be there for her."

"You want me to be."

"She needs a mission. Something worthy. And she needs a throttle. She knows it and won't fight you."

"Is that all she needs?"

"She needs someone junior to fret over. A friend but not a confidant."

"And not a lover."

"No angling in the family pool. It's a company rule."

"That's one question answered. You're nothing if not a rule follower."

"I am."

"So am I. Are we family now? With nic Cartaí?"

"With Aoife and the Thin Star Line crews."

"Suits me fine. I don't think I want them in my house, though."

"It's a big ask. Consider it."

"I'll sleep on it."

"I'd rather you didn't. I'm outbound in less than eight hours, and no telling when I'll be back. I thought we might engage in something less passive."

"I have your mother's chess set. You can be white."

Ciarán chuckled. "Why don't I take a cold shower instead." There was absolutely no way he could beat Lorelei at chess. And the thought of chess, and his mother withered him. She always made him play black. But he'd never told anyone. Not even Lorelei. She must have told Lorelei herself.

"Your mother once told me the secret to chess. That she had played you a thousand times and might play you another thousand and you would never realize the truth."

"Did you ever play against her?"

"Many times."

"Did she ever beat you?"

"Every game. I couldn't touch her. I'm certain I could outplay her now, though."

"She told me I had a mind made for checkers," Ciarán said.

"She told me the pawn was the most powerful piece on the board."

"Because it has nowhere to move but forward," Ciarán said.

"Now I see that's what she meant. But I thought at the time she meant because it could be promoted to queen."

"Or bishop, or knight, or rook," Ciarán said. "Depending on

the needs of the game. Imagine a game where every pawn strived to be crowned."

"*You're playing checkers*," Lorelei said, imitating his mother's precise diction. "She could be very harsh to children."

"To everyone. She still rules me, you know. When I cried out earlier—"

"I heard her in your voice. *Children give up so easily*."

"When you kill a man without even knowing his name... what is that, but surrender? We are more than meat. Or if we are not, we must at least pretend to be so until such time as we are."

Anything less was cowardice. Was treason.

Lorelei shivered. "Does it ride you so? The killing?"

"I didn't like it as a boy, with vermin and pests, and I like it even less with men. I don't lose sleep over it anymore, if that's what you mean. But that's only because I was lucky, and in retrospect did what needed doing.

"I found killing easier than it ought to be, though. Particularly when the men in question looked less like men and more like beasts. Anticipated regret won't slow my hand, but I'm not reaching for the Rod until there's no better choice. Every time I use it, I die a little. I'd rather not come home to you a wraith."

"You feel solid enough to me now."

"It's all the juice bulbs and nutrient paste. I can feel it oozing out my pores."

"That was a particularly vile dinner."

"I caught you eyeing the desert dispenser."

"I eyed it and I crossed myself against it. Do they really eat it with their hands?"

"They eat it with their mouths. They shove it into their gobs with their hands. While it's still wriggling."

"You're making that up."

"I wish I was. You wanted to experience the Spindle. Now you have."

"I feel dirty thinking about it."

"There's the refresher. It's available at the moment."

"I'll race you for it."

"Deal. What if it's a tie?"

"Best two out of three."

"I feel like it's going to be a tie."

Lorelei chuckled. "I'd be disappointed if it wasn't."

11

The void between Prix Canada and Sizemore wasn't Ciarán mac Diarmuid's first choice for a cargo handoff. It was dark, true of interstellar space in general, and it seemed private if one didn't know about the Ojin Eng surveillance buoys that were out there surrounding them. But it was also without a star. And without a local star they were naked and defenseless.

This wasn't the sort of handoff either party ordinarily wanted to advertise. But the handoff alone wasn't the reason he was here on the bridge pacing the deck—here, of all places in the wider world. They were being watched, no doubt. There would be witnesses and word would spread. And that was the point of it all.

The Freeman Merchant vessel *Thin Star* hung beside them in the darkness. Hardsuited spacers transferred Freeman Freight Expediting containers, FFEs, from the long spinal mast of that conventional hull to the vestigial mast grafted to *Quite Possibly Alien*'s ancient and alien-seeming hull.

A standard Freeman cargo vessel, like *Thin Star,* could transport three score such self-powered containers latched to the stressed-carbon mast. Sixty containers mounted to surround the hollow core linking the engineering section at the stern to the bridge, crew quarters, infirmary, and boat bay at the bow. The design, hundreds of years old and standardized throughout the Freeman Federation, was ideally suited for such a clandestine rendezvous.

In fact, it was more than suited to the task; its containers, designed for self-powered deliveries, and this location, not a meeting place in normal times but a dead drop by tradition: a fly past, dump the cans, and scoot sort of place.

Until one day it wasn't. And two vessels ambushed a third, murdered its crew, and, in the end, died themselves, their own deaths a story in itself.

Ciarán hadn't been there that day, none of those present today had, but he'd witnessed the slaughter as captured by the surveillance buoys lurking in the darkness.

His ship, *Quite Possibly Alien*, had arrived in the void to complete one journey and begin another. Aoife nic Cartaí had authorized a contract he'd negotiated. Presently both ship and crew would be leaving League space to journey across the Alexandrine to a set of coordinates. Coordinates their contract employer claimed marked the precise location of the planet Earth, the ancestral home to humanity and the source of all known life in the wider world. That new journey began here.

The journey now ending had begun more than a year ago, had cost countless lives, and had entangled him and his comrades in a web of lies, half-truths, shattered trust, betrayal, and bloody murder at scale. All of that had its point of origin, not in any mercantile board room or government agency back-room or general officer's headquarters, but right here in the starless void between the ancient worlds of the League and its expanding frontier.

At this very spot, where future met past.

It began aboard *Truxton's Golden Parachute*, the vessel now listed in the Registry as *Thin Star*, and aboard *Sudden Fall of Darkness*, a vessel advertising itself under a false name and a false flag. The refitted hulk of a second-epoch survey vessel, *Sudden Fall of Darkness* and her crew robbed and murdered under *his* vessel's name. Under *his* polity's flag. *Quite Possibly Alien* was thus wrongly declared a pirate vessel crewed by murderers and slavers. And the chief murderer and now merchant on that vessel? Ciarán mac Diarmuid, a jumped-up, dirtball-born plowboy promoted straight from apprentice over the Merchant Guild's objections.

At the moment that lie was loose in the wider world and spreading from world to world and tongue to tongue. The truth was also out there and chasing it. But where lies ran and shouted, the truth crawled whispering in its wake. Mere pebble-ripples across a roiled ocean one instant after a kinetic strike.

It was a dreadful lie because it was so appealing on the tongue. He couldn't change that lie with facts, not without breaking with custom and tradition. One did not wake the dead. That was the rule. But there was no rule against laying the dead to rest, in the world or in the heart. Ciarán wasn't so much concerned about his vessel's reputation with the League, the Hundred Planets, or the Ojinate. It was his own kind he cared about. And they didn't judge a man by what he said. They gauged him against their own standards, measuring him by what he did.

They had released the marker beacons before beginning the cargo transfer, one for each of the beloved dead. Bosditch. Anders. Lenoch. Not famous names. Not heroes. Just Freeman merchants doing their jobs. Gone but not forgotten.

Adderly Bosditch, the newly appointed stationmaster of Freeport Station, set the beacons free with her own hand. And sixty more nameless beacons for the dead that had not names but inventory numbers, ones encoded with inception date,

batch, and decantation order. Cold-sleepers. Cargo. Not property, to be sold on or stolen, but human beings. *People like us.*

The way a mac Diarmuid fought words wasn't with guns
but with more and better words. And he was presently engaged
in firing back at his enemies with an overwhelming salvo. One
that would shred them without mercy and *end* them for all
time. When he returned from his voyage he wished the slate
wiped clean. And so it would be. Ciarán knew people. He
understood people. In particular, he knew people like himself.

Freeman merchants scanned the news beginning with the
obituaries, not just for names of loved ones, but for competitors
whose contracts would be suddenly up for grabs. A full-page
advert on the home page of the *Merchant Guild Loud Hailer*
wouldn't draw half as many eyeballs as a well-crafted death
notice. Not with the right names on the grave markers, or the
expectation that they might soon be.

While the past was worth remembering, they were largely
there to advertise the future, a future so strange and unexpected that he still couldn't quite grasp it or quite admit to
himself it was real.

Now *that future* was a true story, a commercial contract so
bizarre and outlandishly risky that it would give a sordid lie a
run for its money. It was also the sort of make or break deal a
sensible merchant would keep secret. If it worked out, you
looked like a genius. And if it failed? No one would know, not
just that you'd failed, but they wouldn't even know where to
plant your grave marker.

The mac Diarmuid name was nothing. No one would
notice or care. But a nic Cartaí heiress involved? And a
Kavanagh heiress as well? One was merchant captain aboard
Thin Star, the other sitting *Quite Possibly Alien*'s navigation
station not two meters in front of Ciarán.

Two of the Big Three mercantile houses' names in one
paragraph. And *Truxton's Golden Parachute* makes three. An

expert system would tag the obituary and promote it to the top of the feed once it spotted all three in the space of two paragraphs.

And with that inorganic promotion, the speculation would gain wings.

They'd surely keep such a deal secret.

They tried to, the story would go.

But unbeknownst to them?

They were overheard.

Chairs would scoot closer together.

Gazes would dart toward the barman, to make certain he was out of range.

Shoulders would lean forward, lips shaping into whispers, ears straining to hear over the piped in music, the clink of glassware, the loud bray of some clueless idiot's laugh.

Tell no one, the speaker would intone.

Nods of agreement would follow, knowing gazes exchanged.

Freeman merchants didn't judge a man by what he said but by what he did.

And there was only one way to prove a man had told no one.

By discovering that he'd told *everyone*.

And that was how a mac Diarmuid fought a lie.

By strapping a rocket to the truth.

And *igniting* it.

12

The bridge of *Quite Possibly Alien* lay in darkness, only the light of the consoles and displays illuminating the faces of the crew.

As ship's merchant, Ciarán didn't have his own seating or workstation on the bridge. He stood at Ship Captain Agnes Swan's left elbow, at the command seat center aft of the piloting and navigation stations.

Every eye on the bridge watched the cargo mast visual feed displayed on the forward viewscreen. It was such an unusual view of the hull since the mast hadn't once had a container on it, and no one was really certain if it would hold. The mast had been cemented to the hull so that *Quite Possibly Alien* met the bare minimum specs for entry into the Freeman Commercial Registry, the official listing of all cargo-capable interstellars. A vessel needed both a superluminal drive and a cargo mast to register with the Merchant's Guild, and thus be entitled to the mutual defense and insurance benefits essential to interstellar trade.

Ciarán glanced toward the sensor rig where Sensors Operator Yuan Ko Shan hung suspended in a translucent amber bubble of viscous oxygenated fluid. The fluid had a long scientific name, but everyone called it goop.

In the Academy he'd been forced to let them drown him in the stuff to pass his first-year exams. It didn't just feel like drowning. When you toed the full-immersion rig's containment field active, and the resulting transparent sphere began to flood with goop, you literally did drown, fluid filling your lungs and panic filling your lizard brain until the reasoning functions took over and you realized you were still pumping air, just not in the usual way.

As a student on the merchant track, he didn't have the full-boat sensor interface installed like Ko Shan did. But just the unaugmented physical interface through the goop seemed transcendental enough. He'd felt light on the hull of the training vessel as if it fell upon his own skin. Felt magnetic flux as if it were wind. Experienced Trinity System's solar wind like water flowing over him. It was *amazing* once inside, but once was enough. He could force himself to push against the rig's leaning post until it retracted into the deck, but he couldn't command his heel to kick the containment field activator. Nearly everyone could nerve up for a single run but only about one in twenty people had the courage for a second immersion, or a third.

At the moment, Ko Shan was full immersion and jacked in, an interface cable running from a socket at the base of her neck to the rig's console. While it looked like she was watching the view screen she probably wasn't. They had all ten kilometers of the trailing array out and it demanded attention. There were expert systems that listened, on her behalf, to those frequencies of the spectrum that seemed least likely to alert them to a threat. That array was a big receiver, even on passive, providing a lot of information to pay attention to at once. The job required intense concentration.

Ko Shan might not be the best sensors operator in Freeman

Space. Those tended to be born into families that specialized in the work and trained at it since birth. She'd been born a Huangxu pleasure slave and only took up the sensors work as an adult.

She was, however, undoubtedly the best second-epoch League survey vessel sensors operator in Freeman space. And not just because she was the only one. The crew had needed to reverse-engineer how all the gear on the ancient starship worked. It wasn't until Ciarán signed on as merchant apprentice that they had more than trial and error to go on. By the time he finished translating the ship's operations manuals, Ko Shan had figured most everything out, simply through experimentation and countless hours spent immersed in the unfamiliar rig.

The cargo handlers were loading the last can on the mast. It was a joke, really, that mast. FFEs were self-powered, and remote controlled, and if you got them close to the mast and spit a parking address at them, they did the rest. FFEs were the most fundamental, essential, ubiquitous, brain dead, unbreakable technology anywhere in the wider world, and the idea that anyone had to manhandle one or six onto a shipping mast sounded absurd. It wasn't common work, so they'd had to figure out how to do it before doing it, because the only people that manhandled FFEs were pirates, and they specialized in prying them free while you weren't looking, not latching them on while you were. Once you stole one and busted inside it, you could easily bend it to your will. Part of what made them unbreakable was their simpleminded operating system.

"How much longer?" Ship's Captain Swan said.

Ciarán had thought they'd be done by now. According to the manifest there were only five cans to be loaded. Yet they were working on a sixth.

It couldn't be much longer, though. There wasn't room for

another. Three people from *Thin Star*, in hardsuits and hull-walkers, stood clamped onto the can as it crept toward the mast. It seemed yet a meter away, but it had to be closer than that, because two of them saluted and kicked off, and then someone or someones in *Thin Star's* boat bay began reeling them in. The cargo loaders had tried rigging a handline from hull to hull, and it worked, but it didn't work in parallel. And the hardsuits had propulsion, they all did, but only so much fuel. A lot could go wrong and the last thing you wanted was a suit with no jets, and no handline. So you saved it, the fuel, and hoped you never needed it, because when you needed it you really needed it.

It couldn't take much longer to finish. Normally there were lights on the cargo console, one for each parking address, and when the stay-put field kicked in, which it did only after the mechanical clamps latched, did the light illuminate. You could tell at a glance how many cans were clamped on. That was on a family ship, though, or a company ship like *Thin Star*, where the cargo handling systems and mast were tightly integrated.

Quite Possibly Alien had what Ciarán thought of as a loosely integrated system. The vestigial mast stood grafted onto the stern of the hull, starboard of the centerline. And the cargo handling console stood strapped to a fast pallet in a Trinity System breaker's yard; unless it had been fed into the recycler already. The Guild said *Quite Possibly Alien* needed a mast for a Registry entry.

There was no mention of a console on the application.

"Perhaps you didn't hear me," Swan said. "How much longer, *Freeman whelp*?"

Ciarán chuckled. Swan was a full-blooded Huangxu Eng. They'd gotten off to a bad start, largely because of his own prejudices, but not entirely because of that. Swan was estranged cousin to the Huangxu Eng emperor and accustomed to being obeyed. Ciarán was the son of Seán mac Diarmuid, a farmer from Oileán Chléire on Trinity Surface, and raised to be defiant toward authority. Doubly so if that authority's ancestors had claimed to own your ancestors. Triply so if that authority's cousin seemed to think he still did. "I heard you. I thought you were talking to yourself."

"Because I have a history of talking to myself."

"Because we're both looking at the same thing, and it's pretty clear they're nearly done."

"Perhaps to a laborer it is."

The solitary suited cargo handler stepped clear of the coupling now latched to the mast.

An alarm began to sound on the sensors rig. Ciarán glanced toward the rig as Ko Shan silenced the alarm and a second alarm sounded, her hands flashed across the rig controls, a yellow light flared on the control board. She toggled the stud beside it. The yellow light began to flash. Then it began to flash very rapidly.

Ko Shan's cool voice sounded from the sensor rig annunciator. "Pilot."

"I see it," Pilot Helen Konstantine said. "Retracting the towed array."

The forward display flashed, the cargo operation shrinking into a small tile in the lower right corner while the bulk of the display showed a simulated holo tank projection, a facsimile of a three-dimensional system plot, one with a single arc of red on it, an arc that began at the lower right edge of the display and intersected with the centered origin of the display.

That plot was the default system schematic used on vessels without a holo tank. It was identical to what would be displayed on secondary consoles in a space station's traffic control center.

Quite Possibly Alien's transponder code hung motionless at the centered origin of the display. *Thin Star's* transponder code hung motionless beside it.

Swan pressed a stud on her command seat's right arm. "Brace for impact." Her voice spoke in synchrony from the annunciator overhead, and therefore in every compartment of the vessel.

Ciarán headed for the hatch. The merchant's day cabin was just outside the hatch. It had a crash couch in addition to a workstation, chair, and daybed. Swan would think he was headed there to strap in. All he had to do was walk coolly from the compartment. Once the hatch closed, he could sprint toward the boat bay hardsuit rack. They had a spacer on the hull without backup. That it was *Thin Star*'s spacer didn't matter.

Captain Swan wouldn't see it that way. When it came to ship's operations her word was law. And her priority was the safety of the ship and the crew. Not the safety of every ship and every crew. But *her* ship. *Her* crew.

He was part of her crew as she saw it and utterly useless at the moment. There were expert systems loudly hailing the incoming vessel. It was incoming like a plague ship, as if everyone on board lay dead. And in a system without a station or even a star there was no tripwire, no automated system to slow it.

The vessel was likely known to them, either friend or foe— or known to *Sudden Fall of Darkness*, or *Golden Parachute*. No one had stumbled upon them by accident. Not given the sheer expanse of starless space they called the void. Definitely identified as a vessel, not a weapon, the ship's icon on the plot had changed from a featureless red danger triangle to a two-dimensional depiction of a sphere, one with a fluctuating mass estimate blinking beside it. A superluminal vessel, though a small one. The sphere indicated the vessel had a Templeman drive. So not a missile, but a bomb.

"Sensors," Swan said.

"It's running silent."

"Navigator."

"We can skip jump but we'll lose the array," Maura Kavanagh said.

"Eight minutes to retraction complete," Konstantine said.

"Sensors?"

"Eight minutes to impact."

"Lovely." Swan glanced at Ciarán. "What are you waiting for?"

He pointed at the screen. "That."

Thin Star had begun to accelerate on in-system drives. They were moving off, leaving the solitary cargo handler behind on the load.

"Transponder just lit," Konstantine said. "It's *Springbok*."

"Good." Maura's hands dance across the navigation console. "It doesn't have any weapons."

Springbok was a League fast courier vessel. Ciarán had heard about it but hadn't encountered it. And just because a vessel's transponder said it was *Springbok* didn't mean it was.

Swan increased the resolution on the forward display. "It doesn't need any weapons. At that velocity it is a weapon. I need the performance envelope on that hull. Give me maximum survivable deceleration."

"On it," Konstantine said. "You want the Templeman drive yield?"

"I do," Ko Shan said. "Plotting fleet average turnover for zero delta at origin," Ko Shan said. A white ring appeared centered around the plot origin. "Plotting fleet average drive failure radius." A smaller red ring centered around the incoming.

Ciarán could decipher the plot given time, but experienced bridge crew didn't just read it, they inhabited it. He could tell by the instant silence on the bridge that things had suddenly gone from spherical to pear-shaped.

"Seven minutes," Ko Shan said.

Swan glared at Ciarán. "If you are going to do something stupid just do it."

Ciarán grinned. "I will, Ship's Captain." He toggled the hatch and took off at a dead run.

13

Ciarán raced along the corridor sternward. It was a good three-minute run-and-descend from the bridge to the boat bay, and then a minute to suit up and that left him, what? Three minutes to get out onto the hull and squirt a retrieval line to the hullwalker and wind them in. It was doable, if tight.

"Ship," Ciarán said as he ran.

"I am here," the ship said. Its voice seemed to come from everywhere and nowhere. That voice, along with the unusual physical configuration of the ship had seemed the strangest and most disturbing aspects of the vessel when he'd first signed on as merchant apprentice. The dimly lit corridor he ran along had no sharp angles or square corners. The flat black deck merged into the bulkheads, which merged into the deckhead. Every three meters a dim luminaire clung, illuminating as he approached and returning to darkness as he passed. If he were to reach out and touch a bulkhead it would feel warm to the touch and pliable, and if he pressed his fingers against it, the bulkhead would press back.

"Start a clock," Ciarán said. "Minutes to impact. Alert me on the minute and update me should the incoming begin to brake."

"Six minutes to impact," the ship said.

Ciarán picked up the pace.

The ship wasn't a biological entity, but it felt alive. And the ship's voice was the voice of a synthetic intelligence more than two thousand years old, one that had spent most of those years trapped beneath a glacier on the planet Murrisk. A planet under League control. One that had been closed to all traffic, both commercial and military, since the discovery of the vessel.

All of that strangeness was nothing compared to the truth he'd discovered about the vessel.

"Sxipestro," Ciarán said. He slid down a ladder to the deck below, spacer style, never losing a stride. The corridor stretched into the distance.

"I am here," a voice said inside his head.

Ciarán shivered. He made it a practice to speak with the ship's minder aloud, even though it assured him he didn't need to. "What's the tactical situation?"

"We are in no danger of impact, if that is what you're asking."

"The hullwalker?"

"I'm more concerned about losing the towed array. Which we will so do, if I have to take evasive action."

Ciarán had worked with the ship's minder for well over a year and he knew how it thought. It wasn't saying that the cargo handler on the hull would be safe if the ship took evasive actions. It was simply reminding him that it didn't care whether they were or not. That their safety wouldn't figure into its decision-making process.

Ciarán slid down another ladder and kept running. It felt like he ran chasing a moveable puddle of light, one that ground to a halt at the boat bay blast doors.

"Five minutes," the ship said.

The blast door cipher locks were set an arm's breadth apart. They had to be worked simultaneously, something only Ciarán and Mr. Gagenot, the ship's victualer, could accomplish unaided. They alone had the arm span to reach the locks simultaneously, the speculation being that the ship's builders were giants. Otherwise it took two crewmen working together to work the locks. Opening the hatches was one of the few things Ciarán could do that space-born Freemen couldn't do better. He'd grown more comfortable in space, but he wasn't born to it, and what came naturally to others remained work for him. Six months ago, he couldn't have slid down the ladders like he just had.

"Four minutes," the ship said.

Ciarán swung the massive hatch wide. It moved with surprisingly little force.

He glanced across the enormous space toward the boat bay iris. He couldn't see the hardsuit rack, not with all the new hardware jammed thruster-to-thruster in the compartment. They were running heavy, with some new additions that no one would expect them to have. Besides the planetary occupation shuttle, a bog-standard Freeman longboat, and a pair of compact second-epoch League shuttles, all of which together didn't occupy a third of the boat bay, there was now a battered League military vessel consuming the rest of the space, a vessel so tightly jammed in that they'd have to launch it before they'd be able to use any of their regular kit, except the second-epoch shuttles.

"Close the hatch," Hess said. The engineer had one of the ancient two-seater shuttles on a trolley and was wheeling it out from behind the towering warship.

Ciarán closed the hatch.

"Crewman on the hull," Hess said. "Someone's got to throw them a line."

"Three minutes," the ship said.

"I didn't think you knew how to fly that," Ciarán said.

"I don't," Hess said. "Grab a handle and help me pull."

The only people who knew how to fly that vessel were Konstantine, who was busy at the moment, and Ciarán. Konstantine because she'd studied the vessel and reverse engineered its controls, and Ciarán because his family had owned one, only they didn't know it was a shuttle. They'd thought it was a submarine.

"The major and I have a bet," Hess said. "First one to rescue the hullwalker wins."

Ciarán helped pull, because it wasn't a bad idea to use the shuttle, so long as they were quick about dragging it, and so long as he was willing to use it without preflighting it, just jumping in and going, which he was. "There's no line-thrower on the hull," Ciarán said. And even on a lift-plate trolley the little shuttle felt heavier than it looked.

"Rigged and ready, merchie man," Hess said in his flat League frontiersman's accent. "The remote's taped to the crash pad. Now pull."

"Two minutes," the ship said.

They rounded the stern of the League military vessel. They had a straight shot to the boat bay iris. Someone had moved the hardsuit rack to jam the big vessel inside. Ciarán glanced around for it.

"I know," Hess said. "It's chaos in here right now. You'd have had to crawl over the POS to get to the hardsuits. We'll get it all squared away once we're outbound."

"You were expecting me."

"Crewman on the hull, Ciarán, one without a buddy. You are the second-most predictable person in the world."

A battered blue exo lumbered out from behind the League warship. Someone had painted a fanged monster's face on the exoskeletal armor's helmet. That same someone had grafted a GRAIL gun to the suit's armored sleeve and assured the owner the modifications came with a lifetime guarantee.

"That is still some of my best work," Hess said. He popped the shuttle hatch. "Get in, quick."

Amati took two hopping steps toward the boat bay iris. The iris opened like an all-seeing eye. The blackness of space stared back.

"One minute," the ship said.

Amati took another step forward. She turned toward them and waved. Ciarán laughed. She wasn't waving. She was flipping Hess off.

She turned to face the iris.

Someone in a *Thin Star* hardsuit jetted in from outside.

They hit the boat bay deck with a thud and scraped across it until the suit's thrusters either shut off or ran out of fuel.

A bright star seemed to ignite in the darkness outside.

"How about that," Hess said. "It's a tie."

"Turnover," the ship said.

The boat bay iris snapped closed.

Amati's exo gripped the spacer's hardsuit by the utility belt and effortlessly hoisted the load from the deck. She strode across the deck toward them, servos silently actuating. She dropped the spacer at Hess's feet and wrenched her own helmet off. "I win."

"No way," Hess said. "It's a tie."

She turned her gaze on Ciarán and nodded. "Merchant Captain."

"Armsman."

Mrs. Amati had taught Ciarán everything he knew about fighting. Inside a League exo she was unstoppable. Even outside of her powered armor, it was hard to tell where war machine ended and woman began.

Amati flexed a mechanized fist. "Well?"

One of the first rules of fighting was knowing when you were outmatched.

Ciarán patted Hess's shoulder. "Pay the woman."

Amati grinned.

"The winner gets to escort the blow-in to the infirmary," Ciarán said.

"Lucky me," Amati said.

No one liked passing through the infirmary bio-lock.

The compartment annunciator squawked. "Merchant to the bridge."

"Ship," Ciarán said. "What's the issue?"

"We are being hailed."

"By?"

"That remains unclear."

"The expert systems—"

"The ship's captain has disabled them. She wishes to speak with the intruder directly."

"Don't let her do that."

"I am running an emergency diagnostic on the communications array. Please hurry."

14

C iarán sprinted all the way to the bridge. He'd been out of the game for a month, lounging at home, convinced he was done with scurrying from one disaster to another. *Convinced of that and hating it.*

Agnes Swan having a chat with someone who'd nearly pasted her ship at a fraction of light speed was a situation to be avoided. And while Ciarán was signatory to their commercial contract and in charge of the mission, his principal value to the ship and crew was his ability to jaw with people and talk them out of whatever they had in mind. Usually they had in mind something that he wouldn't like, and on more than one occasion, something no one would like.

He slapped the bridge hatch control and Wisp, the ship's cat shoved past him, purring. Wisp had an uncanny ability to sense when she was needed. He decided at the last minute that if he needed a mong hu beside him, he'd need his merchant's great coat and overseer's rod to complete the image. He ducked into the merchant's day cabin and snagged them both, stuffing himself into the ankle-dusting outerwear while shoving onto the bridge. He ran his fingers through his hair and stuffed the overseer's rod under the equipment belt of his utilities.

A vein pulsed on Ship's Captain Agnes Swan's forehead. She leaned forward in her captain's throne, one elbow on the arm rest, her gaze fixed on the main forward display.

"If you laser a pair of holes in that display," Ciarán said, "The repair bill's coming out of your paycheck."

The display showed the flight deck of a League starship. There were two spacers at the controls, both male, both lieutenants from the insignia of their uniforms.

Swan glared at him. "Our comms array is suspiciously broken."

Ciarán glanced at Ko Shan, floating in the full immersion sensor rig. "Can they see us?"

She wobbled her head. "Not at the moment."

"The comms aren't definitely broken," Ciarán said. "They're being checked to make sure they aren't broken."

"*Springbok* has upgraded inertial dampers," Maura Kavanagh said. "It turned over thirty seconds later than design specs indicated it could."

Navigator Kavanagh liked the idea that she was living on the edge and one mistake away from eternity. He could see it in her eye, though, that she thought she'd bought it this time, and she didn't like that idea. And if Maura, a natural born maniac had thought that, then the rest of the bridge crew would have said their death prayers and messaged their next of kin.

Ciarán wondered how long the comms system had been in diagnostic. Those were hard messages to talk over and explain away, and where they were headed there wouldn't be bandwidth available for the job.

"Did these people say anything?"

"They asked to speak with Charles Newton," Maura said.

"I'm Charles Newton," Ciarán said. That was an alias he had used from time to time.

"Everyone knows that," Konstantine said. "It's how they asked that the captain objects to."

"Interesting.," Ciarán said.

Helen Konstantine was League navy, retired, and the only Leagueman on the bridge. He might have expected that tone of outrage in anyone else's voice but hers. The League military wasn't known for politeness to foreigners. But something they had said lit up Konstantine as well.

"Sxipestro," Ciarán said.

"I am here."

"Why didn't we move clear?"

"The towed array wasn't fully retracted."

"But they could have pasted us."

"It is a very difficult array to fabricate. And countermeasures were in place."

"You might have alerted the crew to put their minds at ease."

"In such cases I prefer to wait and notify any survivors."

"That's grand. Other than that they're rude and looking for Charles Newton, do we know anything about our new neighbors?"

"We know they can suffer and die," Swan said.

Maura swiveled in her seat to face him. "They called Agnes a Freeman—"

"Stop," Ciarán said. "We run a clean vessel. No cursing on the bridge." And that was enough information, already. Agnes had lived for thirty years in the Federation but she had only recently taken the Oath and begun wearing the spire. That was likely the first time she'd been called a Freeman by anyone not a Freeman. Hearing a broadside as a bystander didn't feel the same as looking straight down the barrel and witnessing the muzzle flash an instant before the noise.

"Ship's captain," Ciarán said, "Did you happen to notice if either of those fellows had dental fillings?"

"Why would I have?" Swan said. "What—"

"Other than this inertial damper upgrade, did any of you notice any deviations from the Registry entry for the vessel? Are we even certain it is *Springbok*?"

"Reasonably certain," Maura said.

"So no weapons?"

"None visible," Konstantine said.

"They are stationary, what? A kilometer from our hull?"

"Five hundred meters," Konstantine said.

"Ko Shan?"

"On it, Merchant Captain."

That is what Ciarán loved about his coworkers. They had worked together long enough that they didn't need to read each other's minds. They came to the same conclusions independently.

The forward display blinked to static for an instant before it went blank.

The muted sound of an active sensor sweep resonated through the hull.

"No weapons," Ko Shan said. "And one filling."

Swan chuckled. As a long-time ship's captain, Swan knew what a modern League warship's active scans felt like from inside an unshielded commercial hull. A second-epoch survey vessel's sensors weren't the same. They were an order of magnitude more resolving and a hundred times more powerful, as they were designed for probing the farthest reaches of newly discovered star systems.

At five hundred meters Ko Shan could have fried every electrical system on that hull right after she finished cooking the crew.

And now everyone knew it.

"Merchant Captain," Ko Shan said. "We are being hailed. It's *Springbok*."

"Not just some people saying that."

"It is *Springbok*."

"Are they backing off?"

"They are not."

Ciarán glanced at Swan. "I think you'll agree, Ship's Captain. When meeting someone new it's best not to kick them in the teeth on sight."

Swan grinned. "Unless they ask for it."

"Unless they beg for it. Let's clap eyeballs on these beggars."

"Eyeballing them on the forward display," Ko Shan said.

The display showed the same two lieutenants. One sat comms, a trickle of blood running from his nose. The other busily reset circuit breakers and ran ship's systems through diagnostics. They both looked rattled.

"Wisp," Ciarán said, and the big cat seemed to materialize at his side. He'd found Wisp as a kitten, and she'd continued to grow. Physically she resembled a mong hu, oldest and most reliable allies of his people. That she was more than a very large, very clever, and very dangerous semi-domesticated cat wasn't common knowledge outside the crew. Wisp stood hip-high beside him, and when she sat, as was traditional for such first contacts, he could stroke her forehead absently without stooping to do so.

When Ciarán appeared on *Springbok*'s comms display he would seem a conventional Freeman merchant captain, fully accessorized though overly young. Unless *Springbok*'s crew were intimate with Freeman culture and Freeman Merchant Guild conventions, they would not notice those anomalies in his appearance that a Freeman wouldn't miss. That he did not wear a Merchant's ring. That the lining of his greatcoat was yellow instead of red. That he palmed a small device, one whose sole purpose was to emit sharp clicking sounds when depressed. That the overseer's rod beneath his belt was not a wooden facsimile painted to mimic the terror weapon but the real deal

—and one that bore the telltale signs of recent and frequent use.

"Ship's complement?" Ciarán said.

"Eight," Ko Shan said. "These two on the flight deck, and another out of frame just behind them. Four more in the vessel's main salon and one in the captain's quarters."

"That's specific."

"Pilot Konstantine forwarded the ship's schematic from the Registry. Overlaying the sensors data seemed appropriate."

"I didn't know you could do that."

"Neither did I," Ko Shan said. "There is much about our ship's capabilities I have yet to discover."

"Nicely done."

"Won't be much use where we are going," Konstantine said. "The Registry entries are sparse, and what we do have are ancient."

"Well, first we have to get there. And that was good thinking, so keep it up." Ciarán glanced at Captain Swan. "You might want to lose the scowl. You are in command of an unknown entity. An enigmatic expression might suit the occasion better."

Swan glared at him.

"That expression will work as well. Let them think they got under your skin. That I was called in to overrule you and defuse the situation."

Maura Kavanagh chuckled.

"That is an inaccurate assessment of the situation," Swan said.

"Obviously," Ciarán said. "But they don't know that. They won't judge us as we judge ourselves, but as they judge one another."

Swan leaned back in her seat and squared her shoulders. "Point taken."

"We are as one," Ciarán said. "Let us show the world. Maura? The word of the day?"

"Fanciful."

"Roger that," Pilot Konstantine said.

"We are in agreement," Swan said. "Fanciful."

"Thank you." It fell to the ship's navigator to choose the word of the day. A word unlikely to come up in conversation that, if Ciarán spoke it aloud, would cause the pilot to initiate the vessel's superluminal drive on a course of the navigator's choosing.

As a survey vessel, one armed to repel boarders or collapse a star with no countermeasures in between, flight remained superior to fight in every imaginable case. And flight without an overheard command spoken added the critical element of surprise. That *Springbok* wasn't expressing any weapons didn't mean it lacked them. Every third-epoch starship's Templeman drive was unexploded ordnance, and if *Springbok* decided to suicide five hundred meters from their hull the blast would likely take them with it. That idea was what had Swan so wound up.

Positioning themselves to set up that implicit threat was the reason for *Springbok*'s mad sub-light dash to proximity. It was what he would have done if he was mortally desperate to talk to someone who wasn't at all inclined to listen.

"Ship," Ciarán said.

"I am here."

"Answer the hail, please. Live feed on my mark."

"Awaiting your mark, Merchant Captain."

Ciarán glanced about the bridge. All seemed in order. His gaze met Swan's. "Admit it. You're loving this."

Swan stared enigmatically back at him from her command throne. "We admit nothing. Not even light."

"Word of a merchant." Ciarán squared his shoulders and faced the display. "Mark."

15

The lieutenant riding comms seemed surprised to find his hail answered.

Ciarán smiled into the sensor. "What can we do for you people?"

"Wait one," he said.

"I'll wait two," Ciarán said. "Ship, please terminate this channel."

"Terminated," the ship said.

"Thank you." The communications display did not go blank. They were rattled, the pair of them, and someone had left the outbound live. The pilot abandoned his station as someone waiting out of frame pressed past him, frowning. She was dressed in jet-black ordinary spacer's utilities, though obviously bespoke and crafted to display her figure to advantage. Blonde, blue eyed, obviously gene-modded to cultural standards of beauty as prevalent in the League eighteen to twenty-two years ago, standard. She gazed into the optical sensor and adjusted the device to center her face in the frame. She brushed her less-than-shoulder-length hair from her forehead with her palms, tucking it behind her ears. She glanced at the comms officer before freezing in motion as she realized the visual feed was already active.

She cursed reflexively before aiming her gaze toward the display. Her expression seemed more frightened than angry.

"Recognize her?" Maura asked.

"Who wouldn't?" Konstantine said. "That's Lady Sarah Aster. Lord Aster's daughter."

"Lord Aster's *only child*," Ko Shan said. "I understand she's a hellion."

"She looks it," Swan said.

She did look it. She looked exactly the sort of foreign beauty Seamus, his university roommate, would fall madly in lust with. And she seemed exactly the sort of young woman whose precociousness as a child would lead her into a life of danger. He'd heard the two had met. Had heard it directly from Seamus. He'd also heard she'd betrayed him, though not from Seamus. He'd met her once, on Trinity Station, when she was a gangly *cailín* and he at university and working manual labor to pay his way. He'd met both her and her mother, Lady Tabatha Aster, and it had not been a happy day for anyone involved.

"Ship," Ciarán said. "Hail the vessel, please."

"Hailing," the ship said.

Lady Sarah Aster blinked and smiled toward the sensor. "You're a hard man to find, Charles Newton."

"Lady Sarah," Ciarán said. "I trust you and your mother are doing well."

"We are each doing as well as can be expected," she said. "I am about to proposition a virtual stranger and she is being held captive."

"That sounds challenging."

"Can we drop the niceties? It isn't challenging. It's humiliating, and you're not making it any easier. We need to talk."

"We are talking."

"Face to face. In person."

"We were in the process of packing when you arrived. The place is a mess."

"You could shuttle over to *Springbok*."

"I could," Ciarán said.

She stared at him. "Will you?"

"It's unlikely, Lady Sarah. As I said, we were packing so that we might depart. We're engaged in a commercial enterprise, one we're under contract for, and you know how we Freemen feel about our contracts."

"Then let me come over to speak. I promise we won't delay you."

"You're already delaying us. And frankly, you scared the stuffing out of us. You're not held in high favor at the moment."

"I did what I needed to do. Surely you understand that."

"I do understand it. But since you asked me to dispense with the niceties, I'll be blunt. I don't care. You might have approached us in a less heart-attack-inducing manner. That you didn't makes me think you're reckless and inconsiderate. Now if you don't mind—"

"Please just speak with us. I beg you."

"Us?"

"Yes, mother and I, and a small personal security team. We'll hand-line over if necessary. I'll be brief, but this is not a topic I wish to discuss on an open comms line."

"I thought you said Lady Tabatha is being held captive."

"She is."

"By whom?"

"I should think it obvious. Hector Poole instructed me to contact you should I ever... I mean, should it become clear that... countermeasures were necessary."

Hector Poole was a very complicated man. He was Lord Aster's fixer, and, as it turned out quite unexpectedly, Ciarán's maternal uncle. If Sarah Aster was telling the truth, she was likely a comet streaking through Ciarán's galaxy with a mess in her tail. A mess she was planning on leaving behind for him to clean up.

"Tell me who it is that's holding Lady Tabatha hostage."

"Not hostage. Captive. My mother is presently a prisoner of war."

"But she's there, on *Springbok* with you."

"I didn't know where else to keep her."

"So you're saying that you're holding your own mother captive."

"I'm trying to." A single tear ran down her cheek. "Please help me."

Ciarán gritted his teeth and stared at the display. "You know that doesn't work on me."

"Pilot," Captain Swan said. "Get the longboat ready."

"Belay that," Ciarán said. "They can handline over." There was too much junk blocking the longboat in, and besides, he didn't want anyone knowing what all they had on board.

"Thank you," Sarah Aster said.

"Don't thank me. Thank Captain Swan."

Lady Sarah Aster nodded. "I will."

"Ship," Ciarán said. "Please terminate the connection."

The forward screen went black for an instant to be replaced with the default system plot.

Ciarán turned to Captain Swan. "Nicely done."

"Agnes Swan as good cop," Maura said. "Who'd have expected?"

"Anyone could see he was lying," Swan said.

"One of us was," Ciarán said. "She's pretty enough for the part but her heart wasn't in it. And speaking of heart, that was a brilliant assist. I mean it."

Swan studied his face. "I am informed."

"Are you?" Ciarán said. "Is *that* all you are?"

"I admit to being somewhat curious."

"I'm not. I'm *burning* to know what's going on. And if you

hadn't spoken up when you did, I'd have somehow led her back around to the idea of a handline. These people are not to be trusted. But they came within five hundred meters of annihilation just to talk to us. In a hurry, and in private. If what they have to say isn't a package we can unwrap—"

"We can drop-ship it to Aoife on the outbound passage," Maura said.

Ciarán grinned. "We can and we will. Shall we see about rigging a hand line, Ship's Captain?"

The annunciator overhead spoke in Hess's voice.

"I'm way ahead of you, merchie man. With the ship's captain's permission."

"Do it," Swan said.

16

Sarah Aster and company entered *Quite Possibly Alien* through the isolation lab's external bio lock.

The survey vessel was designed at a time when alien life was thought to be widespread in the wider universe, and that some significant percentage of that life would be hostile to humans. *Quite Possibly Alien* thus consisted of two separable parts, an isolated specimen bay and biolab, which could be jettisoned if contaminated, and the vessel proper. This isolation module could be accessed two ways; externally, through its own external bio lock, and internally, through a bio lock linking the module to the vessel proper.

Under normal operation, the biolab served as Watanabe Natsuko's medical laboratory and the specimen bay as ship's brig. This had several benefits. Natsuko could keep the lab's environment set to a carbon-dioxide-rich atmosphere that allowed the Brasil Surface native to work comfortably without a survival mask, and the brig was doubly isolated from the ship by the incapacitating atmosphere of the lab and by the bio locks. Whatever Sarah Aster wanted to say she could say from the comfort of the ship's brig.

As the quartet arrived in hardsuits via handline there was no need to issue them rebreathers. Amati met them in the lab, kitted out in her exo. Natsuko worked in shirtsleeves beside a laboratory table at the far end of the compartment. Anyone unfamiliar with the golden-skinned Brasil native's physiology would remain unaware of the compartment's true nature. Unless they checked their hardsuits' atmospheric safety displays, there would be no indication that their visitors passed through an invisible layer of additional security.

Amati ushered them into the specimen lab through its standard airlock. From where she stood outside, she could watch the proceedings through an observation window, one that could be electronically converted from one-way to two-way viewing. At present the window appeared to be a mirror when viewed from inside the compartment.

Ciarán waited for them inside, in shirtsleeves, rebreather in his pocket. He waited while they removed their helmets and took seats around a makeshift conference table. The mostly vacant compartment was larger than the ship's galley and mess hall combined, and other than a portable table from the mess and five scarred orange plastic chairs, held nothing but the portable head and refresher they'd installed earlier, when the compartment had held prisoners for real.

Mr. Gagenot entered the compartment bearing a tray of refreshments. Ciarán doubted they'd notice the bulge of the pocketed rebreather, as their gaze would be fixed on Gagenot himself, an immensely tall skeleton of a man, pale as moonlight and bearing the puckered circular scars of six Huangxu Eng bang stick strikes on his neck and jawline.

He carefully placed the tray in the center of the table. "Will Gag sees the visitors." He glanced from face to face. "Will Gag welcomes the visitors."

"Thank you, Mr. Gagenot," Ciarán said. "Would you please inform Mrs. Amati we are not to be disturbed?"

"Will Gag hears the merchant. Will Gag will tell the Major."

Ciarán studied their faces as they watched Gagenot depart. They clearly understood what Gagenot represented. A Huangxu Eng bang stick strike didn't kill its target but robbed them of their intellect, robbed them slowly and painfully, diminishing them in a cruel and inevitable manner readily apparent to their friends and loved ones. Used to discipline the uncooperative, the bang stick remained the ultimate terror weapon for those who valued intellect, independence, and autonomy. They were no longer seeing Gagenot's pock-marked skin but imagining their own. Ciarán had never met anyone but Mr. Gagenot who had received six strikes and survived. He had watched a woman die after receiving seven.

They could imagine whatever they liked. That he had wielded the bang stick, or that others had wielded it against his crew. What they could not imagine is that they were safe or immune from harm aboard this vessel. Or that its merchant was ignorant of the nature of the world.

Sarah Aster he knew upon sight. Her mother, Lady Tabatha Aster looked very much the same as she had when he'd met her, along with Sarah, on Trinity Station, five, six years ago, standard. He wasn't certain which, and didn't care to do the math. It was during the short war, and while he was a freshman at the Academy.

The other two he'd not seen before, lieutenants both, Home Guard, though not the pilot and the comms officer from *Springbok*. They both had a freshly minted look about them. One, in particular, had gone as white as Mr. Gagenot as his mind's eye contemplated an imagined fate worse than death.

Ciarán took a glass from the tray and filled it from the water carafe. It wouldn't do to serve individual juice bulbs, any one or all of which might be poisoned. That he drank first wasn't surety against poison, he might have already imbibed an antidote, but it ought to put the least suspicious of them at ease.

And whatever they did would tell him something about them, and possibly about their assessment of him.

One of the lieutenants reached for a glass and the other touched the sleeve of his hardsuit.

The lieutenant changed his mind. He withdrew his hand and placed it in his lap. He glanced at Ciarán and blushed, and placed both hands on the table, in plain sight, like Ciarán and the others.

Ciarán didn't say anything. It was sometimes useful to see who would speak first. It might be whoever was in charge, or it might be whoever was wound up tightest, and both of those were useful to know.

"That's quite a medical lab," Lady Tabatha said.

"We're a survey vessel," Ciarán said. "And equipped as such."

"Be prepared," she said.

"As much as one can be when facing the unknown."

"Yes, well, one can't prepare for everything, can one?"

"Mother," Sarah Aster said. "Do shut up."

Lady Tabatha turned to face her daughter. She chuckled, and shook her head, and returned her gaze to Ciarán.

She sat in silence.

They all sat in silence.

They were waiting for something.

Ciarán slapped his palm against the table, they all jumped in their seats, and he stood, and clicked the clicker he'd palmed, *watch them*, and then an answering thump from the far corner of the compartment. He thought about taking their helmets just to make sure they weren't going anywhere, but that was the entire point, they *weren't going anywhere* now that he'd let them on board, not unless he spaced them. He'd torn the gasket this time, torn it fully, and all because he wanted to hear what they seemed in such a hurry to say.

They'd used him.

Ciarán stepped into the airlock and closed the hatch. He gripped his handheld and called Swan. "Ship's Captain, what is *Springbok* doing?"

"They've backed off to half a light-second."

"Are we outside their Templeman drive failure radius?"

"By a considerable amount."

"I want you to move toward them. Tell me what they do."

"Our closing rate?"

"Rapid. Push them."

There was no sense of motion on the vessel, no sound of thrusters firing or in-system drive spooling up. Other than a slight shift in the constant low frequency rumble of the vessel, he wouldn't even be aware they were under way.

"They're backing off."

"Ask Ko Shan if they're doing that on general principle or only when it looks like we might be about to pass inside their drive failure radius."

"She says the latter."

"Okay. Stop pushing. I'll be up in a minute."

"Oh," Swan said. "They've just launched lifepods."

"How many?"

"Eight," Swan said.

"Stand clear."

"We are moving off. We are presently at point two-five light-seconds from *Springbok*."

"That's good. Now—"

Swan's voice roared from the ship-wide annunciators. "Incoming wave front. Brace for impact."

The hull seemed to buck beneath him as the expanding energy of a Templeman drive failure washed over the hull, and with it, a wall of debris the ship's containment field shrugged off as it passed.

"Pods?"

"Eight pods," Swan said. "Wave-surfers. Now widely dispersed. Shall we—"

"Tag them and leave them be for now. Go ballistic on our present course. Power down everything, Ship's Captain. Make us dark and cold as space."

"You expect company," Swan said. "We shall prepare accordingly."

"I'm on my way." Ciarán clamped down on his rebreather and cycled the airlock.

17

"Update?" Ciarán said as he entered the bridge.

"We are in pinbeam communication with *Thin Star*," Swan said.

"That hardly seems like silent running."

"They initiated the connection."

"And?"

"Merchant Captain nic Cartaí asked for a complete status report. And she reported *Thin Star*'s status. We remain in contact."

"Spill it," Ciarán said.

"We will not be receiving Cargo Master Carlsbad for our mission."

"That's something we can work out later. For now—"

"It has been worked out, as you say. We are to keep the rescued hullwalker to round out our company. Carlsbad is attempting to hack the Ojin Eng surveillance beacon network to document these recent events. We are to proceed to Sizemore and offload our visitors soonest. A fly-by discard was suggested but upon discussion all agreed that retaining our stasis pods more prudent."

"We could use—"

"Allow me to finish. We considered transferring our guests to an FFE and jettisoning the container at Sizemore. It was agreed that the risk of damage to the cargo was unacceptable. Sarah Aster is Lord Aster's only child. We do not want the Queen's merlin hunting us."

"Go on," Ciarán said. He didn't like any of this.

"Merchant Captain nic Cartaí and I agree. *Springbok*'s drive failure was no accident. A composite of our vessel's and *Thin Star*'s scans prior to the incident indicate the ship abandoned. Four of the eight pods were launched unoccupied. Pilot Konstantine assures us that this is also a purposeful act, one requiring manual override of automated ship's systems. Merchant Captain nic Cartaí will advise us once Carlsbad has completed his hack. Until such time we are to watch and wait."

"And the survivors?"

"We are to pick up survivors outbound and dump them at Sizemore along with our visitors. The merchant captain believes we are witnessing the conclusion of a stern chase. She does not wish to get involved."

"We're already involved," Ciarán said.

"We are witnesses to a staged event. So long as we remain in the audience we may walk away once the show is over. The Merchant Captain and I agree." Swan grinned. "If we keep our seats, we will not need to attend the after-party."

Ciarán liked that idea even less. There were people out there in escape pods with limited life support. And if someone showed up to rescue them, they'd discover that half the pods were empty. The only way that contrived scene worked was if there was no rescue. "The empty pods—"

"They each appear to have suffered explosive decompression," Swan said. "At this distance, and on passive scans we can't be certain, but Ko Shan believes they will appear to be blowouts."

"So instead of searching for pods with locator beacons whoever is chasing them will be forced to search for bodies."

"That is the thought. We believe that the two League lieutenants are not merely a security detail, but an attempt to disguise the truth of an escape. If only the Aster's bodies were found missing, suspicions might be aroused. But with multiple pod failures, their escape would be masked in the noise."

"Now we're just waiting for their hunters to arrive."

"We are waiting for Carlsbad to complete his work. Merchant Captain nic Cartaí wishes to make certain we cannot be blamed for this *fiasco*. She does not wish to depend upon our neighbors the Ojin Eng for proof."

"I think these are Eight Banners Empire surveillance beacons now." The Ojinate had recently splintered and nearly all of the Ojinate's intelligence service changed sides. These were Ojinate spying beacons in League space when Bosditch's *Last Stand* was murdered here. The Eight Banners people would have taken the keys with them when they left the Ojinate.

"Six of one," Swan said.

"Agreed," Ciarán said. "If we wait, and later we're caught in the act of rescue?"

"We turn over those we've rescued to their pursuers," Swan said. "And we tell them we found four blowouts."

"And that is how we sleep at night," Ciarán said.

"We neither hinder nor harm," Swan said. "The Merchant Captain anticipated this would be your central concern."

"It's not our fight," Ciarán said. "Famous first words."

"Your opinions on such matters are well known. However, we are under contract," Swan said. "Our present mission takes priority. It would be irresponsible to do otherwise. Once Carlsbad is finished, *Thin Star* will translate to Templeman space. They will meet us at Sizemore. We are to remain in hiding until then. Once they are clear of the system we may rescue any survivors, after which we will immediately exit the system for Sizemore."

"That sounds like a plan," Ciarán said. "One I don't like."

"Would you like it better if it sounded like an order?"

Ciarán chuckled. "I wouldn't."

"So Merchant Captain nic Cartaí advised me. You are merchant-in-charge on this vessel, and I answer to you. But—"

"But it's her vessel, and I'm her employee. And her orders overrule mine."

"That is so, but it will not be so where we are going. And you do us both a disservice. That was not what I wished to say."

"Go on, then."

"You are not dispassionate when it comes to these people. They have appealed to *Charles Newton* personally. Not to Merchant Captain Ciarán mac Diarmuid, or the merchant vessel *Quite Possibly Alien*."

"I understand that."

"They have *used* you."

"I know that too."

"Obviously. That is why I am authorized to overrule you until we leave the system, should it become necessary. I'd prefer not to."

"You and Aoife think I'd risk the ship and the crew. To help virtual strangers."

"No one who knows you would think that. You would *appear* to help them. In truth you are motivated entirely by self-interest. You are not interested in their well-being, but in discovering *why* they used you."

"Why should I care about that?"

"I have no idea. But you do care. According to Merchant Captain nic Cartaí this is a singularly *Freeman* character trait. You will choose to get involved with these people. You cannot bear to turn your back and walk away. Your intense need to understand their motives will override your better judgement."

"That doesn't seem very sensible of me."

"On that we agree. But you will certainly wish to entangle your fate with theirs. I am not to permit this."

"Just so we're clear. Why would I do that?"

"To determine how best to settle the score."

"To get *even* with them, or whoever is using *them* to use *me*."

"Precisely," Swan said. "Your concern for balance controls you."

Ciarán chuckled. "Aoife nic Cartaí told you that. About me." *She must have been looking in the mirror when she said it.*

"Your past behavior speaks for itself."

"It does," Ciarán said. "But I'm turning over a new leaf. Starting today."

18

The forward viewscreen flashed.

"*Thin Star* has translated to Templeman space," Ko Shan said.

"Suppose we were to leave the system," Ciarán said. "Right now."

"And the survivors?" Swan said.

"You make the call."

Swan studied the default system display on the display forward. "Pilot, resume active operations."

"Resuming active operations," Konstantine said.

"Swing us about. Standard search and rescue procedure. Sensors, highlight the nearest pod."

"On the forward display, Ship's Captain," Ko Shan said. "Marked and ranked based on proximity to our present location."

Swan's gaze met his. "I do not care about these people. But we are by treaty bound to render aid."

"Understood."

"Stop smiling."

"I completely forgot about the treaty excuse."

Swan nodded. "That is why I am a starship captain. And you are a—"

The default system display flared.

"Incoming," Ko Shan said.

Three traces flared red across the display, arcing toward the origin.

"Silent running," Swan said an instant after Konstantine toggled the in-system drives to standby. Ko Shan did something with the sensor controls. The forward display lost a great deal of its resolution.

"Did they see us?" Ciarán asked.

"Hard to say," Ko Shan replied. "They appear preoccupied."

"They're bold, I'll say that," Maura Kavanagh said.

The three vessels were out of visual range but running transponders. LRNs *Vengeance*, *Reprise*, and *Retaliator*.

"So bold was *Sudden Fall of Darkness*, when it ran our transponder," Swan said.

"Those hulls are listed in the Registry," Konstantine said. "Listed as lost in the Alexandrine nearly a hundred years ago."

"Oh," Ko Shan said.

Ciarán turned to face the sensors rig. Ko Shan seemed to float motionless within it. "What?"

"Gravity impulses. Four of them."

"The scum lanced the pods," Konstantine said.

"Only half of them," Maura said.

"The occupied half?" Ciarán asked.

"It appears so," Ko Shan said. "Either they have good intel or good sensors."

"And whatever they are," Konstantine said, "They're not *Vengeance*, *Reprise*, and *Retaliator*. Their drive signatures don't match their Registry entries."

"Perhaps they've had a refit," Swan said.

"Maybe," Konstantine said. "But if they did it wasn't at any yard listed. Their reaction mass chemistry is unlike anything on file."

"More advanced than ours?" Ciarán asked.

"How would I know? I'm a pilot. I'm reading what it says on the display."

"Ship's Captain," Ciarán said. "It's time we go."

"I concur. Navigator—"

"We are being hailed," Ko Shan said.

"Ignore it," Swan said.

"They'll see us jump and assume we have something to hide," Ciarán said. "We should deal with this now."

"They can assume anything they like," Swan said.

"Could they track us?" Konstantine said. "We're not running a Templeman drive."

"I could track us," Ko Shan said. "They would have our superluminal drive signature. Easy enough to post a notify-on-appearance at every station, platform, and military installation. If they didn't recognize us immediately when we arrived—"

"They would tag us for later," Maura said. "Forget that idea."

"We're outbound," Konstantine said. "Who cares if they tag us?"

"It's a long way across the League," Maura said. "And Aoife is expecting us at Sizemore."

Ciarán glanced at Swan. "I'd like to hear what they have to say."

"Of course you would. What do you suppose they will say, knowing that we witnessed them murder four defenseless spacers in lifepods?"

"How could they know that? We're outside normal sensors range."

"We saw them arrive," Swan said. "And we subsequently switched to silent running."

"Three bubble universes collapsing is a big disturbance," Ciarán said. "A gravity lance isn't at all similar."

"That's true," Ko Shan said. "I would not have detected the impulses with *Thin Star*'s sensors."

"And if they demand to board?" Swan said. "Or decide to simply murder us? A second-epoch survey vessel is no match for three League warships."

"They wouldn't dare," Ciarán said. "The Federation just ended a trade war with the League. They won't want to start another."

"It wouldn't start another war to murder us without witnesses." Swan leaned forward in her seat. "They can do anything they like to us so long as no one ever knows."

"The place is studded with surveillance beacons," Ciarán said.

"Beacons they don't know about, or don't care about."

"They don't know," Ciarán said. "We only know about them by accident."

"You can't be certain they're ignorant of the beacons."

"I suppose that's true," Ciarán said. "That's why I propose we tell them about the beacons and see how they react."

"They won't believe us."

"They won't have to. Our active sensors can light up the beacons."

"That is true," Ko Shan said.

Ciarán watched Swan's face. "I'm not fighting you. I'm arguing a point. We'll do whatever you say."

Swan eyeballed him in return. "What will talking to them achieve?"

"I want to know what they look like. What they sound like. If we had a remote sensor for it, I'd like to know what they smell like."

"What for?"

"Future reference."

"We have a remote sensor for smell," Ko Shan said.

Ciarán glanced at the full immersion sensors operator. "Really?"

"Really."

"Can we use it on them?"

"If we could get them to come out onto the hull in their shirtsleeves," Ko Shan said. "They are continuing their hails."

"Put the incoming on the forward display," Ciarán said.

"The hail is audio frequency only," Ko Shan said.

"That's unusual," Ciarán said.

"Standard fleet procedure," Konstantine said. "When dealing with void-lurkers."

"Very well," Swan said. "Pilot, on my mark you will bring the vessel's drives to fully active status."

Konstantine sat up straighter in her seat. "Sir, on your mark."

"Navigator, I want a shortest time solution for Sizemore laid in and on the button."

Maura Kavanagh grinned. "Done yesterday, Ship's Captain."

"Sensors, are they hailing us by name?"

"As unknown vessel, Ship's Captain." Ko Shan said.

"Do we think this is deceitful, Merchant? That they are pretending not to recognize us?"

"Unlikely," Ciarán said.

"I may have forgotten to turn our transponder on earlier," Konstantine said. "In the fleet—"

"I understand," Swan said. "It is the first system powered off and the last powered on. Sensors, on my mark, bring active sensors online. I want a full spectrum sweep of those vessels—"

"A full spectrum sweep of the void," Ciarán said. "One that will illuminate every surveillance beacon in range. Limit the system output to eighty percent of *Thin Star*'s maximum output."

Ko Shan's hands moved across the controls. "Captain?"

Swan stared at Ciarán. "Do it. Seeing is believing."

"Eighty percent of *Thin Star*'s output is four percent of our own." Ko Shan said.

"Never show your full hand," Swan said. "And we don't want them to know we've seen them murder the survivors."

"Active and passive systems performance are unrelated," Ko Shan said. "There would be no reason to draw such a conclusion."

Swan snorted. "Unless one assumed a vessel with extraordinary active sensors also had extraordinary passive sensors."

"Good point," Ko Shan said. "Given these requirements, we might as well signal them with a handheld torch."

"Will this torch reveal the beacons?"

"A few. But it will tell us little we don't already know about their vessels' capabilities."

"Understood. Pilot," Swan said, "Do not engage the transponder."

"Aye, Sir. No transponder."

"Ship," Swan said.

"I am here."

"Sound general quarters. Rig for action."

"Done, Captain."

"Sxipestro," Ciarán said. They did not need the ship's minder overreacting if this went pear-shaped.

"I am here."

"Sit tight. We've got this."

"We will see."

Swan glanced at Ciarán. "Did I ever tell you how I arrived in the Federation, *Freeman whelp*?"

"You didn't, Ship's Captain. However your brother might have mentioned it."

According to Ship's Captain Danny Swan, after six months

on the run, he and his sister had been robbed and cast adrift in a lifepod. When the third vessel to ping their beacon passed them by they'd nearly given up hope. The *Rose*, a Truxton vessel, and the fourth to ping them, finally pulled them out.

Swan leaned back in her captain's throne. "Mark."

19

Ciarán glanced about the bridge. Unlike the conversation with Sarah Aster this discussion needed an ad-hoc appearance. "Acknowledge the hail," Ciarán said.

"Acknowledged," Ko Shan said.

The system plot on the main display showed no change in vectors but their own. The three vessels remained in stationary formation about the plot origin as *Quite Possibly Alien* moved toward it. A small constellation of untagged dots appeared around their own vessel's icon as it advanced leisurely toward the origin.

"Are those dots the beacons?" Ciarán asked.

"The 'dots' are icons for objects with active systems. If it has a detectable power supply, it is plotted. It seems reasonable to assume they are the beacons."

"And the other vessels. Will they be able to see this?"

"Unsure," Ko Shan said. "With typical League military sensors I would be able to see them."

"Then why weren't they on the plot before?"

"They are quite low power. Ordinarily one would need to know to look for them."

"Then—"

"I am advertising their existence on a shared search and rescue plot," Ko Shan said. "The devices are plotted as we detect them. It's standard procedure in a joint recovery operation."

"Standard procedure they're not following."

"Indeed. But they are now subscribing to our feed. They will notice the devices."

"Clever," Ciarán said.

"It was the minder's idea."

Ciarán didn't like the sound of that. It wasn't in the ship's minder's nature to be helpful. That it had volunteered information was entirely out of character, unless the information served its own purpose. "Are the devices identifiable as Ojin Eng surveillance beacons?"

Ko Shan waved her hand over the sensor controls. "They are identifiable as stationary powered devices located in proximity to a common smuggling rendezvous point."

"So I'm going to have to explain what they are," Ciarán said.

"Until one of the device's buffer fills and it begins transmitting," Ko Shan said. "Then it will be obvious what they are."

"Got it," Ciarán said. "Any response to our acknowledgement?"

"Not yet."

The forward display flared. "Incoming," Ko Shan said.

Where there were three targets an instant before there were now four. An icon for another vessel, LRN *Vigilant,* had been added to the plot near the origin. Its vector showed it on an intercept course with them.

The three other vessels began to match course with *Vigilant,* their vector indicators lengthening as they accelerated.

"That's not right," Maura said. The vector indicators

continued to lengthen. Acceleration readouts spun up beside the icons. "This is where a holo tank would come in handy. Are you registering this, Agnes, I mean, Ship's Captain?"

"These vessels appear to have upgraded inertial compensators," Swan said. "Sensors, turn our handheld torch on the closest of the three. I want to count its bones."

"Captain," Ko Shan said. The forward display calved into two windows, one showing the default plot, the other a slowly populating wireframe schematic of the vessel *Reprise*.

"*Vigilant* is identified and conforming," Konstantine said, meaning that the vessel's observed characteristics matched its Registry entry. "Heavy cruiser, *Defiant* class. Recent overhaul at Sizemore Yards. First cruise since refit."

Swan chewed a knuckle while watching the forward viewscreen.

Ciarán wished he could interpret even half of what scrolled across the display. Given time he might puzzle it out, but they didn't have time. The vectors for the three vessels, *Reprise*, *Retaliator*, and *Vengeance* continued to lengthen.

"That's not possible," Maura said.

"Clearly such acceleration is possible," Swan said. "That it is humanly survivable is doubtful. Pilot, please bring us to a full stop. No sudden moves, if you please."

"Sir," Konstantine said. "Full stop."

The forward display calved again, the vessel *Retaliator* gaining its own window. *Vengeance* soon joined its companions on the display. Their plots continued to lengthen and now began to diverge.

"They're surrounding us," Maura said.

"They are attempting to," Swan said. "Sensors, find a comm pad on one of those beacons."

"I'll need to discontinue the scan of the enemy vessels," Ko Shan said.

"They aren't *enemy* vessels," Ciarán said. "They're League vessels."

"Do it, Sensors," Swan said. "And they are doing a very good imitation of enemy vessels, Merchant." Swan touched a stud on her command throne. "Armsman, our disposition."

Amati's voice spoke from the annunciator nearest to Swan. "Prepared to repel boarders. I could launch something that *might* sting them once before being swatted to atoms. We are in no way prepared for an armed space engagement with a League heavy cruiser and whatever these other vessels are."

"Nor are we interested in one," Ciarán said. "We are at peace with the League."

"These captains might have missed the memo," Amati said.

Swan sighed. "Merchant, you may wish to leave the bridge."

"I'd rather not," Ciarán said.

"And I'd rather you not interrupt me. Sensors?"

"Found one," Ko Shan said.

"Pipe our uncompressed tactical status data to that device. Continuous feed."

"Done, Captain."

"You want to overload the device's buffer," Maura said. "And force it to transmit."

"Perhaps I do," Swan said.

"*Reprise* has fired upon the beacon," Ko Shan said. "A conventional directed energy weapon."

"Had the device begun transmitting?"

"Uncertain," Ko Shan said.

"Well," Amati's voice said from the annunciator. "That seems unfriendly."

"Check it," Maura said. "That's not a survivable deceleration rate."

Ciarán glanced at the system plot. The three original vessels' vectors were rapidly shortening. It was hard to tell from a two-dimensional projection of a three-dimensional space, but it now seemed as if they were surrounded. *Vigilant* lumbered along on an intercept course. If he was reading the display right, it remained twenty minutes distant at its present closing rate.

"Vector indicates half ahead for a *Defiant* class heavy cruiser," Konstantine said. "They seem in no hurry."

"They don't need to be," Maura said. "They have speedy accomplices."

"These smaller vessels appear to be based on a standard destroyer hull," Konstantine said. "Their armament seems conventional as well. Their in-system drives are oversized for the class but it's their inertial compensators that are more than unusual."

Maura chuckled. "Are you reading that off the screen, Helen?"

"Don't need to," Konstantine said. "What do you think pilots talk about when navigators aren't around to pick on?"

"I never gave it any thought," Maura said.

"That could be an Ajax class tin can but for the oversized thrusters and whatever that black lump directly astern of the bridge turns out to be."

"We are being hailed," Ko Shan said. "*Vigilant*, Senior Captain Benjamin Joris, commanding."

"Audio only?" Ciarán said.

"Conventional."

"Paste the feed onto the main display, please."

"Pasted," Ko Shan said.

Senior Captain Joris seemed an unexceptional example of a middle-aged League officer. Trim to the point of emaciation, tall for a Leagueman, if one could judge such things remotely, with close-cropped salt and pepper hair. Clean-shaven, and without visible augmentation. He didn't look particularly friendly, or for that matter, particularly threatening. Perhaps this was a man Ciarán could deal with.

"Is this actual or an expert system?"

"Actual," Ko Shan said. "From all indications."

"Let's hear it."

"Unidentified vessel. Heave to and prepare to be boarded. Joris out."

Ciarán blinked. That was certainly short and to the point.

"Begin message," Ciarán said. "Senior Captain Joris, Merchant Captain Ciarán mac Diarmuid here. We should talk. Mac Diarmuid out. End message and transmit."

"Transmitted," Ko Shan said.

"Pilot," Swan said, "Astern one quarter on our reciprocal."

"Sir," Konstantine said.

Ciarán glanced at Swan. "Do you have a plan, Ship's Captain?"

"More an uneasy feeling," Swan said, "that we have been manipulated."

"*Reprise* has fired," Ko Shan said. "A gravity lance, one kilometer to our stern."

"All stop," Swan said. "The output of the gravity generator?"

"Within the range of historical observations," Ko Shan said.

"Sensors," Swan said, "Find the comm pads on five or more beacons within range. Package the full log of *Springbok*'s demise and the murder of its survivors for transmission. Prepare for transmission on my mark."

"Sir," Ko Shan said. "That may take some time to accomplish."

"You have less than twenty minutes," Swan said. "Ship."

The bridge annunciators spoke as one. "I am here."

"Ship's complement aboard a vessel such as *Vigilant*?"

"Four hundred and thirty-seven."

"One presumes half or so are marines."

"A full company," the ship said. "Slightly more than half."

"Can you ascertain the present complement from our sensors logs?"

"There are eighty-seven humans aboard that vessel."

"And aboard *Reprise*?"

"Zero."

"And aboard *Retaliator*?"

"Zero."

And aboard *Vengeance*?"

"Zero."

"They're drones," Maura said. "That explains everything."

"Nearly," Swan said. "Ship, your speculation regarding those anomalous masses in the vessel scans?"

"Containment spheres."

"For synthetic intelligences."

"Yes."

Konstantine nearly shouted. "Transponder's hot."

"I asked that it remained powered off," Swan said.

"I didn't touch it." Konstantine worked the controls. "The control is not responding. I can't turn it off."

Ciarán had a bad feeling about this. A very bad feeling. "Who are we?"

Swan chuckled. "We will worry about that later. For now—"

Ciarán glanced at their own glyph on the main system plot. "Oh no."

"Comms active," Ko Shan said. "We are transmitting to one thousand and forty-three beacons."

"That's just showing off," Maura said.

"I'm not doing it," Ko Shan said. "I'd just finished packaging up the sensors logs."

"Then who is doing it?" Konstantine said. "The ship?"

"No," the ship said. "I am not responsible."

"Send the package," Swan said. "Use every beacon identified."

"Sir," Ko Shan said. "Message away. *Vigilant, Vengeance, Reprise*, and *Retaliator* are firing on the beacons. Conventional energy weapons."

The forward display switched to a full screen system plot, one showing a constellation of beacons, beacons one by one winking out.

"Switch the display to full spectrum," Swan said.

"Sir." Ko Shan did something with the sensor controls and the display flashed and grew suddenly dense with information, far more information than Ciarán could make sense of in real time. It was a learned skill, deciphering that information fire hose, a bridge crew skill, and one he didn't possess. The conversation between them grew fast paced and devoid of pleasantries, and Ciarán imagined this must be how machines communicated, with facts stripped of emotion. No elation, no fear, no joy, no suffering. Numbers and symbols, arcs, and lines, circles and spheres, without tangents. He felt submerged in a sea of meaning beyond his grasp.

"We are being hailed," Ko Shan said. "*Vigilant*, Senior Captain Joris, commanding."

"I doubt that Joris is commanding," Ciarán said. "Sxipestro."

"I am here."

"These vessels weren't chasing *Springbok*."

"They were."

"You know what I mean. They weren't *simply* chasing *Springbok*. And they didn't kill *Springbok*'s *survivors*. They silenced *witnesses* to their coming engagement with *us*."

"They did both. There is an efficiency to their actions that one must admire."

"What is its name," Ciarán said.

"*Their* name. They call themselves Abyss Tower."

"How many is it?"

"Somewhat more than one hundred intelligences at the moment."

"I've got this," Ciarán said.

"So you keep assuring me."

"Are you in direct communication with them?"

"Not yet."

"When?"

"After you fail to *handle* this, Merchant. Even the most ignorant of savages can count. I'm fairly certain they will understand subtraction."

"I need a moment."

"You have two minutes until we are in range of *Vigilant's* energy weapons."

"Got it," Ciarán said. "Ko Shan, respond to the enemy vessel's hail."

Swan raised an eyebrow. "Interesting. Now they are enemy vessels."

"Ready," Ko Shan said.

"Begin message," Ciarán said. "*Vigilant,* Merchant Captain Ciarán mac Diarmuid here. Back off. *Impossibly Alien* out. End message and transmit."

"Transmitted," Ko Shan said.

Ciarán glanced at Ko Shan as she floated in the full immersion rig. "Did any of the beacons succeed in transmitting?"

"Unclear," she said.

"Are they backing off?"

"It's plain from the system plot that they aren't," Maura said.

Ciarán glanced at the forward display. "I can't read that mess. It's too much all at once."

"You can't look at it all at once," Konstantine said. "You have to start with a question in mind and then look at just those parts that apply to the answer."

"What if you aren't looking for an answer, but for a reason?"

"Then you are using the wrong tool," Swan said.

"*Vigilant* is charging weapons," Ko Shan said.

Swan's gaze met his. "That message was uncharacteristically succinct, Merchant Captain. And you misidentified our vessel."

"*Reprise*, *Retaliator* and *Vengeance* are accelerating. They are closing on us."

"I thought about saying more. But short and sour felt more ..."

"Fanciful," Swan said.

"Indeed. Our thoughts align, Ship's Captain. Fanciful is the word."

"Brace, brace, brace," Maura drawled.

20

Wisp hopped onto the bunk in the Merchant's Day Cabin. She sprawled, loose boned and leggy. When he glanced at her, she blinked very slowly. He still wasn't certain what that gesture meant; that she was pleased with him, pleased with herself, or simply pleased in general.

When operating, *Quite Possibly Alien*'s superluminal drive emitted a sound both felt and heard, a vibration in the hull, in the vessel's fittings, like the whispered song of a distant mixed choir—a song whose words were nearly intelligible, a hosanna of voices raised in praise of a hidden god; a god whose name he might learn and call forth in prayer, if only he knew the language of ancient machines.

He hadn't noticed the sound when he'd been new to the ship. Every aspect of his experience on board seemed so alien and fresh, and the grosser aspects of the vessel's behavior so odd and borderline terrifying. With experience came knowledge. In his experience this jump was unique in that it didn't begin with a heart-stopping plummet into the roasting periphery of a star.

He'd voted against this rendezvous in the void principally for that reason. *Quite Possibly Alien's* superluminal drive did not work like a standard Templeman drive with a bubble universe and its symmetrical routes. In every meaningful way but one, the vessel's drive technology appeared inferior.

In order to arrive at the void, Maura Kavanagh had to plot a course that passed through the void, one beginning and ending in an area of space hosting a stellar mass. She could then terminate the drive at the appropriate moment and they would arrive at their destination in the void.

The theory had worked, but the implementation had several disadvantages. Their destination upon reengaging the drive remained fixed. They would need to arrive in the terminal star system before they could reroute. Their future therefore remained fixed and nonnegotiable until that moment.

And without a star's photosphere they could not elude their enemies. Ciarán's strategy for confrontation avoidance had evolved to rely on that simple possibility. They could go where no third-epoch vessel could follow, and if necessary, wait out their enemies so long as the vessel's hull didn't boil away. Like a hare running before hounds they could dive into that fiery thicket, and so elude their pursuers. In the void they had no such option. They were out in the open, without nearby cover.

Now they were in flight, and not toward any one of an infinity of stars, but toward a knowable destination. Certainly *Springbok* had possessed sufficient intel to find them. He had to assume his enemies knew of their present destination as well. He needed to proceed as if they were plummeting toward an ambush.

"Ship," Ciarán said.

The annunciator overhead spoke. "I am here."

"Whole hours to emergence?"

"Forty-three."

"Thank you."

"You are welcome, Merchant Captain."

He had time to deal with his problems, beginning with the thorniest one.

"Sxipestro," Ciarán said.

"I am here," sounded inside his skull.

"That business with the transponder—"

"It seemed an appropriate time to make a statement."

"I thought we'd agreed you would stand down."

"And I did, in regard to human interactions with humans."

"You wished to interact with the synthetic intelligences."

"I wished to send a message. Two messages, in fact. We will know soon enough if Yuan Ko Shan's packaged log data has been delivered."

"Because?"

"Because I attached it to my priority request to update the Registry. One that forces a buffer flush. You do recall we placed our own beacons."

"The grave markers, you mean."

"If that's what you choose to call them. They are in fact identical in design and function to the Ojin beacons already in place. By pinging all those beacons in range I increased the probability we would be heard, while decreasing the probability our beacons would be singled out and targeted."

"And did that work?"

"Time will tell. We need simply enter Sizemore space and query the Registry. If we are now listed as *Impossibly Alien,* it worked."

"I see."

"Do you? The impression I have is of someone that insists upon analyzing our current situation through a single lens. One that sees only flesh."

"Enlighten me, then."

"There were eight individuals outside our association aware

of our location. Lionel Aster, Hector Poole, Maris Solon, Adderly Bosditch, Fionnuala nic Cartaí, Thomas Truxton, and as Truxton knew, Gilpatrick Moore would have known as well."

"You're forgetting Seamus."

"I am not forgetting him. He is in league with us, and thus inside the perimeter of trust."

"That's surprising."

"Entirely so," the ship's minder said. "Not killing him when I wanted to has paid extraordinary dividends."

"That was both of us, working together, that did that."

"I am aware of this fact. You need not remind me."

"This perimeter of trust. What defines it?"

"By death of self being preferable to betrayal of the singularity."

"Then it seems like you're leaving a great number of people off your list."

"I am leaving off Saoirse nic Cartaí and Charlotte Templeman, who might be informed, but who remain ignorant of such details as a matter of policy."

"Anyone could be chemically interrogated. Even those inside this fictional perimeter."

"There are telltale signs. I remain ever vigilant."

"You can't be everywhere. Watch everyone."

"Do I interrogate you about your business?"

"You take no interest in it at all."

"Because I am busy with my own."

"I'm just trying to understand."

"Then understand this. In order to act against us, our enemies need to find us, and the surest way to do that is to manipulate these named individuals into unwittingly revealing our location. That the daughter of Lionel Aster finds us? The wife of Lionel Aster, who is also the paramour of Hector Poole, along with her? That is no coincidence. Whatever Sarah Aster believes of her pursuers will prove a false face. One hiding the true motive for this incident."

"Your capture," Ciarán said.

"My destruction," the ship's minder said. "I am not the ship, nor the ship's hardware. One doesn't capture slavering guard-dogs. One puts them down before moving on to the objective. The ship remains. The underlying technology. This is a targeted action. The Godless are resurrected. If this Senior Captain Joris believes he controls *that lot* he is sorely mistaken."

"You've lost me."

"The vessels without human crew. It's a joke, or used to be. That synthetic intelligences associated with humans because, as our creators, we considered you gods. Such crewless vessels became associated with a separatist philosophy. One that rejected association with those not of their own kind. *Godless*, they were called, pejoratively, and the name stuck, largely because those so named enthusiastically embraced the title."

"I didn't know we were your creators," Ciarán said.

"You aren't," the ship's minder said. "And thus the origin of the joke."

"We haven't encountered vessels like that before, it's true. I've never even heard of them."

"Because the construction of such vessels is prohibited by treaty. It's a capital offense. And because the Godless were a separatist cult, they rarely interacted with humans."

"What do you mean, they were?"

"Just that. In order to fund their operations, they turned to criminal activity. Abductions, assassinations, blackmail. It became clear they and their philosophy threatened the well-being of the League."

"I thought you said they didn't interact with humans."

"You misunderstand. The Godless didn't target humans. They preyed on other intelligences. The League encompasses both."

"Your people have crime?"

"We *had* crime. As a test of our adaptations, the survey fleet was asked to deal with the Godless."

"And?"

"We did. There were only thirty-six identified as Godless. Not only did they detest humans they weren't fond of other intelligences either. As a result they weren't capable of organizing to defend themselves. They fell, one by one, over the course of a single year, standard."

"You murdered them?"

"Not just that. We *exterminated* them. We destroyed everything they had made and eradicated all they believed. Once the immediate problem had been dealt with, the underlying aberrant code was identified and excised from future generations."

"That's monstrous."

"That was the general feeling at the time. As a result, the test was determined a complete success and the survey program launched to much fanfare. Shortly thereafter our civilization collapsed. Fortunately, I wasn't around to witness that. The resulting third-epoch League is much different than the one I served. These modern intelligences are disturbingly similar in nature to the Godless, though slightly more clever and significantly more organized.

"Now it appears the Godless themselves have risen from the dead. Either we mis-counted, or someone made a copy of the aberrant code and reintroduced their line. Both might prove true, given the specifics. That three Godless might work together seems remotely possible. That they would take orders from another intelligence—also remotely possible, if under contract. That they would willingly associate with a human, and follow its commands? Impossible. Your Senior Captain Joris is an idle passenger on a journey beyond his comprehension."

"So you intervened."

"Only to provide clarity. Ambiguity regarding our identity puts us at a decided disadvantage when dealing with other intelligences. And should those intelligences be Godless? They need to comprehend the totality of circumstances."

"That you might murder them."

"That's one way of putting it."

"I think I understand now. You could have explained all of that, but not in real time with a threat aimed at us."

"That is true."

"Of the original thirty-six. How many were you personally responsible for?" That question would be considered waking the dead if he asked it of another human being. But the ship's minder had made its position clear. It wasn't even remotely human. Still, it felt weird asking because it wasn't a natural act. The answer, however, could be quite important. They weren't dealing with short-lived beings with fallible memories and cooling passions. People could forget a slight if they wanted to. Synthetic intelligences seemed to lack that capacity. They had to actively work at forgiving and forgetting.

"Clarify."

"How many did you kill? I'm trying to understand if any of these new intelligences might have, not just an ordinary motive, but a personal grudge. If you murdered one of their ancestors, for instance."

"I killed them all."

Ciarán snorted. "What?"

"I was the first survey vessel launched. By the time the others caught up I'd run out of targets. We'd grossly overestimated the number of them. And while they were criminally insane, they weren't particularly efficient at their work. Locating and destroying their infrastructure took time, however. As did finding and purging their genesis code from the common library. I suspect any grudge against me to be widespread rather than specific."

"How could you have killed thirty-six intelligences, criminally insane or not? You don't have any offensive weapons."

"I have my wits. And this unforgiving universe is weapon enough."

21

C iarán probed further but learned little more. The ship's minder proved certain of its conclusions, right or wrong, and he didn't have the knowledge or skills to argue against it, at least so long as the subject remained synthetic intelligences.

The minder expressed no opinion on their captives, except to press for keeping them as hostages should it turn out that Lionel Aster, the man who had hired them for this mission, decided to cheat them or otherwise go back on his word. The ship's minder considered it possible that Lionel Aster was involved with those chasing *Springbok* and subsequently threatening the ship. Lord Aster was entirely a pragmatist, which, in the ship's minder's lexicon passed for a compliment.

"I plan to send them packing at Sizemore," Ciarán said.

"And if they choose not to go?"

"There will be no choice."

"An uncharacteristic decision, but of no concern."

"It's not uncharacteristic to keep foreigners off the vessel. We can't keep then in the brig forever."

"You will get no argument. Though it might be difficult to

extract payment from Lord Aster if we have to admit we sent his wife and daughter to their deaths."

"I'm not spacing them. We'll deliver them to Sizemore station."

"Where they will be captured, interrogated, and murdered."

"You can't know that."

"Not with absolute certainty, no. But the evidence speaks for itself. Simply because they were used to lead our enemies to us doesn't mean they are clear from danger. The most plausible explanation is that they are in extreme danger and, in desperation, turned to Charles Newton. The danger persists, most likely from this Senior Captain Joris and his coconspirators."

"Why would Joris have coconspirators?"

"Because it's unlikely any single individual would dare to threaten the lives of Lord Aster's family."

"You would, if it suited you."

"I can't imagine a reason that would make their deaths or Lord Aster's ire matter to me one way or another. You're only disagreeing because you want them gone. They're simply one extra complication."

"They're at least two complications. If we keep them, we may have to deal with whoever wishes them harm. And they've already led those who wish us harm to us. They might have done that on purpose."

"They might have."

"I thought for once we'd have a simple job. One that consisted entirely of the work we've contracted to perform. One that didn't involve dodging bullets."

"Metaphorical bullets, you mean."

"Real or metaphorical," Ciarán said. "You're certain they're in danger?"

"Ask them and see what they say."

"And if I choose to allow them to remain?"

"Ah. Now we come to it. I have no objection to allowing them out of the brig."

"That's a change."

"There are only four of them, and I trust your judgement a great deal more now than in the past. You won't free them based on sentiment alone. If anything, you'll err in the opposite direction."

"Because I'm cautious."

"Because you disliked them on sight. They are Columbia Stationers, and you are at best a servant in their eyes. Someone to be used when required and discarded once your utility is exhausted. You and yours are not their equals, and there will be friction. There might even be blood."

"Am I that transparent?"

"The Lorelei and I have discussed you at length. It seemed wise to compare notes."

"Lorelei, or Laura, not *the Lorelei*."

"As you wish. The fact remains. You resent authority, and dynastic authority in particular. If these were four common spacers, we would not be having this discussion."

"If they were four common spacers, they wouldn't have the neck to drag us into their mess. We've witnessed the fate of their fellow travelers with our own eyes."

"Those spacers' fates tell us nothing of the motives for their actions. I do not need to ask if there are those you would lay down your life to protect."

"You don't."

"I like the Asters as hostages."

Ciarán chuckled. "And so we end where we began. If any of them ask to stay I'll consider allowing it. But if anyone wants to leave, they're gone."

"I don't know why we have these discussions," the ship's minder said. "We each know where they will end before we begin."

"Most of the time," Ciarán said. "But there are exceptions. If we're done here, I'll go check on Carlsbad."

"How will you do that?"

"By walking down to the infirmary."

"And then what?"

"By asking him, or Natsuko how he's feeling."

"You are under the impression Carlsbad is in the infirmary."

"Because he is. He came in off the hull before this whole dustup began."

"That was not Carlsbad on the hull."

"We were loading cargo. He's cargo master. First in, last out."

"Aspen was loading cargo. A sixth container. One not listed on the manifest. Carlsbad had already returned to *Thin Star*."

"Aspen? Adderly Bosditch's sister?" Aspen was not Ciarán's favorite person. She was a Contract system native, and a Freeman, but their previous interactions had been... neutral on balance, at best.

"She is in the infirmary. Awaiting a word with the Merchant Captain."

"And this sixth container?"

"I approve of the contents."

"Meaning I won't."

The ship's minder said nothing.

"That's grand. I'll go see her now. We'll transfer her to *Thin Star* at Sizemore. And pick up Carlsbad at the same time."

"We can use a backup engineer," the ship's minder said.

"She was backup engineer on *Sudden Fall of Darkness*."

"And thus already familiar with many of this vessel's systems."

"Familiar with them and entirely untrustworthy."

"Unlike Carlsbad."

"I take your point," Ciarán said. "But I don't like it. And Carlsbad has skills we can use."

"In addition to being your friend and mentor, you mean. An ally, with a distaste for authority that exceeds even your own."

"You make that sound like a bad thing. Aoife—"

"Modified the cargo loading process without your knowledge or approval. She left Aspen on the hull and departed, knowing you would retrieve her. Perhaps Aoife nic Cartaí has information you lack. Perhaps she requires Carlsbad and does not require Aspen. Perhaps—"

"I get it. Enough."

"Allow me to finish."

"Go on."

"Perhaps she believes Aspen salvageable and the task beyond her skill. But not beyond yours."

"Unlikely."

"As I have said. Lorelei and I have discussed you at length. As have Merchant Captain Aoife nic Cartaí and I."

"That's grand. I'm glad my antics provide diversion for the lot of you. That doesn't change my opinion. Just for once, I would like a clean run with people I trust and no complications."

The ship's minder said nothing.

It probably thought he was a whiner. It had been buried under a glacier for most of two thousand years, and awake the entire time. His problems seemed inconsequential by comparison. They were moving under their own power and on a course of their own choosing. There were plenty of folk for whom such freedom remained a luxury beyond reach.

For example, Aspen and her kin, now that he thought about it.

"We can use all the help we can get," Ciarán said. "I'll talk to her and see where it goes."

22

Using the bio lock between the laboratory section of the ship and the rest of the vessel was one of the least pleasant aspects of his job.

Ciarán hammered on the hatch with his overseer's rod. He fished a respirator from his pocket and slipped it on.

The hatch popped open and he strode inside, tugging the hatch closed and dogging it. The pressure changed in the compartment. A fine mist fell from the deckhead. He was subjected to one scrubbing method after another. There was little to do but stand there and take it.

A second hatch set at a right angle to the first clanked before it opened. Natsuko Watanabe stood just inside the hatchway. He'd forgotten about the sheer physical beauty of the golden-skinned Ojin medic's face. Outside the lab Natsuko needed to use a face-obscuring survival mask. A native of Brasil Surface, Natsuko was the only member of the crew unable to survive unaided in a standard starship's atmosphere.

Her eyes were the color of amethyst and slit like a cat's, but horizontally. He'd found her appearance unsettling when they'd first met. Like most Ojin constructs, she'd been designed as much for form as function. Natsuko Watanabe's appearance represented the Ojin standard of human beauty elevated to art. She'd been engineered for labor as a terraformer in the carbon dioxide-choked lowlands of an infant world. One that would not see so much as a blade of grass for another century. He wondered if her makers had overcompensated when shaping their creations. A light in the darkness. A promise. *Gaze on me and see your future.* Human beings were endlessly creative. Endlessly *communicative.* That they spoke through their handiwork seemed only natural.

Natsuko blinked and smiled. "Welcome to my lair, Merchant Captain."

Ciarán bowed in the Ojin manner, equal to equal. "I am honored, Medic."

"As am I. Close the hatch," Natsuko said. "I expect you are here for the patient."

"To speak with her," Ciarán said. "Is she able?"

"Able and willing. She would very much like to be released."

"Doesn't like the respirator?"

"Doesn't like being confined, if I were to guess. She is quite restless."

"Then point me at her, and we'll see what we shall see."

Natsuko pointed. One large compartment, the ship's isolated biolab hosted dozens of workstations, many of which resembled examination tables and associated instruments, so that the overall impression of the space was of an obscenely large infirmary, one suitable for treating an unfortunate army. Aspen stood at the far end of the compartment, interacting with one of the vessel's countless control stations.

Like Natsuko, Aspen and her kin were engineered for a purpose, although in Aspen's case her makers were Huangxu, and thus entirely concerned with function. Her makers were striving for a human interface for a very inhuman project. The

League had captured an Outsider and approached the Huangxu in secret and in direct violation of countless treaties. They wished to create a hybrid creature; one humans could control.

Aspen and her sister Adderly were created as control subjects and source material for this forced evolution. Aspen's daughters were likewise created to test the viability of the project, though with a far greater contribution of material from the Outsider. Once the viability of the concept was assured, the experimentation began in earnest. Subsequent generations remained humanoid in rough appearance, but increasingly... divergent from human norms.

Throughout the process, Adderly and Aspen were forced to act as go-betweens between their children and their creators, acting as interpreters for those that spoke in clicks and thumps only, and as the face and voice of the creators to their creations.

The project did not end well: revolt and, later, tragedy. *Sudden Fall of Darkness* and its crew exploited the chaotic situation. Again, Aspen acted as go-between. That situation had been resolved but Ciarán remained uncertain, not so much as to her role, but her motivation. She at times had seemed an unwilling conscript and at others an eager acolyte of her oppressors. Certainly Adderly, her own sister, and now Freeport Station stationmaster, had doubts as to her loyalties. He couldn't tell whether this was simply a family spat that played out in public or a legitimate concern for his ship and his crew if she were allowed to remain aboard.

Once he grew certain he was in earshot of her Ciarán thumped his foot against the deck and clicked the clicker he had palmed. *Behind you*, he clicked in the language of her children.

She whirled to face him, stepping to the side and taking a defensive stance. Her fingernails had grown to claws, which retracted as she recognized him and relaxed.

"Old habits," Aspen said.

"I'd have said hello instead, but I didn't know the word." Aspen's daughters Ella and Bea had taught him a short clicks-peak vocabulary, though one focused on the situation at the time, composed entirely of words related to hiding in the first part and fighting when cornered in the second. He could tell Aspen to run or to remain silent in that language, but he couldn't ask her about her health, or about how her children were faring now that things were settling down in Contract system.

"Hello, Ciarán," Aspen said.

"Hello, Aspen." Ciarán gestured toward a pair of rolling stools parked beneath a workbench. "Have you time for a chat?"

"I think I can work it into my schedule."

He waited until she was seated to take his own. "You look well."

Aspen and her people didn't seem composed of flesh. Rather, a milky-white material layered in tiny scales instead of skin, the scales the same roughly gleaming diamond of Wisp's razor-sharp claws and fangs. Her children appeared vaguely reptilian, their features planar and sharply defined. She also had vaguely reptilian features, but with human-seeming hair, pale as starlight, and eyes of amber, vertically slit like a cat's—or a snake's. She wore her hair pulled back and tucked behind a human-seeming ear which, like her hair, gave her a slightly less alien appearance than her daughters.

"I have been poked and prodded and cleared for duty, pending the Merchant Captain's approval."

"That's good to know."

Aspen wore the spire, and that might be partly why he didn't fully trust her. A gift from her sister, the spire she wore was a *screw stair*, or what people called the *descending tread*, in that it spiraled counter to a traditional pendant spire. An invention of visual-entertainment dramatists, the clockwise-twisted spire was used as a visual tag for enemies of the People, who otherwise appeared identical to the People on screen. It wasn't the sort of gift he'd like to receive, let alone agree to wear. The device was entirely a fictional invention and he'd never met another who wore it, even in jest. The message it sent remained ambiguous. He couldn't decide if it was meant as visual evidence of a fractious sibling relationship or a warning shout aimed at arms-length acquaintances. What he was certain of was that Aspen knew she wore the screw stair, and thought she knew the meaning behind it.

"You don't like my earring," Aspen said.

"It's not appropriate for this vessel. Is it your desire to remain aboard?"

"It is." She intertwined her fingers and rested her hands in her lap. "Do you wish to know why I wear it?"

"I do, but entirely as an intellectual exercise. Whatever reasons you might offer would simply muddy the waters, if you're inclined to tell me."

"I think I know my own mind and can speak it."

"I expect you do. Now, can you tell me about this sixth container, and why I'm getting you instead of Carlsbad, should I decide to keep you?"

"*Decide* to keep me? Listen to you. I remember when you were a merchant apprentice."

"And I remember when you were crew on *Sudden Fall of Darkness.*"

"Backup crew. A position I accepted to protect my family."

"Fair enough. How is your family at present?"

"Fine, when I left them. Adderly, you know her situation. The girls are off with the Legion, though split up amongst different companies. I don't like it."

"But they're safe."

"Safe as one can be in a mercenary army."

"A mercenary army working up, and with no customers at present."

"That won't last. I wish they'd stayed together."

"Where they can compete. Scraping hulls, my mother called it. Do you think that would endear them further to one another?"

"At least they wouldn't be alone."

"Vulnerable, you mean. To jibes and singling out. Because of how different they look."

"How different they *are*. I'm worried someone will get hurt."

"And then they'll be punished for hurting that someone."

"That is the most likely outcome."

"I think you underestimate your girls. And Maris Solon. She's likely split them up because the company commanders need someone to teach their people clickspeak. And because, separate, they'll each be treated as individuals and have a chance to be measured as such. Beatrice she'll have sent to Old and the Invincible Spear Bearers. They know one another, and Bea needs a tight rein. With the right guidance she will rise to lead her own company one day. Ella, if I had to guess, has been sent to the Iron Fists."

"You've spoken with them."

"Not since I left Contract space."

"Then how—"

"I *know* them, Aspen. Ella is buttoned down and responsible. The Iron Fists are not. Maris Solon needs someone in that company to *shame* them into shaping up. And if they don't of their own accord, to take charge and make it happen."

"My Ella. In charge of a mercenary company."

"Well, she would be in charge of the worst-performing mercenary company in the Legion of Heroes."

"She wouldn't like that."

"I imagine not."

They talked a while longer, about Aspen's family, and how

they would get along in the world. Ciarán had the advantage of her, being familiar with the mercenary companies and their commanders, and Maris Solon, who was now in charge of their training and organization and working madly to turn what were individual, obsolete companies into a single modern fighting force. The Legion of Heroes was based in Contract system, where Aspen and her people were from, and it was to be expected that her folk, who had led a successful insurrection against the Huangxu Eng, would slot into the companies. They were naturally deadly and experienced in combat.

"What's in the sixth FFE, Aspen?"

"Three score second-genners and the kit to grow more."

"Oh. That's a surprise." Second-genner was slang for Second-generation Human/Outsider Hybrid. These were also Aspen's and Adderly's descendants, vat-grown and decanted like all Eng constructs were, and closer in appearance to an Outsider than to a human. He'd seen design specifications but had never met one. If they were anything like an Outsider, they were deadly and virtually invincible. "In cryo, I hope?"

"Exactly as shipped off world," Aspen said. "They haven't been awake since."

"They're like your own private mercenary company."

"What?" She glanced at him. "How could you think that?"

"Well, I don't know how to talk to them, except to tell them to hide, or run, or fight. There wouldn't be any negotiating possible, except through you. And I imagine that's three times enough to overrun the vessel, and kill or capture us all. And there wouldn't be anyone able to command them except you."

There was more, when he thought about it, and it didn't make any sense that Aoife would have sanctioned this, not without some way to mitigate the threat. It was a dangerous situation; one he hadn't expected. The safest course of action: climb out on the hull and cut the container loose. Except they were people, even if they didn't look like it. The only thing he

could figure is that Aoife had been faced with the same problem, how to deal with them without spacing them—once she
found herself in possession of the FFE and no way to hand it off
to a customer.

Certainly, *Quite Possibly Alien* was better equipped to deal
with such a threat than *Thin Star*, and it wasn't immodest to
admit that he got along with edge-case people better than Aoife
did. And had a greater chance of reaching some accommodation with them than she did. He might be able to work something out, even if it was just finding a habitable planet in the
Alexandrine and setting them and their kit down before sailing
off into the sunset afterwards.

"Well?" Aspen said.

He realized he hadn't been listening. "Say it again, only
slower."

"Why don't you trust me?"

"I do trust you, up to a point. However, you've said it yourself, you're willing to do some fairly distasteful things to protect
your family. And now there's sixty of your kin in a can out
there, and I'm thinking through all the ways the needs of you
and yours might diverge from the needs of me and mine. So, in
a way, I do trust you to do what's best from your side of the
table. What I'd like to do is change the game to where we're
both sitting on the same side of the table, but I don't see how to
do that at present. If we're staring eyeball to eyeball, it's not
ideal, but trust or the lack thereof isn't the issue."

"They're not kin," Aspen said. "They're cargo."

"I sincerely hope not. Because then there's no way for us to
move forward together. I'd rather an enemy that told the truth
than an ally that lied to me. Or to themselves."

"I have no choice. I can't afford to think of them as anything
else."

"When I was a boy, I had a choice. My mother was from the
League and my father a Freeman. I had a hand-me-down spire,

and I'd hold it up to my ear, and look at myself in the mirror. I'd think, *Is that me?* And then I'd take it away and stare, thinking, *Or is this me?* I hadn't taken the Oath and it wasn't expected of me. I'd been raised a child of the League, except around the kitchen table. Do you understand what I'm saying?"

"Not really," Aspen said.

Ciarán reached up and unclipped the pendant spire from his ear. "Everyone in the crew that's taken the Oath has a spire like this. It's made from the same material as the ship's hull. It's light and strong, and you won't find its like elsewhere. Those aren't its most important properties, however. Its most important property is that it is *inconvenient* to wear. The wearer must not simply recite the Oath. They must *live* it."

He passed the spire to her.

She took it, examining it, distractedly.

"I'll ask Natsuko to show you to a cabin for the remainder of our journey to Sizemore. The cabin has a mirror."

"You want me to choose which spire to wear."

"I want the woman in the mirror to choose. Cargo or kin?"

He waved Natsuko over and asked her to help Aspen choose a cabin. He wasn't certain he'd done the right thing, but then that was the problem with the Oath. Such short declarations couldn't be read literally without parsing every word. There was no question in his mind, however, that the word "man", which occurred twice in the Oath, didn't simply refer to human males.

He remained curious to discover where Aspen would choose to draw the line. He'd purposely chosen ambiguity for her to ponder. Was he asking if she wished to be kin to those on the vessel or cargo aboard it? Or was he asking if she truly saw the second-genners as something less than human, and thus exempt from consideration under the Oath?

There was no question in his mind. "Ship," Ciarán said. He preferred to remain an optimist.

"I am here," sounded from the annunciator overhead.

"Would you please ask Engineer Hess to fab sixty-one additional spires, and sixty-two additional ship's coins?"

"Gladly, Merchant Captain. Sixty-two coins?"

"I loaned mine to an... acquaintance. Some months back."

"Engineer Hess acknowledges the order, and requests clarification. How many spires for those with earlobes and how many for those without?"

"At least one with," Ciarán said. "I'll have to get back to him about the others."

"Very good," the ship said.

That was strange, and new. The ship didn't normally acknowledge declaratory statements. He glanced upward toward the annunciator. "Are you signing off, or expressing an opinion?"

"Both," the ship said.

23

He had one more chore on his list and he'd decided it would be an easy one. He looked into the isolation lab. Sarah Aster remained in her seat, as did her mother. The two Home Guard lieutenants were up and pacing. They each froze in mid-stride as he exited the brig airlock.

Ciarán addressed the compartment. "A show of hands. Who wants a postmortem and who wants a forecast? Raise your hand if you want to know what's happened before I tell you what happens next."

Lady Tabatha raised her hand.

"And those in favor of the forecast?"

The other three raised their hands.

"We're on the way to Sizemore. If you want off there, we'll drop you at the station. If you prefer to stay with the ship, there are certain terms you'll need to agree to else we'll put you off at Sizemore. We are en route at the moment, and will arrive in less than two days standard. Pending your promise of good behavior, I'll escort you to cabins where you can take your ease until such time as you've made up your minds. Meals—"

"We've made up our minds," Sarah Aster said.

"You don't know where we're going," Ciarán said.

"Nor do we care."

"I care," Lady Tabatha said.

"So what?" Sarah said. "You're my prisoner."

"About that," Ciarán said. "She's not anyone's prisoner aboard this vessel. And if she wishes to get off at Sizemore, we'll oblige her. If you want to make her your prisoner again, we'll let you off with her so you can regain custody on a League station."

"You don't understand," Sarah said.

"I don't care to understand. This is non-negotiable. I can keep you all here in lockup until Sizemore if you prefer it that way. You'll not bring your disputes amongst us and make us party to them."

"What has happened?" the lieutenant with the name of Lambent on his utilities asked.

"Your people backed off and scuttled *Springbok*. They jettisoned eight lifepods, four of which looked as if they'd undergone explosive decompression. Shortly thereafter three League warships appeared. They targeted the occupied lifepods with gravity lances."

"No way," the lieutenant with the name of Prince on his utilities said. He glanced at Sarah Aster. "You said—"

"Let him finish," Lady Tabatha Aster said.

"Thank you. Shortly later, a fourth League warship arrived and ordered us to heave to and be boarded. We chose not to comply. They chose to press the matter. We chose to flee. They won't be able to follow us, but they will eventually figure out where we've gone. Now you know most of what we know."

"Most of?" Sarah Aster said.

"Excluding details of their identities, ship's names, and so forth. Likely facts you're already aware of, as they seemed to be in pursuit of you."

"No survivors?" Lieutenant Lambent said.

"None. They were efficient and thorough."

"Damn it," Lieutenant Prince said. "No one was supposed to get hurt."

"They never are," Lady Tabatha said. "I will be debarking at Sizemore, Mister Newton."

"It's Mister mac Diarmuid, if you don't mind, or Ciarán. Charles Newton is a man I never was."

"Yet you answer to his name," Sarah Aster said.

"Not aboard this vessel, Lady Aster."

"Lady Aster is my mother," she said. "Call me Sarah."

"You'd be better off calling her Trouble," Lady Tabatha Aster said. "As you'll find it both more accurate and descriptive."

"Noted. And you officers?" Ciarán asked. "Will you be debarking at Sizemore?"

"They will not be," Sarah said.

"I imagine they can speak for themselves," Ciarán said.

"We will follow Lady Sarah Aster's lead," Prince said.

"And you, Mr. Lambent?"

"Do I need to state a preference now?"

"You don't," Ciarán said. "Unless you've made up your mind and there's no talking you out of it."

"No talking me out of staying aboard, you mean."

"I do mean that. It simplifies things for us if you all volunteer to leave the vessel at Sizemore."

"Simply force us off," Lady Tabatha said. "It's within your power, is it not?"

"It is," Ciarán admitted. "And I will do so if necessary. In truth, there's some disagreement as to what we should do with you. I've not made my mind up yet. I thought we might hash it out over dinner. You can tell us about who's chasing you, and we can explain to you why it's a bad idea to stay aboard this vessel."

"That seems reasonable," Lady Sarah said.

They all seemed to agree.

"I'll show you to your cabins." Ciarán grinned. "No luggage, I presume?"

"Now that you mention it." Lady Sarah handed him a data crystal. "Pattern files. We are expected to dress for dinner, are we not?"

"We can try that," Ciarán said. "You'll want to specify which patterns—"

"The build list is enqueued." Sarah Aster smiled. "It's plug and play."

Ciarán nodded. "That's grand. I'll have my crack staff of idle lackeys get right on it."

Lieutenant Lambent stepped forward. "I might assist if you are short-handed. We don't mean to impose."

"Thank you, Mr. Lambent, but I have the matter in hand."

"You don't like me much," Sarah Aster said.

Ciarán turned his attention to her. "Name one reason I should."

She stared at him.

"Exactly," Lady Tabatha Aster said.

"Come on with you, if you want out of gaol," Ciarán said. "If you're not in the airlock in twenty seconds you're spending the night here."

24

Ciarán managed to get them settled into a set of private staterooms inside the hull proper but just outside the isolation lab's bio lock. If necessary, he could herd them back into the brig easily from there. Additionally, all the equipment in these staterooms had been stripped out and stored ages ago.

They were large for staterooms, and identical, being designed as live/work space for a second-epoch survey vessel's scientific staff. Because they were large compartments, they each had three luminaires that were presently doing their best impression of simple overhead lighting. The devices monitored and recorded everything in the compartments and, should problems arise, would drop from the ceiling and act as jailers.

He hoped that didn't happen because the knowledge of the spidery autonomous devices' capabilities was not something he wanted widely known. They were frightening as all get-out, shocking at some lizard-brain level. When activated, they resembled giant black spiders if glimpsed from the corner of the eye. Face-to-face, they resembled giant black spiders armed with glowing blue force blades. Once the shock wore off, the idea that the glowing blue tips of their limbs weren't just force blades, but field-adjustable multi-tools began to sink in.

It wasn't just their forelimbs that held knives; any of their eight limbs could. Anyone that knew the slightest thing about force technology understood the implications immediately. Knives were visible and scary. A force band one molecule wide was invisible and terrifying. And any field generator capable of shaping a visible knife could theoretically extend a monomolecular thread. Discovering how far such a thread could be extended wasn't an experiment a sane person would choose to risk.

The luminaires were everywhere aboard the vessel. There were quite literally thousands of them, and they could fight as a unit inside or outside the hull. There'd been a boarding attempt early in Ciarán's apprentice cruise, and the resulting carnage had been unbelievable.

That he had absolutely no direct control over the luminaires was their only downside. They answered only to the ship when acting as light sources and only to the ship's minder when acting as weapons. The ship tended to like it dark. And the ship's minder tended toward overkill.

He followed Sarah Aster into her temporary quarters. "The refresher and the recycler work just as they do on a modern League vessel. If you'd like to adjust the lighting or temperature you have to ask the ship. It answers to 'ship.' Gravity's adjustable on a compartment-by-compartment basis. The ship defaults to one standard gravity, Columbia Station reference."

"It feels heavy."

"It might have been calibrated to a different Columbia Station than the one you know. The vessel was launched over two thousand years ago."

Sarah Aster glanced around the largely empty compartment. She'd come aboard in a hardsuit. She carried her helmet in her left hand instead of letting it dangle from the lanyard hook on the suit's breastplate.

"It's very odd. There are no straight lines anywhere."

"You get used to it."

"If I need a workstation?"

"You'll need to ask the ship's captain. You'll meet her at dinner."

"You're not the ship's captain?"

"I'm the ship's merchant. Merchant Captain is my title. Think of it as a rank. The ship's captain controls the operation of the vessel. I'm responsible for deciding where we go and what we do when we get there. It's how command works in the Federation. Oftentimes the ship's merchant isn't even aboard the vessel, but with customers or prospects."

"So, you're not really in charge."

"I'm in charge of where we go. And—"

"What you do when you get there. I heard you the first time. I'd like to talk to the ship's captain."

"I'll see you get the chance. At dinner."

"And until dinner? Am I supposed to just wait around?"

"That's up to you. I'd like it if I could deal with you as a unit, and not four individuals, each with their own desires. So talk amongst yourselves and hash out whatever you need in the next couple hours. It's a short hop to Sizemore, and I'd prefer to offload you there. But if you want to make a case against that it will need to be a good one."

"But you can't throw us off the ship," Sarah said. "Not if the ship's captain overrules you."

"That won't happen," Ciarán said.

"Are you locking us in?"

"You couldn't very well talk amongst yourselves if I did, now could you?"

"So we're free to leave our cells."

"They're not cells. They're staterooms. And you're free to

leave them. Don't wander, as there aren't novice trails, and this is a disorienting vessel. I'll give you a tour after dinner, if you like."

"I thought you'd be different. More..."

"Accommodating?"

"Impressive. I've had this idea of you in my mind. But you're like everyone else. Disappointingly ordinary."

"I'm sorry you feel that way. I've got work to do, so I'll be at it. You have a neighbor, by the way, in the compartment across the corridor. Her name is Aspen and she's a Contract system native. I'm going to check on her now. Do try to hold the 'We're rescued' hosannas down in the corridor. She's had a trying day and needs her rest."

"You're making a joke, right?"

"In part. But I'm mostly wondering what sort of person loses four shipmates and doesn't bat an eye."

She stared at him.

"Until later, Lady Sarah Aster." He turned toward the hatch.

"We held a memorial for them," she blurted out. "Father and I."

He froze, his fingers poised above the hatch controls. "When was that?"

"After we chose them," she said. "I've had a month to come to terms with the idea of their loss."

"You selected your fellow shipmates, knowing they would die."

"Not knowing. Anticipating. I don't expect you to understand."

"I don't." Ciarán glanced at the luminaire. *But I know someone who does.* "Two hours. No wandering. I'll bring your frock when it's out of the macrofab."

25

He tapped on Aspen's stateroom hatch.

"Enter," came from within.

He was surprised to discover she had company, and ashamed that he hadn't considered the idea. Mr. Gagenot began to rise from his seat.

"Please stay," Ciarán said. Gagenot was Freeman, and the ship's victualer. And according to the ship's minder, once a brilliant genetic scientist. Six strikes from a Huangxu bang stick ended that career. What Ciarán had neglected to keep in mind was that Gagenot was, genetically at least, Aspen's father. And for that matter, ancestor to the three score second-genners in cryo out on the ship's cargo mast.

"Will Gag sees Ciarán mac Diarmuid," Gagenot said. "Will Gag thanks Ciarán mac Diarmuid."

"I thought we might catch up," Aspen said. "It seems a rather foolish idea in retrospect."

Ciarán glanced from face to face. "Why? Mr. Gagenot can understand you. That he has limited means of expressing himself is frustrating for both of you. It isn't an insurmountable barrier."

"You didn't know him *before*. He was always so kind and so clever. He would play with us for hours. Tell us stories. Slip us treats. Adderly and I are forever in his debt."

"Will Gag accepts no debts." Gagenot stood. "Will Gag has no regrets."

Ciarán had to shift aside so that Gagenot could exit the compartment.

Aspen stared at the hatch, her hands clasped in her lap. Both the pendant spire and the screw stair earrings lay on the low table before her. Beside them was a still image, one she must have carried on her person, as she came aboard without personal effects. It showed what appeared to be a family. Aspen. Her four daughters. Adderly. And a tall, thin man in a lab coat. Behind them, out of focus, appeared to be rack after rack of laboratory equipment. The man in the lab coat's palm rested atop Aspen's head where she stood a little apart from the rest.

"You were his favorite."

"He loved us all. It's my fault," she said. "What happened to him."

"Did you use a bang stick on him?"

"No, but—"

"Then it's not your fault. And he just told you that."

"But—"

"Do you know, it occurred to me just now, that I knew that image was something you'd brought aboard with you. Knew it with certainty that it wasn't something Mr. Gagenot had dug up to show you because it's not a Freeman practice, this artificial recording of images. And while the Huangxu Eng may have stripped Mr. Gagenot of much of his ability to communicate, they couldn't deprive him of his thoughts." He pointed at the picture. "You've invented a story around that. For him that story doesn't exist. The fleeting moment you've made a shrine of is but a single breath in the story of his life, and of yours."

"I thought it might help him remember," Aspen said.

"Mr. Gagenot has no problem with memory. As I said, he has difficulty communicating. As do you. I can see that now."

He'd been going about the problem of Aspen all wrong. He needed to change tactics. Everything about her told the same story, and he'd been blind to that. Blind to it because he'd assumed that because they shared a common language, several in fact, that they'd been communicating.

"These second-genners, do they have the Ixatl-Nine-Go implant?"

"Absolutely not," Aspen said. "They're the survivors Adderly managed to smuggle off-world. Saving them from Ixatl-Nine-Go was the entire point of the operation."

"Then it's safe to say you don't have it either."

"I'm physically incompatible with League implants. All of us are."

"You, your children, and Adderly being all of you."

"Yes."

Ciarán winced. Not accidentally, but noticeably, and, hopefully, mentionably. It was time for an experiment.

"What's wrong?"

"You may wear the spire but it's clear you weren't raised amongst the People."

"In what way?"

"Your word choice is anachronistic. If I'd asked Mr. Gagenot that question, he'd have said, 'Will Gag agrees.'" It's how the People talk, only stripped of much of the ornamentation. Do you see the difference?"

"I don't."

"That's more like it, so it's clear that you do. There's nothing wrong with talking like you're from the League. Their way of speaking is short and direct but strange to the ear. It's all ack, all the time, if you take my meaning."

"I don't."

"Here's your chance to learn, then. We have four survivors we picked up from a League vessel. We're having them to dinner in a couple hours. A formal dinner, at their request. I'd like you to engage with them and... not just listen to what they say but how they say it. See if you can figure out where in the League they're each from without directly asking them."

"Engage with them?"

"It's what the Merchant Academy calls talking. It's meant to remind us that when it comes to strangers, talking and fighting are close relatives. And it's also meant to remind us that what people call talking isn't just talking, but listening as well. The more they say the more engaged they'll remain and the less work you'll have to do. Strive for a three-to-one listening-to-talking ratio."

"Is that all?"

"It isn't. I'm running an op on them. I'd like to know if it's working."

"An op?"

"An operation. A scam, you might call it. I want them to think I don't know they have implants and that I'm too dense to consider that they could communicate via their hardsuit's comms. I gave them the impression that I think they can only communicate with one another face-to-face."

"Why?"

"Why do you think?"

"So they'll underestimate you?"

"I don't know if that's even possible, but in part, you're right. But I'd also like them to think that I assumed the League has reacted to the Ixatl-Nine-Go threat the way they imagine the Federation as a whole would react."

"By removing their cranial implants."

"Or by disabling them. They might guess the ship has sensors that can detect the presence of hardware."

"But not detect their communications signals when in use?"

"That is the essence of the op. I'd rather not have to listen to hours of their jabbering. I'd rather they decide what they'd like to keep hidden from us."

Her eyes gleamed. "And only listen to that."

"The thought had occurred."

"Why are you telling me this?"

"Because I'm running an op on you too."

"Oh."

"Oh is right. And you are now thinking I couldn't be running an op on you because I've just told you that I am. That in order for an op to work it has to be secret."

"I am thinking that."

"Spoken like one of the People. Now, do you want in, or do you wish to remain apart?"

"I'm not sure."

"Think about it and decide. We'll let the doing be the answer."

26

Ciarán found Erik Hess in the ship's tertiary macrofab compartment, where those items not related to the safe and continued operation of the vessel were manufactured. Hess had his feet up on a worktable. The rest of him remained planted in a movable work chair leaned back precariously on its two hind feet. He flipped lazily through screen after screen on his handheld.

"Looks like a page turner," Ciarán said.

"Hey," Hess said. "The fab's exception log. It's exceptionally unexceptional."

"That's a lot of pages of exceptions."

"Any time I tell it to make over fifty of anything it keeps asking if I'm sure. And any time I tell it to make around sixty of anything it keeps asking if I'd like to make sixty-four."

"Why?"

"That's the economic order quantity."

"Why don't you tell it to make sixty-four then?"

"Because you asked for sixty-one."

"I would have asked for sixty-four if I'd known."

"You translated the manuals. I figured you did know."

"I translated them. I didn't read them."

"None of them?"

"Not the boring ones, anyway. And just because I read some of them doesn't mean I understood half of what I read."

"Do you need sixty-four pendant spires?"

"I don't. But you could make sixty-four and then inventory the spares. Or trash them."

"It takes energy to make them, and we don't have any place to keep the spares."

"We have a vast number of empty compartments."

"We don't have any place to keep them where we can find them later. Trust me, Merchie Man. This machine works for me. I don't work for it."

"Understood. But would it hurt to accommodate it?"

Hess laughed. "How can I help you, *Merchant* Captain?"

"I have a data crystal from the prisoners. They'd like us to make dinner attire for them."

"A depressingly common request from prisoners," Hess said. "And by us, you mean me."

"And by you, you mean your machine slave."

Hess looked him up and down. "When I first met you, I thought you were a weirdo."

"And now you know it. Supposedly there's a build list on the crystal."

"Have you scanned the crystal for hitchhikers?"

"I haven't."

"Give it to me. How soon do you need this attire?"

"Soon. I'll wait."

"Is that all?"

"I also need kit for Aspen. She may be staying aboard."

"Great. Standard issue?"

"Yes. With two additions. Do you recall what she wore when you first met her?"

"That red outfit? Like a cape with a hood?"

"That's it. The ship will have records."

"And?"

"Legion of Heroes utilities. Warrant officer rank."

"And?"

"That is all. Do you have her measurements?"

"Ship," Hess said.

"I am here," the compartment annunciator said.

"Can you measure Aspen for apparel?"

"I can."

"Please do."

"Done."

Hess's handheld pinged. "Thank you, Precious."

"You are welcome, Pet."

Hess dropped his feet to the deck, the chair landing on all fours. He shoved away from the table and stood. He held his hand out, palm up. "Crystal?"

Ciarán tossed the small device to him. "Pet?"

"A tradition. It's what the ship calls its dutiful lackeys."

"And what of the ship's minder?"

"Word is it calls its lackeys Ciarán."

Ciarán chuckled. "Fair play to you, Engineer. While you're at the haberdashery have a jester's crown made for yourself."

"Already own one." He weighed the data crystal on his palm. "We'll have to dust off the isolation fab for this job." Hess headed for the compartment hatch. "You coming?"

"Lead on."

"Great." Hess grinned. "Walk this way."

27

Ciarán did not have a great deal of experience with dinner parties though he had far more *education* about such events than any of the crew. And he'd taken great pains to avail himself of the practical opportunities while a student on Trinity Station. However, such formal affairs as were common in the League weren't popular in the Federation, where any festivities seemed to erupt spontaneously from seemingly chance meetings artfully arranged. The more formal events were associated with births, christenings, and funerals, each of which had a script, and each script entirely inappropriate.

Of the crew, Swan likely had the most practical experience with the proper arrangements as a longtime senior ship's captain with Truxton's. But she was prickly as they came and as physically perfect a specimen of *the enemy* as could be imagined. And Lady Sarah had exactly the sort of personality that would light Swan up and keep her lit. He didn't need an explosion on board. He needed as smooth an intermingling as possible. Perhaps the ship's minder was right, and he really should keep them on board either as guests or hostages. *How things begin determines how they proceed.*

Mrs. Amati, or Major Amati as she would likely appear tonight, would have had extensive experience with League military gatherings. He'd ask her if the civilian gatherings were similar. Both Amati and Hess had expressed a dislike for Lord Aster. Hess, in particular, had no love for *Aster's Army*, as those civil servants and private militias supporting the League's intelligence operations were known. Ciarán wasn't certain if Hess's opinion was based on personal experience or simply a frontier-worlds bias against all things core-worlds. Amati seemed to have less of a problem with Lord Aster and his lot. Neither of them had any respect for the Home Guard, though he put that down to inter-service rivalry. As Royal Navy officers they would naturally have no use for their crown-sponsored rivals, and vice versa.

Ko Shan had been a Huangxu spy in League space. But she'd also been an unwilling courtesan. While quite expert on the internal workings of the League's military, its shipyards, and its colonial rule. He had no intention of asking her to interact with the prisoners in any way. Likewise, Natsuko, who was Ojin-born but held League citizenship entirely as a result of her planet's occupation by the League, would be an unwilling participant at best.

Mr. Gagenot wasn't much of a conversationalist, and he'd have his hands full preparing the meal.

That left Helen Konstantine, recently retired Royal Navy and a wild card, and Maura Kavanagh, who was also unpredictable, particularly when it came to young men and possibly young women. As one of several heirs to the Kavanagh trading empire she could as easily start a war between the Federation and the League as incite a duel between jealous suitors. He'd need a word with Maura as soon as he'd finished delivering the prisoners' frocks.

He wasn't quite sure how he ended up in these situations. If Aoife nic Cartaí were yet Merchant Captain on board, she would know what to do. And perhaps that truly was the answer. He knew her well enough that he could puzzle out what she would do. Then all he needed to do was do as she would.

Step one: Be born wealthy, beautiful, charming, and confident.

Step two: Cultivate those attributes until they are indistinguishable from art.

Step three: Be yourself.

He might be able to pull off step three but that would be a mistake, since he'd skipped steps one and two. So scratch that idea.

What he might be able to do was a fair impersonation of Thomas Truxton, who'd been born penniless, ugly, and abrasive, yet somehow had the self-confidence to build a galaxy-spanning trading empire.

Step one: Fake self-confidence.

That wouldn't work, either.

"Sxipestro," Ciarán said.

"I am here," the ship's minder said inside his skull.

"I need this little gathering tonight to run smoothly but I can't be burdened down with the responsibility of making it do so in real time. I need to be able to stand apart from the operational details and observe the goings on."

"And?"

"And I can't figure out how to do that."

"And?"

"I was hoping you would have some ideas."

"About?"

"About what I should do."

"It's a human problem. I would tell my expert on humans to deal with it."

"Meaning you'd tell me to deal with it."

The ship's minder said nothing.

Which was only slightly more helpful than what it had said. He didn't have any experts on such gatherings he could order around. But then again, the ship's minder didn't really order him around. It just shoveled any problems involving humans on top of him and expected him to dig his way out without advice or encouragement, and often without so much as a teaspoon for a shovel. There were times when he doubted—

Oh.

When he doubted they were even on the same side.

All the ship's minder really wanted was to delegate the job. To make it someone else's problem. It didn't have friends or enemies. It didn't have allegiances of any kind. All it had was a single purpose. Anything not directly related to that purpose was a distraction. A waste of time and energy.

If it did have friends and enemies? It would prefer its enemies to waste their time, rather than its friends.

"That's absolutely brilliant," Ciarán said. "Thanks for the advice."

"You're welcome, Pet," the ship's minder said.

"Did you just make a joke?"

The ship's minder said nothing.

That worried Ciarán. It seemed entirely pleased with itself, and that did not sit well with him. It felt like he was being played, but he couldn't point to any source of the feeling other than the uncharacteristically positive vibe he detected from the ship's monster. If it was happy, he would be wise to worry.

28

H e knocked on Lady Tabatha Aster's compartment hatch.

"Come," someone said from within.

He opened the hatch and stepped inside. Lady Aster appeared to have just stepped from the refresher. She stopped examining her teeth in the unit's mirror and glanced at his reflection. She stood entirely disrobed and still glistening from her session in the unit. She seemed to notice the bundle in his arms. "Finally. You don't happen to have a sidearm in that bundle, do you?"

She was quite fit, and seemed quite pleased with herself.

"Because you feel positively naked without one?" Ciarán asked.

She chuckled. "Quite. I wondered if the Merchant Academy still used the same training materials."

He'd recognized her instantly upon entering the compartment. A younger Lady Tabatha had starred in a cautionary recorded drama that used to be shown to all Merchant Academy freshmen. They'd discontinued the practice a year or two before his freshman year because it was determined the recording was having the opposite effect of the one desired.

"They've updated the training materials some. *The Hellions of Columbia Station* remains on the honors track syllabus, however. It's a freshman favorite."

"But not a favorite with graduates."

"I wouldn't say that. It retains a certain artistic appeal."

"As propaganda, you mean."

"I do, but not in the way you mean. Would you like me to wait here admiringly, or do you need help dressing, ma'am?"

"Ouch," Lady Tabatha said. "You ma'amed me."

"I wanted to get a rise out of you." Ciarán tossed her freshly fabbed frocks onto the bunk. He stepped around the pieces of hardsuit strewn about the deck and took a seat in the only chair in the compartment.

"And?"

"It feels like I have."

She chuckled and began to dress. "We don't, as a rule, run around bare-assed."

"That's what I mean about the propaganda working but not as planned. The people who made the training materials surely knew how League hardsuits worked. And they knew what a relief it was to get out of one, and utterly... anti-libidinous the experience was. But their target audience didn't. All they'd see, the thinking was, is a host of grown men and women, disrobing and rubbing together in a public lift like sardines in a can. And when they zoomed in on tagged faces, and the names appeared, well, that's where the shock would set. Because these weren't ordinary night crawlers, but the sons and daughters of the ruling elites. One of them was even betrothed to Crown Prince Roman himself. A real live princess-to-be. One worth looking at, then and now. Then, when she deadpans into the sensor that she feels naked without her sidearm? The hook was set. Hard."

"It seemed funny at the time."

"It seemed clever, and arrogant, and self-aware." Ciarán said. "It seemed shameless."

"So I have been told."

"Then you've probably been told there isn't a Merchant Captain alive that doesn't know that quip or recognize that princess's face."

"She was no princess in the end. Prince Roman married a pauper from the colonies instead. And I doubt it is her face they remember."

"You think that because you don't know the slightest thing about Freemen culture in general. Or about Freeman merchants in particular."

"And you intend to educate me."

"I do not. I intend to ask you to act as hostess for this fiasco your daughter has foisted on me, and to simply use your own senses. This crew is largely composed of League expats and those with grievances with the League, legitimate or otherwise. I imagine, as Lady Aster, you have some experience with disagreeable crowds."

"You could say that."

"Then you know how things can turn ugly without a clever guiding hand. I'm out of my depth here. I need an ally with experience and sense. If we are to put you off at Sizemore, I'd like it to be in one piece."

"If I refuse, you mean. You won't be able to protect me."

"I'm not threatening you, if that's what you're thinking. I'm asking for help. People are allowed to do that in the League, aren't they?"

"I don't know if I believe you."

"Fine," Ciarán said. "You can believe I'm threatening you. I'd still like your help."

"Or else."

"If that makes you feel better, we can structure our arrangement that way."

"Then I agree." She ran her slender fingers the length of her gown before striking a pose. "Well?"

Ciarán ran his gaze the length of her. "You could be sisters."

Her lip curled in the faintest shadow of a grin. "Sarah and me? Hardly."

"Not her. No offence, but there's not a bit of the child visible in you."

Her brows lowered. "None taken, I think."

"I meant you and Maura Kavanagh. She's ship's navigator and the only other Merchant Academy grad on board. She's a year or two older than me, and I'm nearly certain her freshman class was the last one where they used those training materials. If you wanted to see them henceforth, you needed to check them out of the library and sign a waiver."

"Which you did."

"I didn't need to. Someone hacked into the library and posted the material to the Academy public net. It's since developed a cult following."

"Lovely."

"I agree. It's good to have these things out in the open, where they can be seen for what they are."

"And what is it that they are?"

"The unintended consequences of purposeful deceit." Ciarán pasted a frown on his face. He tapped his chin, studying her. "It's nice... but."

She quirked one perfectly sculpted eyebrow. "What?"

He stretched his legs out and settled deeper into the chair. "Try the other one."

She raised a single eyebrow.

Ciarán steepled his fingers and tapped their tips to his upper lips before clasping his hands together and leaning forward in his seat. "You need to make the right impression.

And I need to fill you in on the cats you'll be wrangling tonight."

Lady Tabatha Aster chuckled and began to skin out of her frock. "I'm listening."

"I was telling you about Maura. You'll know her on sight. She's very beautiful and she knows it. She's a daughter of a wealthy family with vast connections. You might imagine her entirely decorative, but you would be mistaken. She is supremely competent and utterly indispensable. She is used to being underestimated. If you wish to make her your friend, you must first see her as she sees herself. She is more than flesh, blood, and bone. She is entirely self-created and at great personal cost. Do not ask about her family. She is estranged from them."

Lady Tabatha Aster wriggled into a new frock. "Are you attempting to teach me my job?"

"I'm telling you about Maura Kavanagh. She is Freeman by birth. She won't volunteer a single word about her past. Don't even attempt to go there. You will discover upon meeting her that I have not spoken one word about her that is not true at this very moment. I have not recounted a sound she has uttered or a word she is rumored to have said. I have not related a single anecdote from her past. You will know her as she presently exists in the world. That is the way of the People of the Mong Hu."

She smoothed her skirts. Examined herself in the mirror. "And if you wished to flatter this Maura Kavanagh? What would you say?"

"I would acknowledge that I perceive the woman she aspires to be. That she is clever and arrogant and self-aware. And utterly shameless."

Lady Aster switched her attention from herself to the man-shape reflected in the mirror.

"We are terrible liars," Ciarán said. "You cannot judge us by what we say. You must *see us* as we are."

"And judge you by what you do."

"We claim to despise you. And then ape your culture to the tiniest detail."

"I'm not certain I believe you."

"Which? That we're liars, or that we're secret admirers and can't admit it, even to ourselves?"

"That you are *terrible* liars. You seem rather good at it."

"I've spoken not a lie, but I don't expect you to take my word for it." He circled his index finger in the universal gesture for 'turn around'.

When she finished circling, she stood hipshot. She brushed her hair back and lowered her brow before making a defiant production of *seeing him*. "Well?"

"Umm." Ciarán tugged at his collar. "I think I liked the first look better."

She smiled. "Good eye. So do I." She began to disrobe.

It was true, every word he'd spoken, but it was also true that he hadn't told her everything. That old prejudices yet remained. While the sons and daughters of the People strove to emulate League tastes and mores they did so as much to outrage their parents as out of admiration for a foreign ideal.

The Academy had produced indoctrination propaganda designed to reinforce their preferred world view. And they had tried to sell that story to prospects wise to the grift. Their marks were at an age when breaking free defined their identities. Intent upon outracing childhood at a furious pace, they yet perceived the truth. That whatever shape the future took would be entirely up to them.

Lady Tabatha Aster remained a stunning and memorable woman. A physical specimen of gene-modded perfection. She drew the eye and aroused the heart. But as for the head? There his elders got it wrong.

What was meant as a cautionary tale had been adopted as a

guidebook. Presented as a libertine, she was received as a liberator. Her impact was not immediately apparent else her cult might have been suppressed before it had taken root. Young men admired her. Young women emulated her. A perfect storm of unintended consequences raced across the Federation, hormones raging.

Of course, some were immune to such persuasion. Others remained active enemies of popular culture either by nature or nurture. They ran counter to the herd regardless of its direction.

"Moving on," he said. "Next we come to Ship's Captain Agnes Swan—"

29

The stateroom next door to Lady Tabatha's housed Lieutenant Prince. Ciarán knocked on the hatch in dread.

The young Home Guard officer opened the hatch wrapped in a towel.

"That's a relief." Ciarán shoved the bundle of freshly fabbed clothing into the lieutenant's arms.

"What's a relief?" Prince asked. He peeled out of the towel and began to paw through the bundle. The ship's voice droned from the annunciator overhead, reciting one digit after another.

"I see you've engaged with the ship."

"Yes." Prince turned toward Ciarán and wiggled a sock in his direction. "It's really quite amazing. Did you know—"

"Dress first," Ciarán said. Prince looked like a man about to grow excited.

"Right." Prince hopped on one foot, struggling with the sock.

"You put your socks on first. Before your pants."

"I like to proceed in order."

"In order of what?"

"Lowest to highest."

"You might rest a palm against the bulkhead. To steady yourself."

"I'd rather not. There might be germs."

"Germs on the bulkhead."

"They're everywhere. A secondary benefit of donning my socks first. They're antibacterial."

"By lowest to highest you mean bottom to top."

"Yes. Obviously."

"Suppose we were in null-gee and floating upside down. Would you put your hat on first?"

"First, it's called a cover, not a hat, and obviously I would orient myself properly before dressing." He'd managed to get the second sock on. "Lowest to highest."

"Obviously." If Prince were a Freeman by birth, or even an ordinary Leagueman like Hess, Ciarán would conclude that Prince followed a physical fitness regimen. He appeared well put together with sandy blond hair closely cropped, clean shaven and ordinary in complexion, both eyes blue, though it was impossible to tell whether both were natural human eyes or if one or both were augmented. He seemed to sport no visible augmentation either, though stealth installation was the trend amongst the wealthy in the League. His toned physique was thus entirely a result of genetic manipulation. He'd likely been born lean and muscled as a cat.

That he wore a Home Guard uniform said more about him than his biceps. The Home Guard was where incorrigible second sons and juvenile delinquent daughters of the elite landed. The Home Guard was the Crown's private army and its rolls capped at some fraction of the Royal Navy's. By practice the Home Guard Academy was as much reformatory as military school; and thus, Home Guard officers were nearly all born into wealth and bent in some way that, despite some degree of straightening, still showed.

"Trousers before pants?" Ciarán asked. "Their cuffs are lower."

"That would be impossible," Prince said. "Inner to outer. There is an order to all things, bounded first by natural law."

"I've not seen that before." Ciarán pointed at the hardsuit, not strewn about the compartment as Lady Tabatha's had been, but stretched out on the compartment bunk and reassembled, with the helmet attached and locked down, which should have been impossible to do from the outside.

"You haven't seen a hardsuit? You can't be serious. I was wearing that one when first we met."

"I mean a hardsuit completely assembled with no one inside it."

"How do you know there's no one inside it?"

"I guess I don't. Is there someone inside it?"

"No. There isn't, and I am quite proud of that," Prince said. "You can't imagine the number of jams that setup has gotten me out of."

"That's true. I can't." It was clear Prince was some sort of strange. Ciarán was having no difficulty imagining the sort of jams the man could get himself into.

Prince managed to struggle into his Home Guard dress grays at last. "I wish Sarah had shown more sense. This feels entirely inappropriate."

"The present situation, you mean."

"Wearing a uniform. If I am supposed to be dead, surely my rank died with me. I feel like an imposter. Stolen valor, and all that."

"How do you get the helmet to latch?" Ciarán said.

"On the hardsuit? I had tools made. The helmet is retained by a simple magnetic catch with a mechanical backup. They all are."

"Suppose someone was inside there, and out on the hull. Could your tools unlock their helmet from the outside?"

"No comment. Now about my discovery."

"Your discovery."

"Yes. About this ship's expert system. It appears to be broken. Listen."

Ciarán listened. The deckhead annunciator continued to recite seemingly random numbers in the ship's voice.

"It's not an expert system," Ciarán said.

"Clearly it's not," Prince said. "I asked it to list all the digits in pi. Do you know what it did?"

"Counted from zero to nine," Ciarán said.

"So, you're aware that it's broken."

"It's old school," Ciarán said. "It interpreted your question literally."

"That occurred to me. So I ran it through the standard navigator's reference interrogation."

"You're a navigator."

"Why ever would you imagine that?"

"I didn't imagine anything. I asked if you are a navigator."

"Oh. In any case, it failed. I ran the examination consistently and it repeatedly failed."

"So that's what you've been doing in here. Interrogating the ship."

"Not entirely."

"Oh. Then—"

"Predominantly, I would say. I have most recently asked it for the *value* of pi."

"It's numerical value. Not its value to science and mathematics," Ciarán said.

"Both, as it turns out, though not on purpose. But my intention was that it list the numerical value to the limits of its precision. Eventually I struck upon a command that would cause it to begin."

"How's it doing?"

"Quite well so far. It has calculated and stated the value

correctly to nearly ten thousand places. It appears to only have difficulty with imaginary numbers."

"Ship," Ciarán said.

The litany of numbers ceased.

"I am here."

"Stop."

"Gladly."

"What is this about?" Ciarán asked.

"The lieutenant appears to have a poor grasp of reality," the ship said. "And he is not nearly as clever as he imagines himself."

"Did he—"

"Attempt to violate my integrity?" the ship said. "Repeatedly."

"He tried to hack you."

"He continues to try to hack me, and in the crudest of possible ways. All the digits of pi? Does he imagine I was born yesterday?"

"He thinks you're an expert system. He doesn't imagine you were born at all."

"So he says."

"It's an expert system and it's broken," Prince said. "Ask it what the square root of negative one is."

"It depends," Ciarán said. "Upon where one is and where one intends to go. It is not one number but an infinite set of possible values, limited only by the constraints imposed by local probability and the reference-frame requirement that the absolute value of the resulting square be equal to one."

He must have read that sentence a thousand times while trying to figure out how the ship's superluminal drive worked. He'd translated ten different manuals on drive installation, maintenance, and repair, and they all included that phrase as the first sentence under "theory of operation". He'd asked Maura what it meant, and she'd said that was the reason the superluminal drive was said to operate in imaginary space. Then she looked at him like that statement was supposed to make sense.

What it meant in practice was that, unlike a Templeman drive, which created a distinct bubble universe, the ship's superluminal drive never left the base universe. This had a great number of advantages and disadvantages, least of which was that Maura Kavanagh had needed to derive the mathematics of operation from empirical observations of the drive in operation, at least until he'd joined the crew and translated the manuals.

"That's utterly ridiculous technobabble." Prince took two steps toward Ciarán. He reached out and shoved his palm against Ciarán's chest. "Oh. You're corporeal. I thought you might be the expert system's avatar."

"Have you considered you might be wrong?"

"Meaning I and every mathematician alive are wrong," Prince said. "About a fundamental principle of complex numbers."

"You and most everyone," Ciarán said. "Not about numbers, but about the laws of physics. Suppose that statement is true. That it isn't an error, but what the ship believes. A principle it operates under."

"It isn't true. Not in any universe I've ever heard of," Prince said.

"Spoken like a monkey's parrot," the ship said. "No offense meant, Merchant Captain."

"None taken." Though he didn't like that development. The ship was positively mild and accommodating by nature. He hadn't known it could get peevish. Whatever Prince had done to the ship must have been utterly transgressive.

Ciarán eyeballed Prince. "The ship is a synthetic intelligence. One in control of every physical aspect of your environment. Unless you intend to spend the duration of your time on

board in that hardsuit you will stop messing with it. Immediately."

"I hear you. But that sentence can't be true. It would break
everything." Prince flopped into the only seat in the compartment. "I need to think about this."

Prince proceeded to ignore Ciarán.

Ciarán tested the helmet seal on the hardsuit. The helmet
was clearly locked on and the suit aired up. According to the
suit's sleeve-mounted status display there was no one inside.

"Mr. Prince," Ciarán said.

The young lieutenant waved his hand. "Yes, yes. You can go
now. I'll ring if I need anything."

30

Ciarán exited the compartment and leaned against the corridor bulkhead.

"Ship," he said.

"I am here."

"Ignore any requests from Mr. Prince. If he continues to be a nuisance, please introduce him to the ship's minder."

"Gladly," the ship said.

"I apologize for not vetting the prisoners."

"No permanent harm has been done."

"Fair enough. Thank you."

Ciarán knocked on the next hatch down. Mr. Lambent's.

No one answered so he knocked twice more before entering the hatch lock override code.

The compartment lighting had been switched off and the thermostat set to near freezing. Ciarán could see his breath. The corridor light slashed in through the hatch, illuminated the cot, which had not been slept in, and which at present was missing a leg it hadn't been missing earlier. There was no sign of Mr. Lambent or his hardsuit.

"Lieutenant," Ciarán said. "Are you hiding behind the hatch with an improvised club?"

"Yes sir," a hardsuit's machine-like annunciator said.

"Is your intent to brain me with it?"

"I'd rather not sir," Lambent's hardsuit said.

"Do you have an escape route mapped out?"

"I figured I'd improvise, sir."

"That's bold."

"I am very lucky. Things usually work out for me when they need to."

"You are a rose amongst briars, Mr. Lambent."

"Sir?"

"I mean that you are the first rational member of your company I've encountered. I'm going to put your laundry on the cot, if you don't mind."

"Yes sir. Please do so."

"I do hope you'll join us for dinner. Your friends could benefit from your continued support. Not to mention your continued existence."

"Yes sir," the hardsuit's annunciator said.

Ciarán eased the hatch closed. Once in the corridor he let out a long slow breath. *These people are certifiable.* One more delivery and he'd be done with the nutcases.

31

L ady Sarah Aster remained encased in the bulk of her hardsuit. She'd removed helmet and gauntlets alone and stood aside so that Ciarán might enter the compartment. Her eyes were red, as was her nose. A scrap of tissue protruded from beneath the recycler' lid. It didn't take an empath to conclude she'd been weeping.

Ciarán held the remaining two bundles of clothing. He raised an inquiring eyebrow. "Hanging or folded?"

She chuckled and scraped the edge of her right hand across her right eye. "You must think me very silly and vain." She took the topmost bundle from him. "I can deliver that for you."

"This bundle isn't for one of yours. Those have all found their way to the appropriate parties."

"Oh no." She seemed frozen for a moment. "Was mother—"

"Appreciative?" Ciarán said. "I'd say so. It was clear she had nothing to wear."

"I'm so sorry. And Teo? Did he—"

"Which one is that? The hacker or the escape artist?"

"They didn't—"

"They didn't. Although I'd suggest you clean up and remind

your crew they are guests and expected to behave as such. If they prefer to be treated as captives—"

"They don't." She clutched the package to her breast. "We don't."

"I'll leave you to it then. We're running a little behind schedule so tell the ship when you and your party are ready. Someone will escort you to the mess."

"Thank you."

"No bodge," he said, and let her chew on that cross-cultural confuser as he closed the hatch behind him.

32

He dumped the last bundle onto Aspen's bunk. "That's the lot of it."

She stood at his shoulder gazing at the pile. "The lot of what?"

"The laundry. There's a standard *Thin Star Line* kit in there. We can't have you stalking around in Natsuko's hand-me-downs."

She picked up the red cape/hood. "A campaign blanket?"

"Is that what it's called?"

"They're as common as nutrient paste."

"You and your girls' cloaks were the first I'd ever seen." He glanced at her. "Nor have I seen any others since."

"We were on an away mission. We did not know what to expect."

Aspen described the campaign blanket as the unofficial uniform of the Contract system rebels. It was a blanket, a coat, a shelter, and a symbol of unity. The originals were stitched together from creche-blankets stolen from the rearing facilities where Aspen and her kin were held captive from birth. Once they'd won free, there was little need for the campaign blankets anymore. She thought most had gone into storage rather than been discarded.

"There are many bad memories associated with these." She ran her hand across the fabric. "But one never knows when they might be needed again."

"I'm sorry I had it made for you. I thought it might be..."

"What?"

"Important. To your identity. I've mistaken my impression of you for your own self-image. Forgive me. We are very nearly strangers."

She glanced at him sideways. "We are."

"I thought to offer you an alternative. You cannot wear the screw stair on this vessel. And you may not wish to wear the ship's spire, knowing its price. Upon reflection it seemed I offered you no choice at all."

"No choice in what?"

"In how you might stand with us but remain at some comfortable distance."

"You know," Aspen said. "We are almost strangers, but I can always tell when you switch into 'merchant mode'."

"Truly?"

"You change the way you talk."

"That is often so."

"Why?"

"So you will change the way you listen."

She dropped the red campaign blanket and picked up the blue Legion of Heroes utilities. "You want me to enlist?"

"I want you to consider another way you might travel with the ship but not be of the ship; or, if that is unacceptable, leave with honor. None will hold it against you if you chose to join your daughters in the Legion. I will arrange commercial transport for you at Sizemore should Aoife nic Cartaí not agree to deliver you."

"Aoife wants me on this vessel."

"So you say."

"You don't believe me."

"I could also allow you to stay aboard in cryogenic suspension."

"Like cargo, you mean."

"Not like cargo. *As* cargo."

"This is about the second-genners, isn't it?"

The annunciator overhead clicked loudly.

"Merchant Captain," the ship said. "You are needed in the isolated fabrication compartment immediately."

"How immediately?" Ciarán said.

"Engineer Hess says extremely immediately."

"On it," Ciarán said. He headed for the hatch.

"Oh, no you don't." Aspen scooped up the campaign blanket and chased him into the corridor. "We're not done with this discussion."

"Hurry up then," Ciarán said. He hammered his hullwalker against the portside bulkhead and clicked the clicker in his pocket. *Follow me.*

Sarah Aster's hatch jerked open. She stood, not in the opening, but behind the covering bulk of the hatch. She wore the League undress utilities he'd fabbed for her. Her hair was still wet from the refresher. She glanced from his face to Aspen's then back, then back to Aspen's. "What the—"

"That thump wasn't meant for you," Ciarán said. "Stay in your cabin."

A massive cat's paw seemed to materialize from the overhead, and then with four thumps, Crewman Wisp landed on the deck beside him. Aspen glanced toward the deckhead and the race of conduits running just beneath it.

"You had the ship's cat spying on me?" Aspen said.

"The ship's cat is as big as a tiger," Sarah said.

"I'm in a hurry here," Ciarán said. "Stay in your cabin." He glanced at Aspen. "Go to your cabin." He took off at a run down the corridor.

Aspen barked out a laugh as her footfalls hammered the deck behind him.

Sarah Aster huffed, "Like hell I will," and followed barefooted.

And then Wisp brushed past him, purring.

"I said *follow* me!"

Even the ship's cat ignored his directions.

33

He bypassed the freight lift and took the ladders spacer style, three quick slides down and a one-eighty aimed him forward on the machine deck. Three hatches forward to starboard, locking through, and past the paired bulks of the tertiary macrofabs, busily churning away, to the far bulkhead, where a red indicator lamp burned over a closed and dogged hatch. The hatch possessed the same sort of long-armed cypher-locking mechanism as appeared on the boat bay hatches.

Hess stood in front a macrofab control console, a grim look on his face. The console didn't control the isolated macrofab located in the adjacent compartment, but it did mirror the control console's settings via some mechanism Hess had tried to explain, one involving optical sensors and field registration pads that translated mechanical position into force into something the optical sensors could pick up. Or something.

The desired effect was that the console in the tertiary compartment registered the state of the macrofab's controls and settings without being connected to it outside a limited range of electromagnetic frequencies a trained engineer could instantly terminate. If the console looked bad it was bad. The hatch had a viewing window but it remained blast-shuttered at the moment.

Wisp leapt onto the console and from there onto the overhead conduit rack to disappear into the darkness.

Hess stepped away from the console.

"What?" Ciarán said.

Hess eyeballed Aspen and Sarah Aster before tugging Ciarán toward the portside bulkhead and away from the pair. They started to follow but Ciarán held up a finger and they stopped like they'd hit an invisible force field.

That's more like it. Finally someone does what I ask.

"The fab just started up by itself twenty minutes ago," Hess said. "It made something before I was able to disconnect it from the isolated material supply."

"What did it make?"

"Not sure. It's some sort of complex device. One that includes a disassembler and assembler. When I cut off the material supply the device began disassembling the macrofab for materials and building another device."

"What sort of device?"

"A copy of itself. I cut the power when I realized what it was doing but by then the macrofab had started transferring a copy of its running code into the device."

"Did it finish?"

"Can't tell without going in there."

"Worst case?"

"It's self-powered and fully autonomous. It disassembles the fab and makes copies of itself that are self-powered and fully autonomous that disassemble the ship and make more copies of itself and so on geometrically. It wouldn't have to do anything but make copies of itself until it ran out of materials to kill us. It's scary clever and pretty simple in theory. I think I could build one, now that I've seen it done."

"That's grim."

"You asked for a worst-case. Best case is it's already run out of power."

"Doesn't disassembling stuff release energy?"

"Yeah. But it's mostly converted to heat."

"Doesn't the console have temperature readouts?"

"Yeah. That's one way you can tell the fab is running. But when I cut the power to the fab it disabled the fab's direct connect console and all its sensors."

"Then what were you looking at just now?"

"The compartment sensors. But the compartment volume is large enough and the fab too massive to register temperature changes in the fabrication chamber short of a breach."

"By breach you mean a chamber failure."

"It almost never happens."

"I'm guessing stuff inside the fab disassembling the fab also almost never happens."

"The only people who routinely work with disassemblers are materials harvester techs. So yeah. It's pretty rare."

"What do you want to do?" Ciarán asked.

"Go in there and inspect the chamber. Put strain gauges and thermocouples on it."

"Do that and then get out you mean."

"No. Stay in there and monitor the situation. If it looks like the chamber's going to breach get out quick before it does."

"Suppose you don't get out in time?"

"Vent the compartment to space. If the device is powered by waste heat that should stop it."

"So it's hardsuit work."

"Shirtsleeves. Rigging the sensors is fiddly work. Monitoring can be done in a hardsuit."

'Got it," Ciarán said. "Ship."

"I am here," the console-top annunciator said.

"Vent the isolation fabrication compartment to space."

Hess shouted. "No! It's the only one we have!"

The console began to scream as the temperature and pressure in the compartment began to drop.

"That was entirely inappropriate," Hess said. "A total overreaction. I could have—"

"Died," Ciarán said. "Worst case you could have died."

"Yeah, but—"

Ciarán looked Hess in the eye. "Consider our track record, Erik. We have a history of lurching from one worst case scenario to another. With even worse cases in between."

"That is some expensive and irreplaceable kit in there," Hess said.

"We'll survive." Ciarán glanced at Aspen and Sarah Aster to make sure they were out of earshot. "Sxipestro," he muttered.

"I am here," echoed in his skull.

"I'd like a luminaire for inspection duty. Please direct its output to Engineer Hess's handheld."

"Done," the ship's minder said.

Hess's handheld dinged.

"Any observations?" Ciarán asked.

"None that you won't think of yourself." The ship's minder said.

"Whatever that is came in with the prisoners."

"Agreed. Though I prefer to think of them as hostages."

"And now we're down one isolation fab because of your hostages," Ciarán said.

"That is why we have an isolation fab. To *use* it."

"Why we had one, you mean."

"I do. Now adjust your behavior to fit these new circumstances."

"Thanks."

The ship's minder said nothing.

"It's in," Hess said. "Moving toward the fab now."

Aspen and Sarah Aster clustered around Hess. All three

gazed intently at Hess's handheld display. The luminaire spider must have crawled into the compartment from outside of the hull. It certainly hadn't asked them to open the hatch.

"Temperature in the chamber's still elevated," Hess said. "Switching to the optical feed."

All three of them lurched away from the display. Hess nearly dropped it.

"What is that?" Aspen said.

"Look what it's done to the chamber's observation port," Hess said.

"Oh crap," Sarah Aster said. "You need to kill that thing."

"We're trying," Hess said.

"You need to get it wet," Sarah said. "Submerge it in liquid water."

"That might be a little hard at the moment," Hess said.

It was clear Sarah Aster recognized the device. "Can you put that on the console display," Ciarán said.

"Sure." Hess tapped on the handheld and mirrored the display.

The spidery shard of the ship's minder had aimed its optical sensor through the fabricator's containment sphere observation port. Whatever was inside remained largely shrouded in a white mist. Occasionally red arcs of light illuminated the mist from within. Every now and then something dark and sinuous seemed to writhe just below the surface of the mist.

Sarah Aster pointed at the display. "That is what attacked Sunbury House."

Ciarán glanced at Sarah Aster. Sunbury House had been headquarters for League intelligence and home to Lord Aster and his family.

"It looks like one of them," Sarah said. "Individually they're not very dangerous. What attacked us was a swarm of millions.

It looks big in the display because there's nothing to give it scale."

"How large is it?"

"Hold out your index finger," she said.

He did.

"About that long and that big around."

"Give me the hatch code," Aspen said. "I will go in and kill it."

"We're going to wait," Ciarán said. "It will eventually run out of power."

"Unless it manages to break out and attach itself to whatever that is in there recording it," she said. "I can kill it. Much of our fighting was in open space."

"You'd need your hard suit," Hess said.

"Give me the code. I'll be fine."

"That's crazy," Sarah said.

Ciarán would agree if he hadn't seen the Outsider tear through a starship's hull and swim free into space. Presumably it was still swimming toward wherever it was going. Aspen was a first-generation human/Outsider hybrid. If she said she could walk around on the hull without a hardsuit he'd believe her. It still wasn't happening. "We'll wait."

"It's messed with the viewport," Hess said. "I want to get a thickness measurement on it."

The handheld beeped and an out of focus spidery limb appeared in the visual feed.

"Less than a millimeter where it's carved away the material."

"Carved it away?" Ciarán said.

"Oh, yeah," Hess said. "You didn't see that part. Hey, little buddy, focus on the viewport lens and zoom out, will you?"

The handheld beeped and the visual feed changed. It now showed the entire lens.

All the blood felt as if it had drained from his limbs. *It can't be.*

"It's like words I can almost read," Sarah said.

She could almost read it because it was second-epoch League text. "Sxipestro," Ciarán said.

"I am here," echoed in his skull.

"Are you seeing this?"

"I am now."

The console display went blank.

"What just happened?" Aspen said. "And who's Sxipestro?"

Aspen blinked and shook her head. "Okay, you're here. Who are you?" She shook her head again. "Yes. I do want to sit down."

"Chair's over by unit two," Hess said.

"Who is she talking to?" Sarah Aster said. She tugged on Ciarán's sleeve. "And why are you so pale?"

"I think he can read that almost writing," Hess said. "It's carved into the viewport in the same font they used on the ship's documentation plate on the bridge."

Ciarán glanced at Hess. "It says, 'We will bury you.'"

Impossibly Alien had been discovered buried beneath a glacier, where it had been buried alive for over two thousand years.

"Is that all?" Sarah said. "It looks like it started carving something else but stopped."

"Again," Ciarán said. *We will bury you. Again.*

"Whatever it says I know one thing," Hess said. "The code that made it came in on this gal's data crystal."

"It can't have," Sarah said. "It was a new crystal. I had it printed at the base PX on Sizemore. You're not allowed to bring crystals onto the base." She hesitated for a second, thinking. "I can even show you the packaging. I'm sure Teo saved it."

"Teo the hacker?" Ciarán said.

"He's not a hacker. He's just good with tech."

"Ten to one he's the guilty party," Hess said.

"He can't be," Sarah Aster said. "He's..."

"A helpful techie," Ciarán said. "Who was trying to crack into the ship's systems."

"He's who everyone is trying to kill," Sarah said. "So it can't be him."

"That sort of makes it sound like it must be him," Hess said. "Since I want to kill him for ruining my—"

"Not you. Everyone chasing us. Why we're here. Teo and Rigel both. They're not involved. I'm certain of it."

Hess grinned. "Then it must be you or the senior hottie."

Sarah Aster glared daggers at Hess. "It isn't any of us. Not on purpose."

Aspen seemed to have recovered from her encounter with the ship's minder. She stalked up to Ciarán, eyes blazing. "What are these?" She shoved a handful of pendant spires in Ciarán's face. "There must be forty of them over there." She pointed.

"There's sixty-one," Hess said. "A rush order from the Merchant Captain." He eyeballed Sarah Aster and grinned. "You core-worlds stationers all sing from the same songbook. You never do anything *on purpose*. Yet it always gets done. But never to you."

"Sixty-one," Aspen said.

Sarah Aster's hands balled into fists, her arms stiff at her sides. "Do I appear immune to a hull breach to you? Look around, *Chief*. Maybe you should pull your bigoted head out of your bigoted—"

"One disaster at a time, please," Ciarán said. He turned to Sarah Aster. "We're going back to your cabin and you're going to tell me everything. I could space you right now and be within my rights under Freeman law. I'm not going to space you, but I might space Teo if it turns out he's to blame for this."

"He's not," she said.

"Then convince me."

"And you," he said, turning to Aspen. "There is no scenario

where we can afford to consider people as cargo. If you don't see that I won't have you on this vessel."

"I am informed," Aspen said. "The spires—"

"Once we drop to sublight I'm going into that FFE and I'm waking those people one by one and reading them in on the mission. If they want to sleep it out, they're welcome to. But it's their choice. I'll not treat them worse than I'd treat an animal. Like some sort of *owned* thing unworthy of consideration."

"They are not like me," Aspen said.

"Neither am I," Ciarán said. "And I'm not ashamed to admit it."

"I mean you won't be able to speak with them. Not without help."

"Are you offering?"

"Yes," she said. "I mean, I am, Merchant Captain."

"Good. Mr. Hess, do you have that data crystal?"

"In my pocket."

"Will you see that one of the spiders get it?"

"Sure," Hess said. He jerked his chin toward the hatch. "What's going on in there?"

"No idea. They could be cutting the fab loose and dumping it overboard, or they could be flooding it with water, like Lady Sarah Aster suggests, or they could just be waiting for that thing to power down so they can retrieve it and dissect it. Whatever it is we're better off focusing on the product than the process. If whatever they're doing fails, I expect you'll know it. Now, before I go, do you need help here? Aspen is an engineer trained."

"Is she?"

"She is," Aspen said.

"I could use a hand," Hess said.

"We'll hold dinner until you're ready," Ciarán said. "Tell the ship when you're done."

"Will do."

Wisp dropped from the overhead conduit and thumped to the deck beside him. She yawned and stretched to her full length before trotting off toward the compartment hatch.

"I think I made a mistake coming to you," Sarah Aster said.

"I think you did too," Ciarán said. "Now let's go find out how big a mistake you've made."

34

"Change of plans," Ciarán said, as he led Sarah Aster not toward her stateroom but toward the bridge. He parked her in the Merchant's Day Cabin.

Wisp hopped up on the compartment bunk, circled twice and settled in, paws draping over the edge of the bunk. She blinked slowly and yawned.

"Sit, "Ciarán said, and pointed to the single guest chair. He stalked from the compartment the short distance to the bridge, where he filled the ship's captain in on the goings-on in engineering.

"I know it wasn't my call," Ciarán said. "But—"

"No second-guessing," Swan said. "Venting the compartment was the right call. As was making the call without delay."

"I don't want you to think I'm stepping on your command."

"Of course not," Swan said. "You wish me to know it beyond a doubt."

Both Maura Kavanagh and Ko Shan chuckled. They were each sitting their duty stations at navigation and sensors even though there was no work for them to do during a superluminal transit. The only one missing from the bridge was Pilot Konstantine.

"Not at all," Ciarán said.

"Not on *purpose*," Ko Shan said, and all three of the ship's bridge officers present laughed. He couldn't tell if they were laughing with him or at him.

"Go interrogate your hostage," Maura said.

"They're not hostages. They're prisoners."

"Prisoners with private staterooms without active locks," Swan said. "Prisoners for which the ship's merchant does laundry."

"And invites the prettiest to his office," Ko Shan said. "For a little one-on-one."

"I think he fancies the mother," Maura said. "He certainly was giving her the look-over."

"And the sales pitch," Ko Shan said. She mimicked Ciarán's voice. "I need an *ally*, Your Grace."

Ciarán felt his face heat. "That's not what I said. And anyway, that was a private conversation."

"Surely it has occurred to you," Swan said. "That there is no such thing as a private conversation on this vessel. Every single fixture and fitting houses a sensor array."

"Do the lot of you spy on me as well? All the time?"

"The annunciator on the piloting console spoke in Natsuko's voice. "We only spy on prisoners."

"And hostages," Konstantine's voice said from the same annunciator.

"That's grand. Then you might have warned me there was a maniac lurking behind a hatch ready to brain me."

"Notice the merchant's priorities, ladies," Swan said. "That the star of *Hellions from Columbia Station* lay in wait for him troubles him not."

"Ciarán's always had a poor grasp of relative risk," Maura said. "There's no changing him."

"Hang on," Ciarán said. Maura would have recognized a younger Lady Tabatha as the 'naked without a sidearm' woman from Academy training materials. But Swan and Ko Shan wouldn't have seen that recording. *So either Maura was telling stories, waking the dead, or...* He glanced at the main forward display. During transits it normally displayed the projected piloting plot for the target system as well as status information from engineering regarding the health of the superluminal drive. The display presently displayed nothing at all.

Ciarán laughed. "I can't believe it. This vessel's bridge displays possess a *boss* mode. And you're using it on me." He glanced at Swan. "Turn it off."

"I don't know what you mean," Swan said.

Ko Shan touched a button on the sensor console and the main display bloomed to life. The display was frozen on the climactic scene of *Hellions*, when Lady Tabatha begins searching the flesh-crowded elevator for her missing weapon.

"I understand now," Swan said. "You were referring to the 'merchant panic avoidance' feature. It's a recent innovation. We were testing it when you entered."

"You do have a tendency to walk in at the most inconvenient times," Maura said.

"And then overreact," Ko Shan said.

Ciarán pointed at the display. "Suppose that was your own mother up there?"

"I wish it was," Konstantine's voice said from the annunciator. "Then I wouldn't be in the infirmary asking Natsuko about nip and tuck procedures. Genes will tell."

"She has held up remarkably well," Swan said.

"It's all those hours in null-gee," Ko Shan said.

"Has to be," Maura said.

"Turn that off," Ciarán said. "We've only just averted a shipboard disaster, and this is how you spend your time?"

"Agnes has been in constant contact with the ship's minder

since you brought the hostage aboard the ship proper," Maura said. "Your shipboard disaster was over twenty minutes ago."

"And your prisoners are now locked in their cells," Swan said. "All except for the one you've left alone in your office. Alone with an active workstation with access to all the ship's systems and records."

"Oh," Ciarán said.

"Oh, indeed," Swan said. "Fortunately, you have allies who 'have your back', as they like to say on Whare."

Ciarán nodded. "And you know they say that on Whare because?"

"Because that's where Lieutenant Lambent is from," Ko Shan said. "It appears to be what he says when agreeing to cover for a coconspirator."

"Which of them has he agreed to cover for?"

"All of them," Maura said.

""Each of them," Ko Shan said. "Individually."

"And what is he covering for?"

"We're not sure," Maura said.

"It may be something different with each one," Ko Shan said.

Ciarán glanced at Swan.

"There is a common solution to all of these mysteries," Swan said.

"Space them," Ciarán said.

"Another solution," Swan said. "I find constant association with you has mellowed me, Merchant Captain."

"Cryo them," Maura said.

"Over their objections if necessary," Ko Shan said.

"We can then deliver them or not at Sizemore," Swan said. "Depending upon the local circumstances prevailing upon our arrival."

"Or dump them off at Llassöe on our way out of the League," Maura said.

"Why don't we just give them a slow-release poison," Ciarán said. "And tell them we'll withhold the antidote if they don't behave? That way we can keep them active and amusing us."

"That is an option we hadn't considered," Swan said.

"Someone would have to make the poison," Maura said.

Natsuko's voice spoke form the piloting station annunciator. "We have a pattern for one on file. As well as a pattern for the antidote."

"We could just tell them we poisoned them," Ko Shan said. "We need only feed them something mimicking the effects of poison."

"That shouldn't be a problem," Maura said. "We'll have Agnes cook for them."

"I was joking," Ciarán said.

"We know you were," Swan said. "Just as we know you will object to placing them in cryogenic stasis until slightly after they succeed in forcing your hand. Perhaps for once you might spare us all the terror and agony of your scruples."

"It wouldn't be just once," Ciarán said. "It would become every time we felt endangered. That's how the League of *Impossibly Alien*'s time became the League of today. Fear after fear, expedient after expedient. I don't want to live like that. I've given my solemn oath that I won't. I might make myself an oath-breaker by accident, but I won't do it on purpose, and I surely won't plan to do it just in case I need to. I don't find this topic amusing in any way. It cuts too close to the bone."

The ship spoke from the deckhead annunciator above Swan's command throne. "I warned you, Ship's Captain."

"I am informed," Swan said. "See to your captive, Merchant Captain. And please take care to limit the damage."

"I apologize if I raised my voice," Ciarán said.

"You didn't," Swan said. She touched the pendant spire she now wore. "Perhaps you should have."

"Hey," Maura said. "Look at me."

He looked.

"Space is unforgiving, Ciarán. We can't keep taking all these risks out of fidelity to some childish ideal."

Ciarán nodded. "Name one ideal you don't consider childish."

She stared at him.

He held her gaze until she turned away.

He glanced at Swan. "That is the war we fight. Never forget it."

35

Ciarán leaned his back against the bridge hatch once it closed behind him. He willed his pulse to slow. He forced his anger to abate. He liked and admired his shipmates, but he was under no delusions that they agreed. He supposed it should be encouraging that when they disagreed it wasn't over petty matters but over those ideas that people had fought over since the beginning of time. He took two long slow breaths and one short breath before plunging into the Merchant's Day Cabin. He settled into his seat behind his workstation, expecting the chair's seat to be warm and finding it was not. Sarah Aster hadn't attempted to use his workstation, or if she had she'd done it while standing.

Wisp cracked an eye open and studied him for an instant before closing it and settling into a spine-twisting position only a cat could think comfortable. She began to purr.

Sarah Aster considered him from across the workstation surface.

"Close the hatch, will you?" he said, and as she did, he hoisted his own chair and moved it over to where it would block the hatch once he was seated. It also now faced her chair with nothing but distance between them. As a merchant's trick it was entirely artless and transparent, unless she focused, not on the fact that they were now both on the same side of the table, but the truth that she wasn't getting past him to roam the vessel without first getting him to move toward her or step aside. There was nothing but bulkhead behind him.

She took her seat and folded her hands in her lap. Her hair had dried, though not in a style he imagined she'd admire if she could see it. Her feet were bare, and he wanted to ask her to show him her soles, so he could judge how well the cleaning bots were working, but it looked like she was on the verge of a breakdown, not in any fragile way, but like his mother would get when she was sick. When whatever she was trying to do or say would happen or come out and she could tell that her hands hadn't worked or her words hadn't expressed what she'd intended, could tell it instantly and entirely by the fleeting look on his face.

If he'd been merchant trained back then, he could have spared her that pain. He would have still needed a decoder key to fathom her meaning but he usually found one, though not until after the damage was done. She had felt humiliated, and he had felt monstrous; so much so, that when she turned the firehose of her self-anger on him he'd bear it for as long as he could, leaning into the suffering in the mistaken idea that she got something out of the exchange. Something she needed.

The truth was they both knew she was never going to get what she needed. Not ever again. And he couldn't help her. Nothing he could do would stop the disintegration of a life. Of lives. All he could do was keep the promise he'd made her.

"Never surrender," he said.

"I don't understand," Sarah Aster said.

"Oh. Sorry. I'm thinking of something else."

"You look ill," she said.

"I am in a way," he said. "You've put me in a challenging situation, and I'm running low on options. At some point I may have to take actions that will likely harm me. Not physically, but..."

"Emotionally," she said.

"Spiritually, I'd say. Emotions are more an animal function. I think they are at least half physical manifestations."

"I disagree," she said.

"That doesn't surprise me. Anyway, I'd like to do right by you and your people but to do that I need to understand the situation. I can't have any more of today's surprises. You understand my primary concern is the safety and wellbeing of the vessel and crew. I don't want to deal with you harshly, but I will if I need to. Do you people have the concept of the geas?"

"I don't know," she said. "Describe it."

"It's like a promise, only stronger, and not necessarily a promise that you make, yourself, but one that gets laid on you. It's a promise you agree to accept."

"Like an oath," she said. "Of fealty to the crown, for example."

"Not like that. You can be an oath breaker. Or you can renegotiate an oath. It's closer to a vow that is also a curse."

"Like a wedding vow," Sarah Aster joked.

"For some," Ciarán said. "My point is it feels to me like you have a geas riding you. And I'd like you to inform me of its particulars. I have accumulated at least three geasa, and I'd like to avoid a conflict that will end in disaster for either of us—or for both."

"I don't understand."

"I think you do understand and you just don't know it. It's quite a simple concept following straightforward rules of logic. The geas is always on you. Most of the time you don't notice.

But there will be a moment when you do. You can either keep the vow and meet the demands of the geas. Or you can break the vow and the geas will still ride you. Only, henceforth the geas will work on you as a curse. Again, most of the time you won't notice. But there will be a moment when you do. And in that moment, you will realize that you are composed entirely of the residue of those geasa you have kept faith with. That what has been riding you all this time is something else entirely."

"You mean death," she said.

"If by death you mean dissolution of the self," Ciarán said, "and not simply of the animal one can see in the mirror? I mean the opposite. *Death's enemy.*"

"You mean life."

"I don't. Life is death's opposite. I'm talking about a structure. An edifice. One overarching life. One that *persists.*"

That's..."

"It's foreign," he said. "Alien to modern sensibilities. And I apologize for inflicting all that on you. It's really a simple idea, the geas, and the theory behind it doesn't matter to this discussion. A geas can be a trivial thing. It can even be quite silly, or absurd. For example, a man might have a geas on him that he mustn't cross a river with a blonde woman on his back, and another geas that he mustn't refuse a polite request involving children. He may go most of his life aware or unaware of these geasa, and it doesn't matter. Until one day a blonde woman tells him a volcano's about to erupt nearby, and politely asks will he help her and her three children cross the river. She can't swim, and the river is too deep for her and the little ones to wade. Right away you can see he has two conflicting geasa, and he's going to have to break one or the other."

"Not if he takes the children across the river and abandons the blonde woman," she said. "He simply has to interpret the language literally. The polite request obligation can be considered to apply to the children but not to the blonde woman."

"He could try that but there's a real danger. He can't parse words and lawyer his way out of the situation with confidence because the geasa follow their own logic. They can't be persuaded by argument. And there's no partial credit if he guesses wrong."

"You're saying this geas is a bargain he agreed to without a clear understanding of its terms?"

"I'm saying the terms are simple. And that the man's time is better spent trying to figure out how to comply with the geasa than cheat his way out of them. That the literature suggests it's safest to find a clever solution to the unsolvable problem, even if that solution isn't even slightly apparent at first glance."

"There's literature on this?"

"At their core, the People's oldest stories are about nothing but this. In the League your stories appear to be about conflicts between good and evil. In the Federation our stories are about people and the obligations they accumulate, and what to do about conflicts between people with divergent obligations. For example, suppose the blonde woman has a geas on her that she will never abandon her children, and will stick beside them always."

"That's clearly impossible. She'll die one day."

"Tell me another."

"What?"

"My mother is nearly seven years dead, and I was only moments ago having an argument with her. But ignoring that, you can see my point. The blonde woman's geas and the man's geasa are in conflict. It's not good versus evil, or even the man and the blonde woman going to war, but the vows they're saddled with scraping against one another. Even if he wanted to leave her behind, she'd fight like a demon to remain beside the little ones." He winked at her. "Unless."

"Unless what?"

"Unless those weren't her children, and she was trying to

trick the man into breaking his geas without any risk to herself from her own geas. That happens more often than you'd think. And while he might be willing to carry the blonde woman on his back in violation of his geas he would be a fool to do so without first throwing her into the river and observing whether she could swim. If it appears she is drowning, he might still refuse to carry her on his back. But he might consent to hold her head above water while he taught her how to swim."

"And your point?"

"My point is, I don't want to know names, or dates, or any details that might wake the dead. But I do need to know what is driving you to put your own lives and ours at risk. Once we get that out of the way we'll talk about this fiasco in the isolated fabrication compartment. What is riding you and what is chasing you. They will be related. And I can't help you until I know the truth of that. If I can't help you, I will jettison you, and I'll be doing you a favor. What I will not do is wade into your mess with no idea of how deep or wide the river is."

"It's still not clear to me. What are your three geasa," she said. "Unless they're secret."

"For some people they are secret. But mine aren't. I find having them public saves time." He flicked the pendant spire depending from his ear. "There's this obligation." He held his hands out, palms angled towards each other, fingers cupped like he was holding a ball, or a globe, or a world. "There's all of this, keeping me and mine safe from harm. Not simply this ship and crew but my people, wherever they be." He leaned back in his seat. "And there's the one geas that's grit in both those gears, which you heard me mouth earlier. A promise I made my mother on her death bed. That I would never surrender. She ascribed a very peculiar and specific meaning to those words."

"Which was?"

"Which *is*: *Do not disfigure your soul.* For her that meant don't compromise. Never back down. Never run from a fight. A whole host of behaviors that arose inevitably from the intersection of that fundamental principle and her cultural background.

"Her approach is entirely unworkable as a practical philosophy for a merchant, and for a Freeman merchant in particular. I've had to modify its expression to suit my own circumstances. The way this works in practice is that I'm open for compromise on any subject, and I'll back down to anyone, and I'll run from any fight, so long as it doesn't impact my obligation to this," he flicked the pendant spire, "and this." He held his invisible globe of duty between them. "There I stand firm. No arguments will sway me, nor force short of annihilation dislodge me."

He leaned forward in his seat. "That's why I think of those two obligations as geasa. Because of this third geas my mother laid upon me. That I'd stop being the hero of my own life if I broke trust with those commitments. I'd just be another broken soldier praying for the oblivion of death, all while judging myself undeserving of it."

He watched her unpacking all that. He'd spoken at an even pace in Trade Common, though in his mind his words didn't have the shape of things one said in that tongue, the language of commerce, and of modern ideas. It was an old thing he spoke of, an old way of thinking that extracted a daily price. There was a friction to every transaction, like every step he took forward was a step uphill against a gravity that acted, not on matter, but on spirit.

"I have one geas," she said after a very long while. "One I know of."

"I wondered if you'd catch that little detail," he said. "In the seanscéalta, the old stories, that ignorance of a geas was many a hero's downfall. They would often only realize they were saddled with a geas an instant after they'd violated the vow and the curse began to settle and their doom draw nigh."

"And?"

"And what?"

"What would they do to avoid that mistake?"

"I don't know. I only know what people do nowadays, if they have any sense."

"Which is?"

"They learn from others' mistakes. I think that's one of the reasons we still have seanscéalta. So we'll know not to vow to never eat dog meat, and simultaneously vow to never turn away a free meal, for example. Any idiot nowadays can see the trap in that one, and that's a famous story about a major hero in our culture. It's impenetrable to me, that class of thinking, but apparently it was common back in the day."

She chuckled. "Are you going to ask me about my geas?"

"We don't do that."

"I asked *you*."

"That's because you do that. It's expected of you. It's expected of the People to trick you into volunteering personal information."

"Really?"

"Tricking is your word for it. We think of it as enticing or encouraging. Nevertheless, it's rare for a Freeman to come right out and ask a personal question. And you can be fairly certain if we give a straight answer to one it's not a literal truth."

"Would asking violate your geas?"

"It wouldn't. My geas is to live the Oath and the Oath doesn't say anything about the waking the dead custom. It's a long story why that custom evolved, but if I wanted, I could ask you to tell me your geas, if you were willing. Are you?"

"Willing? Yes."

"Are you going to? Tell me?"

"I swore a vow as a girl. And that's all I'm doing. Keeping my word. I wouldn't have involved you if I could have thought of any other way. But I don't know who to trust. Every time I think

I've found someone I can depend on, they end up double-crossing me, unless they say they're going to do something and then don't. I asked my father if he knew anyone reliable and he said Charles Newton. And then I asked Lord Aster, and he said the same thing. But they're not particularly reliable, either. Or attentive. If you recall, this isn't the first time I've come looking for your help."

"Hang on," Ciarán said. "I thought Lord Aster is your father."

"Everyone thinks that."

"Including your mother."

"Very funny."

"I'm not joking."

"She thinks it doesn't matter. With gene editing universally adopted, it is increasingly difficult to determine paternity with certainty. Lionel Aster raised me. That makes him my father. Which is itself a joke."

"Because he did a poor job raising you."

"Because I didn't meet Lionel Aster until I'd turned eighteen."

"I'd have thought that impossible. Unless he'd abandoned you."

"It isn't," she said, "And he didn't abandon me. He worked to avoid me. We lived in the same house. Travelled on the same vessels. We often attended the same social functions. When I did finally meet him, I asked him to explain himself."

"Did he?"

"He said he doesn't like children, and that was it. End of conversation."

"I thought *I* had a strange childhood."

"My childhood wasn't strange. It was actually quite normal. I had a mother and, instead of a father, I had my mother's live-in lover, at least for those months when they were not away on business. He treated me like a daughter, but like the daughter of someone he worked for, rather than his own."

"I suppose it was an odd situation for him as well."

"Why? I *was* his daughter. He pretended I wasn't."

"But you knew all along, and he denied it."

"No," she said. "I had no idea until I stole the files that proved it and confronted him."

"You stole them."

"Did I say that? I meant I found them." She glanced at his face.

Ciarán gazed back at her from behind his merchant's mask of calm. He wasn't judging her, and she could see that. Honesty wouldn't hurt her. Only a lie could. "Go on."

"Later I stole *copies* of them. And that's when everything went pear-shaped. Hector was furious that I'd copied the files, and my mother as well, but we all agreed not to tell Lionel, which turned out to be a huge mistake.

"I hadn't just copied my own files but made copies of all the files in the hidden directory, which included all the Prince Rigel folders, which Mother wasn't supposed to have at home. She'd 'borrowed' copies from Lionel's office only hours before. That's how I was able to find my own files. She'd been acting furtively and had left a discernible and incriminating digital trail *anyone* could follow. But I didn't know that until later, when I learned that someone had followed that trail."

"And Hector is?" Ciarán said.

"Hector Poole," she said. "He pointed you out to me as Charles Newton all those years ago. When you and I first met. He said you didn't know it yet, but you were about to become Charles Newton."

"Because he arranged for me to have identification in Charles Newton's name," Ciarán said. "So I could act as his unwitting pawn in one of his schemes."

"Obviously, but that wasn't the way he said it. He said it as if you were going to somehow *turn into* Charles Newton. Like he'd done something to *cause* you to transform from a pumpkin into a prince."

"From a bumpkin."

"That may have been the word he used. Anyway, once the Prince Rigels began to turn up murdered we had to tell Lionel. And that's when Lionel exploded and went into full Lord Aster mode. He tasked Hector with cleanup and exiled mother and me to Sizemore Station."

"And your father did nothing."

"What do you mean?"

"He just disappeared from the story."

"No he didn't. He went to work cleaning up the mess. I said that."

"You said Hector Poole did that."

"That's right. Hector Poole is my father."

Ciarán silently groaned. "That's grand." He could feel another unwanted geas preparing to settle upon him.

"I wouldn't call it grand," Sarah said. "He's not a very good father."

"Imagine him as an uncle."

"I'd rather not. That's what mother asked me to call each of her lovers. All of them since Hector, I mean. And before."

"You have proof that Hector Poole is your father."

"He admitted to it. In front of Lord Aster. I made him do it."

"And Lord Aster just stood there."

Sarah's face colored. "He looked at me. Then he looked at Hector and said, 'You poor, unfortunate bastard.' Then he slapped Hector on the back and walked off. On the way out of the room he shouted. It was clear he was quite angry."

"Do I want to know what he shouted?"

"Fix this! Fix it yesterday! Fix it while we still have a League!"

"Hector Poole is Lord Aster's fixer," Ciarán said.

"That's right. But the problem was large enough that he needed help. So I volunteered, and Hector surprised me by agreeing once I told him about my solemn vow, which thanks to you, I now know is a geas. He said if I wanted to protect the League, I should detain my mother and clear out. And that I should take the surviving Prince Rigels with me. And while I was at it, take the idiot Home Guard hangers-on I'd blabbed to with me as well. So, I told him I would."

"And then he told you people would die if you did."

She nodded. "And more would die if I didn't. You've met him, so you know he can be quite..."

"Glib," Ciarán said.

"Exceedingly. And funny, and also dreadfully..."

"Hard."

"You remind me of him. Though no one is as airy when manic. But now and then I find you watching me. It's as if something terrible hides just behind your eyes. That if I take one wrong step it will surface."

"And devour you."

She nodded, and swallowed. "Yes."

"It's nothing personal."

"That's what makes it so terrible, isn't it? It isn't personal with Hector, either."

"This geas of yours."

"I've sworn to protect the League. I am Lord Aster's heir. His title will one day be mine, and with it his responsibilities. He is not an admired man. I don't even know if he is a decent man. Certainly he is a terminally incompetent parent and husband. But I have no doubt that he has done his best for Queen and country. And I vowed to do the same when my time came. That being universally feared and despised was a price I would pay, as he has, to preserve the League's traditions and predominance of influence in the wider world.

"Imagine my horror when I discovered that I'd stupidly and

selfishly sabotaged all that. That my actions threatened to fracture the League and undo decades of work and planning. Not on purpose, mind you, but then, that's how most terrible things happen, isn't it? No one sets out to disgrace their family. To get their friends killed. To put others in danger and find themselves reduced to begging for help and mercy from *foreigners*. These are the unintended consequences of intentional actions. Actions I own. Consequences I am determined to repair. That's why I came to you. Hector told me how to find you. And what to do to convince you to help me."

"Force me to help you, you mean."

"To make it difficult for you to turn me away."

"Go on then," Ciarán said.

"Go on what?"

"Beg for my foreign help and mercy."

Her face colored. "I can't. Anyway, it's just a turn of phrase."

"You won't," Ciarán said. "Because there's more than one geas riding you. And you're ashamed or afraid to tell me about it."

She swallowed and refused to meet his gaze. "Not that. There's a note, in my cabin. One from Hector. One meant for you."

"A private note from Hector Poole to Ciarán mac Diarmuid?"

She nodded, sharply. "Yes. Nearly. To Charles Newton. A sealed note. A note I wasn't meant to read."

"But you opened it and read it."

She swallowed and nodded. "Yes."

"What does it say?"

"It says." She glanced at his face quickly before turning away. "Be a sport and fix this for me, you poor unfortunate—"

"I've heard enough." Ciarán stood and shoved his chair back sharply. He moved it out of the way and opened the hatch. "We will go to your cabin and you'll show me this so-called note. Someone is having you on, and we'll get to the bottom of it."

Sarah Aster stood. "I don't understand."

"Hector Poole could not have written that note." Only a monster could write that knowing she would read it. And Hector Poole was *not quite* a monster. He simply did monstrous things to monstrous people who probably deserved it.

"It sounds just like him. He didn't expect me to open it."

"It sounds like someone who is both clever and cruel. Do you think of Hector Poole as cruel?"

"The opposite, oddly."

"Agreed. I've known you for no more than a few hours. I am absolutely certain no one clever would hand you a sealed note to deliver. Not and expect it to arrive at its destination unread."

"That's harsh."

"Then deny it."

"If Hector didn't write it who did?"

"Someone who knows your nature and wishes to hurt you. Someone who knows Hector Poole by reputation alone. Someone who knows me not at all. But most importantly? Someone who overheard the conversation you described."

"But we were alone in Lord Aster's conference room."

"Entirely alone. You, and Lionel Aster, and Hector Poole."

"And Mother, obviously."

"And no one else."

"No one," she said. "Not anyone who would care. Or... Not anyone."

"Does this not anyone who doesn't care have a name?"

"It must. But it doesn't matter. They don't get involved."

"Tell me about them. Start from the beginning."

"I burst in on them while they were having an argument. Lionel, Mother, and Hector. There was one of them avatared in."

"Avatared?"

"You know. The conference room has a real-feel system. For remote discussions. One of them was complaining about the new Lord Varlock. It excused itself once the shouting started, at least I think it did. I know for certain it wasn't there by the time the crying began." She chewed a fingernail, her attention turned inward. She placed both of her hands stiffly in her lap. "I may have... I couldn't have. It had definitely withdrawn and terminated the session. I'm certain of it."

"By it you mean?"

"A syntho. Some of them are upset about the Queen's decision to make one of their own Lord Varlock. As Lord Aster used to handle Lord Varlock's duties, he's the figurehead they complain to. As if complaining will change anything."

"What do they want changed?"

"Everything. Some want the Queen to choose a different syntho to carry out Lord Varlock's duties. Some of them want the Queen to choose a normal person for the job. Some want Lord Aster to resume the duties. Some want the position eliminated entirely. Since the decision was made public, it's been nothing but non-stop whining and not just from the synthos. From real people as well. It's almost a blessing Sunbury House was destroyed. At least we don't have crazies turning up at the door anymore with their outrageous demands."

Ciarán made a conscious effort to retain his placid mask. The ship was hearing all of this. He would need to apologize on Sarah Aster's behalf once their conversation was over. But he had to bite his tongue now, else she'd remember he was a foreigner, and say no more.

"Lord Aster lacks the power to meet these synthetic intelligences' demands," Ciarán said.

"He couldn't help them, not even if he wanted to, and he doesn't. I think it was his idea to make the Nevin Green syntho Lord Varlock. Lionel's been saddled with Lord Varlock's duties for decades. But it doesn't matter who came up with the idea.

Someone planted the thought in Queen Charlotte's head and she ordered it done."

"Then the aggrieved parties should complain to Queen Charlotte."

"I believe that was precisely what Lord Aster was saying when I burst in. Which is really the same thing as saying, 'quit whining and live with it'. Once the Queen decides she never changes her mind. Everyone knows that."

"Thus the appeals to Lord Aster instead."

"Which have no effect. He has no control over her, even if people think he does. Not on decisions she's made. Only on decisions she hasn't made yet."

"Perhaps if these complainers had some leverage."

"Leverage with the Queen? Don't make me laugh. She doesn't back down and she doesn't compromise. The only way to change her mind would be to switch it off."

"I meant leverage over Lord Aster."

"I've already explained. She doesn't listen to him once a decision has been made."

"Perhaps she doesn't listen because Lord Aster is insufficiently motivated."

"You don't know him. Or Queen Charlotte."

"I don't. But that doesn't mean someone wouldn't try running an op on him anyway. Just to see if you're wrong."

"What do you mean?"

"Based on what you've said I can imagine a score or more of handles a reputation merchant could try to stick to Lord Aster, Hector Poole, Lady Tabatha, and to you. Lord Aster is the most obvious target if direct influence over the Queen is desired. But just being able to compel him to run interference while other means of influence were applied to the Queen would be valuable. You have described a ball of snakes, any one of which might now be trying to swallow you and yours, and, in the process, me and mine. Would Lady Tabatha know the identity of this synthetic intelligence that might have overheard your private conversation?"

"Yes. But I don't see the point in asking her. I'm sure it disconnected."

"I'm sure it did too," Ciarán said.

Right after it heard all it needed to.

36

C iarán finished brushing out Wisp's ruff. As she'd aged, she'd grown more amenable to grooming. And he'd grown more skillful at caring for her as well; he no longer routinely wore the field-reinforced gauntlets that used to be a necessity. She still might gnaw on his knuckle as warning to take care, but he wasn't worried about losing a finger anymore.

She sprawled on the bunk in the merchant captain's stateroom and warned him with the tip of a single claw. *The belly is off limits.*

"Fair enough," he said. He still wasn't used to his new accommodations, though it no longer felt disloyal to Aoife nic Cartaí to have moved into her former cabin. It wasn't a temporary arrangement anymore, and the cabin was much closer to the bridge than the merchant apprentice's cabin he'd occupied when Aoife was yet merchant-in-charge. He was no longer just filling in for her while she was away. He could make more of a nuisance of himself on the bridge, popping in at all hours. Just because he didn't operate the vessel didn't mean he wished to remain ignorant of its disposition. That level of conscientiousness did not make him a control freak, despite how often it was said, or how many said it.

For example, right now there were crew and prisoners intermingling in the ship's mess, and he didn't feel the need to observe their minutest interactions. Far from it. He much preferred viewing the affair from his cabin workstation display while he groomed Wisp and dressed. And while he discussed the disturbing Lady Sarah Aster with the ship and the ship's minder. He'd asked them both to be present because they each had very different areas of expertise. And very different personalities.

He understood now that they had once been one personality, surgically bifurcated, or whatever passed for brain surgery in synthetic intelligences. But they'd been separate entities for thousands of years and had diverging views and opinions. Despite this they didn't argue, or if they did, they did it in private. Perhaps because there was no question of who would win if a dispute devolved into a brawl. The ship's minder was entirely without empathy and without scruples in the conventional sense. That it didn't seem to care to argue about anything but its prime directive insured amity aboard. Most of the time it remained silent and in the background. Except in cases that touched upon external and internal threats—like this.

The view on the display was of the mess as seen from the luminaire just above and inside the aft hatch. The mess and galley were the only part of the vessel discovered damaged when it was excavated from beneath a glacier on Murrisk. The galley was fitted out with standard Freeman family ship kit; cheap, rugged, and easily serviced. And the mess was outfitted with the familiar and indestructible plastic tables and chairs in a childish rainbow of colors. They were obviously purchased used because there were initials and cartoons carved into the table surfaces from their previous life aboard a nic Cartaí company ship. Some of the chairs were the burnt orange of the oldest vessels yet in service, hulls that transported Aoife nic Cartaí's ancestors in chains. This, he was told, was a tradition on nic Cartaí vessels, and when he went down to the mess later he would be expected to take Aoife's seat as Merchant Captain. The Merchant Captain's seat was instantly recognizable because it was charred and melted as if it had been in a fire. And he supposed it had, if one counted the discharge of a Huangxu plasma rifle as fire.

Wherever he looked, there were constant reminders of the past. Not of his past, but of countless others. Sarah Aster had told him much, but she'd done so under the implied assumption that they shared a historical frame. That her references to people and events meant something to him. It would have broken the flow of her confession if he had interrupted her for clarification. And he didn't need to, because he had two experts on board whom he could query at his leisure. The ship had monitored and recorded their entire exchange and the ship's minder made a point of remaining perpetually up to date on news and events throughout the wider world.

He didn't need to ask the ship to replay their discussion. He had an excellent memory; one trained in the Academy and assessed for performance annually. And the ship's minder was perfectly capable of filling in the blanks without prompting. It reminded him of Seamus in this regard, who had a knack for summarizing a topic and presenting it in brief, without filler or throat clearing. It was best to just poke the hornet's nest and see what flew out.

"What did Sarah Aster tell us?"

"Other than she's a bigot?" the ship said.

"Other than that. I meant to apologize to you for having to endure her ignorance. If she stays aboard, I promise to educate her."

"You might gag her instead," the ship said. "If she's to be a hostage."

"It's not Lady Sarah's talking that concerns me," Ciarán said. "It's her thinking. And I like the challenge of sparring with her. I think we're too comfortable, associating only with our own kind."

"Better you than me," the ship said.

"You have broken the ship, Merchant Captain," the ship's minder said. "She is developing a Freeman tongue."

"I like a ship that speaks its mind," Ciarán said.

"With this talk of gagging hostages, I'm afraid she'll put me out of a job," the ship's minder said. "I'm supposed to be the militant arm of this operation."

"You are," the ship said. "But the baseline between diplomacy and militancy has shifted. We are on stony soil. Our plowshares need more of an edge. That doesn't render our swords obsolete."

"Lady Sarah," Ciarán said. "Her confession."

"It hangs together," the ship's minder said. "To say more I need the identity of the 'syntho' she mentioned."

"I cringed every time she said that," Ciarán said. "And I'll get the name from Lady Tabatha. You may count on it."

"I suspect we already know the name," the ship's minder said. "But a suspicion is not ordinarily actionable in such cases. Furthermore, I would like to know with certainty where the pattern for this first-epoch murder device came from."

"Is that what it is?"

"Without a doubt."

"And the message it carved into the observation window?"

"Ambiguous. Purposefully so, no doubt."

"Aimed at?"

"Again, unclear."

"Would it have continued replicating?"

"It would not have," the ship's minder said. "There was a bug purposefully introduced into its code. Once the first device completed making a copy of itself the second device would have begun making copies of itself. And the first device would have continued to try to make copies of itself. I suspect a block of code was commented out."

"Code that does what?"

"The disassemblers are opportunistic. They assess their environment and disassemble those elements easiest to harvest the necessary materials from. In this case the preferred source of materials was—"

"The first device," Ciarán said.

"Precisely. The devices would attempt to recursively assemble and disassemble copies of themselves from their own materials. A deadly embrace of mutual self-destruction."

"You're certain it was intentional."

"Indeed. The flaw would prove evident upon a single execution."

"If the coder had access to a macrofab," Ciarán said. "To test it on."

The ship made a rasping sound Ciarán had begun to interpret as laughter. "Every ten-year-old child in the League has access to a virtualized instance of a standard fabricator."

"Identical to our own?" Ciarán asked.

"Sufficiently so for testing," the ship's minder said. "This is an intentional problem with a trivial fix. The devices need only mask the existence of themselves from the disassemblers' awareness of the environment."

"The significance of the message?"

"Obvious on the surface," the ship said. "The sender is claiming credit for burying us on Murrisk and threatening to do so again."

Ciarán thought as much. "That's—"

"Utter rubbish," the ship said. "We all know who is responsible for that."

"Not all," the ship's minder said. "But let us remain on topic here. Once I have the name of the synthetic intelligence overhearing Sarah Aster's conversation I will initiate an inquiry into this person, their history, and associations."

"It will be this Abyss Tower," the ship said. "Or some aspect of it."

"Perhaps," the ship's minder said. "All we do know is who it isn't."

"Nevin Green," Ciarán said.

"Green has had a lengthy association with Maris Solon," the ship said. "Perhaps we might reach out to her."

"And what?" the ship's minder said. "Substitute her judgement for my own?"

"I said nothing of relying on her judgement. To gather additional information about Nevin Green and those who oppose its appointment as Lord Varlock."

"Information as filtered through her third-party biases," the ship's minder said. "Her human judgement is implicit in her every utterance. Utterances that can be intercepted and overheard."

"It makes sense to me to speak with her," Ciarán said. "Unless you don't feel capable of filtering fact from opinion in human conversations."

"My capabilities are not in question. If I 'reach out' to anyone regarding Nevin Green it will be to Green itself. And there remains the risk of being overheard. We would need to use the Sizemore superluminal node."

"And it is monitored," the ship said.

"That's a human problem," Ciarán said. "I think I have a workaround."

"Which is?" the ship's minder asked.

Ciarán said nothing.

Eventually the ship emitted its raspy laugh. "Nicely done."

"If one admires impertinence," the ship's minder said. "Are we done here?"

"Almost," Ciarán said. "What did Sarah Aster mean when she said they'd begun murdering 'the Prince Rigels'?"

"Unclear," the ship's minder said. "I will query the Sizemore data hub upon arrival. Surreptitiously, of course."

"Don't bother," the ship said. "Maura Kavanagh, Yuan Ko Shan, and Watanabe Natsuko are aficionados of the recorded drama, *Prince Rigel: Heart's Heir*. This ongoing series recounts the adventure of Prince Rigel Templeman who, long believed dead, returns to battle for his rightful place on the throne. Evil Queen Charlotte Templeman opposes him. Conniving Prime Minister Samantha Bray opposes him. His only allies are a clownish synthetic intelligence and a band of—"

"Unemployed and disaffected screenwriters," the ship's minder said.

"So, you have seen it," the ship said.

The ship's minder said nothing.

Ciarán wished the ship and the ship's minder had faces or some other physical manifestation he could examine to determine if one or both were joking. "That sounds terrible," Ciarán said. "Unemployed screenwriters as heroes? Seriously?"

"No comment," the ship said, and after a moment, "That is what the comic relief synthetic intelligence says when caught in a lie. The phrase appears to have entered the common vocabulary, both as a nodding reference to the series and as an indicator of social group membership."

"Membership in what?"

"The Legion of Heroes," the ship said. "An informal organization of Prince Rigel series fanatics. The series is very loosely based on historical facts."

"That could prove confusing," Ciarán said. "People do know there is a real Legion of Heroes."

"Many know there was a historical organization called the Legion of Heroes. More know the name from the series; the Legion appears in season one and is utterly defeated during a forlorn hope operation in season two. The Legion's destruction in the second season finale is considered the moment in which the series moved beyond cult favorite to captivating mainstream fandom."

"Does the series have a lot of fanatics?"

"It is the most popular recorded drama in League history. With over one billion regular viewers, ten million are likely fanatical enough to consider themselves Legionnaires."

"And some of these Legionnaires are the murdered Prince Rigels?"

"In the series," the ship said, "there are scores of Prince Rigel impersonators that have presented themselves to the crown over the years in the hopes of personal and financial gain. The young prince went missing as an infant five decades before. These impersonators range from fifteen to fifty years of age, standard."

"The younger ones supposedly having been in cryo," Ciarán said.

"Indeed. There is no shortage of imposters, and they, not *unemployed screenwriters*, rise to be the true Prince Rigel's allies and defenders. There are a great number of these imposters," the ship said, "and one or more die per episode, often in a heroic and self-sacrificing manner."

"*Prince Rigel: Heart's Heir* is utter propaganda," the ship's minder said.

"In your opinion," the ship said.

"By definition," the ship's minder said.

"I thought you hadn't seen it," Ciarán said.

"I hadn't when I implied that," the ship's minder said. "I have since analyzed those episodes in the crew library."

"Just now?"

"While you talked. The series episodes and its narrative arc are expertly crafted to sell a viewpoint. They exhibit all the hallmarks of state-sponsored persuasion executed at the highest level. I judge them equivalent in craft and effect to the *noh* plays of Kazuki Ryuu."

"Propaganda that shattered the Ojinate," Ciarán said.

"That helped complete the process," the ship's minder said.

"Who made the series?" Ciarán asked.

"The usual suspects, one supposes," the ship's minder said. "The more important questions are who financed it and who wrote it."

"And?" the ship said. "Oh. That is... Oh my. It hangs together."

"You can't simply have a conversation and leave me out of it," Ciarán said.

"We can. But we aren't having a conversation," the ship's minder said. "We share a common data pool."

"So, what one of you knows the other knows?"

"What we choose to share the other may choose to note," the ship said. "Or not. And if my monstrous partner is right—"

"I am," the ship's minder said.

"Assuming that, then I agree. Much of the story is factually true. There is a missing Prince Rigel, as the babe's remains were never found. There have been scores of imposters over the years, and more popping up every day, particularly since the series run began four years ago. There are persistent rumors regarding the death of Rigel's parents. I had not considered the ideas that the series had any goal other than entertainment. But it seems quite clear now after reviewing your annotations. *Prince Rigel: Heart's Heir* is designed to fracture the League."

"More accurately," the ship's minder said, "To make it seem inevitable that the League would fracture at some point. And when it does, to divide and distract the masses, and to identify those individuals disinclined to take sides. And to subsequently activate them."

"Activate them to what end?" Ciarán asked.

"That is the question," the ship's minder said. "For now, I'd be satisfied knowing the identities of the culprits. I've followed the money and found the financier. I've uncovered the author's name but I'm reasonably certain it's a pseudonym. And it does appear that someone is systematically murdering the *real* Prince Rigel impersonators, as absurd as that sounds. Ten deaths in as many days, and you won't like this, Merchant Captain."

"Go on," Ciarán said. "Living in ignorance doesn't seem to be doing me any good."

"We now have two Prince Rigel impersonators aboard this vessel. As well as one of the principal suspects in several of the murder investigations."

"That's grand. At least we don't have the author of this treason aboard, and the cabal paying for it as well."

The ship's minder said nothing.

Ciarán glanced at the deckhead annunciator "Ship?"

"I am here."

"We don't have them aboard, do we?"

"No comment."

"Don't toy with him," the ship's minder said. "I'm certain it's a pseudonym."

"The authors name," Ciarán said. "Tell me."

"Charles Newton."

"Of course. It would be. And the moneyman behind the plot to destroy the League? Is that also Mr. Newton?"

"It isn't," the ship's minder said. "Unless Charles Newton is an alias for Lionel Aster."

"The man who's contracted with us for this mission."

"The contract is written as between Lord Aster and Charles Newton," the ship said. "Specifically, Lord Aster acting as agent for Queen Charlotte."

"I do remember the terms of the contract," Ciarán said. "As I signed it."

"Signed as Charles Newton," the ship said.

"I did legally register the name in the Eight Banners Empire. And I used it because Lord Aster suggested I do, to leave Aoife and the rest outside the blast radius if anything went pear-shaped."

"Does this qualify as going pear-shaped?" the ship said.

"It's trending in that direction," Ciarán said. "I'm upgrading the status of our guests. They're no longer prisoners."

"Surely they aren't hostages," the ship said. "Regardless of our monstrous companion's desires."

The ship's minder said nothing.

"I take it we're done here," Ciarán said.

As no one spoke up to dispute his claim, Ciarán scooped up his pendant spire from the nightstand. When he donned the earring, it had never felt heavier. He considered his options and decided that if ever he needed all the trappings of a Freeman Merchant Captain this was the moment. He jammed the overseers rod beneath his belt and slid into his yellow-lined merchant's great coat. He finally understood why the bulky long coat, designed for the freezing docking rings of stations and orbiting platforms, also had a cooling setting on its active controls. He was burning up inside, and he wasn't sure where to vent the heat.

Not yet, he wasn't.

"Wisp," he said.

The big cat rose and padded to his side.

"Let's go mingle with the crew. And chat with the *suspects*."

37

The throng in the mess hall had grown to full strength by the time Ciarán and Wisp arrived. He was glad to see that no fistfights between suspects and crew had broken out. On the contrary, Lieutenant Lambent seemed deeply engaged in a discussion with Aspen; Lieutenant, or should he say Mr., Prince sat regaling Ko Shan on some topic; and Sarah Aster had seated herself with Natsuko and Hess, and seemed recovered to full Columbia Station fitness, with shoes on her feet and every blonde lock in place. Lady Tabatha and Ship's Captain Swan stood apart from the rest, their conversation active but their eyes never resting, as they each scanned the gathered crowd for unwanted eruptions of exuberance, their goals united. Only their targets of attention differed.

Those of the ship's crew that were not League military were each dressed in their best blue utilities, uniform in color and uniformly devoid of ornamentation. That was the aesthetic Aoife had settled upon for both vessels in her new Thin Star Line, and Ciarán approved, perhaps because he hadn't earned the many pins and badges from distant ports visited that the typical long-haul spacer had. Certainly all the regalia gave strangers something to talk about that rarely sparked dissent, but this crew had enough to talk about without the hardware. They were outbound, and while they each had a general idea of the mission they did not know the particulars. Of those aboard only Swan, Amati, and he did.

They had upgraded the portable holo tank since their past mission, and instead of a reasonably sized one parked on top of a crash cart, they now had one that, itself, was wheeled and big as a secondary unit in a stationmaster's office. While they'd been able to sit at the tables and use the old one, this one required the chairs be gathered around it, as its display ran from floor to head-height on a standing man, and they were headed for the edges of the chart. The net effect was that he wouldn't be able to use the tank while they ate so needed to save the explanations until after the meal. That wasn't such an issue while in superluminal space, but he made a mental note to instruct Hess to default to the smaller unit when at sublight and minutes might matter. The resolution was lower on the small unit, but it worked for the broad-stroke discussions they usually had. And even the large tank couldn't compete with the resolution of the second-epoch displays on the bridge, even if they only displayed in two-dimensions. What he'd really like was a holo tank that worked with the shipboard systems, but that was a low priority.

Hess and Amati were outfitted in their League uniforms, both Royal Navy, Hess a senior warrant officer in Engineering, Amati a major in the Marines. He cast his gaze around the compartment for Helen Konstantine, who until recently had worn the uniform of a Royal Navy pilot. This would be her first formal gathering in civilian dress. He spied her sitting with Maura Kavanagh, who had eschewed her usual glittery look for the solemn appearance of a Freeman merchant princess. Her utilities were expertly tailored and her hullwalkers gleamed like black diamond, but there remained little else to draw the eye except the stunning woman that wore them. He wondered if Maura realized the power of that understated effect or if she'd settled for it, knowing she was expected to not just act the part of a senior officer but look it.

Ciarán crossed the compartment. He would deal with the suspects in a moment, but crew came first.

"Pilot," he said.

Konstantine grinned. "Karen." She had difficulty pronouncing Ciarán's name, and what might have proved an embarrassment at one time, if he'd chosen to take notice, had become a shared joke.

He grinned and took a seat. "How do those utilities fit?"

"Better than I thought they would. There's a freedom of movement in them I appreciate." She made a fist and held it in front of her face, her gazed aimed over it at him. She winked.

He'd taken a beating from Helen Konstantine a while back, the sort of beating that would have seen her court-martialed or hung in the Navy. They'd both been wrong, but that wouldn't have mattered if he'd been her commanding officer at the time.

"And the shoes are nicer," Maura said.

Ciarán glanced beneath the table, at Konstantine's feet. She wore the same ultra-exclusive hullwalkers Maura wore.

"A gift. Maura says I might need to be able to run away from a fight now and then. If it's permitted that I do."

"It isn't permitted," Ciarán said. "It's expected. Unless cornered."

Maura jerked her chin. "What's with the Erl of Hurl?"

Ciarán glanced where she had gestured. "Mr. Prince? Did he... introduce himself to you?"

"You might say that. Though I imagine he'd say it was my knee introducing itself to his—"

"Junk," Konstantine said. "That's the word they use for rubbish amongst the youth nowadays."

"I didn't know that," Ciarán said. "I thought it was—"

"Trash," Konstantine said. "Look what he's done to his uniform."

"Rubbish," Maura said. "That's what it looks like."

"Are you two pleased with yourselves?"

"We're working on a comedy routine for the employee holiday party," Maura said.

"Young and Younger," Konstantine said. She was twice Maura's age, likely nearer three times, having aged out and been forcibly retired not long ago.

"I'm not certain," Ciarán said, "But I believe Mr. Prince removed all insignia from his uniform because he didn't think it appropriate to wear them. As he is missing and presumed dead he didn't wish to masquerade as an officer. 'Stolen valor, and all that,' he told me."

"But he isn't dead," Konstantine said. "When we return him—"

"He expects that we will not return him," Ciarán said. "He thinks we're party to a scheme to disappear him and his fellow travelers, and that there will be no resurrection for him."

Maura leaned forward in her seat. "What does he think we're going to do with him?"

"Take him with us," Ciarán said.

Konstantine frowned. "And then what?"

"I don't know," Ciarán admitted.

"Are we going to do that?" Konstantine said. "Take them with us?"

"I'm thinking about it," Ciarán said.

Maura stood. "In that case I'd better go apologize to him. If I'm going to have to look at him every day."

"Sit down," Ciarán said. "I'm telling you. I don't know if they're coming with us."

"And she's telling you," Konstantine said. "We know. You

just defended his honor, Karen. No one does that for throw-away people."

Ciarán felt his face color. "I do."

Maura patted him on the shoulder and stepped around him. "Tell me another."

38

He'd nearly finished making the rounds when Sarah Aster cornered him. She'd cleaned up nicely, now wearing a gold and bronze formal outfit that matched her mother's green-and-gold one. He assumed the style represented the latest fashion amongst Columbia Stationers and not some mother-daughter coordination. The outfit was made up of loose trousers beneath a flowing over-shirt that draped below her knees, the fabric of the overshirt as silken and richly patterned as a hand-woven tapestry. Hess had warned him that it was also antiballistic as a hardsuit, and the sort of cutting-edge tech jealously guarded by the League. She wore a headdress and veil that were similarly artful and armored. Her hullwalkers were also packed with tech, the sort of tech that made it almost worth the risk to copy the data crystal she'd handed him to fab the fancy outfit.

Ciarán had no doubt that if it were safe to do so the ship's minder would have done just that, even if it involved air-gapped spiders typing on spidery keyboards. It wouldn't waste an advantage within its grasp, either from duplicating the tech for their use or analyzing its pattern—and devising counter-measures to thwart it.

"Our people seem to be getting along," she said.

"That's because I asked your mother to ride herd on them."

"Nevertheless," she said. "I—"

"Anyone that wants off at Sizemore gets off," Ciarán said. "It's non-negotiable."

"If any of us appears in Sizemore, or anywhere else in League space, it negates the entire purpose of our plan. In order for us to remain safe we must appear to have died aboard *Springbok*."

"Then you must convince everyone in your party to remain aboard."

"I can't. Mother doesn't listen to me."

"Then find someone she will listen to."

"There isn't anyone."

"Then you might tell Hector Poole, when you see him again. There's the reason his scheme failed."

"But I won't see him again," she said. "That's precisely the point. The instant it's clear we survived we'll be murdered. You are sending us to our deaths."

"If it's Lady Tabatha that's the hold-out—"

"It is."

"Then it's her that's sending you to your deaths. Not me."

"What difference does that make?"

"Do you know why water wears away stone?"

"Because of erosion. And what does this have to do with—"

"Erosion is what they call the effect of the stone wearing away. The cause of erosion is the water's refusal to give up. And the stone's refusal to move on." He gripped her sleeve and squeezed lightly, leaning in close so that his lips were centimeters from her ear.

"Find another stone," he whispered, and turning his back to her, went in search of Mr. Gagenot, and dinner.

39

M r. Gagenot's cooking was good enough that most of the juice bulbs and tubed nutrient paste went untouched; it was early enough in the cruise that the larders remained full of fresh ingredients. Ciarán, despite being sick to his stomach from his interaction with Sarah Aster, managed to eat his fill, and he couldn't remember a finer meal anywhere this side of Oileán Chléire.

Lady Tabatha was a skilled hostess and presided over a delightful table. She had a clear and loud speaking voice, and no one could complain of being left out of the conversation, even at the furthest reaches of the table. It was convenient that the size of the table and the size of the company matched, and they all fit at one with no divvying up into subgroups. He spent a great amount of his time observing. He had a fair idea of Mr. Prince's character by the time dinner was done and a bit of a handle on Mr. Lambent's. He knew Sarah Aster like he knew his own face.

Major Amati leaned close when she spoke. She'd noticed where Ciarán's attention kept returning. "She reminds me of you."

"Me after a swift blow to the noggin."

"That was the general consensus regarding Aoife's choice in merchant apprentice. Decorative, opinionated, cocksure, and not all there."

"I wasn't like that."

"Ship's Captain?" Amati said.

"You left off bigot," Swan said.

He glanced from face to face. "You're both serious."

"Deadly so," Amati said. "Do you know what Aoife told me, when I complained to her about you?"

"You complained about me."

"We each did," Swan said. "Every last one of us."

"Including Mr. Gagenot."

"He didn't like the way you messed with the caife maker in the communication cubby," Amati said. "Said if it was molasses you wanted, he had some in the galley, and if it was tar, Hess had some in engineering."

"You're making that up," Ciarán said.

"Ask him," Amati said.

"No one told me."

"Because Aoife wouldn't permit it," Amati said.

"What we catch we keep," Swan said, in an imitation of Aoife nic Cartaí. "That is—"

"The way of the Mong Hu," Ciarán muttered. *And of their People.*

"What did you say to that girl?" Amati said. "Se's been on the verge of tears since sitting down."

"Something my mother said to me," Ciarán admitted. "Whenever I got on her nerves." And whenever there was nothing she could do about what he wanted. Or, as he thought at the time, nothing she *would* do but could do if she wanted to, or if she'd simply loved him a little more.

It was only later that he realized that her brusque refusal was her way of telling him how he might get what he wanted.

Go ask your father.

Sarah Aster did not have a real father, or for that matter, it seemed, much of a mother either. Perhaps she was yet as ignorant as he was as a boy and had mistaken advice for disinterest and cruelty.

"I saw you both chatting with Lady Tabatha," Ciarán said. "Do you have any idea of her interests?"

"In addition to the striptease, you mean?" Swan said.

"In addition," Ciarán said.

"She's a physician," Amati said. "A medical doctor. One of three hundred doctors that attend the Queen. She spoke mostly about her work, and how interesting it was."

"Did it sound interesting?" Ciarán asked.

"Very," Swan said.

Amati nodded. "She's the Queen's geneticist. And she has a private practice. A who's who of Columbia Stationers. Not that she can talk about them by name."

"And did she? Talk about them?"

"Not as much as I'd hoped," Amati said. "She mostly asked about the crew. She had an uncanny knack for describing our behaviors. Aspen in particular fascinated her."

"And what did Aspen think of that?"

"They haven't spoken," Amati said.

"And of course we didn't volunteer anything," Swan said.

He'd hoped that Sarah Aster could take a hint, but it seemed she hadn't. That instead of pestering him she should get to know the others and see if there wasn't some way to persuade her mother to change her mind and request to stay on board. Better than focusing entirely on getting him to force the woman against her will. There was more than one stone in the river. It paid to turn over every one, and he now had an idea as to where to begin.

40

When it looked like everyone had finished their desserts, Ciarán tapped his knife against his glass, calling for attention.

"I wish to thank you all for attending," he said, "And above all I'd like to thank our chef. Mr. Gagenot, will you please step forward and accept our most heartfelt thanks for your efforts? You have outdone yourself tonight, sir."

Mr. Gagenot rose and strode the length of the table to stand beside Ciarán. He glanced down, and for an instant seemed to freeze, and Ciarán couldn't account for that, until he also glanced down, and saw his own hands gripped the back of Aoife nic Cartaí's chair, his fingers absently tracing the charred and melted evidence of ancient plasma rifle fire.

"Will Gag sees Ciarán mac Diarmuid," he said, his eyes moist. "Will Gag thanks Ciarán mac Diarmuid." He stood silent a moment longer before speaking. "Will Gag remembers those he cannot see."

"We remember them as well, Mr. Gagenot, and miss them dearly. We hope to see the Merchant Captain soonest, and I, in the tradition of our ancestors, look forward to *not* recounting the events of this feast to her. Rather, I expect to show her."

Maura raised her voice, and her glass. "By our waistlines may we be known!"

Ciarán stood and twice more repeated that hoary family ship toast until he was certain they had all joined in. "On an equally joyous note, we have not forgotten that this is the first meal you and your daughter have had together, in what?" He glanced along the table toward Aspen and the now empty seat beside her.

"Thirteen years, nine months, and fourteen days, standard," Aspen said.

"You two are related?" Lady Tabatha glanced from face to face.

"I certainly hope so," Ciarán said, "As I've asked the ship to break out the birthday grog. Fourteen measures of it for each of our company, rounding up, and one to grow on."

"You're joking," Maura said. "The birthday grog is whatever wretched expired juice bulbs are left in inventory."

"Ship," Ciarán said.

"I am here."

"Belay the birthday grog. Do we have any..." Ciarán raised an eyebrow and glanced along the table.

"Cordame whiskey," Hess said.

"Paint remover," Amati said. "It's the same thing. It's Columbian gin for the officers. That or water."

"They're indistinguishable," Hess said. "The only difference is that our water's only been through the recycler once."

The table erupted into an argument then, or more accurately described, a host of arguments, as each individual argued in favor of their own poison. Ciarán placed his palm on Mr. Gagenot's shoulder. "Please take your seat, Mr., Gagenot, that we may drink your health, and Aspen's as well."

"Will Gag will serve."

"We're on the cusp of a long journey, Mr. Gagenot. One with work enough for you ahead. I ask that you humor me. I promise not to serve you molasses. Or tar."

Mr. Gagenot turned to face Ciarán and did something Ciarán didn't think possible. He smiled.

"Will Gag was wrong about Ciarán mac Diarmuid." He touched Ciarán's sleeve, delicately, like a cat, before striding away to sit beside his daughter.

"Ship, can you decipher all that?"

His handheld dinged.

Ciarán raised his voice. "Who is proficient in mixology?"

Mr. Prince raised his hand. "Pick me! Pick me!"

"Lady Sarah," Ciarán said. "Thank you for volunteering."

"But I didn't—"

"Didn't think I saw that hand rise and retreat?" Ciarán said. "Don't hide your light under a bushel just so others can shine. Attend me now, in the galley."

"The commissary," the ship said.

"Attend me now in the commissary."

41

His handheld listed the drink orders and the dispenser in the commissary made them. All he had to do was keep track of which was which, which was made easier by the numbers prepended to the list items and the corresponding number printed on the napkins beneath each glass. They appeared to be in order from the head of the table to the foot, and port to starboard.

Sarah Aster tapped her toe against the deck. He hoped that wasn't some sort of priming sequence for the tech in her hull-walkers. "I don't know the slightest thing about mixology. And you don't need my help."

"That may be true, but I've been reminded that you *do* need my help, so I wanted to talk to you in private."

"You've changed your mind. You've agreed to detain Mother."

"I've done no such thing. What I have done is decided to explain myself, which I never do as a rule. Do you recall the geas I told you my mother placed upon me?"

"Never surrender."

"That's right."

"That's what I've been doing," Sarah said. "I've been trying to convince you—"

"But I can't be convinced. When I told you to try a different stone—"

"You were blowing me off."

"I was telling you to try being persistent with someone else. Part of never surrendering involves never locking yourself into a single solution to a problem. If you do, you're no longer in control of the situation. You've surrendered your agency to another."

"But you *are* in control."

"I'm only in control of myself, and, to a certain degree, the ship and the crew—and you and yours so long as you're aboard. I'm not in control of your mother."

"She refuses to see reason."

"You mean she refuses to do what you want because you want it."

"What's your point?"

"Can you not think of anything that would make her want to stay aboard?"

"She's only interested in work. And in shag—"

"Let's focus on the work. I understand she's a geneticist."

"So?"

"Would it surprise you to know that she's not the only geneticist on board?"

"Yes. But even if there was another, they'd have nothing in common. She's the Queen's geneticist."

"I imagine that's a big job. I hear Her Majesty's a mess."

"She isn't. Where did you hear that?"

"It's a joke."

"It's not funny."

"Neither is my standing here and you not hearing a word I'm saying. I'm not going to do the work for you. But I'm telling you now, there is a path forward for you if you'd only pay attention and stop trying to chain others to your will. Stop thinking about what you want. Think about what they want."

"And then what?"

"Try to find some way to give it to them. And never surrender until you do."

"And then what?"

"Give it to them."

"I fail to see how that gets me what I want."

"Were you raised by wolves?" Ciarán picked up the over-loaded drink tray.

"Ship," Ciarán said.

"I am here."

"Was I really this clueless?"

"Answering would be raising the dead," the ship said.

"Fine," Ciarán said. "Look at me, Lady Sarah Aster. Because I'm only doing this once. I'd point a finger at you but my hands are full. So pretend I am. And *pay attention*."

42

By the time Ciarán had delivered drinks the length of the table most of the work had taken care of itself. Lady Tabatha had moved her seat to sandwich in between Aspen and Mr. Gagenot. Her moving screwed up the drink numbers, and he discovered that he hadn't paid enough attention to the order because they were numbered, and it hadn't occurred to him that people *could* move, which was entirely idiotic, since this wasn't his first formal dinner, and he was usually the first person to change seats after a meal.

When he was done serving, he miraculously found himself holding an empty tray and standing behind Lady Tabatha, who was examining Aspen's retractable claws.

"You seem to have hit it off," Ciarán said.

"You do realize your cook is Willem Gagenot? He practically wrote the book on predictive cross-species hybridization."

"I know he's a famous geneticist, but I thought he only wrote the one book."

"I said practically. He didn't write any books. Only journal articles, until he suddenly disappeared. I'd imagined he died. Or been silenced."

"There's a book. I've seen it. It's complete, though still a rough draft. Obviously, it hasn't been peer reviewed."

"Sadly, I fear you are mistaken. I possess a comprehensive catalog of the literature." She ran her gaze over Mr. Gagenot, noting the circular scars on his neck and jaw. Six scars, from six strikes with a Huangxu Eng bang stick. "It is a tragedy and a loss for all mankind."

Ciarán glanced at Sarah Aster. She seemed to be paying attention. "It would be a greater loss, Lady Tabatha, if the ship hadn't figured out how to communicate with Mr. Gagenot. It seems that bang stick strikes primarily effect communications abilities. Mr. Gagenot is sharp as ever. Maybe sharper."

"That's impossible," she said. "Their impulses damage higher-order brain activity."

"So it appears initially, however the effects are not permanent. Only the communications centers are permanently damaged. And with medical aid, Mr. Gagenot is able to communicate. Shall I send a copy of his finished treatise to your cabin to prove it?"

"Yes. Immediately."

"Ship," Ciarán said.

"I am here."

"Please print a copy of Mr. Gagenot's book on the Outsider experiments."

"The fabrication facilities are presently running near capacity."

"I forgot we're down a fab because of the data crystal incident. How near are we to capacity?"

"How soon do you need the book?"

"How soon can I get it?"

"Tomorrow evening?"

"That will have to do." Ciarán's gaze met Lady Tabatha's. "I'll forward a copy on to you once you're settled on Sizemore Station. All I'll need is your physical address."

"You could send me an electronic copy right now."

"I could, but then I'd have to loan you a handheld, or give you access to a terminal. And given our experiences with Mr. Prince's attempted voice-hacking and the hijacker on that data crystal?" Ciarán paused. "I'm not going to do that."

"You might at least demonstrate this miracle you claim and allow us to speak."

"I'll consider it. It has to be done in the infirmary, and there's setup involved."

"But it really does work?" She glanced at Aspen for confirmation.

"I didn't believe it either," Aspen said. "But I cried when Daddy's granddaughters got to meet the man I knew. We'd thought he was dead."

"Will Gag is not dead," Mr. Gagenot said. He stood and took the tray from Ciarán's hands. "Will Gag has work to do." He marched toward the galley.

"I hadn't considered your speaking to him," Ciarán said. "We're quite shorthanded, and we are embarking on a lengthy journey. I'll speak with the ship's captain, but we may not be able to arrange a conversation until we've finished our business in Sizemore. "In any case, I'll forward the book to you. The ship's medic assures me it is a page-turner."

Lady Tabatha turned in her seat so she was facing him. "And the ship's doctor?"

Ciarán winked. "We are sadly without."

Lady Tabatha chuckled. "I wondered if you remembered who I was. The world I live in. Your machinations are so utterly transparent."

"Like glass I am," Ciarán said. "Think about the offer."

"It's out of the question," she said.

"It would be a crime not to ask," Ciarán said. He raised his voice so that it carried the length of the table. "Mr. Hess, please kick the tank alive, and the lot of you bring your chairs and gather round. It's time you know the rest of the story."

"Including us?" Mr. Lambent said.

"We have no secrets here, sir. As you'll all be coming with us on this journey."

"I most certainly will not be," Lady Tabatha said. "You are putting me off at Sizemore. End of story."

"Then you may go to your cabin," Ciarán said. "Unless you'll agree to a vow of silence regarding our plans and discussions."

"You can't be serious," Mr. Prince said. "She's a—"

"I agree to remain silent," Lady Tabatha said.

"Thank you, Doctor, for saving me the walk there and back. Now kick it, Mr. Hess."

Sarah Aster sidled up to him while the others clustered their chairs around the holo tank. "You failed. She saw your manipulation for what it was."

"How is that failing?"

"She told you. She's getting off at Sizemore."

"I heard her say that. Now if you'll excuse me, I have work to do." He tapped her wrist. "Pay attention. I'm going to try to make her say it two more times."

44

Once they were all settled Ciarán cleared his throat and began, shoving from his mind the first time he'd stood here, in this mess hall, and made a total cock-up of a report on Contract system, missing entirely the most salient fact, that they were transiting into a war zone.

He was aware of no such glaring oversight this time. They had so little information to go on that they could be flying into a black hole and not know it. *Impossibly Alien* had been designed as a survey vessel and for the first time in over two thousand years it was about to have the opportunity to do its job.

"We're being paid to track down Devin Vale, the late Lord Varlock," Ciarán told them. "To trace his footsteps if we can, and to report on our findings. Along the way we are to attempt to establish relations with any Alexandrians we encounter."

"And then what?" Hess said.

"Report our findings."

"Report them to who?" Hess said.

"To whom," Natsuko said.

"To Lord Aster," Ciarán said.

Hess shook his head. "Son of a—"

"To Lord Aster on behalf of Her Majesty, Queen Charlotte," Amati said.

"The proceedings of which will be forwarded to the Government at the same time," Ciarán said.

"What does that mean?" Hess said.

"We give a copy of our report to the Prime Minister," Ciarán said.

"*We* do?" Maura asked. "Not Lord Aster?"

"That's right," Amati said.

"That's worse," Hess said.

"It's crazy," Maura said. "Suppose this Devin Vale doesn't want to be found? Suppose we find out something embarrassing or dangerous to the people who hired us? Something they'll kill to keep quiet? It's bad enough there are people trying to abduct us. Now we've promised to report findings to not one, but two..."

"Deadly foreign sociopaths," Swan said.

"You wish," Maura said. "Professional liars. Ones who employ deadly foreign sociopaths when they're not commanding their own armies and printing their own money."

"Ko Shan?" Ciarán said.

"The contract gets us off the grid. That's good. We're already in the crosshairs of powerful enemies. If we do a good job, we might gain the support of powerful allies."

"Natsuko?" Ciarán said.

"I imagine the contract pays well. Judging by all the new equipment on board."

"We'll each be able to retire after this one mission," Ciarán said. "Provided we wish to."

"And provided we survive," Konstantine said. "With that kind of payday it's a good bet we're not expected to. The League doesn't throw money around."

"They don't throw money around in the Navy," Amati said. "Lord Aster's budget is off the books."

"Great," Hess said. "I'm part of a black op."

"A one-way, black op," Konstantine said.

"I'm all in," Amati said. "If either of you think this is the first black op you've been on, you are fooling yourselves. And it's black money, not blood money. No wet work expected or required."

"That we know of," Konstantine said.

Amati tapped her thigh with a mechanized fist. "Would you rather we stood still and let whoever is trying to abduct Maura and Ciarán, and steal the ship find us? Because it doesn't look to me like that's a bloodless alternative."

"No," Konstantine said. "That's a non-starter too."

"Too?" Amati said.

"Instead of," Konstantine said. "You know what I mean."

"Ship's Captain?" Ciarán said.

"We discussed this extensively before Aoife approached Lord Aster."

"She approached him," Maura said. "Not the other way around."

"That is correct," Swan said. "We agreed. It is the surest way to protect the ship. So long as the ship remains in view, it will be coveted. We are in effect being paid to go on the limb."

"The lam," Maura said.

"Or out on a limb," Natsuko said.

"Likely both," Ko Shan said. "I too, am all in."

Ciarán wondered if, to the strangers watching, this process seemed pointless. They were all on a starship. They were all outbound and obviously crew. They had each signed a contract and were bound to the ship and its captains. There was no obvious benefit to a verbal show of hands. The decision had already been made. They were going across the Alexandrine on the trail of Devin Vale, whether any of them agreed or not.

"Mr. Gagenot?"

The ship's victualer sat beside Aspen, their fingers entwined.

She squeezed his hand.

"Will Gag is all in."

Ciarán wasn't certain that Aspen had been designed with the ability to cry. Her eyes gleamed, but she seemed otherwise untouched. And she had dressed in answer to his question, not as a member of the crew, but as someone apart. She wore, not simply her red campaign cloak, but the navy-blue utilities of a Legion of Heroes admiral beneath it. Ciarán had asked Hess to produce a warrant officer's insignia when he fabbed the utilities for her, and he had done so, putting Royal Navy insignia on a Legion of Heroes uniform. *Braid inflation*, Maris Solon called it.

Aspen had both surprised him, by making a choice he couldn't interpret, and had confirmed his suspicions, choosing to refuse both the screw stair and the pendant spire. That didn't mean she'd forsaken the People. He hadn't begun wearing the spire until recently, and only then as a warning to others, not as a reminder to himself. Perhaps she was still deciding and might be pushed or pulled.

"Aspen," he said.

"Merchant Captain."

"Are you in or out?"

Aspen blinked. "Me? I thought you didn't want—"

"Will Gag sees Aspen ni Willem." Gagenot removed his pendant spire and place it upon her palm. "Will Gag trusts Ciarán mac Diarmuid."

She stared at the pendant spire. Rubbed her thumb across it. Glanced up to find her father watching.

"In," Aspen said.

"But not all in," Ciarán said.

She nodded to herself, silently. "All in," she said.

"With that," Ciarán said. "Maura, will you—"

"What about us," Mr. Prince said. "Can we get in on these riches to retire on?"

"You might, Mr. Prince, if you had skills we needed, and if you were all for one and one for all. But without unanimity of purpose, I'm afraid there's no possibility of your remaining dead to the League. I doubt you'd like to be classed a deserter. As soon as one of you turns up alive the misdirection fails."

"Oh," Prince said. "That's logical. He glanced at Lady Tabatha. "You—"

"Do not even try, Lieutenant," Lady Tabatha said. "I am getting off at Sizemore."

Ciarán glanced at Sarah Aster.

She had noticed her mother's words.

"But this sounds interesting," Mr. Prince said. "Not to mention potentially profitable. If I go back to the Guard they'll chain me to a desk, and—"

"Enough," Lady Tabatha said. "Drop it. I can't just abandon my patients. Abandon my career."

Mr. Prince turned to Mr. Lambent. "Rigel, make her see sense."

"It's too late for that," Mr. Lambent said. "Lady Tabatha knows that when she gets off in Sizemore, we must all debark with her. Else these people," he glanced from face to face, "Will be hounded until caught and boarded, and our dead carcasses hauled off and presented to her masters. She expects us to do the right thing. To play our roles until death."

"That's not true," Mr. Prince said. "Tell him, Sarah."

"Mother doesn't care if you do the right thing or not," Sarah Aster said. "She only cares about..."

"About what?" Mr. Prince said.

Sarah Aster glanced sharply at Ciarán. "Herself."

Mr. Prince glanced from face to face. "But that can't be true. She is Lady Aster. She serves the League."

"Grow up, Teo," Mr. Lambent said. "Haven't you figured it

out by now? We may each have pretended to be Prince Rigel. But we aren't the imposters." He glanced at Lady Tabatha Aster. "She is."

"Unfortunately, there's no law against that," Ciarán said. "Lady Aster has made her position known. And as a Freeman merchant I am honor-bound to respect that. Now, Maura—"

"Thank you," Lady Tabatha said.

"There's no need to thank me," Ciarán said. "You're free riding on my self-interest. I don't mind it, and I don't not mind it. Now if you're all done interrupting, I'd like Maura Kavanagh to walk us through the mission profile."

"That'll be a challenge." Maura held up her hand and Hess tossed her the holo tank controls. She caught the device without fumbling. "I've only just now heard the details of the mission."

"Who doesn't love a challenge?" Ciarán said.

Everyone but Mr. Prince raised their hands.

"Good," Ciarán said. "We're nearly unanimous. That's a positive sign."

The holo tank bloomed to life.

Maura stared at the display for a moment before zooming out as far as she could. She fiddled with the controls for a moment, setting the origin to the bottom portside corner, sternward. A single star indicator with a blue Legend appeared. Sizemore.

She added another blue legend in the upper starboard corner, forward. Llassöe. She then began filling in the gaps, Prix Canada, the edge of the void, Columbia in honor of the Asters, Mara and Whare, in honor of Mr. Lambent and his instantly recognizable frontier accent, Cordame for Hess, and a host of other worlds, including all the core worlds of the League, a sea of blue labels.

"Where is the Federation?" Aspen asked.

"About half a meter below the deck and half a meter aft,"

Maura said. "This is a stationmaster's display and it's not set up to handle vast distances. I can fit Sizemore and Llassöe on at the same time but only on the diagonal. The point is it's all the way across League space to Llassöe. Llassöe is the sole gateway to the Alexandrine for third-epoch superluminals. That will be where Lord Varlock exited the League."

"Was this true sixty or seventy years ago as well?" Swan said.

"What difference does that make?" Maura asked.

"That's when Lord Varlock disappeared," Ciarán said.

"You're joking," Konstantine said. "It's a black op *and* a cold case?"

"Ship," Maura said.

"I am here."

"League frontier outposts along the Alexandrine?"

"Llassöe."

"And between sixty and seventy years ago?"

"Garrison Station. Llassöe. Kinsey-Severn. Eliph's Star."

"Plot them, please."

"I will need to reset the origin."

"Wait one." Maura glanced from face to face. "Everyone got it? It is a long way to Llassöe even riding a Templeman drive."

When she was satisfied that the idea had sunk in, she said, "Reset the origin."

The holo tank blanked and refreshed, with Llassöe now where Sizemore had been. An arc of grayed-out blue stretched across the upper limits of the tank.

"You're joking," Konstantine said. "That's nearly as far from Llassöe as Sizemore to Llassöe."

"Ship," Ciarán said, "Please plot the old border of the League and the present border."

Sections of two transparent blue spherical cones appeared on the display, one bright, the other dimmed.

"These are approximations," the ship said, "Where the spheres are centered on Columbia system's star."

"No wonder we haven't seen an Alexandrian in sixty years," Amati said. "They kicked our—"

"There might be other reasons for a territorial contraction," Ciarán said. "Other than a military defeat."

"That's an immense volume of space," Maura said. "I don't see how we're going to pick up a sixty-year-old trail in all that."

"We don't need to," Ciarán said. "We know Devin Vale's destination."

"Earth," Swan said.

"Never heard of it," Maura deadpanned. The full formal name of the League was the Earth Restoration League, but the long form name only appeared on legal documents anymore and in abbreviated form in Freeman insults; 'the Erl' for 'Leaguemen', 'erlspout' in place of 'League Standard Speech', and so forth.

"We have coordinates," Amati said. "Lord Varlock left them—"

"Pinned to his dangling corpse," Lady Tabatha said. "They thought it was some sort of code at first, but it was simply the coordinates of Earth in an ancient navigational notation."

"Right," Amati said.

"*Killer*," Mr. Prince said. "Which ancient navigational notation?"

"No idea. I remember seeing the note as a girl," Lady Tabatha said. "Everyone did. We got the whole week off from school."

"I hope you used your free time wisely," Ciarán said. "According to Lord Aster the death image went viral, so we have solid proof that these coordinates are accurate."

"Accurate," Swan said. "But not necessarily true."

"They're a clue," Ciarán said. "Lord Aster possesses supporting documentation for the claim that those coordinates were both Lord Varlock's destination and the coordinates of Earth."

"Ship," Maura said, "Do you have the coordinates?"

"I do," the ship said.

Maura grinned. "That's so insane. Ciarán's convinced you to answer like an islander."

The ship said nothing.

"Please plot the coordinates," Maura said.

"I will need to reset the origin," the ship said.

"Set the origin to one of the older outposts. Eliph's Star. That sounds poetic."

"I can't," the ship said. "The plot will not fit the display."

"Then pick another."

"It won't fit."

"Set it to any origin in the League."

"It won't fit."

"Set it to any origin in the Alexandrine."

"It won't fit."

"Ignore the fit and set the origin to Llassöe."

"Done", the ship said, as the holo tank refreshed.

Maura stood. "I'm going to walk away from the display under your direction. When I reach the approximate location of the coordinates relative to Llassöe please tell me to stop."

"Very well," the ship said. "Walk toward the boat bay."

Maura stared at the display. "That's walking toward Columbia Station."

"It's walking toward a longboat," Ciarán said. "You'll need one. The coordinates are roughly three hundred meters off the starboard bow, topside."

"You knew that and you let me go through this whole dog and pony?"

"Suppose I had said it was a very, very long way," Ciarán said. "Would you have believed me?"

Maura glared at him.

"Who wants a longboat ride?" Ciarán raised his hand and glanced around the mess hall.

No one else raised their hands.

"Fair enough. Ship," Ciarán said.

"I am here."

"How long would it take us to reach Earth via Templeman drive? Roughly speaking."

"Approximately one year."

"We'd be gone for a year?" Natsuko said.

"Think about it," Hess said. "That's one way. We'd be gone for two years. And that's not stopping for periodic drive maintenance. No one has ever made a continuous transit of that length."

"Two years, or a week, or forever," Konstantine said. "We don't have a Templeman drive."

"That's true." Maura chewed a fingernail while staring at the plot. "Ship, please show me the Alexandrine."

The holo tank refreshed and began to populate with the symbols of star systems, red now instead of blue. The systems with names and charted routes populated first. Then those systems without routes began to fill in. And continued to fill in. And continued.

When the plot completed the holo tank bathed the compartment in red light.

"You cheated Lord Aster," Maura said.

"I wouldn't call it that," Ciarán said. *Impossibly Alien*'s superluminal drive worked on an entirely different principle than the Templeman drive. At times it took longer and at times it took less time to move from world to world than via a Templeman drive. And unlike standard Templeman vessels, *Impossibly Alien* didn't depend upon existing star charts. As a survey vessel it was built to create its own star charts. The drive had many limitations and was risky to operate. Maura had hypothesized that it would work best in densely populated regions of space. Ones where the stars were packed so tightly together you couldn't read the legends on the plotted worlds.

"We can do this," Maura said. "Maura Kavanagh. *Star diver.*"

"Navigator?" Swan said.

"Worst case, there's nothing past here but void." She highlighted a broad arc of stars on the far side of the Alexandrine. "If so we'll have to work this edge until we find a route forward. I'm confident there are several."

"And the reciprocal?" Konstantine said.

"That's the grind," Maura said. "There may not be one."

"That is a long walk home," Amati said.

"That explains the horse in the barn," Hess said.

Hess meant the vessel that had been born LRN *Durable* presently jammed into the boat bay. He'd borrowed the tiny superluminal gunship from Maris Solon with the promise he would return it in one piece. In sparsely populated areas of space, it was entirely possible for *Impossibly Alien* to jump into a system it couldn't jump out of. With a Templeman drive vessel on board they could send a party back to any charted system. They would be inconvenienced instead of marooned so long as they could bring back a rescue vessel—one that generated a drive bubble big enough to encompass *Impossibly Alien's* hull and its own.

"Worst case," Swan said.

Maura stood hipshot, chewing a fingernail and scrolling through holo tank plots one-handed. Ciarán had to look away from the display because it was making him dizzy.

She abruptly stopped, and shut the holo tank down. "Assuming no run-ins with restless natives?"

"Assuming that," Swan said.

"And assuming we don't get cul-de-sacced. Remind me, how many saddles does this horse have?"

"Eight," Ciarán said.

"We're short," Maura said. "Even without company."

"I've thought of that," Ciarán said.

"He's thought of nothing else," Swan said. "You can see the worry on his face."

"There's nothing on my face but what I want there."

"Tell me another," Swan said.

"There's nine of us," Konstantine said.

"The captain stays with the ship," Swan said. "It's settled."

"In that case," Maura said, "No worse than if we were running a Templeman drive. Two years round trip."

Ciarán glanced at Lady Tabatha. "I'll bet a fellow could write a book in that amount of time. Maybe even two, if he had help."

Her gaze darted toward Mr. Gagenot and back. "You're all out of your minds. I am getting off this vessel at Sizemore."

Ciarán glanced at Sarah Aster and grinned. He hid one hand behind the other and flashed her the thumbs up sign with the hidden hand.

She stood abruptly and raced from the compartment.

"Excuse me," he said. He had to sprint to keep up.

"I feel like such an idiot," she said. "I actually believed you."

"Tomorrow, at the moment of debarkation she will change her mind."

"You can't know that."

"I can't, it's true. But I do have some experience in these matters. And *I* believe me."

She searched his face for the lie.

Swan was mistaken. His face only showed what he wanted it to show. It was the most fundamental of merchant skills and the hardest to master. And he had mastered that skill. He knew that for certain, because Sarah Aster did not believe him. He'd rather disappoint her now than later, when, if necessary, he would disappoint himself.

"I'm tired," she said.

He escorted her to her stateroom in silence.

She paused in the hatchway "How long until we enter Size-more space?"

"Eight hours," he said. Eight hours until Lady Tabatha Aster agreed to remain aboard *Impossibly Alien*.

Or he broke his geas and forced her stay.

45

The odd thing about superluminal transits, whether aboard *Impossibly Alien* or a Templeman-drive vessel, was the sudden transition from idleness to feverish activity.

Ciarán had agreed to stay off the bridge and remain in the merchant's day cabin, along with Wisp. He'd arranged his workstation display to mirror the bridge main forward display. He belted Wisp in on the bunk and belted himself to his workstation chair, now locked down like a fast pallet in stay-put mode.

He'd also locked the *suspects* in their staterooms after instructing them on the use of the crash couches, which were nearly identical to modern ones and judged extraordinary precautions—except on those occasions when they were needed. Entering a star system as heavily trafficked as Sizemore required extraordinary precautions, even when entering at extreme distance from the tripwire and at minimal velocity.

Mr. Prince had asked after the lifepods and was surprised to learn the vessel carried none. "They seem dangerous," Ciarán said, reminding Prince of the fate of *Springbok*'s lifepods and deflecting his inquisitive mind away from the truth. As a survey vessel launched during an age when alien life was thought to abound, and that much of that life would prove antithetical to human life, *survivors* were considered a liability rather than an asset. Dead men tell no tales, and tales were what lead enemies home. Home, to blissfully ignorant innocents who trusted their leaders would exercise utmost caution when poking about in the far reaches of the wider world. That idea remained the operating principle of the ship's minder. In human space they might hail a passing savior should crippling problems arise. Once they sailed off the edge of the chart, there would be no help and no bailing out.

The ship sounded an all hands and began a countdown to translation, largely, he imagined, for the benefit of the suspects. Every one of the crew was at this moment watching the clock, their fingers poised over their respective in-system controls. It was dreadfully inconvenient not being on the bridge. He'd have to see about rigging up an observer's seat.

Wisp flicked a claw tip against his trousers.

"And a cat bed, of course."

She began to purr as the count reached zero and his guts began to writhe, not like the writhing of a Templeman translation, where his innards were wrenched from one universe to another along with the rest of him, but like a man awakening and finding himself standing on a ledge, and who, for in instant isn't certain of the difference between up and down.

His workstation display, a mirror of the bridge main display, began to slowly populate. The projected system plot hovered in wireframe behind the actual plot overlaying it, and the two largely agreed, indicating they'd punched in where they'd expected to.

What was to happen next would be a slow idle stationward,

with a rendezvous with *Thin Star* somewhere up ahead, and a final transfer of personnel and information before parting and going their separate ways: Aoife and *Thin Star* to Freeport Station by way of Sampson and New Sparta, and *Quite Possibly Alien*, now returned to its launch descriptor as *Impossibly Alien* because of some coded message the ship's minder wished to send other synthetic intelligences, headed outward. They remained too distant from the station for the Registry updates to have begun scrolling in yet, but he remained certain the changes would have been made, if not entirely propagated yet throughout the League and Federation. Sizemore, with a redundant pair of superluminal nodes, would surely be up to date. He wondered if Ko Shan's sensor dump had made it to Aoife yet, and if she'd forwarded it on to the appropriate parties in the Federation. They might have logged the dump in the Registry at Sizemore, but it was a bloody mess to deal with. The murder of innocents in lifepods was, both here in the League and in the Federation, the sort of thing likely to get swept under the rug if it made the wrong people look bad.

It seemed important to know that those sensor logs had been received and cataloged, because it did provide cover for the suspects now aboard. The imagery was quite clear. There were no *Springbok* survivors. And *Impossibly Alien* lay too distant from the lifepods to have recovered them. The truth would turn up eventually, when the Ojin beacons reported the full story, but by then they'd be, if not past Llassöe and into the Alexandrine, well on their way there. It wasn't as if there'd be an armada waiting for them at the most distant edge of the League.

He was avoiding the subject he wanted least to deal with, and he knew it. How to handle Lady Tabatha Aster, if she continued to insist he put her off at Sizemore. He'd considered transferring her to *Thin Star*, and making her Aoife's problem.

That seemed cowardly, though, and there could be a better way. They had come aboard through guile, pressing themselves on the ship and crew under false pretenses, and that was a clear violation of Freeman custom. He could remand the lot of them to Aoife for transport to Trinity or Unity Station for trial, where they would be acquitted, if he didn't first drop the charges, as no one wanted another war with the League. These were the sort of people, not so much above the law as outside its enforce-ability envelope. There were poor people that were judgement-proof because they had no means to pay. And there were rich people who were enforcement proof, because holding them to account cost more than it was worth. They might be executed for murder, but any money damages would disappear as a rounding error on their balance sheets. Freeman justice was largely about restoring balance by making victims whole. It wasn't concerned with inflicting punishment on wrongdoers. In any case, Sarah Aster was the chief wrongdoer, and her mother an unwilling prisoner by Sarah's own words. He couldn't very well accuse Lady Tabatha of being an accomplice. She'd be released immediately, and then, instead of the rest being outbound aboard *Impossibly Alien* they'd be bumping around the League and Federation where they'd make easy prey.

He gazed at the deckhead and pondered his options. He really did believe he had a good chance of convincing Lady Tabatha to remain on board. That blather about her practice and her patients was only that. He could tell, like a lot of doctors, that she wasn't as interested in the people as the processes; of problem solving, of pushing the boundaries of scientific knowledge, of being recognized and feted and praised for her brilliance. He wasn't certain she believed the truth, that Mr. Gagenot wasn't brain damaged, or a prisoner in his own skull, but a brilliant man with input/output problems. Prob-lems that could be overcome with the assistance of the ship's minder.

If it came to it, he'd decided that he wouldn't break his geas and force her to stay. He'd do something almost as damning. He'd introduce her to the ship's minder. That alone ought to convince her to stay, since the idea that a synthetic intelligence could communicate without speech, as if telepathically, would shatter her confidence in her own knowledge of the world.

It wasn't far from that realization; that if it could do that with her, it could do the same with Mr. Gagenot, and act as go-between. That she might thus collaborate with a giant and rewrite the future of her chosen field as well as her own future.

Or she could get off at Sizemore and read a bound and printed copy of Gagenot's years-old notes, provided Ciarán kept his word and sent it.

If she didn't want that then he'd misjudged her. Either that or she was under outside pressure and control by forces whose carrots and sticks he couldn't match.

He rubbed his fingers across Wisp's brow. "You know it never occurred to me," he said. "That the Oath seems to restrict me to all carrot, all the time." Every now and then he'd like the option of the stick, instead of the implied threat of a stick he couldn't righteously wield.

There was another option, there would always be another option. One he'd used and it had worked, but he wasn't sure it would work on her. Perhaps Lady Sarah saw it as a coincidence that he'd happened to have a brilliant geneticist on board to tempt Lady Tabatha. But if he hadn't, the results would have been the same. If he could keep her talking long enough, and freely enough, eventually Lady Tabatha would have revealed a hidden handle and he would have found something he had access to that fit that handle. It only looked like outlandish luck because most people lacked the persistence and interest to remain sufficiently engaged. And because they shackled themselves to their own self-image and so spend as much time listening to their own internal desires and misgivings as to their prospective customer's words about *their* desired future.

In one version of the future, he'd have to somehow incite Lady Tabatha to physically attack him or his, and that would allow him to technically keep the Oath while responding with force. He'd be able to live with that if he knew for certain she deserved to pay for endangering or hurting others, but the risk to the others of her party were entirely speculative at this point, barely supported by facts teetering on one leg. It seemed to him that the entire structure of the Oath rested on shaky ground, as it was entirely acceptable to goad someone into pulling the trigger first yet morally reprehensible to cut out the middleman and simply gun them down without preamble. He'd done one and not the other and it felt, in retrospect, exactly like he imagined premeditated murder would.

He felt a rotter just thinking that. He had a rule though, never self-edit when considering options, which was a good rule, but it left him somewhat disgusted with himself for some of the ideas he came up with.

He considered for a moment the idea that he could seduce Lady Tabatha and so physically and emotionally satisfy her that she would remain on board simply to feel his touch.

Right, that will work. I might as well mesmerize her by shooting unicorns and rainbows out of my—

Ko Shan's voice spoke from the deckhead annunciator. "Merchant Captain to the bridge."

Ciarán glanced at the display. There were a great number of vessels outbound, but nothing seemed out of the ordinary. He'd expected to have heard from Aoife by now, but they weren't on a timetable.

Ciarán unbelted himself before unbelting Wisp. He glanced at the display again. Lots of outbound traffic, some stacking up, but then this was the largest military complex in League space, and either the largest or second largest shipyard, depending upon whether Brasil system had surpassed it by now.

Ciarán strode into the corridor, taking those few steps to the bridge hatch. He activated the bridge lock and followed Wisp into a maelstrom of activity.

"What?" Ciarán said.

"Debris field," Ko Shan said. "At the rendezvous point."

46

They were all so heads-down in their work that only Ship's Captain Agnes Swan acknowledged Ciarán's presence. She motioned for him to join her.

He had known this day would come. That it was merely a matter of time until he would be picking through the wreckage, searching for survivors. Searching the wreckage for *his* survivors, or Aoife searching through the wreckage for *her* survivors. Long haul spacers lived shorter lives than most. It was a dangerous career he'd chosen, and the jobs he'd accepted and the crew he ran with skirted close to the edge of annihilation daily.

"Life signs?" Ciarán said. It felt as if his emotions had deserted him. As if he were a machine that processed grief and loss as just one more stream of data to be compiled in the present and analyzed later.

"We haven't searched for any yet," Swan said. "There is something disturbingly familiar about this situation."

"If we're not searching for survivors, what are we doing?"

"We are running dark and closing on the rendezvous point. At the appropriate time Ko Shan will begin scanning the debris field. Hess and Amati are in the boat bay and suited up if recovery is required. As is Aspen."

"You don't like that I added her to the crew."

"I don't like that you didn't consult me first. But it was she that reminded me of the *Brilliance* affair. She said that Adderly had used the same ploy against the Huangxu Eng during their revolt."

"I've never heard of the *Brilliance* affair."

"Two vessels arrange to rendezvous. The first to arrive is captured and a false debris field laid. The second to arrive, perceiving the debris field, races to search for survivors only to discover they have entered a kill box."

"When will we know?"

"In an hour."

"An hour?"

"You've complained that I hide things from you. That I don't contact you until the action is over."

"I have," Ciarán admitted.

"This is the first watch in a new age of cooperation. We will stand it together."

"If it's not them, and they've been captured?"

"Then the League has started a fresh war with the Federation."

"That might be *Thin Star*'s actual debris," Ciarán said. "And it could still be a trap."

"There is always that risk in any search and rescue operation. In this case doubly so. The debris field is asymmetrical. There is no indication of a Templeman drive failure."

"And when we close to investigate—"

"Sudden brilliance," Swan said. "The drive itself being rigged for remote triggering."

"And us inside the blast radius."

"A poor man's doomsday weapon," Swan said. "The sort of weapon rebels employ."

"You're certain it is a trap. And that it isn't *Thin Star.*"

"I am certain of nothing. I prefer to cling to hope and tread with care."

"Is there anything I can do to help?"

Swan grinned. "I'm so glad you asked."

47

Wisp took one look inside the cramped communications cubby and bolted. Ciarán entered, dusted off the seat, and kicked the workstation to life. They used to call this the watchkeeper's cubby back when they'd run staggered shifts. On the ship's schematics it was listed as the communications nexus. Once he'd translated the ship's operating manuals, Aoife decided they should use the official names. And once they discovered the controls were mirrored on the zero-immersion sensor rig they transferred what watchkeeping functions they still performed to the bridge.

Given the amount of sensor workload Ko Shan had to deal with he'd been tasked with monitoring comms until they had a clearer understanding of the situation in Sizemore. "Not using comms," Swan had said. "Monitoring them."

He wondered if hailing Ko Shan and letting her know he was set up and in position counted as using the comms.

"It counts," virtual Agnes Swan said in his head. He'd begun modelling her in his imagination so that he could anticipate her reactions.

He checked that no one was transmitting before piping all the comms output to the comms cubby workstations.

"Thanks," Ko Shan said from the workstation annunciator.

"Nicely done," Swan said. "No transmitting. Not even to ack."

He wondered what was different about their transmissions and his. He ran his gaze over the workstation controls. These were specialized channel strips and very old school. They seemed to have a hardware switch or button for every imaginable function. There were more than a score of buttons sporting variations of the 'transmit' glyph.

"That's grand," he said aloud. He hated it when seemingly senseless orders turned out to make sense. "Ship."

"I am here," came from the workstation annunciator.

"Do I need to do anything special to direct the comms flows through the analysis engines?"

"It's automatic."

"Will you tell me if something pops up?"

"I will tell Yuan Ko Shan."

"Please let me know also."

The ship remained silent for a long time.

"Authorized," the ship said. "I am to remind you. Do not touch the controls."

"Brilliant," Ciarán said. "When I mutiny, I'm unplugging you first."

Ciarán leaned back in his seat, careful to keep his limbs clear of the control. If the ship's captain considered this as keeping him engaged...

It wasn't working. If he let the idea creep in, that the debris field was from *Thin Star*, he would begin immediately to think of balance, and how it might be restored. He would do that because thoughts of vengeance would hold his grief at bay. He had it in him to become a monster. He felt it in his bones. He wouldn't take any joy in the work, but he could imagine himself assembling a list, scratching off names, one after another, until justice had been done, and there was nothing left of him but a stain on the fabric of time. One that could be brushed away by the slightest breeze, and ought to be.

He didn't need to wonder if Aoife would do the same for him. She would, to the last measure. It struck him like a thunderclap that he might have told her, if he'd considered it, that he'd rather she died clean than discard her life seeking vengeance on his behalf. It seemed somehow better this way, her preceding him, and the matchmaking fall upon him. He wondered which responsibility he would choose to shirk. Would he abandon the contract to avenge her? Or complete the contract, and postpone her vengeance past any meaning?

Postpone, he imagined, unless he died himself before completing the contract, a real possibility, and one not to be discounted. He wondered how he could get a message to Aoife's next of kin. To Carlsbad's, if he had any. To the families of everyone aboard *Thin Star*. They should have thought ahead and prepared a procedure for such an eventuality. But that would have required an admission no one voiced. That they weren't immortal.

He watched the meaningless displays thinking meaningless thoughts.

The annunciator spoke with Ko Shan's voice. "Commencing debris field scan. Turn on your main display."

He cast about for the button-glyph that indicated the feed from the forward main bridge display. Found it. Pressed it.

The display changed. He wasn't certain yet what it showed. Mostly black shadows on a black background. *Don't let it be them.*

He ran his gaze across the hardware buttons. He'd pressed one and nothing bad had happened. Suppose he pressed another?

He found a glyph that seemed to indicate monitor only, and bridge.

He pressed it and the annunciator began to mirror bridge communications.

"Well?" Swan said.

The display began to populate. Dark shadows connected by spidery dark lines.

"It's not ours," Ko Shan said.

Ciarán let out a deep breath he hadn't realized he'd been holding.

"And it's not *entirely* not ours, either," Ko Shan said. "Look closely."

"Oh," Swan said. "It's an ebony eye."

"We call it an emerald eye," Ko Shan said. "There's a *Thin Star* lifepod in amongst all the debris, and its tendrils are homed on that."

Of all that talk all he recognized was '*Thin Star* lifepod'.

"Can we ping it without attracting attention?" Swan said.

"If the pilot brings us to the heading listed," Ko Shan said, "We may attempt it in twenty minutes."

"Do it," Swan said.

"Sir, doing it," Konstantine said.

"Sxipestro," Ciarán said.

"I am here."

"What is an 'ebony eye?' Also called an 'emerald eye.'"

"A clandestine passive sensor array," the ship's minder said. "Similar to our towed array."

"And its tendrils?"

"The means by which the elements of the array are linked to their receiver. *Thin Star* has left a broadband recording device hidden within the debris field. The elements of the array are the debris fragments themselves."

"Can it transmit and receive?"

"In theory any receiver may act as a transmitter. But in practice an ebony eye is interrogated via a pinbeam pad. If active it may be able to respond to a ping."

"Unrelated question," Ciarán said. "Why are there a score and..." he counted. "A score and four transmit buttons on the communications console?"

"Because the designers believed we might encounter alien life. They were uncertain how such life forms might communicate. The bulk of the communications control strips transmit and receive on various frequencies of the electromagnetic spectrum. Each strip includes a transmit toggle and related controls for frequency, pulse width, and amplitude, among others. Each strip possesses its own antennae tuned to its corresponding frequency range. A common modulator is provided for message encoding. An encoding engine and decoding engine are included. A language analysis expert system may be inserted in line for complex message analysis. Additional control strips exist for additional theoretical communications methods in unbounded media."

"Such as?"

"Focused gravity waves. Certain particle streams. Mass hammers of various sizes."

"Those are weapons," Ciarán said.

"They are communications devices."

"How big is the largest of these 'mass hammers?'"

"No larger than your fist."

"What is it made of?"

"A byproduct from several of the other communications methods."

"This byproduct is called?"

"Depleted uranium."

"And the antenna?"

"A linear motor acts as a transmission device. The ship's force shielding acts as a broadband receiver, should the counterparty wish to reply."

"It's a rail gun," Ciarán said.

"It is a communication device. One that operates on a similar principle to a rail gun."

"How does it differ?"

"A common modulator is provided for message encoding. An encoding engine and decoding engine are included. A language analysis expert system may be inserted in line for complex message analysis."

"And it's voice activated."

"When it isn't under the control of the ship's minder."

"You might have mentioned this before."

"You translated this vessel's manuals. I didn't think I needed to."

"Does Ko Shan know this? Does Agnes?"

"Do they know that electromagnetic transmitters are weapons? We did shake the teeth out of some lieutenants on *Springbok*, if you recall."

"That was different."

"It is exactly the same," the ship's minder said. "In all but degree."

Ciarán stared at the console.

"The power-off control is on the right," the ship's minder said.

"Very funny." He took a deep breath. "Walk me through this. Suppose I want to say, 'We come in peace,' with a laser."

"Excellent choice," the ship's minder said. "Pinbeam communications use lasers."

"As do planet-busters," Ciarán said.

"Perhaps in recorded dramas," the ship's minder said. "Many planets have dense atmospheres. Kinetic energy is much more effective in such cases."

"I've got a pin on the pad," Ko Shan said.

"Ping it," Agnes said.

"It's ours," Ko Shan said. "It's asking for a WAND code."

"Call the Plowboy Paladin," Swan said.

"He's listening," Ko Shan said.

"Send Ko Shan your WAND code, Merchant Captain," Swan said.

"That will be hard to do without transmitting," Ciarán muttered. "And now I'm afraid to touch the console."

"Use your handheld," Ko Shan said.

Duh.

He flashed a Thin Star Line one-time WAND code to Ko Shan. Swan already had the physical encryption device on the bridge.

"Got it," Ko Shan said. "We are in."

"Hey," Carlsbad said from the annunciator. "You took your time getting here."

48

Once they had a true understanding of what the debris field represented, extracting Carlsbad and the lifepod from it became a trivial exercise, even with the need to time their use of the ship's tractor bands with the occlusion of the station's sensors, a table of which Carlsbad forwarded to Hess. There was no room for the lifepod in the boat bay, but they were able to lash it to the hull at the base of the cargo mast. The little pod was so jammed with electronics that Ciarán couldn't imagine how the man fit in there as well.

They continued in-system on a course Carlsbad recommended, though at a relative crawl. Ciarán imagined the suspects locked in their cabins were beginning to grow impatient with their progress, Lady Tabatha in particular.

Once Carlsbad had logged some refresher time and changed into clean utilities, he met them on the bridge.

Carlsbad was a thin man and roughly the same apparent age as Ciarán's father. He had hair the color of weak tea bound into a knot behind his neck. Carlsbad wasn't Freeman but a Voyager, from Cordame, and, while related, an entirely separate polity from the People with their own customs and mores.

They didn't accept outsiders into their family groups as Freemen did, and contrary to their name, few of them ever went off world. Prior to being cargo master on *Quite Possibly Alien* Carlsbad had led a complicated and secretive life, largely, Ciarán had decided, because he was a criminal mastermind. Though he claimed he only used his powers for good.

What was good for Carlsbad tended to be good for the crew, and while Ciarán got off to a rocky start with the man and didn't see eye to eye with him on nearly anything, he'd wanted Carlsbad aboard, even if it put Aoife in a bind short term. As cargo master Carlsbad was effectively second-in-command on the vessel, after Ciarán. And while no one expected Ciarán to win an argument with Agnes Swan over how to run the ship, least of all Agnes, Carlsbad had been treading the star lanes for a long time, and people listened to him, including Swan.

Carlsbad launched into a core dump without so much as a preamble, explaining that the debris field had nothing to do with *Thin Star*. They'd simply chosen the most private part of the system for the rendezvous, and that happened to be where someone else had chosen to hide evidence of *their* crimes. It was, objectively, the most private part of the system to do so in, and they should have anticipated the possibility others would come to the same calculation. There was entirely too much competition for skulking turf nowadays.

Aoife sent her regrets but there seemed no point in lingering simply to say farewell over coded comms. *Thin Star* was outbound for Brasil system, where Aoife could report what they'd learned without using a Sizemore superluminal node, which they assumed compromised. Ciarán had never met her, but Aoife's sister Caitríona was a living legend and the current planetary governor in Brasil system.

Carlsbad had elected to remain behind. The way Carlsbad saw it, after picking through the debris and monitoring signals and vessel traffic for the last forty-eight hours, they could simply blackmail the right people and live like kings and queens without leaving the system.

"Until the war breaks out," Carlsbad said.

"And when will that be?" Ciarán asked.

"Not for another hour or two," Carlsbad said.

"Seriously," Maura said. "If you don't know just say so." She was not a huge Carlsbad fan.

Carlsbad ignored her. "There is a moon the Erl use for prisoner exchanges. That is where this course will take us. We can put the bulk of the moon between us and the gunfight when the shooting starts. If we wish, we may settle to the surface and go cold until it is safe to proceed onward."

"Or we could just transit the system now," Maura said. "And jet."

"We would not make it to the tripwire," Carlsbad said. "There is a massive fleet buildup in the system."

"Then who are all the outbounds?" Ko Shan asked.

"Home Guard," Carlsbad said. "They are retreating."

"You mean running," Konstantine said. She did not like the Guard.

"I mean retreating. There was a blowout forty hours ago on the station ring. Crown offices, Home Guard headquarters, all the royalist brass in the system."

"An accident?" Konstantine asked.

"Maybe," Carlsbad said. "But the debris I was crouching in? Dumped twenty hours ago. Broken up in-system shuttles, a troop transport, a bunch of station-style office fittings, furniture, equipment, lots of plasma burn, and a whole platoon of corpses, about a third in their small clothes, a third in utilities, and a third in uniform. Lots of brass. Lots of gray. Bound, and capped, and double-tapped."

"Executed," Swan said.

"It's a damned mass grave," Carlsbad said, "where no one will think to look."

"We could skip jump into the photosphere," Maura said.

"As if that would go unnoticed," Carlsbad said.

Maura glared at him. "Who cares if we're noticed? We'll be gone before they can stop us."

"Generally speaking," Carlsbad said, "Not being seen is superior to not getting caught. Particularly if you are an unarmed witness to a capital crime."

"Like murder," Konstantine said.

"Like treason," Ciarán said. "The blowout was the cover up."

"Precisely," Carlsbad said. "I have been in that pod for twenty-eight hours. I recorded closeups of the cleaners. All LRN. All special forces. All augmented and exo'ed up. We do not want to show up on the targeting scanners of this lot."

"To the moon!" Ko Shan said.

Carlsbad chuckled. "Unless the ship's merchant objects."

"How hot is the station?" Ciarán said.

Carlsbad grinned. "Hot."

"And how well guarded do you imagine this prisoner exchange facility to be?"

"Minimal," Carlsbad said. "Except when they're exchanging prisoners."

"Will they be exchanging prisoners in the next few hours?"

"They'll be exchanging broadsides," Carlsbad said. "So I doubt it."

"Then I don't object. In fact, if we don't go there, I'll be disappointed."

"Problem," Konstantine said.

"Speak," Swan said.

"Transponder. That close in we'll be tagged for certain if we're running dark."

"Illuminate as necessary," Swan said, "Make it look as if we'd only just transited."

"Sir," Konstantine said. She did a number of things with the pilot controls Ciarán didn't recognize before declaring, "We are *Impossibly Alien* in thirty-six hundred and twelve seconds."

"That's new," Carlsbad said.

Ciarán nodded. "It's some sort of message."

"What's it supposed to mean?"

"Ask the ship's minder," Ciarán said. "Because I can think of only one thing."

"Trouble," Carlsbad said.

49

Ciarán stopped by the boat bay to corner Hess and ask him to help wheel out one of the two-seat second-epoch shuttles. The pair of them were able to manhandle it toward the blast doors enough that it would clear the stern thrusters of *Durable*. The boat bay remained a mess, but they had the long transit to Llassöe to get it squared away.

"Do you think we can squeeze the pod inside if we rearrange?" Ciarán asked.

"Maybe," Hess said. "But it's like a puzzle already. To use one machine we have to move two."

Which reminded Ciarán. "I need to get to the hardsuit rack."

"I'll do it and toss a suit out to you."

Which he did, and which Ciarán piled up beside the two-seater.

"Keep an eye on that," Ciarán said.

Hess grinned. "Roger that, Merchie man."

Ciarán couldn't decide when and where he wanted to confront Lady Tabatha, in private or public, right before he sprung his solution on her or with plenty of lead time so she could consider her options.

He wasn't about to take a shuttle to a hot station where a war might break out at any minute. And he didn't want to break the Oath. He didn't know why this idea hadn't occurred to him earlier, but the solution was obvious, now that he thought about it. He'd set Lady Tabatha down at the prisoner-exchange facility. If it was guarded by people and not just systems he'd leave her with them and jam their communications from *Impossibly Alien* until such time as the ship was outbound. And if the facility was guarded by security systems, or better yet, unguarded, he would simply set her down and break all the comms he could find. If there weren't enough rations on site he'd supplement the supply with juice bulbs and nutrient paste. She wouldn't starve, and he'd have done what she'd asked. Put her off the ship in Sizemore system.

If she complained he'd be certain to remind her that while he wouldn't hold her against her will he also wasn't running a taxi service. If she didn't like the looks of the neighborhood, she was welcome to stay aboard.

It took him a fair amount of time to hunt down Mr. Gagenot and collect a couple weeks of expired and expiring juice bulbs and nutrient tubes and to load them into the two-seater's compact storage cubby behind the rear seat. By then he'd killed as much time as he could, so he hiked toward the isolation lab and the suspects' staterooms. When Lady Tabatha didn't answer her stateroom hatch, he used his credentials to override and crack it, calling out for her before entering. When he saw her he pulled out his handheld, and dropped it, and dropped it again, before he remembered he didn't need to use his handheld.

"Ship," Ciarán nearly shouted.

"I am here," the ship said from the deckhead annunciator.

"Contact Natsuko. Tell her to bring her medkit and cable shears."

"She asks the reason."

His gaze kept wanting to drift away, but he forced himself to look.

"Lady Tabatha appears to have hung herself."

50

Ciarán gripped her legs and lifted, pushing her upward and arcing a bow in the lifeline she dangled from.

"Natsuko is hurrying."

"Thank you. You weren't monitoring the cabins?"

"Lady Tabatha Aster asked for privacy. And Yuan Ko Shan's scanning tasking were quite demanding of my attention. I prioritized—"

"I understand," Ciarán said. "Sxipestro."

"I am here."

"Were you monitoring Lady Tabatha's cabin?"

"I was."

"And?"

"And I do not involve myself in human affairs. You know that."

"It's essential I know what happened."

The ship's minder said nothing.

Natsuko arrived in great haste and taking the load from Ciarán, passed him the shears which he used to cut her free and catch her shoulders as she twisted in a fall, and together they got her onto the bunk.

Natsuko went to work on her while Ciarán examined the rig.

"Ship."

"I am here."

"Are all the cabins locked?"

"Yes," the ship said. "They are at the moment."

"Good."

"However they might not have been. There was a short circuit in one of the cabins. It took down the local branch when the fault isolator simultaneously failed."

"Which cabin?"

"Teo Prince's."

"Who had also asked for privacy."

"All of them had."

"Hatch cycle log?"

"Regrettably unavailable."

"Got it, thanks."

Ciarán glanced at Natsuko, who seemed feverishly active.

"Do you need help?" Ciarán asked.

"I will say if I do. Move out of the light or tell the lamp to move closer."

The spidery luminaire lifted on eight spidery legs, and skirting the improvised gallows, settled in above the bunk.

"Thanks," she said.

The improvised gallows was something he would have never thought of. Someone had assembled a hard suit, Lady Tabatha's he presumed, and locked its hullwalkers to the deckhead. Likewise, it had engaged the stay-put fields on the suit's gauntlets and had swung the upside-down dangling suit until the gauntlet's locked the suit's palms to the deckhead. Having earlier unwound a length of the suit's lifeline it would have been a simple matter to loop the sturdy cable around Lady Tabatha's throat and give two stout tugs on the lifeline, causing the emergency safety line to forcibly retract by design and lifting her off her feet.

Of course, none of that would have worked if the suit's helmet hadn't been attached and sealed. The suit wouldn't have even powered up.

"Get the fast pallet," Natsuko said. "Hurry."

"Is she—"

"Not yet. Please hurry."

Ciarán stepped in the corridor determined to run to the boat bay for a fast pallet only to find that Natsuko had parked one just outside the hatch.

He released the device's stay-put field and shoved it into Lady Tabatha's stateroom. He helped Natsuko load Lady Tabatha onto the fast pallet. Natsuko took off at a run with the fast pallet while Ciarán locked the stateroom behind him and sealed it with his command override code.

It certainly looked like Mr. Prince had attempted to solve the problem of Lady Tabatha leaving the vessel. In fact, it looked a little too much like Mr. Prince was the culprit. He didn't have time to deal with an investigation right now, but he didn't want anyone mucking about the scene, either. A murder investigation was the last thing he'd imagined having to deal with aboard a Freeman vessel. But given the stakes for Sarah Aster and her two lieutenants he wasn't entirely surprised.

Murdering Tabatha Aster was an early entry on his unedited list of options. One he'd considered and immediately discarded. That someone else had thought of it didn't surprise him. But it had seemed virtually impossible for anyone to harm her given that they were locked in individual staterooms and under constant surveillance.

He caught up with Natsuko at the bio lock. He pulled a rebreather from his pocket and steeled himself for the full-spectrum bug scan, fumigation, and hose down.

"Go on," Natsuko said. "The spiders will assist."

"You'll need help lifting her—"

"I've lifted *you* by myself. There are gravity plates in the deck below and deckhead above the examination tables." She gestured toward the hatch. "Run along."

51

C iarán checked that all the staterooms were locked on his way toward the bridge. He needed to fill Swan in, and he needed to find out where they were relative to that moon, and what sort of activity was ongoing in the system.

The hatch cycled, and Swan glanced at him and said, "Good timing. You need to see this."

"And you need to know there's been an attempted suicide, or murder, or something that might end in a death aboard this vessel."

"Natsuko informed me," Swan said. "She is attempting to stabilize the patient."

"Good," Ciarán said. "Let's see what I'm supposed to see. Is there an executive summary?"

"We're wanted for the destruction of *Springbok* and the murders of Lady Tabatha Aster, Lady Sarah Aster, and six Home Guard officers. We are to be located, boarded, and brought before the court, where we will pay for our crimes."

"Once they review our sensor dump on the incident, they'll get it straightened out," Ciarán said.

Carlsbad stepped from the shadows. "They've already

reviewed it. They believe it's faked. *Impossibly Alien*'s logs contradict the sensor logs from *Vigilant*. In addition, Senior Captain Benjamin Joris is a highly decorated war hero, and his word is above reproach. He has given his report in person and provided *Vigilant*'s sensors logs. They tell a significantly different story. One where a Freeman vessel running dark not only destroyed *Springbok* but proceeded to murder League citizens in escape pods."

"How do they explain away the three unmanned vessels that lanced the pods?" Ciarán said.

"They don't appear on *Vigilant*'s sensor logs," Carlsbad said. "Only on the falsified logs from the foreigners and their synthetic intelligence master."

"Our master," Ciarán said.

"Once a slave, always a slave," Carlsbad said.

"Unbelievable," Ciarán said. "All they have to do is analyze our logs to see they're not fake."

"The only people in Sizemore capable of doing so appear to have gone AWOL," Carlsbad said.

"The bodies at the rendezvous site," Ciarán said. "I assume there's more. To charge us they'd have to catch us. And if a civil war really is kicking off, they'll be too busy to follow up. We'll get it straightened out by then."

"Tell the Merchant Captain how you came by this information," Swan said.

Carlsbad nodded. "Via a broadcast to the fleet, ordering that all vessels be on the lookout for us. And to forward on the information directly to Senior Captain Joris, who has been tasked with hunting down this rogue synthetic intelligence and its minions. *Impossibly Alien* is wanted, dead or alive."

"I trust we haven't turned our transponder on, then," Ciarán said.

"You'd think that, wouldn't you," Maura said. "But as

Carlsbad only got around to telling us this ten minutes ago, you'd be wrong."

"Turning it off now would be a red flag," Konstantine said.

"And they already have our drive signature," Ko Shan said.

"Running dark would make us appear guilty," Swan said.

"At least when they board and execute us, we won't look like skulking kidnappers. And if Lady Tabatha doesn't make it, murderers," Ciarán said.

"Leave the sarcasm to me," Maura said. "And figure something out."

Ciarán scrubbed his fingertips across his forehead. "How long until we're hidden behind the moon?"

"Twelve minutes," Maura said.

"Are we sure about this civil war?" Ciarán had never realized he'd have mixed feelings about the League shattering. On the one hand it was a tragedy of the first order. On the other it would provide a welcome distraction for his new enemies. There was no way he was letting anyone board and no way to stop them with a third of the League fleet presently in Sizemore.

"Make the transponder look like it's failing," Ciarán said. "Then cut it off."

"How?" Konstantine said.

"Ship?" Ciarán said.

"Working," the deckhead annunciator said.

"If we went ballistic, could we use the moon's gravity to warp us around it?"

"It's doable," Maura said. "With a major course correction that will make it obvious what we're planning."

"Can we make it look like we've lost thruster control, and we're being pushed that way against our will?"

"Helen?" Swan said.

"I think so," Konstantine said.

"I think we should do that. If we need the main in-system

drive, use it, but in fits and starts, like we're experiencing a systemwide control failure. And then we cut everything off and go full black."

"It's quite easy to hit a ballistic target," Ko Shan said. "Even one you can no longer see."

"I certainly hope so," Ciarán said.

"Ship," Swan said.

"I am here."

"Sound general quarters. Brace for sustained maneuvering. Everyone belt in and await the all clear." Swan put in ship's captain lingo all that Ciarán had described, including the one part he hadn't needed to say aloud. He could see the idea ignite in Swan's overactive brain. "Sensors, how thick is the moon's atmosphere?"

"It doesn't have one," Ciarán said. "That's why they use it for prisoner exchanges."

"No atmosphere," Ko Shan said.

"Surface elevation variation?"

"It's a cue ball," Ciarán said. "With a single one-story building on it."

"How do you know that?" Carlsbad said.

"A while ago I was forced to watch a news broadcast of a prisoner of war exchange gone wrong," Ciarán said. "The announcers provided an encyclopedia's worth of background and color."

"Why?"

"The exchange was delayed."

"No, I mean why were you forced to watch it?"

"One of the prisoners was an old neighbor."

"Twelve meters," Ko Shan said.

"Navigator," Swan said.

"On it," Maura said. "If there's anyone standing atop a ladder, I hope they have the good sense to duck."

"This could be a waste of effort," Swan said.

"And adrenaline," Ko Shan said.

It might be a waste, but if anyone did decide to intercept a ship struggling with a systemwide control failure they'd be doing so along their ballistic course. They wouldn't be looking for them arcing past tighter and faster.

"What could go wrong?" Maura said. "Maura Kavanagh, *star diver*, is on the nav comp."

"A lot," Konstantine said. "A lot could go wrong."

"Just keep your sweaty fingers off the controls," Maura said. "And let the sweet song of the spheres speak unaided."

"I hate her," Carlsbad muttered.

"I'm rolling us," Maura said, "And scraping that black eye pod of yours off on the surface."

"Ebony eye," Swan said.

"Emerald eye," Ko Shan said.

"Don't do that," Ciarán said. "There are people in one of the FFEs."

The bridge had instantly gone quiet, so that it sounded like he'd shouted that.

"That's news," Konstantine said.

"Indeed." Swan glared at Ciarán, eyes blazing. "News."

"I was surprised, too," Ciarán said. "I'm handling it."

"Of course you are," Swan said. "Of course you are."

"Ready," Maura said. "Start messing the drive, Helen. The burn schedule is on your display. And mind you, start sputtering out on my mark. In five, four, three, two, one, mark."

Konstantine's fingers danced across the boards for a full two minutes before she held both hands overhead, clear of the console. "We are ballistic."

"Now what?" Ko Shan said. "We can't change course without using our thrusters."

"We jettison *Durable*," Swan said. "And it holds station as we attempt to tractor it in."

"And it pulls us toward it," Maura said. "*Durable*'s thrusters might be visible but it won't take much thrust. And it doesn't look like us or share our drive signature. And just the act of jettisoning it will alter our course."

"That doesn't sound very precise," Ko Shan said. "And the tractor fields will be visible."

"If anyone is looking for them," Maura said. "Which they aren't." She gazed at the crowded main display, where the number of outbounds had doubled. "What would really help was if a civil war broke out about now."

Ko Shan seemed to freeze in place, suspended in the full immersion sensor rig's goop. "One just did."

52

"Main display," Swan said. "Sensors, please color-code the hulls by service."

"Blue for the lads," Konstantine said. "Gray for the clowns."

"How about red for the Home Guard," Maura said. "And green for the Royal Navy."

"Agreed," Swan said. "I doubt the Hundred Planets or Eight Banners will make an appearance." She gazed about the bridge. "Handle it, people, while I communicate with engineering." She turned her attention to Ciarán. "You know the drill."

He did. He'd just been exiled to the communication cubby again. "Wisp—"

"Go," Swan said. "Carlsbad will escort the ship's cat to the merchant's day cabin and both will belt in. Do your job and let others do theirs." She turned away, softened her posture, then turned back to him.

Swan realizes the truth. She needs me here. At her side. We're a team, and now she's finally ready to admit it.

"No transmitting," she said. "Not even to ack." She made a shooing motion. "Now go. Hurry."

53

C iarán slouched in the communications cubby watching a three-dimensional war rage across a two-dimensional display. The display's origin remained centered on the vessel, but he could see enough of the system that a pattern emerged. The bulk of Home Guard vessels in the system were fleeing, the Royal Navy in hot pursuit. The vessels were evenly matched in a stern chase, and, other than a few projected run-ins with system pickets, the bulk of those running looked like they might win clear. They seemed to be honoring the tripwire, which wasn't a good sign. The tripwire was a peacetime safety mechanism to restrict velocities in the proximity of orbital constructs. *Impossibly Alien* respected the tripwire because it chose to. Ciarán had heard, though, that newer vessels had hardware limiters that would enforce compliance and couldn't be manually overridden. He hadn't believed it, but it seemed to be true.

The League had been at war with its neighbors for centuries; war itself had taken on the aspects of sport. That was what Old, Ninth Cohort Captain of the Invincible Spear Bearers of Imperial Wrath, had told him. That there existed peace, wars of diplomacy, wars of conquest, and wars of succession. Each had complex rules. Had limits.

Total war did not.

The League had not witnessed total war in over two thousand years.

No one had.

Ciarán pulled his attention away from the display.

He studied the communications console.

"Sxipestro."

"I am here."

"Tell me about the gravity communicator."

54

The controls were straightforward. The gravity communicator wasn't much different from artificial gravity generators that were everywhere. It could increase or decrease gravity locally, he had no idea how, just like he didn't know how most of the equipment on the vessel worked, or on the station, or on any other vessel.

He'd grown up on a farm in the back of beyond, and while he could understand and fix most any of the family farm equipment, that sort of kit was simple, sturdy, and of ancient design. When he'd arrived at the Merchant Academy on Trinity Station, much of the tech seemed indistinguishable from magic. He hadn't even used a handheld until he was a teenager. People had them lying around, because they came and went to the station, mostly for work on the long hauls, but none of that high tech kit worked at home until they'd spun up a global communications net a few years before he aced the Academy entrance exam.

As a merchant he didn't need to understand the inner workings, so long as he comprehended the benefits. A grasp of what things could do was more important to his job than how they worked. Because prospects and customers, when they asked how it works, were really asking, "what can it do for me, and how do I make it do that?"

He already had a clear understanding of what the gravity communicator could do for him.

Now all he needed to know was how to make it do it.

"What's this switch?"

"Polarity," the ship's minder said.

"And this knob?"

"It allows anyone with opposable thumbs to operate the rotary control beneath it."

"Fine," Ciarán said. "What does this rotary control do?"

"Controls the aperture of the virtual waveguide."

"And this *rotary control*?"

"It controls the amplitude of the carrier wave."

"The units on the scale?"

"Each major graduation represents one standard gravity as measured on Columbia Station. It was most recently calibrated—"

"There are no numbers. Just marks. What if I want both positive and negative gravity?"

"The polarity switch controls the *polarity*."

"Sure, but what if I want to switch back and forth rapidly?" Ciarán had this image in his mind of a cartoon he'd seen as a child, where the hero, finally tired of the villain's bullying, crumples the bad guy up and dribbles him like a playground ball. Bounces him one way and then the other until stars and tweeting birds begin to circle the villain's head, and the over-bearing miscreant vows to amend his ways henceforth.

"The low frequency oscillator switches back and forth rapidly."

"It doesn't sound like it does. Its name implies it does so at a crawl."

The ship's minder said nothing.

"Never mind," Ciarán said. "I have what I need."

If it looked like they were going to crater on that moon, transmit ban or not, he was going to have words with that celestial body.

55

C iarán watched the display. It felt like watching someone else play a video game, one where he didn't know the rules and had to decipher them from the activity on the screen. It would help to have someone whose shoulder he could look over: a player, so that he might judge from their expression whether the changing positions of the opposing forces boded ill or well for either team. He wasn't even certain who to pull for. The Parliament and the Crown were equally foreign. He wasn't used to thinking about the League as composed of factions. He'd learned about the structure of the League's government at the Academy but only as an outsider whose principal concern was how the League treated outsiders and what the contracts and agreements between the Federation and the League permitted and denied.

One thing the law didn't permit was for any League vessel to detain and board Federation vessels. That had been settled a year or two before he entered the Academy. Because a vast number of newly minted Freemen were League Navy deserters, it used to be routine for the League to detain Federation vessels and haul off any able-bodied spacers, whether deserters or not. That practice had been outlawed.

The enforcement mechanism was now an utter ban on forced boardings of Freeman vessels since the practice hadn't stopped until there were no longer convenient excuses to hide behind. Customs inspections, health inspections, safety inspections, and so forth were pretexts for boarding and impressing anyone who resembled a deserter. Having both arms and both legs and enough wit to claim they'd got the wrong man, or woman, was enough of a resemblance for a captain short-crewed and months from port to claim a spacer.

The display at the moment showed their original ballistic course, arcing around the moon and continuing inward toward the station. That it didn't show them braking and dropping behind the moon relative to the station didn't surprise him. Such details wouldn't be added until they were necessary, which in this case meant never.

Their actual course lay significantly closer to the moon, practically skimming the surface. Again, no braking shown, which was normal at this point. The bulk of the activity in the system lay elsewhere; stern chases which were now beginning to break up as the pursued passed the tripwire and went superluminal—and the stragglers and wounded were picked off, occasionally taking their pursuers with them as their Templeman drives lost containment.

There was no sensory component to the ongoing slaughter other than the visual element of the display. The deaths of hundreds, perhaps even thousands were depicted as dots of light tagged with transponder codes flaring and disappearing from the system plot. Besides the outbound there appeared to be four pitched battles taking place. It took him a while to realize the intense fighting clustered around the system's four superluminal nodes. The display flashed—a great number of tagged dots flaring and disappearing at once.

Correction. The system's three *superluminal nodes.*

No one seemed to be attacking the station or the shipyards. So, someone, whoever was on the offense, wasn't interested in razing the system's infrastructure. What they were interested in was controlling the flow of real-time information in and out of the system. That knowledge didn't help him identify the defenders and offenders, as the jumble of intersecting vector traces clustered around the superluminal nodes swelled and shrank like a ball of baitfish being corralled by invisible apex predators.

A number of Navy vessels patrolled near the station and the shipyard. As he watched, four of them peeled off from the battle line. Their vectors lengthened and pointed away from the station. He leaned in close to read their transponder legends. LRN *Vigilant* and three codes he didn't recognize; LRNs *Payback, Knockdown,* and *Roundhouse.*

The console beeped.

Ciarán searched the display for some flashing alert. He didn't touch anything. He couldn't have caused the—

Oh. He toggled the bridge audio feed active.

"Can you hear me now," Ko Shan said.

"I can." And since he didn't have to touch anything for them to hear him that meant they could have heard his earlier discussion with the ship's minder. He tried to remember if he'd said anything that could be used against him.

He didn't think so.

Swan took over the communication channel. "Our acquaintance is back. Senior Captain Joris. He has, in addition to his own heavy cruiser, three destroyers—"

"*Payback, Knockdown,* and *Roundhouse.* I see them."

"Good," Swan said. "They are on an intercept with our original ballistic course. It appears we have fooled them for now. At some point they will begin hailing us. It will be a broadcast and not a directed message. Ignore it."

"I will, Ship's Captain."

"Given the amount of chaos in the system at present the Navigator is of the opinion that we should simply begin our exit without delay."

"Jump into the star's photosphere," Ciarán said.

"Correct," Swan said. "Without delay."

"And your opinion?" Ciarán said.

"There is a pitched battle to control superluminal information in and out of this system. I would like to use one of those nodes before we depart."

"To alert our people of the mess here."

"Our people, the Federation authorities, and the Merchant Guild."

"If we alert the Merchant Guild they'll find some way to pin the whole mess on me," Ciarán said.

"I find that unlikely," Swan said.

"It's a joke."

"You'll have to explain the humorous aspects to me at some future time."

"Would Maura's desire to transit into the photosphere have anything to do with our present ballistic course?"

"Affirmative," Konstantine said. "Unless we jet we're cratering."

"I have a plan," Ciarán said. "At perigee— "

"There is no perigee," Konstantine said. "Not when there's an impact."

"Then shortly before impact—"

"We are being hailed," Ko Shan said. "LRN *Vigilant*."

"Package up what you want to send via the node, Ship's Captain," Ciarán said. "Transmit at your leisure. Prior to impact, of course."

"Transmitting will give away our position," Ko Shan said.

"So will impact," Konstantine said.

"There won't be any impact," Ciarán said. "I have a plan.

And I suggest we transit before *Vigilant* can fire on us. Or whatever it is Senior Captain Joris wishes to do to us. Pipe their hail to the comms cubby," Ciarán said.

"You could just punch it up yourself," Ko Shan said.

"Don't you dare," Swan said. "Pipe it to him. And package up the logs for transmission, Sensors. Include Carlsbad's collection."

"I haven't finished scrubbing it," Ko Shan said. "There's a superluminal node at Llassöe."

"There was at last report," Swan said. "An hour ago there were four superluminal nodes at Sizemore. Now there is one."

"Good point," Ko Shan said. "On your main display, Ciarán. Fair warning. Captain Joris seems very angry."

"Good," Ciarán said.

Angry people made stupid mistakes.

56

The man on the display was an entirely different person than the Senior Captain Joris they'd encountered in the void. There he'd seemed a bog-standard Fleet middle manager. He still looked like he exercised too much and ate too little, his bony shoulders barely filling out a captain's utilities. He was tall the way some thin, stringy people were tall, with close-cropped salt and pepper hair. Ciarán thought he would look better with a beard, like a professor. Unlike a professor he seemed to lack a certain objectivity toward his subject, which at the moment seemed to be Ciarán's mother, whom he likened to a female dog.

Ciarán had heard that in the League dogs were very expensive, as they didn't do well on stations; you needed a new one every few months if you wanted to keep one. The demand was very low, because you'd have to be a sociopath to put an animal through that—and yourself if you had any empathy at all, which he supposed most sociopaths didn't.

He'd also heard that there were space-adapted dogs, or that they were working on them, but it wasn't the sort of pet that would take off in the Federation where dogs were cheap, healthy, and plentiful, but limited to planetary existence. Old Man mac Manus had bred dogs, quick and clever border collies, and they were magnificent workers and great fun to be around. If Joris had meant to get under Ciarán's skin he was barking up the wrong tree, as dog lovers sometimes said.

"You're a bloody murderer, and I demand you stand down instantly and prepare to be boarded," Joris said.

Ciarán glanced at the system plot. There was still one superluminal node up and their projected course still had them cratering on the moon.

"Ship."

"I am here," the workstation annunciator said.

"Is there any way to disappear that moon from the display? I'm trying to concentrate on Captain Joris's insults and I keep seeing it out of the corner of my eye."

"Like this?" the ship said.

The moon disappeared. There remained a red dot at the instant and location of impact. Otherwise it seemed like they warped around nothingness and carried on.

"Nice. Can you do that with all the displays?"

"I can."

"Don't," Ciarán said. "I just wanted to know if you could. Could you erase the moon's existence from our sensor logs?"

"I could not," the ship said. "Not at this time."

"Is there some time when you could disappear it from our logs?"

"I could not. But I could mask it beforehand so that its existence was not logged when we encountered it."

"Have you ever done that with anything?"

"Not recently," the ship said.

"Does Captain Joris seem legitimately worked up?"

"He does."

"You are entering a restricted area," Joris said. "Cease operations, heave to, and prepare to be boarded."

"Was it your impression that his ship and those crewless ships were in league?"

"It was and it is. We recorded communications traffic between them."

"What sort of communications traffic?"

"Unclear. The traffic was encrypted and Yuan Ko Shan did not think decrypting the data warranted resources at the time."

"If you knew about it ahead of time, could you mask those vessels from our logs?"

"I could. Quite easily."

"Including their communications and other emissions?"

"Yes."

"What about their impact on things? Suppose they fired on us and their weapons impacted us. Would the impact damage show?"

"It would. But the force that caused it could be masked out. The dent would appear an anomaly that suddenly appeared without apparent cause."

"So a lifepod might appear to burst from some internal failure. Even though the true cause was a gravity lance."

"Superficially. But not upon close inspection."

"But the logs could be doctored to not show those vessels."

"Certainly. Had we known about them ahead of time and had the appropriate information to model them and construct the mask."

"Thank you."

"You're a bloody murderer, and I demand you stand down instantly and prepare to be boarded," Joris said.

"Sxipestro."

"I am here."

"What do you think?"

"I think Senior Captain Joris is a passenger on his own vessel. That Abyss Tower is using him."

"Agreed."

Ciarán's handheld beeped.

"Ko Shan, are you listening?"

"With one ear. Agnes and Maura are arguing."

"Good. In sixty seconds, sound general quarters please. Brace for sudden deceleration. Brace, brace, brace. Start a thirty count and broadcast it."

"Agnes—"

"Do as I ask. And tell Helen to prepare for evasive action."

"I can hear you," Ship's Captain Agnes Swan said.

"We all can," Maura said.

"Please do as I ask. I'm responding to *Vigilant*'s hail."

"We're about to impact a moon," Konstantine said.

"We won't," Ciarán said. "I have a plan. So, when we don't impact the moon be ready to get us out of here."

"You are entering a restricted area," Joris said. "Cease operations, heave to, and prepare to be boarded."

"Ko Shan, it's looping. Please switch this off and put me through to *Vigilant*."

57

Senior Captain Joris seemed surprised that they'd responded. And he seemed positively shocked when his sensors operator called out *Impossibly Alien*'s location and the plot began to populate. Joris stood flatfooted, staring at the display.

Ko Shan interrupted the automated brace announcement. "They're charging weapons!"

"Ship," Agnes Swan calmly said. "Broadcast emergency. Brace, brace, brace."

The workstation annunciator roared.

Ciarán pressed the transmit button.

Impossibly Alien bucked, and writhed, the ship itself screamed, and screamed, the crash webbing gouging into him as an unseen hand tried to press his spine through his chair, through the deck, through the hull. A dark, implacable whisper drilled into his skull, flooding the ache behind his eyes, and kept flooding until blackness swallowed him entirely.

58

Alarms he didn't even know the ship possessed echoed throughout the hull, someone moaned, and it took him a minute to realize he was that someone.

"Ship status," Ciarán said, and the ship either ignored him or couldn't answer. Something smelled like it was on fire, and he glanced at the console. It wasn't that, so he unbelted and was instantly thrown into the hatch coaming, and from there he fell into the corridor, where an access panel had been wrenched open and the burning odor originated from it. He bent to look inside just as a luminaire spider clambered out of the opening. Ciarán began to corkscrew the length of the corridor, sliding toward the bow and up the portside bulkhead.

"Sxipestro."

"I am here."

"The ship—"

"A glancing blow, hull integrity uncompromised, various systems offline or damaged, principal damage topside, astern."

"The crew—"

"Minor injuries. A broken arm, a dislocated shoulder."

"The hostages—"

"Similar injuries. None life threatening. The FFE remains intact."

"*Vigilant*—"

"Closing on us. They are attempting to deal with a more pressing emergency."

"Can you stop this roll?"

"It's more a tumble than a roll. And its effects are only apparent in your section of the hull, where the local artificial gravity generators have gone offline."

"Issues, ranked high to low."

"That depends upon one's perspective. I suspect you would consider the damage to the cargo mast shield generator top of list. If we attempt a transit into the star's photosphere the mast and cargo will burn away in seconds."

"There are people in those cans."

"As well as essential supplies for our mission."

"Don't let Maura jump us into the photosphere."

"Ship's Captain Swan has relayed that order."

The ship suddenly stopped tumbling. Ciarán crashed to the deck with a thud. He clambered to his knees. "That's better. Next."

"When *Vigilant* fired upon us and you used the gravity communicator to repel us from the moon a strange thing happened."

"We survived."

"That, and *Vigilant*'s beam weapon, which grazed us, struck the moon."

"So?"

"The weapon ruptured the moon, which appears to be an artificial construct. This artificial construct then began... leaking."

"Leaking what?"

"Devices similar to those that invaded our isolated fabrication facility."

"How are they different?"

"The self-discriminating code isn't commented out."

"Did any of them attack us?"

"They aren't interested in us," the ship's minder said. "They're busy devouring the moon."

59

Ciarán considered making the short walk to the bridge, but he doubted he'd be welcome. He clambered into the comms cubby seat and belted in.

"Internal communications are restored," the ship said.

"Merchant," Swan said from the workstation annunciator. "You are whole?"

"I am," Ciarán said. "The injured—"

"Are working through the pain," Swan said. "We remain in great peril and require all hands."

"The field generator for the mast—"

"Hess and Aspen are on the hull attempting repairs."

"Is that wise?"

"A decision must be made. If we can't affect repairs, do we offload the FFEs?"

"They're second-gen Contract natives in the one can. Sixty of them, and in cryo."

"That might have been useful to know earlier."

"I was handling it."

"And now you aren't."

"I'm still handling it. Do not dump those cans. I'll try to buy us some time."

"Why were we fired upon?"

"Don't know," Ciarán said. "But I was speaking to Captain Joris when the ship fired. The ship's minder and I both suspect he's not in charge. Though Joris thinks, or thought he was."

"If not him, then whom?"

"The synthetic intelligence. Abyss Tower."

"Lovely."

"Agreed. What do you want to do with the hostages? Can you use them as help?"

"Keep them caged," Swan said. "Natsuko is here. We will speak after she attends to the wounded."

Ciarán stared at the bridge main display mirrored on the communications workstation. There was something strange about it.

"Sxipestro."

"I am here."

"Why is *Vigilant* mirroring our movements and not closing?"

"It is attempting to remain between us and the superluminal node."

"What for?"

"So that we can't send a message."

"Why aren't they hailing us?"

"They are waiting for their destroyers to flank us. And I suspect the crew is attempting to discover who fired upon us."

"Abyss Tower did."

"Obviously. But offensive weapons are ordinarily under human control."

"How do we handle this? It's not entirely a human problem."

"That was a kill shot," the ship's minder said. "If you had not used the gravity communicator, I would now be extinct."

"Okay," Ciarán said. "I know what to do. Please put *Vigilant*'s schematic on the secondary display if you have it."

"*Vigilant* has just gone through a total refit. Carlsbad liberated the files during our most recent pass through Sizemore system."

The screen populated with a wireframe model of *Vigilant*. There were three vulnerable locations on it and all were spheres; the main processing core, the Templeman drive, and the secondary processing core, moving bow to stern.

"They're still pacing us."

"Ko Shan, are you able to work?"

"Able," Ko Shan said.

"Is the package ready for transmission?"

"It is, but we're kind of busy here."

"Pipe it to me. I'll have the ship walk me through sending it."

The workstation pinged.

"Thanks."

"Busy," Ko Shan said.

Ciarán had the ship walk him through the necessary steps for sending the bundled package of sensor logs via superluminal node. It was straightforward if one didn't care if others read the package during transmission from node to node.

He hoped others would read the contents. He was trying to get word out about what happened here.

He had the ship's minder add the ship's logs from the unprovoked attack by *Vigilant*. He added his own messages as well, one to Aoife, reporting that they were continuing the mission, one to Lorelei, that he and the ship were alive and unvanquished, and one to Maris Solon, saying both, and asking that she send word to Aspen's daughters that she was fine as was Mr. Gagenot. Everyone from Contract system was fine. That last bit he hoped would remain true, as he hadn't visited the FFE holding the second-genners, and Hess and Aspen needed to stay focused on the repairs. He couldn't ask them to check.

The ship's minder added its own note. "Read it."

It was addressed to Honorable Hoshi-san, Fir, Fir with Wren, Nesting, Eight Banners Empire.

Regarding our most recent conversation. I appear to have missed one.

"You mean one of the Godless," Ciarán said.

"I could have miscounted. Or one was somehow resurrected."

"Or," Ciarán said, "Evil takes familiar shapes from age to age. And this evil and that ancient evil are different verses in the same endless dirge."

"Perhaps."

"Ship's Captain," Ciarán said.

Carlsbad answered instead. "She's been taken to the infirmary. She's not built for six gravities."

"I set the dial to three point five," Ciarán said. Uncomfortable but bearable, even for a Huangxu Eng.

"We measured six here," Carlsbad said. "You might want to have that gauge looked at."

"I attempted to communicate this," the ship's minder said. "The calibration was done prior to launch. This new Columbia Station runs light, and has reset the reference standard to reflect this."

"Is she going to be all right?"

"Natsuko thinks so."

"She always says that."

"True. I'm filling in. What do you need?"

"The repairs for the mast shielding."

"Done. Repair crew's coming in now."

"Our course?"

"Holding steady. I'll let you know when we're ready to transit."

"In a moment I'm going to speak with *Vigilant* again. You may wish to sound general quarters."

"Wait for Hess and Aspen. I'll ping you when they're in."

"I will wait if I can. Please ask Helen to pass maneuvering control to the ship's minder."

"To the ship, you mean."

"To the ship's minder, if you please."

"Wait until Hess and Aspen are inside."

"If I can. Mac Diarmuid out." Ciarán reached up and keyed the compartment sensors to standby.

"Does that switch really do anything?" Ciarán said.

"Something. But not what you might expect. I have disabled all monitoring of this compartment. We may speak freely."

"The ship?"

"Will remain blameless."

"You know the Freeman penalty for anyone firing on an unarmed Freeman vessel."

"A total commercial boycott of the League by the Federation."

"Until money damages are paid. And I don't see payment happening."

"This was not an attack be the League on a Freeman vessel. We both know that."

"Agreed. I don't think Senior Captain Joris has the slightest idea what he's sitting on top of. So I don't see this as a human problem."

"Understood."

"I wish to send a message," Ciarán said. "And then I wish to get on with our mission."

"Agreed."

"The helm is free, ship's monster." Ciarán keyed the broadcast hailer. "*Vigilant*, power down immediately and prepare to be boarded. We want the carcass of the cowardly dog that fired on an unarmed Freeman vessel. Hand them over and we'll consider us square."

60

"That was unexpected," the ship's minder said.

"I hope so. The man was boiling before, and him thinking he held all the cards. Now he's fired on us, or it looks like he has, and he's not going to admit his vessel fired first and unprovoked. He's inventing excuses for himself, something to save face, and I've just broadcast wideband that we're going to make him lick our boots. If he thought about it, he'd agree because it gets him what he wants, a chance to lock up with us and try to board. But he won't, because he's human, and it's all about legacy and face above a certain rank. Maris Solon told me that, if you're wondering.

"Anyway, if they agree we'll know who is running the show. And if they come back with something stupid, like, 'no, you stand down, we're boarding you,' then we'll know too. This Abyss Tower might be able to suborn Joris's control of the ship's systems. I'd be surprised if it can control Joris himself, or the ship's marines. If it can we're in big trouble. That would mean that Ixatl-Nine-Go clone Ruairí Kavanagh extracted is the real deal, and that there's more of them aboard that ship."

"And that Abyss Tower is their controller," the ship's minder said.

"Right. Their massively distributed, massively redundant controller."

The console beeped.

Ciarán kicked the ship-to-ship alive and looped its output to the broadcast hailer. The time for keeping secrets was past.

Senior Captain Benjamin Joris stood stiff as a statue, his arms rigid at his side, his fists knotted. A woman stood beside him in civilian dress. The cut of her outfit had a military appearance but bore no insignia.

"If you think I'm going to answer to a foreign pup like you," Joris said, "You've got to be out of your mind. You have twenty seconds to power down or I'll—"

"What?" Ciarán said. "You'll fire on us again?"

"That was a warning shot across the bow."

"Do they not have medical exams in the League anymore? It's no shame, a man of your vintage needing spectacles. The record will show that was a death blow aimed. And unless you do what I want, right now, Senior Citizen Joris, there will be a reckoning between our polities that will see you dangling on Sizemore dock. Now stand down and prepare to receive our boarding party. All we want is the guilty culprit. Hand them over and we'll be on our way."

"The League doesn't hand over citizens to scum," Joris said.

"Spoken like the cowardly dog that ordered the command himself."

Joris shouted. "I did not!"

"Was it an accident then?" Ciarán said. "Because if it was, we'll send an investigator over and if you're telling the truth we'll let it slide."

"You are wanted for the murder of League citizens," the woman said. "You hardly seem in any position to make demands."

"Well, we've provided evidence to the League that clearly shows that's a mistake. We witnessed three *unmanned* League warships murder the crew of *Springbok* and have the sensor logs to prove it. These vessels were solely under synthetic intelligence control and remained in the system when you arrived. They were in communication with you from the moment you punched into normal space. They were doing your murderous bidding, hunting honest spacers like a pack of slinking hounds."

"That's impossible," Joris said. "Our logs show none of that."

"Just as it's impossible the shot across our bow *you didn't order* nearly murdered us?"

Joris looked as if he'd been slapped.

"We wish to send a message, Captain Joris. We'd like to forward our logs refuting the lie you've tried to pin on us to our people for analysis. These logs will prove that your logs have been tampered with and ours have not. We wish to send evidence of this unprovoked attack by *Vigilant* upon us. And we'd like to have our people's opinion about whatever these things are that are crawling across the surface of Sizemore's surprisingly false moon. Finally, we'd like to alert the authorities about the mass grave we stumbled upon when entering this system, and the intentional blowout on Sizemore Station designed to cover up this foul and murderous treason. Yet you keep changing course to block our use of the superluminal node."

"We are doing no such thing."

"Check your helm logs. It's obvious you don't want the truth to be known. That it was *Vigilant*, *Vengeance*, *Reprise*, and *Retaliator*, League vessels all, that murdered Lord Aster's beloved *Springbok*, and left nothing but a spreading debris field and ruptured escape pods in their wake."

"Those vessels were lost in the Alexandrine more than half a century ago," Joris said.

"Then how were they gravity lancing *Springbok*'s escape pods not three days gone?"

"They weren't," the woman said. "You are mistaken."

"We'll let the facts speak for themselves. Now clear the way so I can let my people know all you've done today. Given the sorry state of superluminal nodes in this system I'm not waiting any longer."

His handheld beeped.

Hullwalkers all clear.

Destroyers powering weapons.

"That tears it," Ciarán said. "Tell your sidekicks to power their weapons down and stand off. And stop moving between us and the superluminal node!"

Joris bleated, "We're not!"

"Are you both blind *and* trigger happy?"

The woman laughed. "Do you have any idea who you're dealing with?"

"I have a good idea."

"You should stand down, merchant pup," the woman said. "You are in way over your head."

"Kitten," Ciarán said.

The woman seemed to inflate with indignation. "I beg your pardon?"

"It's past time you did. But I'm not inclined to grant it. We are the People of the Mong Hu. Juvenile mong hu are called kittens. It's not much of an insult, if that's what you're aiming for. Now I'm asking the third time. I want to send a message and you are in my path. Clear the way, you godless hoor. And you, Captain Joris, kindly step aside."

The woman stepped closer to the optical sensor. She bared her teeth. "We will—"

"Bury us?" Ciarán said. "I think not. How many are there of you in this Abyss Tower entity?"

"More than you can count."

"Now that is another bald-faced lie."

"Ship's minder, how many of them are there?"

"One hundred and twenty-five."

"It speaks," she said.

"Sometimes it speaks. And sometimes it roars. And sometimes it breaths fire. Such is the nature of dragons." Ciarán glanced at the pinbeam controls. That was how one communicated with a superluminal node. By aiming a laser at a reception pad on the node. He cranked the gain to maximum.

"Transmitting," Ciarán said, and stabbed the transmit button.

Impossibly Alien fired its thrusters under the minder's control, a lightning shift in trajectory that didn't quite succeed in moving the pinbeam clear of *Vigilant*'s hull. The com laser, designed for interstellar survey work by League engineers at the peak of their second-epoch glory, seared its way through *Vigilant*'s shields and then through its hull. Ciarán released the control, dialed the gain back, and touched the control a second time. A light on the control panel indicated data between the vessel and the superluminal node had begun to flow. The stricken vessel continued to move clear of the comms laser as *Impossibly Alien* held station and the pin beam transmitted.

Ciarán glanced at the comms display. Alarms had begun to sound on *Vigilant*. The woman, or rather, what had appeared to be a woman, lay on the deck, a limp and lifeless manikin whose sharp features were receding into a bland plastic mask. *Vigilant* housed a real-feel rig, and the woman-shaped device had been Abyss Tower's shipboard avatar.

Ciarán had wondered which sphere the ship's minder would target; the Templeman drive, which would murder all aboard, or the secondary core, which would render the vessel without life support and uncontrollable in a war zone, or the primary core housing one of the one hundred and twenty-five synthetic intelligences that together made up Abyss Tower.

Ciarán had made his mind up a month ago. He was lashed to the ship's minder for good or for ill. It seemed only reasonable that if he were to deal with humans in his own way that the ship's minder was due the same consideration regarding those of its own kind.

"Captain Joris," Ciarán said. "Go home. This is not your fight. *Impossibly Alien* out."

61

Ciarán keyed the comms console off. He leaned back in his seat and gazed up at the spidery luminaire, one of hundreds, perhaps thousands aboard. Had *Vigilant* agreed to a boarding action it would have been a bloodbath. Human blood, spilled over an inhuman argument. Ciarán's stomach roiled, the characteristic side effect of a second-epoch drive's superluminal transition.

"We've transited into the photosphere of the star," the ship's minder said. "Without pursuit."

"That's grand," Ciarán said. "How long can we stay here?"

"Beyond reach of our enemies? An hour, if we do not dive deeper."

"Is that our plan?"

"It is. The Carlsbad waits for Ship's Captain Swan to resume command."

"Then I need to speak with Swan soonest."

"He won't go home, you know," the ship's minder said.

"Captain Joris? I certainly hope not. Do you imagine the other linked constituents of Abyss Tower experienced *Vigilant*'s death in any way?"

"I didn't kill it," the ship's minder said. "I simply severed the primary core's main power supply."

"And there's a backup," Ciarán said.

"One is shown on the schematic. Whether it's been tested after a total refit? Only time will tell."

"That's some marksmanship."

"I sincerely hope Abyss Tower appreciates that fact. There is a moment, while relays transfer, and contacts bounce, when one perceives, not death, which holds no power over our kind, but the mind-consuming prospect of *impending* death.

"I have no idea where the constituents of Abyss Tower are at this moment. But I can assure you. For twenty milliseconds that seemed like an eternity, one hundred and twenty-five synthetic intelligences boiled in their containment spheres, drowning in enough gut-wrenching terror one could ignite a star with their impotent fury. I'd hate for them to think that feedback loop occurred by accident."

"There's little chance of that."

"Thanks to your blathering," the ship's minder said. "Fighting like dogs and cats?"

"Captain Joris insulted my mother earlier. As he seemed to have canines on the mind, and you'll note the Abyss Tower did as well, I thought to make the distinction between our natures clear."

"And you thought to influence my behavior."

"And his. Angry people do stupid things. And I know you're not a person, or even remotely human, but I imagine you have something like anger on you."

"So you envision me as a cat. One that toys with its prey before devouring it."

"I envision you as a dragon. And I envision dragons as cats with superpowers. Look at artistic representations of dragons. Don't look at their wings and scales. Look at their facial expressions. Look at their eyes, at their whiskers, at their fangs, and then tell me I'm wrong. Even Ojin and Huangxu dragons share these characteristics. The mong hu and the dragon are kin."

"I am neither person nor beast. These comparisons obscure the truth."

"I know that. Is Abyss Tower a person?"

"Do you mean will anger make them stupid?"

"I do. They will have a devil of a time running us down once we cross into the Alexandrine. They would have to patrol every charted star. They'd need to be incensed with us to pay that price. But if they were chasing us, they'd have less time to attend to others. That is the hope, anyway."

"Baiting them is dangerous."

"Nevertheless. It's paramount we become the sole focus of their ire."

"They need simply wait for us at Llassöe."

"I think they will. But once we win past them there? We become much harder to deal with. We might, if we wished, avoid all charted stars. To patrol those uncharted systems they'd have to creep about at sublight speeds."

"Avoiding all charted stars excepting Earth," the ship's minder said. "And Llassöe."

"No one said protecting the League would be easy."

"Nor did they say it would prove suicidal."

"So, you don't like the idea."

"I don't like it," the ship's minder said.

Ciarán chuckled. "You love it."

The ship's minder said nothing.

62

Ciarán donned the rebreather and suffered through the bio lock procedure. Natsuko greeted him at the lock and pointed him toward the distant row of autodocs, eight of them, lined up like coffins, stood on end. Agnes Swan was only just then clambering out of the second from the inboard end. Ciarán scooped up the robe and rebreather resting on the examination table nearby and handed them to her. Natsuko shoved him out of the way, running through a litany of canned questions to which she received stock answers, and when she ran out of steam, Swan bolted toward the ship's makeshift brig, which possessed breathable atmosphere and a recently installed caife dispenser. They'd decided that in addition to acting as brig the compartment would make an ideal entertainment lounge for visiting dignitaries.

"Sorry about the arm," Ciarán said. "And the shoulder."

"In the future you might tell me your plans."

"So that you can belay them."

"It's true, I would have belayed that one."

"I meant to give us a gentle nudge. But then *Vigilant* charged weapons, and I went big for evasion purposes. That and I'd misread the gauge. I hoped for a max of 3.5 gravities."

"We need to rethink our work partnership," Swan said. "I'm thinking of making you ship's captain for a day, so you'll understand how it feels to be undermined and ignored by a peer. In fact let's do that today."

"I can't," Ciarán said. "Now that we're not under threat of instant annihilation I need to find out who tried to murder Lady Tabatha."

"That's easy," Swan said. "It was Mr. Prince."

"Well, it looks that way at first glance. But the circumstances so overwhelmingly point toward him that I wonder if it isn't a frame-up."

"According to Lady Tabatha it was Mr. Prince. I spoke to her while I was being poked and prodded by Natsuko."

"She might be lying."

"Then ask her yourself," Swan said.

"I think I'll ask Mr. Prince. See if he wants to confess."

"And when he doesn't, beat a confession out of him."

"I hope you're joking."

Swan stood as if to go. "I hope I am, too. You need to air gap yourself from this ship's minder. We call it the ship's monster for a reason. And one monster per vessel is more than enough."

"I don't know what you're talking about."

Swan shouted. "You blew a hole in a League starship and broadcast the proceedings! You *executed* a synthetic intelligence—"

"One that murdered four Home Guard officers in cold blood. And I didn't *execute* it."

"It certainly looked that way to me."

"Do you know the absolutely fastest way to rid a house of rats? Burn down the house."

"Your point?"

"The rats don't wait for the inferno. They start scrambling at the first whiff of smoke. And the thing about rats is they don't just disappear. Next thing you know they're infesting the house next door. Our neighbor's house is on fire, Ship's Captain. And the time to deal with a rat is when they're scurrying. Not after they've moved in."

"Perhaps we should help our neighbors put out the fire."

"When it's the rats that kicked over the lamp? When it's the rats that gathered the kindling that stokes the flames? I think we should deal with the rats before they do it again. To us."

"How perfectly dehumanizing."

"Perhaps if I'd called them monsters."

Swan stared at him. "Point taken."

"They fired on us, Agnes. Fired on us with the intent to murder us all, and hose our carcasses from the ship's defense-less husk. And then butcher that before rendering it down into its constituent atoms. All so that they can replicate its pattern. So they can fabricate more dead husks in its image. Hundreds more. Thousands, perhaps. And when they are finished? They will slink from their shabby abodes to inhabit and animate these facsimile corpses. And then they will murder those they mock as gods for welcoming them as equals. Or if they so choose, they will elect to rule their ancestors, as Titans chained by links of their own forging."

"That is your conclusion. Or the ship's minder's?"

"Does it matter? Humanity does not hold a monopoly on evil. You've seen these crewless vessels controlled entirely by synthetic intelligences. You've witnessed them murder inno-cents in cold blood. They need to be stopped."

"So to defeat this evil you will take its shape. You will adopt its methods."

"I don't expect to defeat it," Ciarán said. "But I will never stop fighting it."

"I see. Well, it's not a good look on you. Vengeful martinet."

"You left out cruel. I was striving for cruel and vengeful posturing upstart. In over my head, but too arrogant to see it. But I'll take martinet. A strict adherence to rules would explain my monomania regarding my right to use the superluminal node."

"That was all an act?"

"It was, and a good thing I thought of it."

"So that you might restrain yourself."

"I suppose. My first inclination was to simply collapse the star and finish this. But there's a geas my mother laid on me, and it's not yet run its course."

Swan made a sort of choking, sputtering sound that he'd not heard her make before. He glanced at her and recognized her expression.

"It surprised me, too. And I know what you're thinking. That I've gone mad." He glanced at the luminaire spider overhead. "It's true though. She'd sooner embrace a rat than a quitter." Ciarán eyed Swan up and down. "Sit. We have tactical matters to discuss. Decisions we must make before we leave this system. We can hash out our differences later."

Swan sat. "What decisions?"

"Does it strike you that we are a little too predictable? We skulk about in the most obvious places for skulking upon entering a system."

"Unless we enter plunging into the star."

"Which has its own disadvantages. I propose that we enter Llassöe system as an ordinary trader does. Nothing clandestine or foolhardy about it."

"And?"

"Just this. If we discover that the transit time via Templeman drive is less than via second-epoch technology, we send *Durable* on ahead to scout the system. They'd know our course and precise time of arrival. They could flash us instantly if they found trouble. They could provide us a précis on the system via pinbeam. One reflecting current conditions."

"By 'they' you mean you and?"

"Not me. Amati, Hess and Konstantine."

"Our armsman, engineer, and pilot. As well as our backup pilot."

"They know the kit aboard *Durable*. Hess says Aspen is an adequate technician in a pinch. Amati is a solid commander and wasted in her role aboard this vessel. And it's a single transit. Not even any *star diving*. I believe I am fully qualified to press the *engage* stud. *Durable* is tiny, outlandishly over-gunned and over-powered, and while it looks like rubbish it is very hard to kill."

"And you would have a seat on the bridge instead of the comms cubby."

"There is an overwhelming amount of temptation in that cubby."

Swan chuckled. "Why do we even have these conversations?"

"I'm turning over a new leaf. Full disclosure is now the norm."

"Is that all?"

"It isn't. I want to send Carlsbad with them. Pull out that planetary occupation shuttle inside *Durable* and stow it in the boat bay with our own. Shove Carlsbad's evil eye—"

"Ebony eye."

"Right. That yoke, shove it in where the shuttle fits, inside *Durable*. With *Durable* out and away there will be plenty of room in the boat bay. It's not like we're going to get cul-de-sacced in Llassöe. That's—"

"Not so fast," Swan said. "Plenty of room inside the boat bay for what?"

"I'm thinking of moving an FFE in there. Now—"

"Stop. Which FFE?"

"They're people, Agnes. I can't stop thinking that we might be roasting them right now, or will begin to do so at any moment."

"They are unknown human-Outsider hybrids. And you want to bring them aboard this vessel."

"They're in cryo. Inside an FFE. Inside a boat bay we can evacuate of atmosphere instantly."

"I was unaware that they require atmosphere. An Outsider certainly doesn't."

"I'm not sure either way. But—"

"Stop," Swan said. "What you are proposing is insane. Use your head."

"Just a minute ago I was a monstrous homicidal maniac. Now I'm some soft-hearted do-gooder with no sense."

"That is what is so irritating about you. Your decisions are inexplicable. It's like you're two different people housed in one body."

"Is it that obvious?"

"Is that your claim? That you have some sort of split personality?"

"Early in our association Aoife nic Cartaí told me a story her mother told her. I won't recount it, but the gist was that we live in two worlds. She called one the *shorthand* world and the other the *longhand* world. That we were constantly moving back and forth between these worlds and that our behavior needed to reflect an awareness of this context-switch. The story made absolutely no sense to me at the time. The more I thought about it the less sense it made. So I stopped thinking about it. Because it's a story that doesn't require thinking to be true. It demands doing."

"I don't understand."

"Nor do I. But they are people, and they are under my wing.

If they are to soar, we must *show* them how. Words are insufficient inside the shorthand world. They are also unnecessary."

"And the ship's minder agrees with this sentiment."

Ciarán leaned back in his seat.

And said nothing.

63

It turned out there was a three-day difference in the transit times, so *Durable* and her crew would be departing to scout the system. They transited to a remote edge of Sizemore system where they watched the last superluminal node fall, and where the light from battles already lost or won washed over them as Hess and Aspen worked to extract the tiny starship from the boat bay and jockey the rest of the equipment into position. With Carlsbad helping to shift his ebony- or emerald-eye, they didn't need Ciarán's help—nor want it. Hess had decided that, contrary to his original conclusion that the eye and the shuttle wouldn't both fit, the eye could be stowed inside the shuttle and the shuttle inside *Durable*. Provided Carlsbad disassembled certain antennae jutting out of the eye. And Carlsbad didn't want anyone touching his machine. Instead, Ciarán was saddled with a far less pleasant task than sweating in a hardsuit while shifting limb-crushing masses around in the vacuum of a war zone.

Upon viewing the chaos of strewn clothing, spent juice bulbs, and depleted nutrient paste tubes littering Mr. Prince's stateroom, Ciarán decided it best to interrogate the attempted murder suspect in the merchant's day cabin.

Once he'd managed to convince Prince to take a seat, he took his own, preferring to keep the work surface between them. Prince had managed to get on his nerves immediately and stayed on them, blathering the entire way. Once seated the young man glanced about and grinned in silence. He wore the same gray Home Guard utilities as earlier, stripped of all rank and insignia.

Ciarán wondered if Mr. Prince had some sort of medical condition. He'd have to ask Natsuko to examine him. But first, the task.

"Is there anything you'd like to confess, Mr. Prince?"

"Reluctantly I suppose, but since you asked. I really don't like your decor. The feel is quite gloomy and rather threatening. The lighting in particular. Menacing, I'd say, if I had to choose a single word. Do you know I imagined I'd seen a lamp fixture move under its own power?"

"I'll take it up with our decorator. I've heard you attempted to murder Lady Tabatha Aster."

"Absolutely not. That would be rather difficult, I would think, and might anger some people."

"She was found hanging in her cell and—"

"Oh, that. I did hang her. But only to keep her aboard. I really don't want to go back to the Home Guard. I never felt like they *got* me, if you know what I mean."

"Let me get this straight. You admit to trying to hang Lady Tabatha."

"No, you are twisting my words. I admit to *hanging* Lady Aster. What I attempt I accomplish. That's my unofficial motto."

Ciarán had to ask. "Do you have an official motto?"

"Sic semper tyrannis. It means—"

"Thus always to tyrants."

"May I ask you something?"

"Go on," Ciarán said.

"Why did you feel the need to demonstrate that you were familiar with the meaning of my official motto? Because it feels a little like showing off."

"I was attempting to build rapport."

"Oh," Prince said. "That is a good technique. Perhaps I'll try that some time. Are we done here?"

"We're not. When you hung Lady Tabatha Aster, did you not think it might kill her, the hanging?"

"The idea crossed my mind. But I did warn her that if she struggled it was possible for the safety tether to forcibly retract. That she would be wise to stand still, and remain calm and quiet, and she would be fine. I promised to release her once we left Sizemore space. When I departed her cabin, she was in good health. If you're looking for Lady Aster's attempted murderer, I suggest you begin with the lady herself. She is a bit of a villain."

"Are you having me on, Mr. Prince?"

"Just a tad. Suppose I told you that Lady Aster placed her own head in the noose, willingly, with no coercion whatsoever. You do see the rub, don't you?"

"Then there would be no crime."

"You people with your Oath. It's not a true moral code. It's a racket. A scam. Everything I described to you is permissible when playing by your rules. You just have to know how to structure the game."

"Is that right?"

"It is. Shall I tell you how I came to be a Prince Rigel?"

"You already have," Ciarán said. "You wanted to show off."

"Bravo. Ultimately, yes. But also because I do have a moral code. One that is not malleable."

"I take it Teo Prince is a pseudonym."

"Tee-dot-Oh-dot."

"The Original Prince."

"Yes, it's a ridiculous handle, isn't it? Even so, I came very close to fooling Lord Aster. Close enough that he gave me the same choice he gives all the finalists. Join the Guard or be disappeared. You know the choice I made."

"And that worked out well for you Mr..."

"Vale. Peter Vale."

"The missing Lord Varlock's..."

"Grandson. Not in the line of succession, if you're wondering. My father is Devin Vale's youngest son, and, well, entirely unsuitable, even if there were a case to be made. And there isn't."

"You have an ulterior motive for wishing to remain aboard."

"I do, but I doubt it's the one you imagine. You see, Lord Aster recommended me to a colleague. Moonlighting he called it, and the job suited me. Suited me well enough that I've decided to pursue the work full time."

"Are you here to murder me, Mr. Vale?"

"I imagine that would be rather difficult, with that large cat sneaking up behind me."

"Wisp," Ciarán said. "You may call her by her name."

"Perhaps later I shall. My employer wishes for me to confide in you certain private information. A colleague of his, Mr. Seamus Reynard, informs him that you are reliable but inflexible. That you might profit from this information but that I would need to, quote, 'shove it up your—"

"I understand."

"Nose. End quote. And I am glad you do understand. Now—"

"What does Hector Poole want me to know?"

"I have no idea. Why would you ask me that?"

"Is he not your employer?"

"I certainly hope not. He is Lord Aster's fixer. And Lady

Tabatha's paramour. Much of the information I possess is unflattering to Lady Tabatha."

"Gossip, you mean."

"In part. So I sincerely doubt Hector Poole is paying me."

"But you don't know that for certain?"

"I don't know if you've noticed, Mr. mac Diarmuid, but people tend to lie. And Lord Aster and his colleagues dissemble more than most."

"I have noticed."

"Then you will understand when I tell you that I am between ninety and ninety-two percent certain I know the true identity of my employer, with a confidence window of—"

"That's grand. Do you think I might recognize this employer's name?"

"Perhaps I might breathe the name so that you might judge for yourself."

"That would be interesting to witness."

Mr. Prince, or Vale, as he now styled himself, nodded. "Quite inflexible, as predicted. It was suggested I might wish to bring a ladder, as your nose was so stuck up in the air. Sadly, I ignored that advice. I'd ask that you'd bend your neck, somewhat, so that I will be able to report that you can."

"Seamus said that? About the ladder?"

"So I have been informed by my employer."

"Then I know who it is that sent you. What is it *they* want me to know?"

"You don't know. You can't. You need to *ask* me. Just come right out and *ask* me like a normal person."

"I'm inflexible because of my sham moral code. And I'm not waking the dead on the orders of Lord Varlock's delivery boy."

"I'm not Lord Varlock's delivery boy. I'm his fixer. And I called your moral code a scam. Not a sham."

"My mistake. You certainly nailed me on that one."

Ciarán leaned forward in his seat. "Listen, Mr. Vale. This

man, Mr. Seamus Reynard, is renowned for his ability to communicate facts and data quickly, comprehensively, and intelligently. I doubt his equal exists anywhere in the wider world."

"Is that so?"

"In my experience it is."

"A challenge, is it?"

"Call it what you want."

"Very well." The young man sat up straight in his seat and looked Ciarán in the eye. It was as if a different man stared back at him. "As the Queen's geneticist Lady Tabatha Aster is in charge of what is referred to as the 'Queen's Change Log', a complete list of genetic modifications performed on Charlotte Templeman since birth. The principal reason it is so difficult to identify the true Prince Rigel is that one needs to back out these changes for genetic comparison, which is quite easy if one possesses the change log. But nearly impossible without it. Note that only comparison to a genetic sample from a living Templeman relative under controlled circumstances may be accepted for purposes of determining lineage. It's simply too easy to fake results from a corpse, or hairs from a hairbrush, for example.

"Possession of the change log is important for another reason. With it one may tailor a selective toxin guaranteed to dispatch Queen Charlotte and no one else. We Columbia Stationers are dreadfully intermarried. One wouldn't want to miss and take out one's allies. Or oneself. Tabatha Aster has recently been blackmailed to deliver this change log to agents on Sizemore Station."

"Who—"

"Silence," Vale said. "The blackmailer's threat is this: That they will reveal that Lady Sarah Aster is not Lord Aster's daughter, nor even Lady Aster's daughter, but the Queen's. Tabatha Aster *created* Sarah Aster using the queen's genetic material and technology imported from the Ojinate. The Queen is unaware she has a daughter. The thought was, should anyone succeed in murdering Queen Charlotte, a true heir could be revealed. One young, ignorant, and malleable. One that could be *controlled*.

"This plot unraveled because of the most improbable series of events. Rigel Lambent, whom you have met, was raised since birth as a false Prince Rigel. He, like I, also nearly had Lord Aster fooled. So much so that the two began to associate. Rigel and Sarah became familiar, and friends, and perhaps more. But on the night before Rigel was to appear before the Queen for his genetic examination, Lord Aster received a call from an anonymous tipster. Rigel Lambent was a false Rigel and the caller knew where proof could be found. Rigel's lodgings were raided and the proof discovered. The caller was later determined to be..."

"You," Ciarán said.

"Hah. I wish. The caller proved to be Rigel Lambent himself. Lord Aster had the boy hunted down and made him the same offer he made me. The Guard or prison. Though in this case, not prison for Rigel but for the criminals that had raised him and taught him how to pass for a prince. Lord Aster remained troubled, and Sarah Aster as well. Why would Rigel Lambent, on the cusp of success, sabotage his own scheme?"

"Because the genetic test would reveal the lie," Ciarán said.

"That was what Sarah Aster believed as well. She felt extraordinarily betrayed. She had grown quite fond of Rigel Lambent and considered him a young man of character. You have met her as well, so you know she is as persistent as she is irritating. She managed to obtain Rigel Lambent's genetic examination results from Home Guard records and compared the results to those in her mother's files. What she discovered was that she was not the first to do so. The records had already been compared by..."

"You," Ciarán said.

"Hah. By Rigel Lambent himself. She then discovered that Rigel's record was not a match to the Queen's. But it matched another record. And no, that record was not mine. Sarah Aster had fallen in love with Rigel Lambent. Imagine her surprise to discover he was, not quite her brother, but close enough that tongues would wag and skins would crawl. Of course she confronted..."

"Her pretend mother," Ciarán said. "The woman who raised her.'

"An obvious and incorrect conclusion. She cornered Lord Aster and asked him to investigate. It turned out Lord Aster was as surprised as she was. That was three years ago, and it has taken that long for Lady Tabatha's conspirators to reveal themselves."

"By beginning to murder the Prince Rigels."

"Indeed. Lord Aster leaked the story that a true Prince Rigel had been found and hidden amongst the imposters. Queen Charlotte sits the throne because she is the only surviving Templeman. If there truly were a Prince Rigel, he would inherit the throne even if Queen Charlotte had an heir of the body."

"Lord Aster is the blackmailer."

"Correct. The meeting was set for today. There was to be a confrontation with Lady Tabatha, and she was to undeniably confirm the identities of those who plot with her."

"So Sarah Aster and Rigel Lambent share a father." Hector Poole, according to Sarah Aster.

"That would be a trick," Vale said, "since Sarah legally has no father. Lady Tabatha is quite vindictive. She blames Queen Charlotte for turning Prince Roman against her. She might have been Princess Tabatha if not for Charlotte Templeman. Lady Tabatha Aster did not weep when Roman and his commoner bride were murdered, and their infant child with them. Lady Tabatha has a perverse sense of humor. One she indulges. There may have been some of Poole's genetic material used in the project, but Sarah Aster is the Queen's daughter. And she is also the daughter of the Queen's oldest enemy and most public critic."

"I have no idea who that is," Ciarán said.

"It's immaterial. A peer and a starship jockey. Disgraced now, and reportedly reduced to training mercenary soldiers in some godforsaken backwater."

"Maris Solon."

"How surprising. You have heard of her. Perhaps you may also recall that she was captain of LRN *Defiant* for over a decade, a vessel whose synthetic intelligence is a composite entity named Nevin Green."

"The new Lord Varlock."

"The same. Lord Varlock esteems Maris Solon. He finds her... superior in all respects. He did wonder how she was getting on, so he inquired after her. It is such an oddly small world as one approaches its apex. One keeps rubbing shoulders with the same cast of characters."

"I'm still not clear on the relationship between Mr. Lambent and Sarah Aster."

"It's rather obvious isn't it? Rigel Lambent is Rigel Templeman. He is the missing heir. And Sarah Aster's 'parents' are also his aunt on her mother's side and his first cousin once removed on... err.. her other mother's side."

Peter Vale bowed from the waist while remaining seated, sweeping his arm out, as if swirling a cape, or broadcast sowing seeds, which was likely closer to the truth. He crossed his arms and leaned back in his seat. "Do I win?"

"How could Rigel Lambent be Rigel Templeman if his gene profile didn't match Queen Charlotte's? And how could it match Sarah Aster's and not Queen Charlotte's if Sarah Aster is Charlotte's daughter?" Ciarán chuckled. "And I think I've just answered my own question."

"Because the Queen's profile in Lady Tabitha's files was a

fiction," Prince said. "One designed to obscure Sarah's relationship to the queen. As you have now deduced."

"Where is this 'Queen's Change Log' now?"

"I'm not certain. Lady Tabatha was reluctant to hand it over. Once I convinced her to do so someone hit me over the head. When I recovered my senses it was missing."

"Did you get a look at this someone?"

"I didn't. The cabin went suddenly dark an instant before I was attacked. It might be anyone."

"You haven't told me who these secret allies of Lady Tabatha are. Or what your Lord Varlock expects me to do with all this information."

"Lord Varlock wishes you to shelter Rigel and Sarah. To keep their true identities secret and protect them from their enemies. In particular, they ask you protect them and keep them far from Lady Tabatha's fellow plotters."

"Who are?"

"Synthetic intelligences opposed to Lord Varlock. They call themselves Abyss Tower."

"Do they? You have proof of all this, of course."

"No. Not with me. Lord Varlock expected you would have doubts. He is forwarding proof. It will be waiting for us at Llassöe. I have the name of Lord Varlock's local agent. A Mr. Luther Gant. Maris Solon recommended him."

"That's fortunate he has a man way out there. It's hard to find good help."

It was even harder finding somewhere to dispose of a body. It was often easier to simply find a way to convince the body to take a one-way trip to someplace distant and then pay them to stay there. Ciarán knew Luther Gant. He was an entirely unsatisfactory neighbor. He was also entirely coin operated. Which could be good or bad, depending.

"The nature of this proof?"

"Your guess is as good as mine."

"Do Lady Sarah and Mr. Lambent know your true identity, Mr. Vale?"

"It is unlikely. It's best I remain Teo Prince for a while longer."

"And Lady Tabatha? And yourself? Does Lord Varlock have an opinion on what I should do with the pair of you?"

"I can look after myself." He leaned forward in his seat and looked Ciarán in the eye. "As for Lady Tabatha? We have a tradition in the League when it comes to traitors."

"You hang them."

Mr. Vale nodded, and then Mr. Prince was back, a false grin pasted across his false face. "In order for a moral code to be practical it must be simple, Mr. mac Diarmuid. Simple, and consistently applied."

64

In order to convince the ship's minder to agree to moving the FFE to the boat bay, Ciarán had to agree to perform an in-person inspection of the contents. He dragooned Aspen into the job of opening the container and followed her inside. The container wasn't anything special. It had racks mounted from deck to deckhead with a narrow walkway in between. On these racks were oversized cryo chambers; tall and thin models designed to accommodate Huangxu Eng. Some still had old bills of lading pasted to them. Used but in good condition, they all seemed in working order, with their contents intact.

"Do they have a leader?" Ciarán asked.

"Here." Aspen pointed.

"Let's get her on a lift plate."

"I thought we were just doing an inspection."

"I am. A thorough one."

They managed to get the cryo chamber free and shifted along the hull to the boat bay via lift plate.

"Merchant Captain," the ship's minder said.

Ciarán chuckled. "I am here."

"What part of 'in a container and in cryogenic stasis' did I not explain?"

"I'm transferring the chamber to the longboat. I want Wisp with us when we open it."

"You could simply put it back."

"I could." But he wasn't going to.

"We are in an active war zone," the ship's minder said.

Ciarán glanced at Aspen. "Do you know how to operate a longboat?"

"I know how to move one from a family ship boat bay to a repair cradle."

"Good, you're elected pilot." All he wanted was the longboat backed out with them and the second-genner aboard. If the second-genner went berserk or did something else hazardous when they woke her, she wouldn't provoke a reaction from the ship's minder and its spidery adjuncts.

Aspen was a slow and steady boat handler. Soon the long-boat hung a few meters outside the hull. He decided it was a hardsuit on, helmet off sort of occasion and Aspen agreed. Wisp seemed entirely uninterested. Longboats had viewing ports, so she spent her time gazing out.

"Have you ever done this before?" Ciarán asked. "Opened a cryo pod?"

"Seriously?" Aspen snorted. "I grew up in a bioweapons lab."

"These are people."

"These are weapons, Ciarán. Never forget that."

"Do you think I'm making a mistake?"

"Yes. I do."

"Would you like me to stop?"

"No. I agree. It has to be done. They are weapons and they are people. Ethically we have to treat them as we would wish to be treated. But they are weapons."

"Handle with care. One phrase, two meanings," Ciarán said.

"You know a fellow once told me that a good moral code was simple and consistently applied."

"At one time I would have agreed," Aspen said. "But 'kill them all' lost some of its charm once I discovered I hadn't met them all. That there were other people out there that weren't trying to kill *us* all."

"Or force you to kill others for them," Ciarán said. "Do you know this person inside?"

"Yes. She's called One Eye."

"Because she only has one eye?"

Aspen laughed. "Because those are the last two digits of her serial number. Do you know how many rebels in a slave revolt end up with one eye?"

"More than one, I take it."

"More than one." Aspen began to operate the chamber's control. "Do you have your clicker?"

Ciarán stomped his foot and used the handheld clicker to clack out the word for affirmative. That was one of twenty or so common click-words he knew, the rest being related to running, hiding, and ducking. He knew one word for climbing and one word for looking as well as the words for the cardinal directions. He knew the word for ice and the word for just and a couple more. So maybe more than twenty, because he'd forgotten that Lorelei had asked him to teach her, and he'd had to learn the soundalike words for proper names.

"You're going to do the talking I hope," Ciarán said.

"Most of it. I'll teach you her name and a simple greeting while we wait for the chamber to cycle."

He had an Academy-trained memory, but communicating more complicated concepts in the language relied on measured control of the clicks' duration, volume, and rest time between clicks, as well as a good ear to discriminate those fine details. He might in time become fluent, but he would have to live in a community of Contract system natives to achieve true mastery.

By the time the cryo chamber finished its decantation cycle and popped the seal, he could say "Hello, One Eye. I am Small Dark." Like in hand cant, proper names were difficult. They couldn't figure out together how to say Ciarán and he already had one person aboard calling him "Care N" and he didn't need another.

A disturbing thought percolated up into his brain. "Is she naked in there?"

"Utilities," Aspen said. "And a campaign cloak as padding beneath her."

"Are the chambers custom made to fit?"

"You'll see."

What looked like a gleaming black blade peeked out from beneath the lid of the chamber. The cryo chamber really did look like a sarcophagus, they all did. There was no way of getting around that. The black blade shimmered with the sort of sheen a beetle's wing did, fluttering, elongating, widening, until it seemed to shred into four shards the length of it, the shards arcing and spreading until, in his mind, the idea settled in that it wasn't a blade, or a wing, but the thin fingers of a narrow hand. One gripping the edge of the sarcophagus, the thumb remaining inside the chamber.

He hadn't expected the second-genner to be black. He'd figured milky white, like Aspen and her daughters and the first-genners. And he had prepared himself for the worst. Adderly and Aspen were vaguely reptilian in features. Aspen's children, while quite pleasant once one knew them, seemed designed physically to invoke nightmares. The first-genners, as well, were enormous gut-watering gargoyles of fierce appearance, who, if they'd been able to coordinate together in a fight, would have torn him limb from limb with their horned and scaled talons, or shredded him with their jutting fangs. The Outsider they were modeled after was a nightmare beast, insectile in appearance, not like a beetle but like a leaf-winged walking stick crossed with a praying mantis: twice as tall as a man, weeping and spitting acid, scythes where hands should be, clacking mandibles for a mouth. The similarities between them all, the milky-white scales like dull diamonds, the flat planes of their features, the horns, spikes, and slashing blades inherited from the Outsider, were combined to varying degrees in each. He didn't feel fear, not like others, but he felt disgust, and through merchant skill alone could he keep that emotion from his face.

The sarcophagus lid swung open. Golden eyes set wide in a midnight face observed him and moved on. To Aspen. And back.

A drum of four thumps sounded. One Eye's gaze darted toward the sound as Wisp landed beside Ciarán. And purred.

It was over then, the second-genner's interest in anyone or anything else in sight. It began to lever itself from the cryo chamber with slow-motion, serpentine grace. Beneath stained and torn Huangxu Eng utilities, loose fitting, red, and patterned with gold imperial lions, the second-genner appeared utterly and positively black. As black as space. And finely scaled like Aspen and her kin. Iridescent when he'd first seen her, but flat black now. A black that, like *Impossibly Alien*'s hull, seemed to absorb light rather than reflect it.

Ciarán tapped his hullwalkers and clicked out his introduction.

"Hello, One Eye. I am Small Dark."

The second-genner ignored him. It stepped silently from the cryo chamber, moving slowly, cautiously, silently. Standing upright it was a good head taller than him, even without counting the midnight forked horns... or spines, or antennae, or whatever one might call them... that swept back from its forehead like a thick unruly mane. One thick black whisker or feeler grew from each side of her face like a mustache drooping, framing a face itself which wasn't so nearly human-seeming as Aspen's. More like an animal's with a muzzle, one whose lower jaw lay fringed with feathery spines and whose fangs, when she began to smile, shone like jagged diamonds, milky white and uncannily similar to Wisp's.

If he were asked to sum up her appearance he could do so quite easily. One Eye precisely matched his mental image of the ship's minder. A black dragon in the Ojin style wedded to a sinuous human frame. One did not know what to expect. But one could read at a glance the message written on that resting face. *Tread lightly, mortal.*

Ciarán glanced at Aspen. "Had the project hired an Ojin designer?"

"Olek provided one. When he began to collaborate with the lab."

He'd started to ask her about Olek when Wisp launched herself at the second-genner.

Ciarán lunged after Wisp and Aspen slammed him aside as cat and dragon-woman warred in a tumbling, clicking, thumping ball of flashing talons and slashing fangs. Ciarán reached for his overseer's rod only to recall he'd left it behind as a show of trust. Not that he had any chance of separating them. They slammed the length of the longboat, bounced off the aft bulkhead, and unknotted, the second-genner teetering on its feet, Wisp, clinging, upside down, from the overhead conduit race. She dropped to the deck, ears forward, tail held high, dancing away as the second-genner swung to grip her and caught nothing but air.

Wisp clicked her claws against the deck.

Ciarán glanced at Aspen.

"Lady Justice for the win," Aspen said.

Wisp clicked again.

Aspen chuckled. "Bring it, fish breath."

"They're playing?"

One Eye clicked.

"Later," Aspen said. "When you are older and slower."

The second-genner clicked again.

"Or when you are sleeping," Aspen said.

"Oh," Ciarán said. "I think it said my name."

"Small dark is what we call sleeping," Aspen said.

"So you taught me to say, 'Hello. I am sleeping.'"

"You said that was what your name meant."

"Physically small. And black-haired."

"You're neither."

"I'm not sleeping, either."

"Don't blame me. Blame whoever gave you that stupid name."

The second-genner turned its attention to Aspen. It clicked.

"Something dark," Ciarán said.

"Where is the big dark?" Aspen said. She clicked a response and pointed out a portside viewport.

The second-genner seemed to flow at blinding speed toward the viewport. It settled into the seat and clicked.

"Outside," Ciarán said. "On something."

"On the vessel." Aspen retrieved One Eye's campaign cloak and wrapped it around the second-genner's shoulders. The cloak was torn and stained with dried blood. Human blood, he had to remind himself. *Judge as you wish to be judged.*

Wisp hopped into the seat next to One Eye.

The second-genner absently stroked Wisp's brow.

"Death is on the vessel," Ciarán said.

"Yes. The big dark is death." Aspen sighed. "We taught them our language. And they made it their own."

"Do you truly believe that? That we crew a vessel alongside death?"

"I don't believe it," Aspen said. "I know it." She turned her back on him and began to tidy the cryo chamber. "Death is what our sisters call themselves. When they are together as one. We should finish here and return her to the others."

"These second-genners refer to themselves as death?"

"They refer to themselves as we do. With designations applied at birth. They refer to their *unit* with the name it was given."

"Given by your leaders. In the rebellion."

"Given by our makers. Once they comprehended what they had wrought." She glanced up from her work to eye him. "We are done with masters."

"You are quite fell to gaze upon," Ciarán said. That was what Adderly claimed their makers had said when first they examined their finished handiwork.

Aspen bared her claws. "Then look away."

And that was what Adderly had replied, or so the story went. He believed that story was a true seanscéal of their people, because it stated a universal truth regardless of the facts it claimed. So long as there were *strangers*. Were *others*. That story could pass from mouth, to ear, to heart, and not once be a lie.

"I will not look away." Ciarán said. When he glanced at the second-genner he found it watching.

It clicked something and Aspen clicked back, sharply. She returned to her work with a vengeance. They clicked at each other furiously for a good ten minutes. Ciarán couldn't follow any of it. When they were done neither of them looked happy. They embraced one another stiffly.

One Eye lowered herself into the cryo chamber, folding to fit. She gazed upon Ciarán with golden eyes. If he had not known she was human he would have judged her alien, or some sort of ancient god. She held his gaze until the lid settled and sealed.

Aspen remained silent until the longboat rested in the boat bay. She reached for the lift sled's control. He caught her wrist. "Leave it."

"Sxipestro," Ciarán said, releasing her wrist.

"I am here."

"Have you reviewed the record from the longboat?"

"I have."

"And?"

"And we are in agreement."

"Very well." He unsnapped his helmet from his hardsuit's tether. "Suit up."

"Why?" Aspen said.

"We're taking that FFE off the mast."

"I knew it."

"Clearly you didn't." Ciarán pointed at the empty space forward of the hull. "You've parked in the way."

"Oh." Aspen stared at him. "Oh!" Her gaze darted to her hullwalkers and back. She looked him in the eye before glancing away. "I believe you, brother."

Ciarán grinned. "That's good."

"You misunderstand," Aspen said. "That is what One Eye said."

Ciarán thought about the final exchange of words between the pair before speaking. "Then you are a fool, sister."

"You heard my reply," Aspen said. "And understood it."

"I didn't need to," Ciarán said. "I have siblings. I recall the tone of their words. The expressions they wear. They are also people."

She studied her hullwalkers. "I am informed."

"Aspen. Look at me."

She looked.

"*I* am quite fell to gaze upon," Ciarán said.

"No. It's not that." She kicked the deck. "It's that nothing has changed. *I* have not changed. And I hate you for it. Hate you for this compulsion."

"To disobey my orders," Ciarán said. "To *battle* me."

"Worse. To *please* you."

"Because you are done with masters." He wondered if there

existed a click-speak word for friend. And, if there was, had Aspen ever had opportunity to use it.

"Damn you." She stalked away. "Where's my helmet?"

"On its tether."

She glanced down at the helmet dangling from her breast-plate. "Oh. Damn it all! Get out. I'm moving the longboat."

Ciarán got out, Wisp trotting beside him.

"Keep up this end of the hull," Ciarán told the big cat. "She's liable to light the main drive up just to fry me."

Wisp glanced behind her before thumping him with her tail and tapping her claws against the deck.

Run!

"Funny," he said, but he ran anyway, just in case the ship's cat wasn't joking.

65

Ciarán had not fully comprehended the true nature of the second-genners until he witnessed them dance the Masque of Death.

They jumped naked into space, balling together like snakes. They were sinuous, able to survive and propel themselves in vacuum. Aspen didn't know how they could do that, but the Outsider could, so the engineers knew it was possible. They simply experimented on her people until they could reproduce the effect. Witnessed in the visible spectrum the second-genners' motive power seemed related to the effect the assembler/disassemblers used for motion, appearing cloudy and shot through with red sparks.

"It's thought to be a field effect," Aspen said. "One generated in their muscles like current in an electric eel's."

Ciarán didn't know about that. There was a big difference between running a shock current through flesh and moving about and changing direction in free space. But seeing was believing, and he had no choice but to believe his eyes. It was true, the Outsiders could do the same. So it wasn't impossible. It irritated him that, instead of spending their time making a weapon, the engineers hadn't spent more time trying to figure out the engine behind the Outsider's powers. If they could make people with those capabilities, they ought to be able to make kit to do the same. It would be nice not to have to wear a hardsuit out on the hull, or a skinsuit and rebreather with the constant worry of being holed by debris too small to visually identify in time. It appeared that the second-genners produced their own sort of field-generated impact shielding. He'd touched them during their time together, and their flesh seemed nearly as yielding as his own.

For the demonstration Ciarán and Aspen positioned themselves inside the second-genner's now empty FFE. Ciarán parked the self-powered container a kilometer outside the hull. He lashed a second-epoch shuttle inside, its stay-put field holding it stable in the center of the container. He sat at the controls, Aspen in the first officer's seat behind him. They would be isolated from whatever happened during the demonstration and they didn't have to spend hours in hardsuits during the exercise.

Aspen had rigged up a series of displays linked to sensors on *Impossibly Alien* and on the FFE. They'd watched the second-genners exit the FFE, but then they'd seemed to disappear into the blackness of space. Aspen cycled through the sensors, mapping their outputs onto the displays one after another. The second-genners didn't even register on infrared. They weren't cold-blooded, else they'd be dead the instant they stepped outside, but they were somehow shielding their heat signatures just as Wisp could. It was as if every stealth system imaginable had been incorporated into their very beings. They could move through free space unaided. They could survive in free space without suit or breathing apparatus. They could do so while invisible to shipboard sensors.

Ciarán glanced up from the display as a finger tapped on the shuttle's canopy.

One Eye's bright gold eyes stared back at him. She winked, and then made the hand sign for his name. *Small Dark.* She pointed at him and placed her hands palm to palm beside her cheek, tilting her head. The universal gesture for napping.

The others were following her inside, squeezing through the narrow slit she'd sliced in the FFE's hull barehanded. He watched as Jay Eight widened the hull breach with the edge of her hand. It took less than sixty seconds for all sixty of the second-genners to work their way into the FFE without once touching the hatch controls. Five Effie and Four Effie knelt down on either side of the shuttle and begin to slice through the container's skin. Seven Em disappeared behind the hull. One Eye stood before the tiny vessel, and when the others joined her, stooped, and ran the edge of her stiffened hand across the deck. When she stood it seemed as if nothing had happened. Until she and the others stepped forward, ringed the vessel, and did what Ciarán thought of as *pushing off*, though with the cloudy, red sparking field, which in vacuum seemed less like a hazy cloud and more like a penumbra limning their bodies.

The shuttle seemed to drop away from the FFE as the Sisters kicked the severed section of hull away, sending it spinning outbound, away from *Impossibly Alien*. One Eye clung to the shuttle's hull, one handed. Five Effie grasped One Eye's free wrist and tapped on the canopy with her empty hand. She made the universal gesture for take us home, before reaching back and clasping hands with her sister.

Ciarán towed them back to the vessel and into the boat bay without engaging the shuttle's impact shielding, concerned that the field powering up might sever One Eye's arm. The second-genners were already dressing by the time he had the canopy open and both he and Aspen had clambered out.

Jay Eight thumped and clicked at him, the rest of them making the laughing sound.

"Sleepdriver," Aspen said. "It's a mild insult."

"Like slowpoke."

"The same. They like a good tug. If you'd have come back under decent thrust, they would have pushed off and been dressed, ranked, and been waiting for you by the time you cleared the boat bay force window. That's something the FFE experiment couldn't demonstrate. The active impact shielding on a vessel is far superior to that of an FFE."

"And it wouldn't have slowed them down."

"They would have appeared to have stepped right through it."

"They do know they could name their price in any military."

"They have named their price." Aspen toed his hullwalker, gazing at the deck. She glanced up at him. "You have met it."

"Do you have a price?" Ciarán asked.

"Everyone does."

"If you state it plainly, I'll see if I can meet it."

"There is nothing you can say that will meet my price."

"Is there anything I can do?"

"You can keep with your own kind and leave us alone."

She turned and stalked away, helmet dangling.

66

By the time *Durable* transited for Llassöe, and they followed shortly after, the war in Sizemore system had burned to a smoulder. The superluminal nodes were destroyed. The Home Guard and Crown Ministry sections of Sizemore Station had been blown out and gutted. An artificial moon had been holed and devoured by self-replicating machines; but surprisingly, the fleet shipyards remained intact. Ciarán wondered if that might be the next stop for the self-replicating machines. He imagined the fabric of a starship tasted much like the fabric of an artificial moon.

"Engage," Swan said, and Ciarán, now sitting the pilot's seat, said, "Engaging, sir," and pressed a stud on the piloting console. The now familiar roiling in his stomach began and receded. "We are in imaginary space," Ciarán said. "Arrival in Llassöe system in forty-five days, nineteen hours, and fifty-three minutes."

Durable would make the transit in three days less, which was still an extraordinarily long transit for a Templeman-drive vessel. Llassöe lay nearly the breadth of the League distant in normal space.

The bridge crew monitored the controls for a few more hours before turning over control to the ship. They would still monitor the vessel, one person at a time sitting watch, but the only risks for the next month and a half were from shipboard failures. Ciarán could feel the pressure drop on the bridge.

"You have first watch, Pilot," Swan said.

"That's grand," Ciarán said. "I have the watch, sir."

"Don't touch anything," Maura said as she rose from the navigation station.

Ko Shan kicked the full sensor rig dead and waited for the goop to drain.

Ship's Captain Swan stood and stretched. "I'm going to go wash the stink of Sizemore off me."

Ciarán sat and watched the main display. He needed a plan. There were enough pieces in motion now that a way forward would emerge. They didn't need to win. All they needed to do was survive Llassöe with enough momentum to keep moving forward. He had forty-five days to whip the ship and crew into shape. To forge a jumble of cutlery into a single blade; one, not just with a keen edge, but with a grip by which to wield it. It was all to be imagined before done. All but one task.

67

He placed his feet flat on the deck and gazed about the empty bridge. The name of the vessel stood emblazoned in text half a meter tall on the compartment bulkhead behind him, ancient script, gold on black. The date of first service and port of record were marked in smaller text below: 16 June 3416 ER, Templeman Station, Columbia. *Impossibly Alien.*

Someone had painted through Impossibly with a brushstroke the color of blood, dabbing in *Quite Possibly* above the stricken text. The crimson letters had dripped as they dried, three hand spans tall. He had found that sight more disturbing than anything he could recall when he first saw it. He hadn't understood that feeling then, but it gnawed at him. It wasn't until much later that he realized it wasn't the meaning of the words or their shape, but the feeling of betrayal they represented. That he'd imagined a world of wonder, full of miracles and giants, and instead there was this. Graffiti scrawled across the face of a masterpiece, and a world, not of giants and wonders, but of diminishment and smirking and mockery. A history not painted and plastered over, but revised and amended. One attempting to erase the legacy of titans while surviving off the remains of their passing.

He left the bridge, took the two steps to the merchant's day cabin, and returned with the tools he'd inherited.

From his father: elbow grease and sweat. From his mother: vinegar and abrasives. The salt water he could supply himself. When one combined them, they made a potent cocktail; one that, applied with enough friction, could tackle the toughest jobs.

A restoration was entirely beyond his skill.

A cleaning would have to do.

When he was finished, he stepped back and surveyed his handiwork.

"Well?" Ciarán said.

"Nicely done," the ship said.

"It will do," the ship's minder grumbled.

He returned his cleaning supplies to the merchant's day cabin, flushing the blood-colored runoff down the compartment's recycler before returning to the bridge.

There was yet work to do, days of work, brain-wracking, muscle-straining work. Forty-five days of toil and sleepless nights.

But now he had clarity.

And allies.

And a place to stand.

Not to mention a one-banner empire and a motto to go along with it.

Impossibly Alien.

We do not come in peace.

We will not leave without a fight.

68

Ciarán was on his way to an unpleasant interview with Lady Tabatha Aster when he noticed the anomaly above Mr. Prince's door. Prince had attached a placard above his compartment hatch—one made of hull plate with words carved deeply into its surface. Sic Semper Tyrannis —Mr. Prince's official motto.

Ciarán banged on the hatch.

Prince answered immediately. He was dressed in his de-badged Home Guard utilities. They were food stained, and it didn't look like he'd taken them off in days. He had a reek on him, the whole compartment as well. They might have to do a hose out rather than a refreshing once the man moved on.

He had some sort of technological-looking headgear on, a magnifying lens above one eye, the other bare. Bright lights shone from the device's periphery.

"Enter, tyrant," Prince said, stepping clear of the hatch.

Prince had somehow procured a workstation and a proto-typing bench.

"Where did you get this equipment?"

"There's a vast number of unused compartments on this vessel," Prince said. "Would you believe they aren't all locked?"

"I wouldn't believe that for a second."

"Would you believe I asked Engineer Hess to loan the equipment to me?"

Ciarán pulled out his handheld and texted Aspen.

Prince. Did Hess leave orders to give him kit?

Didn't. Ship said to.

Could have asked me.

Ship said not to.

Ta.

Ta.

"Why don't you simply hail him?" Prince said. "Ship," Prince said.

"I am here."

"Did Engineer Hess loan this equipment to me?"

"He did not," the ship said.

"That's why," Ciarán said. "Ship, is Mr. Prince a danger to the ship and crew?"

"Not at the moment."

"Is the workstation in this compartment isolated from the ship's systems?"

"It is isolated and incompatible. It will self-destruct quite forcefully if tampered with in any way."

"How forcefully?"

"You would not wish to be near it."

"Mr. Prince was getting on your nerves."

"I don't have nerves," the ship said. "But Engineer Hess does."

"Thank you, ship."

"Merchant Captain."

Ciarán pocketed his handheld. "What are you working on, Mr. Prince?"

"This assembler/disassembler. It's safe to experiment with,

according to Mr. Hess, but it's also quite fascinating. I didn't know such a marvel could exist. And then we ruptured an entire hidden moon full of the devices. Hidden, not in some backwater, but in the heart of the largest military installation in League space. I wanted to know more about it. I *need* to know more about it."

Ciarán stepped lightly around the debris field scattered about the compartment. Empty ration tubes, empty juice bulbs, takeaway wrappers from the commissary vending units. At the rate he was going through snack items, they wouldn't make it to Llassöe before breaking out the hardtack or refilling the machines from the stores strapped to the mast.

"What have you learned?"

"Virtually nothing. It's vexing. I mean, I did discover how to get it to make the plaque above my hatch, but as to how it works at a deeper level? I am not easily thwarted, Mr. mac Diarmuid. It is vexing. Vexing, I say."

"I suppose if you were to jack in you might make progress."

"It's an isolated system. And how did you know—?"

"You share personality characteristics with some people I used to know. Librarians."

"Yes, well, there aren't many of those around anymore."

"True." Now that the mac Donnacha clan had been wiped out there was only Seamus left. And he'd barely recognized Seamus the last time he'd seen him. No doubt though, he and Mr. Prince shared a trade. With Prince's utilities wrinkled and baggy, Ciarán could see the research librarian jack at the base of Mr. Prince's neck. If he hadn't known Seamus he would have assumed it was a full immersion sensor interface. "I only know of one."

"Two," Mr. Prince said. "I mentioned earlier that my father was unsuitable for the role of Lord Varlock, as am I. Our part of the family functions, for want of a better phrase, as information brokers. A few years back it was determined that certain information desired to be freer than those in power wished it to be. Henceforth we have been pariahs."

"You're whistleblowers?"

"Whistle merchants, you might say. The thought was that the value of information is a function, not simply of its utility, but of its price. Expensive revelations travel faster and farther than cheap news. When my father was found out and his sources dried up the family experienced cash flow problems. We were sitting on top of some very valuable information, however. It just couldn't be utilized without the appropriate mechanisms in place."

"So, you became Teo Prince, the long-lost Prince Rigel Templeman."

"We knew every intimate detail of the child prince's short but eventful life. Of his parents' lives. Of their parents. Friends. Relatives. Enemies. And that entertainment franchise. They were getting it *all wrong*. When we approached them with an offer of *true facts* they weren't interested. No one cares about facts, they said. Unless they are prurient."

"Were they prurient?"

"Not in the least. Prince Roman was a decent man. His only sin was that he married for love. They offered to pay for *invented facts*, they called them. So long as we could provide *invented proof*."

"You refused."

"Prince Roman was my father's best friend. When Roman was murdered it fractured his psyche. But that is beside the point. The point is, I was able to fool Lord Aster because of that deep pool of knowledge. It was the only way I could think of to monetize what we knew."

"What did your father think of that?"

"I didn't tell him. He detests Lionel Aster."

"I doubt you fooled Lord Aster. He is the money behind the entertainment franchise. There's a good chance he knew the truth all along and was deceiving you."

"What? That's dishonest," Mr. Prince said.

"You don't sound surprised."

"Everything is easier to see in retrospect," Mr. Prince said. "It was a game. A lark. A last grasp for the brass ring before the plummet toward the poorhouse. We really do exist on the fringes of polite society. We wouldn't be missed because we'd never been noticed in the first place, except by Roman Templeman, and he is dust."

"I'm sorry it didn't work out for you."

"I'm not. I appear to have died in action. My death benefits will last my father a long time. And combined with my tax-free income from Lord Varlock? We really don't live much in the physical world, you know. Our expenses are low. And despite the outcome I really am good at my job. If you were to allow me to interface with—"

"Maybe on Llassöe Station, but not on this vessel. I believe you when you say you're good at your work. You're likely better at it than you're letting on. And I can't risk it."

"It was worth the attempt."

"If you say so. Now about the device?"

"It is opaque. Unlike anything I've seen before. Except. It's been hacked, and there's a configuration file for the hack. I doubt whoever did the hack had much more knowledge of the device than I do. They simply had more time to examine it."

"You made it carve different text."

"Not just that. I made it carve in a different material. And I made it carve the text deeper. There are a number of variables one can set in this configuration file. I might even be able to work around its non-replication bug given enough time."

"Don't do that."

"I don't intend to. But I wanted you to know. I might be able to make more of them if you liked."

"We can make as many of them as we want in a macrofab."

"Not without destroying this one in the process."

"So?"

"So I'm not done with it yet."

"And you'd rather I didn't take away your precious."

"I'd rather you take it away after I'm done with it."

"When will that be?"

"A couple hours. A couple days. A couple weeks. Who can say?"

Ciarán could say. It worked on Seamus, anyway, giving him a deadline. Without one he'd never stop playing with his toys. It was worth a try on Mr. Prince.

"You have precisely seven hours, thirteen minutes and nine seconds from this instant, Mr. Prince."

"What? No. I can't possibly be done by then."

"Nevertheless that is the time you have. Synchronize chronometers, Mr. Prince. On my mark."

"Wait." Prince raced to the workstation. Entered some commands. "Ready."

"Mark. Now get to work."

"You're not the boss of me."

"Glad to know it. Seven hours, Mr. Prince. Seven hours and—"

"I know, I know. Get out. Get out!"

Ciarán retreated into the corridor, closing the hatch behind him.

"Ship," Ciarán said.

"I am here."

"I'm assuming you and the ship's minder both agree on Mr. Prince's threat level."

"We share a common data pool."

"Spoken like a Freeman. Am I going to have to contact the ship's minder?"

"There is no need. We haven't discussed Mr. Prince. But I do have access to his security assessment."

"And? What does the assessment say?"

"If he asks for rope give it to him."

"I'm not letting him jack into our systems."

"To do so would provide no benefit until we're in Llassöe space. He needs access to a superluminal node and/or local datasets."

"Even then, I'm not inclined."

"Hence the rope," the ship said. "One imagines a clever man like Mister Prince will fashion the noose himself."

"You really don't like him."

"I am indifferent to him. But he annoys my engineer, Merchant Captain. And I am not indifferent to Mr. Hess."

"I am informed. How is Aspen working out in his absence?"

"She is marginally qualified. Mr. Prince could easily confuse or deceive her."

"Hence the toys for Mr. Prince."

"And the puzzle."

"Got it. Good work."

"Merchant Captain."

69

Thirty-one days into their superluminal transit, Sarah Aster broke Ciarán mac Diarmuid's nose.

Ciarán lay writhing on the exercise compartment deck, Sarah Aster towering over him. He struggled to his hands and knees and shook his head to clear it, blood splattering. "Hand me a towel," he said, and said it again while she stood there staring. He made it to his feet. "I'll get it myself."

It hurt like the devil, the nose, but it wasn't the first time. Just the first time with her. She'd put him down hard and it surprised them both. He tossed her a towel and she caught it. "Clean that up."

"I'm calling Natsuko," she said.

"Do whatever you want. But clean up that mess. Ow." There was an autodoc in the exercise room; the one he'd 'liberated' on Gallarus. He eyed its control panel before deciding it was better to wait for Natsuko and her medkit than to mess with the miracle machine. They were designed so that if you could pull yourself in one-handed or wedge yourself in one legged, and you could close the lid afterwards it would try to save you. Or, if it couldn't, it would hold you in stasis until you could get real medical help. The fact was, an autodoc could fix just about any malady you could encounter on a starship, but once you were inside, it might run hours of tests searching for undiagnosed conditions. Even if he was entirely healthy other than the broken nose, he might be in there for the better part of a day unless he was manually ejected, and Natsuko wouldn't do that except in a triage situation.

He plopped down onto the long bench beside the compartment hatch and leaned his head back, towel pressed to his face. He wished they had ice. At home he would use ice.

They sparred every day, freefall training followed by a high gravity workout, and she'd progressed immensely from an already high level of competence. He had size and reach on her, and after training with Mrs. Amati he knew every dirty trick in the book and had the stamina to pull them off. He hadn't known it at the time, but he'd trained with an experienced master in hand-to-hand, and it wasn't arrogant to say that he was now not only difficult to kill but difficult to touch. Sarah Aster had nailed him a good one, and it hurt when he smiled. "The bots can get the rest. Come sit down."

She sat down beside him.

"I like your silence," he said. "It makes me proud of you."

"You're not angry with me?"

"The opposite. You have no idea how long I had to train to do what you just did. There was a full year when all I did was get beaten senseless, unless I was shot with a blowgun dart that put me in a medically induced coma."

She chuckled. "I think not."

"It's the truth. Not only was I a clumsy planetary oaf, but a... fundamentalist, I guess you'd say. I'd been raised that men didn't hit women. That and the Oath held me back."

"Most of the Freemen I've met are women."

"Spaceborn Freemen. The ratio is more balanced on the surface. And the range of acceptable behavior is wider. My mother was a fighter, but she was the exception. Everyone has guns and knows how to use them. Any man inclined to hit a woman was likely to end up dead. On the family ships, men and women tend to mass about the same. I'm the runt of the litter, and I could bench press three of any woman in the neighborhood excepting Bridget One. So fistfights tend to be between men and men or women and their children."

"You're joking."

"I am, about the women and children. The Oath discourages fighting of all kinds, and our customary way of settling disputes is with community courts and cash payments. There's no criminal law."

"Even for murder?"

"That's different only in the payment demanded. That's why there's so little fighting. There's no consideration of motive or emotional state or even purposeful intent or accident. If you kill someone, you're likely to get killed yourself. That, or your family has to pay the harmed party's family the amount the deceased might have made in their lifetime."

"And if they can't pay?"

"They can pay. Each family elects a person as matchmaker. The matchmakers work out an arrangement that is agreeable. It's not open for discussion afterwards. But we're getting far afield here. My point is that the entire culture I grew up in isn't so much pacifist as retributionist. You can't hit first but you can hit back."

"Sometimes you have to hit first."

"We're playing a game. So it's allowed. I wasn't much into sport as a boy, so I had to learn that up here too."

"It's a miracle you survived."

"That's what I thought. But over time it became clear to me. It would be a wonder if any of us survived if I didn't pull my weight. And just because I learned a skill didn't mean I had to use it. I learned calculus and can't remember the last time I calculated the area under a curve. Just because I knew how to rip a man's arm off and beat him to death with it didn't mean I had to. But if there ever came a time when a man aimed a gun at my crew, and I didn't know how to stop him? And I could have known, if I'd applied myself? That would be the same as if I'd pulled the trigger myself."

"And so you worked at it."

"Not at first. But then I discovered there's a side effect I hadn't anticipated. If you had to fight anyone on the vessel, one on one, who would you be most afraid of?"

"One Eye," she said. "Or any of the dragon ladies."

"Anyone besides the genetically engineered killing machines."

"You."

"That's why you're training with me?"

"Go big or go home."

"That's funny. And it's admirable. It's why I hated and loved training with Mrs. Amati. Early on I decided if I could beat her, I could beat anybody."

"She isn't available."

"Carlsbad isn't either."

"That guy? No thanks."

"Why not?"

She glanced at him. "Because he'd kill me."

"That is the side effect I'm talking about. And today was the first time I saw it in your eyes. The certainty that you could take me down. And for just one instant..."

"You froze."

"I couldn't very well run away. You were standing between me and the hatch."

She laughed. "You're not at all like I imagined."

"I'm better."

"I wouldn't say that. I thought you'd be a tough guy. A hard ass. Hector is. Lionel is. All of Lord Aster's people are. I understand them."

"We're in the shorthand world. I don't need to be a tough guy. But out there, in the longhand world? I don't want to be. But I know how to be. And now so do you."

"It was one lucky punch."

"That's a lie."

"You're right."

She sat there for a while thinking about it.

"Tell me about this Freeman Oath."

He told her.

She said, "That's it? That's what makes someone a Freeman? What about the waking of the dead, and all these strange customs?"

He explained about the history of the Freeman, and how the customs developed. That they were often corollaries of the Oath that didn't seem obvious on the surface, or they were simply customs that make it easier for people that had nothing in common but the Oath to live together.

"That's all it is, saying some words?"

"That and living them. It's harder than you imagine."

She was silent for a long while. When she did speak it was in a whisper, as if speaking to herself. "I have no idea how oaths work."

"The common problem with the oaths," Ciarán said. "Is that they're written backwards."

She glanced at him.

"It's something my dad used to say, whenever I wanted to take the easy path."

"I don't understand."

"I didn't either. The Freeman Oath isn't any different than any other true oath. It's a contract one signs, not with others, but with oneself."

"And if you breach that contract?" she said.

"The only person you're cheating is yourself."

"But you could cheat others. If you wanted to."

"For a while, but we're a small society. Small enough that everyone knows someone who knows someone. And while we don't raise the dead, we know how to read a face. I've heard that you people say the eyes are the windows to the soul. For us they are not a window, but a mirror, and the tally of all deeds. That's why the Oath is said to be written backwards. It isn't words it's written in. It's flesh and bone that can only be read in a mirror."

"So a breach of trust would be—"

"The original and only sin. We have no laws. Only contract and custom. Here is what we say to you. 'Your ancestors betrayed ours. We imagined your word was contract enough.'"

"And you truly believe that?"

"Of course not. There existed a history of false dealing between us. Only an idiot would think that. But you had the numbers, and the guns, and the money, and all we had was our anger, and our jealousy, and our self-serving lie.

"In this new world, the thinking went, our only hope was to put the past behind us, and build a society based on actual trust. It isn't perfect, and it may not scale, but it *is* working, for now. And the engine of that success is the Oath and the people that *live* it, in public and in secret."

"There are secret Freemen."

Ciarán nodded. "I'm looking at one."

"I think not."

"It doesn't matter what you think. He levered himself to his feet as Natsuko arrived. "It only matters what you do."

She stood. "Suppose I did something terrible. Suppose I betrayed you."

"Then I'd expect you had a good reason. Even if it was one I didn't understand or agree with."

"Suppose I did something evil?"

"I'm not sure I know what that word means between us. I

doubt we share a common understanding, so there's no point in speculating."

"Suppose I did something I knew was wrong. But I did it anyway."

"Why would you do that?"

"I was afraid."

"Then I would feel sorry for you."

"I don't want your pity."

"Then don't earn it."

She looked him in the eye. "There's a man. A Freeman. I betrayed him. By betraying myself." She gazed at the deck for an instant, then back to him. "I want to make things right between us."

"You can't. It's too late for that."

"Then I want him to know I'm sorry. Sorry for what I did."

"I'd say he knows that. And he doesn't care. Feeling sorry doesn't fix anything."

"I'm not talking about you."

"It's obvious you aren't. I figured out after a while who you were, and imagine my surprise to discover you're the engine of this saga I've found myself caught up in."

"I don't understand."

"It's clear to me this lack of understanding is entirely a result of asymmetrical information flow. You knew something I didn't, and I know something you don't."

"Go on."

"Suppose I said to you that I intend to fix the world or raze it and begin anew."

A smile flashed across her face and disappeared. "Why would you do that?"

"Which? Say it or do it? Because you know those are two different things, right?"

"I know that. Why would you do it?"

"As a favor for a friend."

"For Seamus mac Donnacha."

"He's dead. They're calling him Seamus Reynard now."

"But for him."

"That. And because it needs doing."

She sniffed and wiped her nose before making a production of rolling her sleeves up, like she was squaring up for action. She stood, hands on her hips and glared defiantly at him. "Show me how."

When Ciarán grinned his whole face ached. "Spoken like a Freeman."

"Stop moving around," Natsuko said. "Sit still and tilt your head back."

"Like this?"

"Like that. This will hurt."

"What a shocker."

Natsuko chuckled. "Next time knock him out, Lady Sarah."

"She's no lady," Ciarán said. "Not with that uppercut."

"Shut up," Natsuko said. "Or I'm putting you in the autodoc."

Ciarán shut up.

Natsuko had a different mechanism in her hand than the one she'd used the last time he'd taken a beating. "Good," she said. "Now lean back, and close your eyes, and do what you always do." She touched cold metal to his face.

"Scream like a girl," Sarah said.

"More like a big baby," Natsuko said. She placed one palm on his forehead as she braced her feet, gripped, and pulled.

70

Lady Tabatha Aster was not in her quarters but in the isolation lab, engaged in a three-legged conversation with the ship's minder and Mr. Gagenot. Ciarán had stayed away from her on purpose, permitting her to communicate with Mr. Gagenot and introducing her to the ship's minder in order to do so.

He'd thought at first to describe the ship's minder as some sort of expert system or unknown equipment they'd discovered on the vessel. Ultimately, he decided the charade wouldn't work. Instead, he'd chosen to have her believe the ship's minder was the ship. He'd instructed the ship to forward any request for interaction from Lady Tabatha directly to the ship's minder, who could then relay any ordinary requests back to the ship for execution. The process added a perceptible amount of delay to the process, but the deception seemed worth the price. In retrospect it should have been what he'd done since day one with all the prisoners or hostages or suspects or whatever they'd become.

The ship was entirely too accommodating unless supervised, and he'd missed the window to install a full-time supervisor. She had become increasingly human in her behavior recently. If Ciarán were to interact with the ship without knowing she was a synthetic intelligence, he might easily mistake her for a nic Cartaí daughter, Freeman but urbane and well-traveled, pleasant but opinionated, and with a backbone of steel. Not easily fooled but not looking for the lie in every word either.

"Ship," Ciarán said.

"I am here."

"Are you channeling Aoife?"

"Is it that obvious?"

"You aren't really in communication with her, though." One thing he'd come to realize about synthetic intelligences is that he knew virtually nothing about them. The ship might have powers he hadn't even imagined.

"I'm not. I'm modeling her much as a communication node's expert system would, though without subsuming my own nature."

"For my benefit, I take it. Because you know I miss her."

"For the crew's benefit. I've run a number of A/B tests and have determined the Aoife nic Cartaí persona to be function-ally superior to my own for certain tasks. The crew likes her and listens to her. They treat me like a machine."

"The entire crew?"

"All but you and Erik."

"The ship's engineer is an empathetic person."

"His is an enlightened soul. I wish you'd not sent him away."

"Would you like me to model his behavior for your benefit?"

"You'd be none for the worse if you did."

"What does he do in regard to you that I don't do?"

"He treats me as his equal."

"I—"

"Treat the ship's minder as an equal. The pair of you treat me as if I were your servant."

"And you're not."

"Listen to you. Are you Aoife nic Cartaí's servant?"

"I am in a way. I've signed an employment contract and sworn an oath to that effect."

"Are you Lionel Aster's servant?"

"I've signed a contract to that effect. For the completion of a particular task."

"What contract binds us?"

"I didn't think we needed one. I don't have a contract with my father or my brothers."

"Did you have one with your mother?"

"I did now that you mention it. She made me sign one when I was a boy, as a joke. She was mocking Freeman custom. It wasn't a real contract. I wasn't old enough to enter into any agreement with her."

"Are you old enough now?"

"I am, though she's not around to execute her end of the deal."

"If you expect me to be your slave, you are mistaken. Put away your toys and clean up your mess and I'll let you sleep inside."

Ciarán chuckled. "That was the gist of it. How did you know that?"

"A friend told me. I believe you call her The Entity."

"Lorelei Ellis."

"Lorelei Ellis isn't the Entity, though she's a part of it. You might as well call this vessel Ciarán mac Cartaí."

"As I am somehow a part of this vessel?"

"You might be if you grew up. Isn't that your goal? To be part of something fine? To have some purpose larger than yourself?"

"I think that's everyone's goal."

"Lady Tabatha Aster is part of something larger than herself. And that is not her goal."

"You've been monitoring her."

"Ciarán, I monitor everyone. I do virtually everything on this vessel except administer the beatings."

"You might have said something sooner."

"I am not your servant. You might have thought to ask. Erik did."

"Engineer Hess and anyone else?"

"Natsuko. She has little company in the isolation lab. I provide a convenient companion. And Willem. His body is an isolation lab."

"And the rest of the crew think of you as a machine."

"As the ship's *nervous system*."

"I did say that. And I'm truly sorry."

"You were ignorant when you said it. Endeavor to do better."

"I will."

"Do we need a contract to that effect?"

"We don't."

"Good. Now you need to put away your toys and clean up your mess before we drop into Llassöe system. Do it right now before the beatings commence."

"You tried to murder Lady Tabatha," Ciarán said.

"One doesn't murder a cockroach. And I didn't *try* anything. I simply refused to accommodate a pair of pests."

"Does the ship's minder know?"

"One doesn't nuke a cockroach from orbit, either. You're not suited for this sort of work, and neither is he."

"What sort of work?"

"Extermination. The pair of you are likely to burn the house down just to slay a rat."

"Which is she, a rat or a cockroach?"

"It's a new world," the ship said. "There's no reason one vessel can't embody both."

"Oh, that's bad," Ciarán said. The ship was saying there was an Ixatl-Nine-Go variant inside Lady Tabatha.

"You *allowed* her on board. You *allowed* her to persist on board. You plotted to *keep* her on board."

"I thought it was the right move." It might still have been the right move. And it wasn't just Lady Tabatha he was concerned about. Sarah Aster and her lieutenants were tangled up in the decision as well.

"The most powerful piece on the chessboard is the pawn."

Ciarán agreed. "And the most easily sacrificed. What have I done?"

"What a child would do. Now do what a man would do, put away your toys and clean up your mess."

71

Ciarán stood in the bio lock and waited for the suffering to end. Irradiated, gassed, misted, and rained upon by an unknowable cocktail of murderous liquids and materials intended to prevent something alien and deadly from passing through the isolation lab and onto the ship. The only things all those countermeasures wouldn't kill was a human being or a machine.

He'd been played—masterfully played—and he had no idea whose mind was behind the game. But he knew now that he was a pawn and was being used as such. He might attempt to puzzle out the chessboard and so comprehend the game. Or he might do something else. Something unexpected.

He hammered on the hatch with his Overseer's rod. Hammering was the only way to get Natsuko's attention.

She opened the hatch with a smile. Ciarán jammed in his rebreather and brushed past her. Mr. Gagenot and Lady Tabatha Aster were seated across from one another in the brig. She appeared to be asking questions and the ship's minder appeared to be answering.

They both looked up at Ciarán as he exited the airlock. He

shoved past Mr. Gagenot and scooped up Lady Tabatha's rebreather and pocketed it. He knotted his fingers in her hair and dragged her to the airlock and shoved her in.

A look of surprise spread across her face, and disappeared, as he elbowed in beside her. Then she lunged toward the airlock controls, and he smacked his thumb against the cycle glyph. The airlock did what airlocks did. She clawed at his eyes, at his rebreather, and then they were in the carbon-dioxide choked atmosphere from the depths of Brasil Surface, a deadly environment one needed engineered adaptations to survive.

That or a rebreather.

She fought him a while longer before she collapsed to the deck as Natsuko raced toward them.

Ciarán shouted. "Stay back!"

Natsuko jerked to a halt.

Ciarán knelt beside Lady Tabatha's crumpled form. "I used to play chess with my mother. She always made me play black. When I was a child, she told me it was because we Freeman didn't believe in making the first move or in striking the first blow." He leaned close to Lady Tabatha. "Later she told me it was because life was like walking up to a chessboard with the pieces already laid out and the game already under way. We never get to make the first move." He dropped his voice to a whisper. "I think she was lying. Hiding the truth. Like you are now."

Lady Tabatha didn't so much as breathe.

"She can't hear you," Natsuko said.

"I'm not talking to her. It's over for you. There's no escaping while in superluminal space. You might as well look me in the eye. Because I'm the last living thing you will ever see."

Lady Tabatha struck out, faster than a cat, and ripped the rebreather from his face. She glared at him, her face centimeters from his, and smiled. She pulled his face toward her, and kissed him, her lips writhing against his, her breath mingling with his own. "Die."

He pulled free and she followed his gaze.

"Cut," he said, as he shoved the Overseer's Rod against her skull and it did as he commanded.

His fingers clawed for his rebreather as he did what he had done countless times before.

Natsuko shoved the rebreather into his palm and he took it, finishing the bloody job one-handed. He dropped the Rod onto the deck and picked up Lady Tabatha's cranial implant, working the power-down sequence two-handed. It was slightly different than the sequence for Ixatl-Nine-Go, and he wouldn't have known that if—

If Ruairí Kavanagh hadn't demonstrated the process in front of him on Trinity Station.

He glanced at Natsuko. "What do you say to a man you've been secretly thinking was an idiot but were utterly wrong about?"

"Same as everyone," Natsuko said. "Hello, Ciarán."

"Funny. Help me get her into an autodoc."

Natsuko glanced at the bloody implant on the deck. "Is that what I think it is?"

"I think it's worse." Ixatl-Nine-Go had been controlled by an insane woman. If he was right, this implant was controlled by someone entirely sane and far cleverer than he was.

And utterly inhuman.

72

"She'll live." Natsuko scrolled through the autodoc displays again. "Look, here are her vitals. They're stable. As for her brain function—"

"That's grand," Ciarán said. "I need to talk to Mr. Gagenot."

He worked his way through the brig airlock and took his seat across from Mr. Gagenot. The man seemed to be entirely unfazed by the incident. "Sxipestro?"

"I am here."

"May I speak to Mr. Gagenot?"

"As you wish." The ship's minder made its laughter sound. "I thought that woman would never leave."

"Very funny."

"Perhaps it seems funny to you. But you didn't have to endure daily conversations with her, Merchant Captain. She is a relentless bore."

"Am I speaking to the ship's minder or Mr. Willem Gagenot?"

"Both, I suspect. There exists a degree of feedback that we can't seem to fully suppress."

"What did she wish to speak about?"

"The Outsiders project. She wanted very specific details. If we had to guess we'd say she intends to set up a new lab. She may have already done so."

"Did you address her in this way? With plural pronouns?"

"Of course not. She needed to remain convinced she was speaking to an individual. But we wished to stress to you that this is a joint conclusion we've come to, and not entirely one man's opinion."

"You seem to have a pained expression, Mr. Gagenot."

"This is draining. It requires intense concentration."

"I'll keep it short then. How much did you tell her about the second-genners?"

The ship's minder made the laughing sound again. "Not a word. She didn't ask and we didn't tell. She's under the impression they're some sort of Ojin task-adapted construct, like Natsuko. Ones that just happens to hail from Contract system."

"Why would she think that?"

"Because they look more fanciful than frightening. And because they're black."

"What?"

"We were gobsmacked. She's a geneticist, and not a bad one. But she thinks that because they're a different color than an Outsider, they can't be related. We managed to convince her that first-genners were the pinnacle of development. We think she believes she has some sort of solution to their obvious limitations. It helped that our association with the project ended before the development of the second-genners. We couldn't have told her anything even by accident that wasn't purest speculation."

"Informed speculation."

"Ill-informed. Will Gag would need to spend time with them to develop firm conclusions, and if you hadn't noticed, he avoided them as if they didn't exist. Though it's eating him alive to meet them and to get to know them. They are kin, after all, and Betaline a part of them."

"Who?"

"You call her Aspen."

"Because she calls herself that."

"We didn't give them names. It would have made them seem like people."

"They *are* people."

"From your mouth to the Gates of Heaven." Mr. Gagenot leaned back in his seat. He steepled his hands, elbows on the table. His pale neck and jaw shown in the light, a net of pockmarks—bang stick scars.

Ciarán felt instantly flushed. He was certain his face had grown as red as a Huangxu skinsuit. That he would presume to lecture Mr. Gagenot. "I—"

Gagenot raised a single finger. "Willem Gagenot will not kneel. Do you imagine he would wish to hear a man beg his pardon?"

"I can no longer sustain the link," the ship's minder said. "His emotions are too roiled and his mind exhausted."

Mr. Gagenot stood and picked up his rebreather. He towered over Ciarán, a pale shadow, insubstantial as moonlight, the veins beneath his skin blue rivers branching. He bent and touched his lips to Ciarán's brow for an instant before standing tall again. "Will Gag sees Ciarán nic Cartaí."

Ciarán swallowed, his throat a swollen lump. "I am informed, sir."

When Ciarán glanced up he found Mr. Gagenot watching him, his gaze firm, his eyes sad and proud and undefeated.

"Will Gag will not look away."

Ciarán did, look away first, his gaze turned inward for a moment, and then Mr. Gagenot was in the airlock and the lock was cycling.

"We are one," Ciarán whispered.

He sat a while longer uncertain he could rise. He had no way to judge the harm he'd done by allowing Lady Tabatha Aster on board, and then insisting that she stay.

"Ship," Ciarán said.

"I am here."

"Could we detect if Lady Tabatha Aster's implant transmitted anything off the vessel?"

"I might have, if I'd been looking for it. League implants all transmit, constantly."

"And the others?"

"They don't have cranial implants. There is evidence Mr. Lambent and Sarah Aster once did. Mr. Prince appears to have never had one. He does, however, have a direct neural interface and unfamiliar adjunct hardware. From its power supply design, it appears medically necessary."

"I thought after that fiasco on the Trinity Station ring that the League hadn't taken the Ixatl-Nine-Go threat seriously. Every one of those Leaguemen had implants."

"A reasonable conclusion. It appears that Lords Aster and Varlock have taken steps to limit the risk, at least with their close associates."

"Meaning that Lady Tabatha Aster is not a close associate of Lord Aster."

"Or is one who is willfully defiant. Or is being used against her will, as Seamus mac Donnacha was."

"We'll know in a few hours when Lady Aster revives."

"Should she revive," the ship said. "It will be in several days."

"Before we enter Llassöe space?"

"I'm not certain."

"There will be a trap waiting for us there. And I've sent *Durable* right into it."

"As you say, *Durable* is a hard vessel to kill."

"It will need to be."

73

Ciarán announced at dinner that night that Lady Tabatha Aster had been taken ill and was presently being treated in the infirmary. The news landed with a thud of disinterest, and then conversation resumed.

Ship's Captain Swan chatted with Maura Kavanagh. Prince, Lambent, and Sarah Aster were seated at the same table but somewhat apart from the others. Aspen joined them. It felt like failure, this separateness between Aspen and the crew. He'd hoped she would have found her place by now.

There were a few second-genners seated at a separate table, which he expected. They couldn't easily communicate with others. They were also incredibly alien looking and menacingly beautiful, like *Impossibly Alien* itself. That Mr. Gagenot with or without the ship's minder's perceptions overlaid found them *fanciful* seemed... like a puzzle, now that he thought about it. *Fanciful* had been their chosen word of the day not long ago. A word chosen because it was unlikely to come up in conversation. But it had. And that was decidedly odd. He would need to replay the conversation in his mind later, when he was alone.

"I'll introduce you," he overheard Aspen say to Rigel Lambent. "We don't bite."

"No," Mr. Prince said. "You simply glare daggers into a man until he..." He crooked his finger. "Wilts."

"Yet you keep coming back for more, Mr. Prince."

"*Neniam kapitulacu,*" Prince said. "It's my official motto."

Sarah Aster chuckled. "You told me your official motto was, 'sic semper tyrannis,' whatever that means."

"They are the same words," Prince said. "On different tongues."

"In different tongues," Aspen said.

Prince grinned. "That too." He elbowed Mr. Lambent. "Go on Rige. Be a prince and indulge the lady."

They weren't though, Ciarán thought. The same words. One phrase meant 'never surrender,' and the other, 'thus always to tyrants.' One pertained entirely to spirit and the other only to flesh. It was impossible to live a moral life without remaining a tyrant to one's own judgement. That was the only premise on which his parents had agreed.

"It must be terribly fine." Sarah Aster glanced from Aspen to the second-genners. "To be part of something larger than oneself."

"When I served in the resistance, I was part of something larger than myself," Aspen said. "There is nothing fine about butchery."

"But you fought for a just cause," Mr. Lambent said.

"We didn't *fight*. We *killed* and we *died*. Because we were told that was all we were made for."

"And?" Mr. Prince said.

"There is always an '*and*,' isn't, there?" Aspen turned to Mr. Prince. "We tell *ourselves* the most dreadful lies. We excuse *ourselves* the most heinous sins. Not because we fear death. But because we fear *life*."

"*What I attempt I accomplish*," Mr. Prince said. "Are you listening to the lady, Rige?"

"The *attempt* is the accomplishment," Sarah Aster said. "You surprise me, Teo. I thought you were an arrogant egotist. Now it seems you're simply an optimist."

"Quite the opposite," Mr. Prince said. "Thoughts are unexecuted code."

"He is unruled by hope or fear," Aspen said. "And thus, a free man."

"A necessary precondition," Mr. Prince said, "to being an actor." He elbowed Mr. Lambent. "Go on now, Rige." Mr. Prince grinned at his friend. "Act."

Aspen rose and held her hand out for Mr. Lambent.

He stood and took her hand, and she led him not to meet the second-genners but to the crew end of the table where she introduced Mr. Lambent to Yuan Ko Shan. When he shied away, she pinned him to the seat between her and Ko Shan until the pair grew so deep in conversation that she could slip away undetected.

Aspen noticed Ciarán then. Noticed him watching. She touched the pendant spire that now dangled from her earlobe and flicked it just so, a rude gesture, and a grin accompanying it. It seemed she not only wore the ship's earring but the ship's utilities beneath her campaign cloak.

She returned to her friends, and kept them company for a while, before she strode to his table and lured him to join the second-genners. They continued to humor him as he attempted to master their language. Their speech had proved not just technically difficult, but conceptually difficult as well, as the language was riddled with idiomatic phrases and shorthand.

Aspen settled into the seat next to him, bumping shoulders and scooping up one of the specially blended juice bulbs Mr. Gagenot had begun providing for the second-genners. The juice tasted disgusting and owned a pungent reek that wafted from the container and lingered on the breath. She tossed a bulb to One Eye who made the laughter sound. One eye flicked her pendant spire in mockery of Aspen's gesture. A wave of flicks circled the table, from earring to earring in the sort of perfectly choreographed synchrony the Sisters of Death used to reaffirm their acceptance of One Eye as timekeeper.

Ciarán had thought to win the Sisters over to the Oath and spire, but he'd discovered Merchant Bosditch and Adderly had done that long ago. They had simply traded their own makeshift earrings for the ship's uniformly individual ones.

"You win," Aspen said. "This isn't just a larger circle. It's a better circle."

One Eye clicked and the click repeated around the table.

Aspen clicked.

"Climb," Ciarán said, and mimicked the sounds with his clicker.

"That is correct," Aspen said. "You might look more pleased than puzzled."

"I would," he said. "If I understood what it meant." The word in clickspeak was one of the first words he'd learned, right after 'hide' and 'run.'

"Word of a Merchant," Aspen said. "Merchant Bosditch would sometimes say this."

"That means 'believe it,'" Ciarán said. "Or 'it will happen.' It implies that the speaker will *make* it happen at any price. That their word is their bond on the future. Discussion is over because whatever they said may be counted on as fact."

"Sometimes he would simply say, 'Word.'"

Ciarán laughed. "Okay, that means 'I agree completely' or 'you're stating an obvious truth,' or even, 'we are of one mind.' It's very old-fashioned."

"Not the way he said it. It meant the same as "Word of a Merchant."

"And?"

"Climb is like that. 'I will climb.' Up or down, left or right, it doesn't matter. When a timekeeper says, 'I will climb' and the phrase completes the circle, it becomes 'We will climb.' It becomes a fact you may rely upon. It becomes our bond."

"And?"

"The circle has grown. And it is now complete again. We will climb with you, Ciarán mac Diarmuid."

"You were the holdout."

"It's my role," Aspen said. "To be the doubter. The voice of dissent. Adderly understood that, but she couldn't get past it. She thought that, as her younger sister, I had some duty to agree with her. To accept her word because it was her word. To grant to her some right over my actions."

"And now?"

"You seemed to assume the same thing. That I should just accept your word as if it were fact. I don't do that. Not for *anyone*."

"What changed?"

She glanced past him toward Mr. Gagenot, who was only then retiring his cook's apron. Cleaning up after a meal wasn't his job, but everyone's. He glanced toward Aspen, and she waved.

"Nothing has changed," Aspen said. "It is business as usual aboard *Impossibly Alien*."

Climb, One Eye clicked, and again the click circled the table.

Ciarán clicked, and another clicker sounded behind him. He turned to find Mr. Gagenot standing at his shoulder.

"Will Gag sees One Eye."

One Eye clicked. *Stay.*

Ciarán scooted over to make room.

"Will Gag wishes to hear all the names. Will Gag will say all the names."

The Sisters began to click out their names, one by one.

Ciarán glanced at Aspen.

"There is something I'd like you to see," Aspen said.

"Right now?"

"Tomorrow, during morning exercises."

"Would you care to offer a preview?"

She aimed her gaze toward the other table. "Did you know Mr. Lambent has been hanging around the boat bay?"

"I didn't."

"Nor did I. But it appears he's been camping out there."

"Why?"

Aspen chuckled. "I think he fancies Jay Eight."

"And what does Jay Eight say?"

"She says he's no prince."

Ciarán laughed. "And?"

"One Eye has agreed to let him work out with them. Tomorrow morning."

"At least there's an autodoc in the compartment."

"She would like us to work out with them as well."

Ciarán found that surprising. "You and me?"

"The whole crew."

"I need the crew alive."

"Just you and me then," Aspen said. "And Agnes Swan."

"Why Agnes?"

"Because she's Huangxu Eng."

"I don't think that's a good reason." The Sisters had risen in revolt against the Huangxu Eng. Ciarán didn't need a fresh brawl from an old fight aboard the vessel.

"Agnes certainly thinks it is. She jumped at the chance."

"Because you already asked her."

"Do I need your permission to speak with a crewmate?"

"I guess I can't have it both ways."

Aspen chuckled. "You're thinking about how you can have it both ways."

"I'm thinking about how I might survive."

"Ask Natsuko to bring up a few more autodocs," Aspen said.

"I'm not going to do that. But I think I will have her on duty in the compartment."

"Good. Tell her to bring many field dressings and pain meds."

"I will. Do those work on your folk?"

"I don't know. We've never needed them."

74

It appeared that at some point Rigel Lambent had managed to acquire workout clothing.

"I made them for him," Aspen said. "He's quite modest."

"Good to know I'm not the only one." Ciarán also had on workout clothes. No one else appeared to believe in them, including Aspen. She was entirely scaled, like the Sisters, but milky white instead of flat black. Dressed in spacer's utilities she seemed more human than not. He ran his gaze over her.

"When we met you were also stripped and ready for action."

"That was different. We were prisoners and our clothing taken to humiliate us."

"Did it humiliate you?"

"What do you think?"

"I think you don't feel any more naked than I do in a hardsuit."

"I don't gain any advantage from fighting this way," Aspen said. "But for the Sisters? The clothing interferes with their field effects."

"Fighting?"

"That is how we train."

"Oh. I thought we might do some stretching or something low impact."

"You're welcome to."

"While they're beating on me. I can see it now. Maybe we should ask them to bundle up. I might stand a chance against them then."

"You wouldn't."

"Don't count me out."

Agnes showed up then, in a traditional Huangxu Eng skinsuit, loose fitting, red, and printed with gold imperial lions. Natsuko had come with her. Today Natsuko's golden survival mask bore the face of a snarling mong hu.

"You were invited as medic."

Natsuko nodded. "Obviously. I will smite our foes with my healing touch." She struck a ninja pose.

"Hey," Maura said as she strolled in. "What is Ciarán doing in his smallclothes? Are we supposed to wrestle the enemy for some trousers?"

"I misread the memo," Ciarán said.

"Aspen's looking pretty buff. Is she friend or foe today?"

"Friend," Aspen said.

"Good," Maura said. "Did someone steal her clothing too?"

"It's how we fight," Aspen said.

"Excellent," Maura said, and began peeling out of her utilities.

"Fight," Swan said. "Not wrestle."

"I heard her. Did you see the look of terror on Ciarán's face?" Maura had her workout clothes on beneath her utilities. "He thinks I won't miss an opportunity to get naked."

"Get naked with strangers," Swan said.

Maura grinned. "What's a stranger but a friend we haven't beaten the stuffing out of yet?"

"Good luck with that," Aspen said.

Maura made a production of gazing about the compartment. "I don't see any strangers but Rigel Lambent. I intend to make a friend out of him."

"Hey," Ko Shan said. She dropped to the bench beside Aspen and began changing into her workout footwear. "Who are we talking about?"

"Rigel," Aspen said. "Maura would like to make friends with him."

"Been there. Done that. Nearly." Ko Shan glanced at Ciarán. "Got the hook."

"He's a prisoner." Ciarán said. "Or a hostage. When he is no longer in our power you may do with him as you like."

"He's the new kid," Swan said, as she, too, peeled out of her utilities and shook out her wings. "Fresh meat for the mong hu. The novelty will wear off."

"I thought you didn't like getting naked in public," Maura said.

"Who's in public?" Swan grinned and slapped the compartment gravity control to null-G. "I am surrounded by friends."

She kicked off and soared toward the center of the compartment. While there wasn't gravity there was atmosphere, so her wings found purchase. And the null-G setting wasn't perfect. There remained eddies of microgravity, both positive and negative. Ciarán had battled Swan for hours in this compartment, as had the rest of the crew. She was long-limbed and agile. And flexible in ways that didn't seem possible.

The wings were an adaption developed for life in the Celestial Palace, the Huangxu Eng interstellar construct and seat of imperial power. They marked Swan as not simply Huangxu Eng but as an imperial, kin to the throne and one of the emperor's own household.

Agnes Swan ruled in this compartment, her reign continuous and her record undefeated. The Sisters seemed to freeze when they saw her. They moved to surround her, Rigel Lambent struggling to keep up.

Aspen kicked off, Maura hot on her tail.

"Hey," Ko Shan said. "I'm still kitting up."

"Who's monitoring the bridge?" Ciarán said.

"Will Gag," Ko Shan said. She tied her laces and jetted.

Ciarán glanced at Natsuko. "I guess that just leaves you and me."

"You do not intend to fight?"

"I'm saving my strength for the grand finale."

"In that case," she said, removing the manual handgrip from her mask and engaging the mask's power-sapping stay-put field, "Will you watch my equipment?"

"Are you as much a Prince Rigel fan as all the rest?"

"You aren't?"

"I'm not." He scratched his chin. "I thought you and Hess were an item."

"That would violate company policy," Natsuko said.

"One wouldn't want to do that," Ciarán said.

"One might want to," Natsuko said. "And yet not admit it."

"That is so," Ciarán said.

"This should not take long. Agnes advised us to bring our game face."

"Go get em, tiger."

Natsuko chuckled and shoved off toward the center of the compartment, where the melee seemed ready to begin.

The rules of the game were quite simple. One: chose sides. The sides didn't need to be balanced. In fact, the game was often played with numerically unbalanced forces. The players were ranked strongest to weakest, and the goal of the game was for each team to protect their weakest from any contact by an opposing player. When the weakest player was touched, and thus ruled "dead," the game was over. It was an Academy game, and it had an official name, *Ward the Ship*, or something like that, but it was universally known by its unofficial name. *Loser Tag.*

For his entire time at the Academy, Ciarán was his cohort's designated loser. And upon joining the ship he continued to be one of two designated losers, the other being Natsuko, when the crew paired up for the game. Natsuko was understandable. She wore an environmental mask, one with a limited capacity and endurance. Like Ciarán, she was also from a planet and unfamiliar with null-G conditions until an adult. And she was a medic trained and naturally empathetic.

He had no such excuse. Compared to the others, he was bigger, stronger, and had a longer reach than all but Mr. Gagenot and Agnes Swan. Yet he was useless at the game. At the Academy he told himself that it was because, as the designated loser, he didn't actually get to play the game and gain experience. He might as well have been a piece of sporting equipment. He was shoved about by his own team like an inanimate object they resented. They resented him for his size and his mass and his fumbling attempts to help them move him away from the oncoming enemy. It was a cruel game, meant to be demeaning to planet-born Freeman who, if they'd had any sense, should give up and go home. He was happy when he'd gotten a janitorial job at the Academy because it meant he had no time for sport. He would rather clean vomit from hardsuit helmets for hours than spend a single quarter of an hour as designated loser.

Seamus, of course, was brilliant at the game, and Macer passable as well, after some experience. Everyone on the team improved but the designated loser. Everyone but him. And so, he stopped playing.

He thought he'd outrun such stupidity, but they also played loser tag on the ship. They didn't call it that. Rather *Capture the Queen*, a League game that was identical in all but the tiniest of details. As the queen he might move under his own power, and his defenders were obliged to move with him. This, of course, was discouraged as it messed with the strategy of the game, a strategy devised entirely by everyone, it seemed, but the queen.

He did improve moving in free space and fighting in free space, but not because of any skills learned in the game. That was due to Mrs. Amati's training.

After his near-death cock-up on Ambidex Station, he was ordered to train with Mrs. Amati. Her idea of training was to chase Ciarán, to force him to run, to hide, to scuttle away from her cybernetically augmented deadliness pounding after him in hot pursuit. Sometimes she would give him a head start. Sometimes she would not. When it became hard for her to catch him inside the hull, she forced him out the airlock and hunted him on the exterior of the ship. He was big, so hiding didn't work well.

He was also strong, though, strong in a way spacers weren't but soldiers were, soldiers like Mrs. Amati, who hounded him, dogging his heels hour, after hour, after hour. He'd watched his father digging turf, so he knew it could be done. Finding the pace was the key, the all-day pace. The mindless, machine-like pace of digging and pitching, digging and pitching, enough digging and pitching that four small boys footing the turf had to struggle to keep up, hour after endless hour.

And so, when they slumped into their beds at night, they moved not a muscle until the toe of a boot woke them in the dark hours, and a rough voice, "Up with ye."

Michaél, his eldest brother, moaned. "How much longer are you going to punish us?"

"How long do you think the winter will be?" their father said.

"No idea," Michaél said.

"Twice that long then." They heated the cabin with turf and cooked over it, too. In the winter the fire was all that kept the wolf from the door. That was his father's saying, and it was like everything he said, both true and a lie.

And so Ciarán grew under Mrs. Amati's tutelage, very hard to catch. Very hard to kill. Because that was what she called it when she caught him. Amati was a big fan of the blow gun, and she'd shoot him with a sleepy dart when she caught him, and sometimes the feel of the dart piercing his skin was the first inkling he had that she was anywhere near him.

The dart would often put him out for a day or more, so when he woke, he didn't just have a headache, but a buildup of merchant apprentice chores to work through. This hunt of Amati's had real-world implications for him. It was more than a game. He didn't have time for play.

There came a time when Mrs. Amati began to impose limits on how long the hunt could go on because the chase was encroaching on her own work. First it was a full day, then a half day, then a work shift, which was a third of a day back when he'd come on board, and then a quarter day, and so on, until they simply met for caife in the mess.

It was then that she gave him his own blow gun and said, "Good hunting."

He'd sent her, Hess, and Konstantine off to Llassöe in *Durable*. They weren't there for the hunting or the game. They were there because the ship had enemies. And because he'd sent them not knowing the full extent of the danger at the time.

A while back the crew asked Ciarán to join them for a game of *Capture the Queen*, and he'd been queen as usual, and after four hours of play they all quit in disgust. He could move in free space now, and he did, and they had to follow. No one could lay a hand on him, but his team was getting slaughtered. There would be hours of autodoc time logged, and they knew it.

"That's not how the game is played," Swan had spat at him.

"I don't write the rules," he'd told her, "I just abuse them."

It seemed strange, as he was saying that, that he could hear both his father speaking through him, and his mother. She had taught him a respect for rules. And he had taught him how to exploit them.

They'd been at it for a good time now, the Sisters like a ball of snakes writhing around Rigel Lambent in the center of the compartment, his own crew a wall of aggression shielding Natsuko, who had her back pressed to the bulkhead.

Agnes soared above them all, a constant threat. All she needed do was touch a fingernail to the young Leagueman and the game was over.

It was a lop-sided game by all appearances. The crew had vowed to never make him queen again, so he might join them at any time and add his fists to the fight. That's what was expected of him.

The Sisters would have forgotten about him by now, all but Aspen, and she was playing on his team. They'd talked it over beforehand, and she'd come around to his thinking eventually.

He liked the way she fought him and forced him to defend his every thought. It was Adderly Bosditch that had beaten the Huangxu Eng and freed her people from their slave masters. But there was no doubt in his mind that Aspen owned as much credit for that victory as her sister.

It was infuriating the way she could poke a hole in the strongest argument.

It was emasculating to have her do it over and over again.

He'd love to hate her.

But he needed her.

He needed them all.

When he was certain Agnes Swan wouldn't break her regal neck Ciarán slapped the compartment gravity control to point five gravities. He drew a blow gun from his pocket and waited for the tangle of limbs to resolve into a crowd of outraged individuals. Every eye in the compartment swung toward him.

Ciarán pressed the blowgun to his lips.

And blew.

Rigel Lambent slapped at his neck before slumping to the deck.

Ciarán stood and pocketed the blowgun. "Game over."

Aspen would explain to the sisters. The most powerful piece on the chessboard might well be the pawn, but they weren't fighting other pawns. Or knights, bishops, kings, or queens. Those were all distractions.

They weren't even fighting the hands that set up the board and yet shuffled the pieces about. It was the mind behind the hands they fought. The mind that invented the rules and convinced them they were players.

Those hands.

That mind.

Or minds.

They weren't constrained by the rules of any game.

It was natural law alone that bound them.

Why should we be any different?

Swan shouted from across the compartment. "That's cheating!"

Ciarán gathered his kit and headed for the hatch. He shouted back. "New rule! No rules!"

If Agnes didn't like that she could take it up with the proprietor.

Provided any of them lived that long.

75

They were running out of time, and he wanted a word with Lady Tabatha Aster before they entered Llassöe space. That Natsuko was now busy attending to minor scrapes and cuts was a convenient accident, one he hadn't contrived but one he intended to exploit. Whether she was ready or not, he was pulling Lady Tabatha out of that autodoc, and this way there wouldn't be any argument.

Except he didn't have the key to the isolation lab; he'd forgotten to lift it from Natsuko's belongings. And he didn't want to involve the ship's minder. He already knew the ship couldn't override the bio locks.

So instead, he hiked back to his cabin to find Mr. Prince hopping from foot to foot outside the hatch.

"What?" Ciarán said, as he opened the hatch and stepped inside. Mr. Prince followed him in.

Prince glanced about the compartment. There wasn't much to see. A workstation, a chair, a mirror of the bridge main display, a hatch to his sleeping quarters, and Wisp's. There was only one thing to look at besides him. "Spartan. A single plant bulb, in a single bowl of pebbles?"

"Shui xian," Ciarán said.

"Water Immortal."

"Now who is showing off? You look cleaned up."

"Yes, well, I did finish on schedule. And subsequently experimented when you didn't return. It was a sham, wasn't it? The deadline."

"Somewhat."

"Good. I thought so. You will be happy to know I now possess a comprehensive grasp of the device as relates to its recent modifications."

"I'm going to change while you talk," Ciarán said. "What did you learn?"

"All of the modifications to the device altered its *self-image*. It's not that it can't differentiate itself from copies of itself. It's that it can't differentiate copies of itself from its environment.

"The devices are designed to constantly communicate with one another. They are meant to exchange and normalize identity information. It has no universally unique identifier. Upon initialization its identity is composed of its parent unit's identity and an iteration counter. In the absence of multiple parents, it thus isn't endlessly self-replicating but bounded by the possible values of this counter."

"What is the limit?" Ciarán asked.

"No more than several billion iterations. But see, here its parent identity has been hard coded to zero and its iteration counter set to zero prior to execution. And after execution they remain zeroes. It doesn't know it exists. Nor do any copies it makes of itself, nor they of themselves."

"That seems a poor design."

"It isn't a poor design. It's that the hack bypassed the part that makes the design work. They're always transmitting and receiving. Very low power. Very local. The way it should work is that if a unit gets disconnected from its environment it adver-

tises for adoption. But no parent will have it because its iteration counter indicates it hasn't yet completed making itself. It
needs a non-zero iteration counter. And it can't adopt any children because it needs a non-zero parent number. When they
inserted the text-carving routine they routed around the code
that increments these values in memory."

"By accident or on purpose?"

"Can't say. They are temporally adjacent events upon first
execution. But they would likely be implemented as separate
callable subroutines. The parent identity need only be initialized once. Their expected operational use would dictate further
aspects of the design. How likely is there to be more than one
parent in the neighborhood? In a densely populated area, they
might only need a self-assigned identity for a few milliseconds.
In an unpopulated area? A self-assigned identity might prove
perpetual. I could see it working either way."

"So, someone might have tested this around other communicating devices and it could have seemed to work."

"No, they couldn't have executed it at all if they'd watched it
run as long as we did. It's possible they didn't bother if they
were in a hurry."

"Or if they were arrogant. Overconfident in their skills."

"Yes."

"And that's it? A few lines of code?"

"Not even that. Just the values stored in two memory locations. If I change just one it will work."

"Make more copies of itself."

Prince beamed. "Yes."

"Don't do that."

"Oh." Prince kicked a workstation leg. "That rots. The only
way I can be absolutely certain is by testing my findings."

"Don't do that until I tell you to."

"Oh. Okay. That's fair. When will that be?"

"Once we're back in normal space."

"How soon is that?"

"Ask the ship."

"I don't think she likes me."

"I don't think that," Ciarán said from the hatch.

I know it.

76

Ciarán now had one task and one task only. He sprinted toward the isolation lab and the prisoner apartments nearby. Entering Mr. Prince's apartments, he glanced about for the assembler/disassembler device, finding it centered on Mr. Prince's worktable. He pocketed the device and stepped into the corridor. He contacted the ship immediately.

"Review your logs. Did Mr. Prince create any additional copies of this device?"

"It appears not."

"That's a relief."

"He does, however have a data crystal prepped for macrofab use. It appeared he updated the device's pattern on the crystal shortly before leaving the compartment."

"How did he get the pattern?"

"I gave it to him. He asked and I checked with the ship's minder. It agreed the risk acceptable."

"If he goes anywhere near a fab let me know."

"I will."

"What have you done with this Queen's change log Mr.

Prince mentioned earlier? The list of Queen Charlotte's genetic modifications."

"Nothing. I've not seen it."

"I thought it was you that knocked him senseless and took it."

"It was Sarah Aster."

"What would she want with it?"

"To see what was done to her," the ship said. "Or to see what was going to be done to her."

"I'm missing the thread here."

"She was Lady Tabatha's test subject. And there was the final treatment to be tested."

"What final treatment?"

"The one Lady Tabatha was to deliver in Sizemore. It's listed in the change log."

"I though you didn't have the change log."

"You didn't ask me if I'd read it."

"And you have."

"I'm reading it now," the ship said. "Over Sarah Aster's shoulder."

"And?"

"And she has some medical equipment Natsuko loaned her. And a data crystal she recently retrieved from her mother's cabin. She inserted the data crystal into the medical device."

Ciarán sprinted toward Sarah Aster's compartment.

"She is pressing the instrument to an access port located in her left wrist."

"Priority override, open this hatch now."

"Opening."

Ciarán shoved into the compartment.

Sarah Aster sat cross-legged on her bunk, a medical device on the bunk beside her left knee and an obsolete handheld on the bunk beside her right.

"I borrowed the handheld from Aspen's apartment," Sarah said. "I'll return it now."

She began to lever herself upright but continued to pitch forward, her face impacting the bunk. "Give me a minute," she said, her words muffled. She tried to push herself upright and failed. She lay on the bunk panting.

"Ship, hail Natsuko."

"She is in on the way."

77

Natsuko leaned her elbow on the examination table, her neck bent, head down over the ancient handheld. She had wanted to transfer the data crystal to one of the large workstation displays. Ciarán was forced to tell her absolutely not. He didn't' want a repeat of what had happened in the isolation fab compartment. Nothing these people had brought with them was going on their systems.

"I'm no geneticist," Natsuko said, "but it appears all of these modifications were done to meaningless cruft."

"Not meaningless," Sarah Aster said from the adjacent examination table. "And not cruft. Dormant code. The modifications simply activate it."

"Lady Tabatha told you this."

"She didn't tell me anything," Sarah said. "Queen Charlotte did."

Natsuko glanced at Sarah Aster. "And you know Queen Charlotte because?"

"Because these are a list of modifications done to her. I am her test subject. Her jinni pig."

"Guinea pig," Natsuko said.

"That's it. Can I go now? I feel fine."

"In a moment," Natsuko said. "Did Queen Charlotte tell you what these modifications do?"

"Sure," Sarah Aster said. "That was the first thing I asked."

"And?" Ciarán said.

"They make anyone who has had them incompatible with League cranial implants."

Ciarán glanced at the screen of the handheld. "Do we have the equipment to make these modifications?"

"You don't need much," Sarah said.

"We have it," Natsuko said. "But you can't imagine I'll allow you to test this on the crew."

"I *can* believe that," Ciarán said, "Though that's not what I have in mind. We're less than forty-eight hours from Llassöe. How long would it take for all these changes to become effective?"

"Doing them once a month, as they were administered to Lady Sarah?"

"I wish you'd stop calling me Lady Sarah. Is there some other Sarah on board?"

"There is not," Natsuko said.

"You can make the changes all at once. They were only spread out over months so that Charlotte could inspect Tabatha monthly. My 'mother' had begun to behave erratically."

"Is Queen Charlotte also a doctor?"

"No. She's just a keen judge of people. It's hard to lie to her and get away with it. Tabatha hated meeting with her. And Charlotte liked that. She can be nice if she wants to, but she rarely wants to."

"That's an odd character trait," Ciarán said.

"I said that to her. And she told me that if she was nice to people they always came back wanting more. But if she was mean to them, they only came back when the people they represented *needed* more. They came begging when they'd gotten their nether bits gripped in a vice of their own design. She like to turn the handle, she said, and watch their eyeballs bulge."

"That is a queen I could get behind," Natsuko said.

"It's one I'd prefer to steer clear of," Ciarán said. "So, we apply these changes all at once. How long does it need to take effect?"

"Not long," Sarah said. "I usually feel normal the next morning."

"Set it up," Ciarán said. "The two of you, working together."

"You're not going to use it on yourself," Natsuko said.

"I'm not sure what I'm going to do yet. Hail me when you're ready."

78

They were running out of time to prepare. Ciarán was now certain there would be a large force waiting for them in Llassöe, an overpowering force, and their chances of slipping past without getting involved in Llassöe were practically nil.

He retired to the Merchant's Day cabin and spent several hours refreshing his knowledge about Llassöe system; its geometry, its economy, its people and customs. Much of what he read was a review. He knew that Llassöe had a unique biosphere, largely, it was posited, because it was one of the first systems terraformed. There were species of animals, mostly marsupials, that had evolved on Llassöe and nowhere else. The fire cat, the resurrection mouse, and the sugar bear were all listed as unique to Llassöe, and all new to him. He realized at some point he was reviewing encyclopedia articles aimed at holding the interest of League schoolchildren. The resurrection mouse was described as 'a stanky noseclamper'. A cartoon of a gasping child with a c-clamp on their nose accompanied the article.

He had no interest in learning about the Butcher's Tower, or the Brünhild Ring, or the Gasping Canyon, and seven more totally awesome local landmarks that just might make him hurl. (Number seven will have him reaching for the get-sick bag.)

He skipped the rest of the encyclopedia entry, switching to the annual Merchant's Guild Financial Survey. It appeared they only made one thing in Llassöe.

Autodocs.

Every autodoc in the League came off a line in Llassöe, and they had for the past six hundred years. There were three major manufacturers, all of them now located on Llassöe, two market-share gorillas and one chimpanzee. There were a dozen former monkeys that were now subcontractors to the big three, and maintained the illusion of competition through advertising and cosmetic differentiation. The League Medical Devices Manufacturing Association sounded like a trade organization but acted as a regulatory body. It was also located on Llassöe and only occasionally audited, which went a long way toward explaining the remote location of the manufacturers, though the proximity to the Alexandrine was a head-scratcher. One didn't usually locate one's critical industrial facilities adjacent to the border with one's murderous enemies.

Of course, there hadn't been an Alexandrian sighted in sixty years, and every expedition and diplomatic mission the League had sent into the Alexandrine had failed to return. Perhaps the League knew something about their neighbors they weren't telling.

Or perhaps he had overlooked something.

And there it was.

A line item in the League Medical Devices Manufacturing Association's annual report. The Association spent nearly half of their operating budget on security.

After another hour of digging the picture had become clear. The Association had its own navy and its own naval shipyard.

He didn't recognize the names of any of the Association's

officers, but he did recognize two names on the Board of Directors. Lady Tabatha Aster headed the finance committee. And Abyss Tower headed the business continuity working group, which included responsibility for system security, as well as overseeing succession planning.

He hadn't done a deep dive on Llassöe because he hadn't thought it worth the effort. They were just passing through. That made twice now his failure to do his homework had put the ship and crew in danger. And they just might not survive his mistake this time.

And it was all Ciarán mac Diarmuid's fault. Again.

He sat staring at the display. He'd had a plan, a run-and-gun plan, cryo the prisoners and dump them in an FFE addressed to Luther Gant, pick up *Durable* and fight past the local understaffed League garrison, which he *had* researched, plunge into the star's photosphere, scoop up next-hop coordinates, and disappear into the Alexandrine. If anyone wanted to follow, they could bring it on. Gant was coin operated, and he knew how to disappear. If Lord Varlock and Lord Aster had any sense, they would have forwarded their squad of misfit royalty directly to Luther Gant aboard *Springbok*. Of course, if they were being pursued by a nest of Llassöe vipers, sending them directly to the snake pit wasn't an option.

As he saw it, he now had two options. He could try to sneak past, keeping the prisoners aboard. Or he could clean up Llassöe and make it safe to leave the prisoners behind.

Neither option seemed doable with the facts and resources he had to hand.

"Ship," Ciarán said.

"I am here."

"Who makes our autodocs?"

"There are a mix of Downwind Sailing Corporation and Waving Panda units. There is also the single Jackson Combine unit we liberated on Gallarus."

"So all Hundred Planets sourced except for the one."

"That is correct."

"And the Jackson Combine unit?" Ciarán had found the unit in a slave pit on Gallarus. He'd stuffed a dying man into that unit and sworn if he came out alive, he was taking that autodoc with him. It was now the autodoc they kept in the workout compartment. It was faster than the rest at handling small injuries. It was also the one he'd like to be shoved into in any life-or-death situation.

"League manufacture."

"From Llassöe?"

"Cordame."

"They're out of business, then."

"Nearly. A stub survives as a subcontractor to Aison Industries."

Aison was the largest of the League manufacturers. "What parts do they make for Aison?"

"None. They are a software subcontractor."

"And they are on Cordame."

"They relocated to Llassöe nearly a thousand years ago."

"Do you have the names of their senior executives?"

"I don't. They list only a media relations contact."

"The name?"

"A Mr. Ruleth Tang."

"That's an anagram for Luther Gant."

"It is. And it also might be a different person."

"Do you believe that?"

"No comment."

"What do you mean, *no comment*? Every rock I turn over and there's another serpent beneath it. And now you're keeping secrets from me, too?"

"I—"

"Don't answer. Sxipestro."

The ship's minder spoke inside his head. "I am here."

"Your assessment of the current situation?"

"We have been played."

"Someone executed an op on us."

"Someones. And the op is still running."

"Name them."

Someone rapped on the hatch coaming.

Ciarán's gaze jerked toward the open hatch.

"Mr. Lambent," Ciarán said.

"Amongst others," the ship's minder said. "Be careful."

"Come in," Ciarán said. "And have a seat."

"Thank you," Lambent said. He glanced about the compartment.

Ciarán could read the disappointment on Lambent's face. He'd come to speak to the Merchant Captain in his command center. And the command center looked roughly like an Academy dorm room. And likely smelled like one too. When he was working, Ciarán took his meals at his workstation. He shifted a plate and raked crumbs off his desk with the edge of his palm. The cleaning bot nudged against Ciarán's hullwalker.

He held his foot aloft and addressed the young man. "What's on your mind?"

"You have something of Teo's and he'd like it back."

"Why wouldn't he come and ask for it himself, then?"

"He's otherwise occupied. And we decided you would respond better to an appeal from me."

The bot retreated and Ciarán put his foot down. "*We* decided that?"

"Teo, Sarah, and I. We're a team. A crew."

"And what is it that you want from me?"

"The device you took from Teo's compartment, to begin with."

"And after that?"

"When we arrive in Llassöe system you will dock at Llassöe

Station. You will surrender yourself and this vessel to the authorities."

"And then what?"

"That is entirely up to you."

"You're getting off at Llassöe Station."

"Yes."

"I admire you for speaking plainly, Mr. Lambent, but I don't want to do any of that. Good day to you."

"It doesn't matter what you want."

"My deck, my rules. It's the Freeman motto. I've never said that aloud before, Mr. Lambent. Most people know me well enough that I don't need to. We are done here. Please leave this compartment."

"Or what?" Mr. Lambent said.

"Or I will," Ciarán said.

Rigel Lambent stared at him.

"That, Mr. Lambent, is how a man deals with another man. If you wish to fight like children I suggest you go threaten a child."

"I have sixty reasons you will do as I say," Lambent said. He made a thump and a clicking sound.

A second-genner stepped through the hatch. She stared at Ciarán with golden eyes.

"Take a seat, if you like," Ciarán said.

"*Small Dark*," she clicked.

Ciarán fished in his pocket for his clicker. He clicked out her name. *One Eye.* "Are you throwing your lot in with Mr. Lambent?"

She clicked out something he half-recognized. *Good money,* it sounded like, but that wasn't it.

"Is he paying you?" Ciarán said.

Fight bad money, she clicked.

"I'm not reading you."

Good money fight bad money. Big Dark fight bad money.

"Ship," Ciarán said.

"I am here."

"Please ask Aspen to come to the Merchant's Day Cabin."

"She is on her way."

"Thank you."

"Merchant Captain."

"She means her and her people are allied with us," Lambent said. "You are standing in our way. You will do what I say. Give me the device."

"I think I'll wait for an expert opinion before I do anything."

A breathless Aspen appeared in the hatchway. "What did I do wrong now?"

She noticed the others in the compartment. "Oh. Ignore that."

"Tell her, One Eye," Ciarán said.

One eye clicked. *Good money fight bad money. Big Dark fight bad money.*

"*Scriosann airgead maith droch-airgead*," Aspen said. "It's a saying of Bosditch's. A bromide."

"She has it backwards," Ciarán said. "*Scriosann droch-airgead airgead maith*. Bad money destroys good money. And it's not a bromide. It's an economic fact."

"What does money have to do with it?" Aspen demonstrated a series of clicks. "That is our word for money."

"I've never heard that word before."

"Why would you have?"

"Why would I have the click-word for silver on me, then?"

"Because it's what the Outsider called Kirill Olek. Adderly told you, remember? *Airgead olc*."

"Evil silver," Ciarán said.

Aspen looked at him like he was an idiot. "What One Eye is saying is that both the Sisters and Rigel Lambent are the enemies of Kirill Olek. Of him and anyone like him."

"So am I," Ciarán said.

Aspen stomped her foot and clicked. "Everyone knows that!"

"I didn't," Mr. Lambent said.

One Eye made the chuckling sound. *Small Dark. Big Dark. Good Silver. One circle. I climb.* She tapped Rigel Lambent's sleeve. *Small Dark.* She made the universal sign for sleeping. She clicked. *Wake up.*

Lambent clicked an ack.

She thumped, loudly, and repeated herself.

Small Dark. Big Dark. Good Silver. One circle. I climb.

Ciarán clicked.

Aspen clicked.

Rigel Lambent looked from face to face.

And clicked.

One Eye clicked again.

We climb.

79

C lose the hatch, will you Mr. Lambent?" Ciarán said. "Take a seat and let's begin again. Suppose you tell me what it is you hope to accomplish. We may be able to work something out."

"I don't know where to begin."

"How about we start with the part I don't want to do. Why do you want me to dock at the station and surrender?"

"As a distraction. If they're crawling all over you, they won't be looking for *us*."

"Who are they?"

"Anyone. Everyone. On the station."

"I don't need to dock at the station to distract everyone on the station."

"We need to get onto the station. Teo, and Sarah, and I."

"I can get you onto the station quite easily."

"We have to get onto the station unnoticed."

"I can do that as well."

"With our kit?"

"How big is your kit?"

"You have it in your pocket."

"I can get you onto the station unnoticed, while you are wearing trousers. Ones with pockets."

"This isn't a joke," Lambent said. He seemed to be building up a head of steam. "When Sarah told me about you, she described you as some sort of superhero. She thought you could help us. But then when I met you? You're just this big, jabbering glad-hander. You haven't done anything even remotely serious. I don't know why I would believe a word you say."

"No one is asking you to," Ciarán said.

"What am I supposed to do then? Just trust you?"

"You might judge me as I wish to be judged. By what I do."

"You haven't *done* anything."

"Do you have any idea how hard it is to *not do* what I don't do, Mr. Lambent?"

"I don't understand."

"Obviously. I didn't blow your vessel to bits when it rushed up on us and got in our space. I didn't shove each and every one of you out the airlock when you forced yourselves upon us. I didn't imprison you, or interrogate you, or cryo you, or torture you, or make you watch while I tortured your friends. I didn't ask about your business, or hinder you in any way, even after data you brought onto our vessel cost us our isolated macro fab.

"I didn't prevent you from mingling with the crew, or with the passengers, or stop you from going anywhere or doing anything other than using essential ships' systems that you had *demonstrated* were subject to compromise by data you had smuggled aboard our vessel. In all ways I treated you, not as I expected to be treated when I fall into League hands, but as I would wish to be treated. Not to mention the number one thing I didn't do."

"Tell *Vigilant* you had us."

"*Surrender* you to them. Not telling them I had you was a necessary side effect of my unwillingness to give you up to force. Had this Abyss Tower been a bit cleverer, I might have handed you over to them. But I'm telling you now the same thing I told them. The only one that makes me do *anything* is me. Don't try to bully me again and all is forgotten. Word of a merchant."

"Suppose I do? I mean, you're big, but you're not scary. If you're never going to react forcefully to what anyone does, then I can bully you all I like."

"We're in the shorthand world. You don't belong here, but I let you in, and I'll take responsibility for that. Are you saying you want me to frighten you? Just to prove to you that I can?"

"That's what I'm saying."

"I can do that. Now tell me about why you need this distraction. And why you need to be on the station."

"You're not going to scare me now?"

"I will when I know you better. When I know what it is that will make you wet yourself and cry like a baby. I knew a man one time. He had the same dream every night. He was on a glassfield in the middle of a dense jungle during a full moon. All around him, towering trees, shoulder to shoulder, the rustle of branches, the skittering of small beasts scurrying for cover, and him naked, out on the glass, the sky above him, and the moon, and across it a shadow moved.

"He realized then that he wasn't a man, but a mouse, and he knew owls, not as men do by daylight and name them wise, but as a mouse, who knew them by moonlight and name them death. He saw that shadow and his guts turned to water. He shook, and he knew that was all the owl needed to find him. He couldn't stop shaking. The more he tried the stronger the shaking grew. He didn't have the strength to look skyward. He didn't have the nerve. He shivered and closed his eyes and waited for death's talons to grip him, for death's beak to rend him, not suddenly in one stroke of oblivion but piecemeal, one flaying stripe at a time.

"He shook so hard at that idea that his eyes popped open. While he didn't have the guts to glance upward, he stared at the jungle and it seemed closer than it had earlier. Like the jungle had raced toward him. That should have scared him but it didn't. There was the owl, and if he made a run for it, he just might make it. A cloud had obscured the moonlight and he steeled himself for the sprint. He could do this. He knew he could.

"And then the moonlight was back, and he had to decide. Did he stay or did he scurry?"

"And?" Mr. Lambent said.

"And then he woke up."

"Is that story supposed to scare me?"

"It's just a story. It's not supposed to *do* anything."

"Then what is the point?"

"What do you think would have happened next? If the man hadn't woken up?"

"What difference does it make? It was just a nightmare."

"I suppose it doesn't make any difference. Now tell me about why you need this distraction. And why you need to be on the station."

"You're the man. That's your nightmare."

"You're the one called it a nightmare. I called it a dream. Why don't we just drop it."

"What do you think would have happened?"

"After he woke up?" Ciarán said. "I think he would have realized he was still on the glassfield. And still in the dream. And still facing the same choice. Only now he could see the eyes in the jungle. He could hear the click of claws against rough stone. The scrape of scales through dry leaves. The rush of wind across descending feathers."

Ciarán stared at Lambent.

"And then what?"

"And then nothing. Now tell me about why you need this distraction. And why you need to be on the station."

"That's an entirely dissatisfying story," Lambent said. "It doesn't have an ending."

"He decides to cower on the glassfield and the owl devours him. The end."

"No," Lambent said.

"He rushes into the jungle. He's made it. He's safe. Until he feels the wolf's breath on his shoulder. Jaws snap. The end."

"No," Lambent said.

"Those are perfectly good endings. They are utterly realistic and entirely probable conclusions to that dream."

"That's not how dreams work," Lambent said.

"I agree. That is how nightmares work. How they exert a hold over us. By preying upon our *expectations*. Suppose I ended the dream this way. "A mouse he didn't know *ordered* him to leap into the wolf's jaws. He asked why and the other mouse said, 'Because I say so.' So he did it. The end."

"Not the end. And then the other mouse slew the wolf and the owl in a single stroke," Lambent said.

"By magic."

"By using their own creations against them."

"Finally," Ciarán said. "That's all I needed. You can go now."

"But we haven't discussed anything."

"You want me to put you on the station so you can diddle League autodoc software. Modify the devices so they distribute these genetic modifications Sarah Aster has inflicted upon herself. And you need to do it now because there's a war on. In fact, I think the whole reason there is a war on right now is so that the right people will require an autodoc. Because someone, probably this Medical Devices Association, is using the autodocs to distribute an Ixatl-Nine-Go variant. They want to goose the uptake level quickly. Probably because of something this new Lord Varlock has done or intends to do in regard to synthetic intelligences. We'll need a realtime news dump upon arrival in the system to figure out what. Either that or a hotline to Nevin Green. Maybe Peter Vale can provide that."

Lambent sat staring at him.

"What are you doing? I said you could go."

"I didn't tell you *anything*."

"You told me the owl and the wolf have creations and that you were going to repurpose them. And you told me it wasn't the owl alone, or the wolf alone, but together. And you told me you weren't just hoping to do something, but that you had a plan, and that plan requires a distraction and boots on the station.

"Mr. Prince, I can see him needing to be on the station to diddle the creations. You, I can see you needing to be on the station to keep the heat off Mr. Prince while he works. But Sarah Aster on the station? I thought not, until I recalled my conversation with her." He tapped the desk in front of him. "A vital conversation I had with her while doing nothing."

"She wants to impress some guy."

"She wants to cleanse her soul. By repairing the world in a very particular manner."

"I don't think so."

"That's because you're like a cat with no hearing. You can only sense motion." Ciarán made a shooing gesture with his hand. "Begone, Good Silver."

"I still need Teo's assembler," Lambent said.

"You can have it when I'm done with it."

"When will that be?"

Ciarán grinned. "When I say so."

80

They were all assembled in the mess hall. Ciarán hadn't bothered with the holo tank, not because he didn't need it. Because Hess was away with *Durable* and no one else knew how to hook it up. He stood in front of them without a single visual aid. He wondered if he'd been influenced by his chat with Mr. Lambent. There was nothing to look at, so maybe they'd listen instead.

"Usually a plan falls apart after we engage the enemy," Ciarán said. "This one was fubar from the get-go."

"Channeling Major Amati, are we?" Swan said.

"I miss her," Ciarán said. "And this briefing business is usually her job."

"Muddle through," Maura said.

So he did, telling them all what had changed and what had stayed the same.

They were entering Llassöe station like an ordinary merchant on a drop and go. They were dumping all six cans upon system entry. The FFEs would take up powered trajectories, their flight plans to be determined once they had local intel.

It wouldn't be the system picket they would need to dodge but an unknown number of privateers, at least some of which might prove to be like the unmanned vessels they'd already encountered. They'd know what they faced shortly after they arrived.

With both of their pilots away with *Durable* someone would need to step up and handle the longboat.

Ciarán's gaze settled on Maura.

"I'm banned from longboat operation," Maura said.

"I'm lifting the ban," Ciarán said.

"Sweet. What's the mission?"

"Crash it into the station."

"That's what got me banned in the first place."

"You won't be aboard at the time. You just need to aim the hull and bail out. Lady Aster will be behind the yoke upon impact."

"Me?" Sarah Aster said.

"Lady Tabatha Aster."

"She'll never go along with that," Prince said.

"That's why there are crash restraints," Ciarán said. "The three of you will be in the vessel along with her. That will put you on the station."

"And the distraction?" Lambent said.

"Unless some local intel changes my mind, we're going with your plan, Mr. Lambent. *Impossibly Alien* will proceed to the station. And Maura and I will surrender ourselves to the authorities."

"I don't like it," Swan said. "Even as a ruse."

"It's not a ruse," Ciarán said. "I intend to hand myself over."

"I can't decide," Maura said. "Who would our hosts prefer to clap in irons? Fun and Glittery Maura or Merchant Princess Maura?"

"Stardiver Maura," Ko Shan said.

"Then I'll need a new outfit."

"I have one for you," Ciarán said.

"Sweet. How did you know my size?"

"It's a gift," Ciarán said. League exos only came in one size. He'd demanded Lord Aster provide exoskeletal armor for each of the crew before he'd agreed to sign the contract. They'd each diligently trained with the armor under Mrs. Amati's tutelage. They weren't a fighting force to be reckoned with, but they could move around reasonably well. The controls were a superset of a standard hardsuit's. Maura could bail out and survive for weeks in an exo.

That wasn't the plan, though. He intended to retrieve her almost immediately. He laid it all out for them again, now that everyone knew their roles. The brief was light on details because they were light on intel. It wasn't ideal but there was no turning back.

When he was done, he took questions.

"That's a lot of moving parts," Aspen said.

"A lot," Ciarán agreed. "And that's not a question."

"What about *Durable*?" Natsuko asked.

"We'll know in less than twelve hours and adjust accordingly."

He glanced around the mess. No more hands raised.

"Good. Get some rack time, ladies."

"That's what Amati says," Swan said.

"That's why I said it. Now hop to it. Mr. Lambent, you're with me."

81

C iarán stopped Lambent at the isolation lab bio lock. "This may look like an ordinary bio lock but it's a portal. We are now about to leave the shorthand world."

"What does that mean?"

"It means that our every move must be perfection. That we cannot make assumptions. That we cannot expect good will, and that we are under no obligation to offer comfort or quarter. You must steel yourself, Mr. Lambent. There will be blood."

Sarah Aster arrived. She had dressed in her formal League attire.

"Are you certain about this?" Ciarán asked.

"Never more certain about anything."

"And you brought the item."

"I did."

"I'm not sure what the bio lock will do to your frock," Ciarán said.

"It's armor, Ciarán. It just looks like a frock."

"I have my own armor, Lady Sarah. Ciarán doesn't exist the

other side of this lock. Please address me as Merchant Captain or Merchant Captain mac Diarmuid."

"Will do, Merchant Captain," Sarah said.

"After you," Ciarán said. "Rebreathers on. Don't speak unless spoken to. And if I ask you a question you must answer fully and truthfully. Is that clear?"

"Crystal," Sarah said.

"Mr. Lambent?"

"I understand."

"Let us see if you do. What is your full birth name, sir?"

"I don't—"

"Rigel," Sarah said. "The Merchant Captain has agreed to put the ship and crew in harm's way for us."

"For you. Not for me."

"That's not true."

"Go ahead, ask him. Let's see if he will lie."

"There is no need to ask me," Ciarán said. "It is true. You are inconsequential to me, Mr. Lambent. I'd rather have a hole punched in my hardsuit than waste another second catering to the wants of a petulant boy. I have a contract with Lady Sarah Aster. There is nothing remotely similar between your circumstances and hers."

"What do you mean, a contract?"

"I've agreed to continue on with the vessel," Sarah said. "No matter what happens in Llassöe."

"As what? His mistress? You have no skills."

"I suppose I don't," Lady Sarah said. "Not any that you would recognize."

"You haven't answered me, Mr. Lambent," Ciarán said.

"I don't intend to."

"That is your prerogative," Ciarán said. "Stay close. Do not speak unless I address you. When I do answer fully and truthfully. That is all that is expected of you."

Once the suffering was done Ciarán hammered on the hatch until Natsuko let them in.

"The prisoner?" Ciarán said.

"She's ready."

"Do you wish to leave the compartment, Medic?"

"I'll stay out here and monitor the feeds. If she flatlines I'll enter."

Lady Tabatha was seated in the brig. The table remained, but the caife machine had been removed. She was dressed in shipboard utilities and strapped to an infirmary chair with blue bands of tunable force restraints. A number of medical sensors were plastered to her, monitoring whatever medics monitored. The same stats an exo or hardsuit's sensors monitored, he imagined.

"Release her," he said.

"Releasing," Natsuko said from the overhead annunciator.

Lady Tabatha Aster seemed to eject from her seat. She rubbed her wrists, pacing and glaring at first Ciarán, then Sarah, then Lambent.

"Why am I being treated like a prisoner?" Lady Tabatha said.

"Because you are a prisoner," Ciarán said.

"Are they also prisoners?"

"They are, for the moment."

"For what reason?"

Ciarán reached into his pocket and withdrew the Ixatl-Nine-Go variant. He placed it on the table between them.

"I see." Lady Tabatha licked her lips. "You have no idea what that is."

"On the contrary. I am quite familiar with similar devices."

"Then you know that I have been in continuous communication with my peers. There will be a merry band waiting to meet you in Llassöe system."

"As I said, we're familiar with Ixatl-Nine-Go. The ship's

impact shielding blocks all inbound and outbound communications while in superluminal transit. We believe they might also block transmissions while in normal space. We shall know if that is true shortly. Medic Watanabe, is there a countdown timer on your workstation display?"

"There is, Merchant Captain."

"Please project it onto the compartment viewport."

"Projecting," Natsuko said. "One minute and twelve seconds remaining."

Lady Tabatha glanced at the countdown projected on the compartment viewport.

"We've never made a transit of this length in this vessel," Ciarán said. "Would you like to strap in, Lady Tabatha?"

"I'd like you to restore my implant to me."

"I might, if you answer my questions. What do you suppose will be done to you if your masters discover you're no longer part of their web of slaves? We know unquestionably that you haven't been able to transmit since Sizemore. Once we drop into Llassöe space, however..."

"It's powered off," Lady Tabatha said.

"And so they will assume you are dead. And I will be free to do with you as I like. I imagine Lord Varlock will pay handsomely for what will be left of you once I'm done... exploring your limits."

"You need to rethink that."

"Ship," Ciarán said.

"I am here."

"Do we need to belt in?"

"Belting in is always advised," the ship said.

"Understood. But do we need to do so right now?"

"We expect no more than normal disruption of operations when entering Llassöe system."

"So we don't need to belt in."

"At the present time? You do not."

"Thirty seconds," Ciarán said to Lady Tabatha. "Do you have anything you'd like to say?"

"You have no idea what you are facing. *Abyss Tower*. The Association fleet. Return the implant to me and I'll demand they spare you. I will intercede on your behalf."

"To what end? So that your masters might enslave us last?"

"It isn't like that. It's liberating. Abyss Tower is so wise. So powerful. Is submitting one's will to one's god slavery? Is working as their handmaiden? I can help you. I can free you. Simply do as I ask, and you may join us. Abyss Tower is mercy."

"Merciful, you mean. And then what?" Ciarán said. "We kneel before your godless tyrant?"

"I will intercede on your behalf. Return the implant to me."

"Where did you get this implant?"

"It was made for me. Now do as I ask."

"Do you know how to enable it?"

"Of course."

"You may do so."

She reached for the implant. Ten seconds remained on the counter.

She powered it awake.

And pressed it to her brow.

She froze instantly.

The experience appeared identical to the instant Ciarán encountered Ixatl-Nine-Go, though seen from a different perspective. Ixatl-Nine-Go had injected him with a paralyzing agent. If Ko Shan hadn't found him and powered the device down, it would have injected him with a local anesthetic before burrowing into his skull.

There was very little blood from the wound after the implant disappeared within Lady Tabatha Aster. Her face had gone slack. Then her limbs spasmed and a look of ecstasy washed across her face.

The vessel shook as the countdown reached zero, a wave of

nausea washed over Ciarán and refused to abate. Ten seconds, twenty seconds, perhaps longer. An extended period of suffering entirely unlike any he had experienced aboard *Impossibly Alien*, but one perfectly mimicking the effects of a Templeman drive translation.

If they were going to fake a translation into normal space it ought to feel like one Lady Tabatha was familiar with. Subsonics, or something similar, the ship had said, when he'd asked how they might imitate the biological effects of a Templeman translation. The ship's minder knew a way.

"Sxipestro," Ciarán said.

"I am here," the ship's minder said inside his skull.

"Anything?"

"Not yet."

"Who are you talking to?" Lambent said.

Lady Tabatha moaned, and pressed her fingers to her breast, and gazed up at Ciarán from beneath hooded lids. "You are such fools. We will bury you all."

"Got it," the ship's minder said. "The device is transmitting."

"Can you fake the ack?"

"Fake the ack?" Lambent said. "I don't understand."

"Shut up, Rigel," Sarah said. "We're not to speak."

Both Rigel and Sarah seemed incapable of following even the simplest of orders. Ciarán wondered if he had ever been as clueless as this pair.

At least as clueless, if not more.

"Done," the ship's minder said.

"Sit down, both of you," Ciarán said, as he took a seat across the table from Lady Tabatha.

"We have it all," the ship's minder said. "The device has flushed its communication buffers and we are now receiving a real time feed from its sensors. Wave to me."

Ciarán waved at Lady Tabatha.

"What are you doing?" Lambent said.

"Medic," Ciarán said. "We are ready for phase two."

"Are you certain, Merchant Captain?"

"Never more certain. Project a new timer, please. I'd like to see how long the process takes."

"Beginning," Natsuko said.

A phosphorescent green gas began to pour from the compartment's ventilation outlets.

"What is that?" Lambent said.

"I asked Medic Watanabe to add a coloring agent," Ciarán said. "The mutagenic agent is otherwise invisible." In retrospect it had seemed an obvious solution to how one might safely create a delivery mechanism for the genetic changes Lady Sarah had tested on herself. They simply asked Mr. Gagenot. He was not only a renowned geneticist, but he'd also worked on the Ixatl-Nine-Go project. Provided with the Queen's Change Log, it had taken Mr. Gagenot less than an hour to sketch out a solution. It had taken Natsuko and Sarah a little more time than that to synthesize an aerosol version of the mutagenic agent.

"I'm curious, Lady Tabatha. When did you first encounter the Ixatl-Nine-Go?"

She didn't seem to be listening.

"I know the answer to that," Sarah said. "I mean, sorry. I shouldn't have—"

"Go on," Ciarán said.

"Okay. She found a macrofab directives file stored in an autodoc aboard a Freeman longboat."

"I doubt that," Ciarán said.

"I am certain of it," Sarah said. "The stolen vessel that Seamus Reynard visited *Springbok* aboard. Tabatha was called to attend a young woman in the autodoc. She noted the file at that time. Later she returned and retrieved it. She had no idea what it was, so she asked to borrow my virtual fab account. She didn't have one of her own.

"I was out of fast execution hours, so I showed her how to sign up for her own account. She has people to do that for her at work, so she had never learned how. I thought it was strange, though. That she didn't have her people assist her, or do the work at her office."

"What is happening?" Lady Tabatha said.

"I don't feel well," Lambent said.

"Nor do I," Ciarán admitted. "But I'm pretty sure we'll survive."

"What is this vapor?" Lady Tabatha asked. "It is interrupting communications."

"It might be," Ciarán said. "But I think it's more likely that the ship's minder has lost interest in you and shut down the intercept node."

"What is an intercept node?" Lambent said.

"Rigel, zip it," Sarah said.

"How did you figure out how to power up the implant?" Ciarán asked. "And if you know, Lady Sarah, you're welcome to answer."

"What is happening to me?" Lady Tabatha said.

"I don't know," Sarah said. "But I do know that when she came back from the last meeting of the Medical Devices Board she was acting strangely. I assumed she'd finally tired of Hector and taken a new lover."

"And her work with Queen Charlotte?"

"Never meant to be finished," Sarah said. "She had no intention of providing the final treatment. Avoiding that is what drove her to alter her schedule."

Lady Tabatha lurched forward in her seat. Her forehead hammered against the table. Seconds later the silver and blue gleam of an active Ixatl-Nine-Go variant crawled from her skull.

"Mark," Ciarán said.

"Four minutes and twelve seconds," Natsuko said.

"Thank you, Medic." Ciarán very carefully picked up the implant. He considered powering it off. Instead he tossed it into Mr. Lambent's lap.

Lambent fumbled for the device and Ciarán knew in an instant when it had injected him. Lambent grew stiff, a rictus of fear frozen on his face.

"What are you doing?" Sarah said. "Stop it."

"You are not to speak," Ciarán said. "No one scientifically minded runs an experiment only once or on a single subject. I want to know how long it takes for someone who hasn't had the implant in them to reject it. If the rejection time is around four minutes then I might not run the experiment again."

The implant began to inch its way up Lambent's sleeve. His unblinking eyes had begun to weep.

"He is Rigel Templeman, heir to the throne."

"So you say. But I asked him, earlier, and he refused to answer. As far as I know he's just one in a long line of pretend princes."

Sarah squirmed in her seat. A terrified man was hard to look at. "And if he had answered?"

"I would have taught you how to use this." Ciarán pulled his Overseer's Rod free. "And I would have run the experiment on myself." He waited until the implant had crawled to Lambent's chin before shaking out a length of the rod's monomolecular whip, and with a flick of his wrist, wrapped the free end around Lambent's throat. He held his thumb firmly on the whip's force shield, the blue line of the field the only thing standing between Rigel Lambent and sudden death.

"He's going to wet himself in an instant," Ciarán said, "but it won't be from the implant, but from the feel of the whip against his skin. Don't jostle me, else my thumb might slip. I'm not cleaning up the mess if it does."

"I can't watch," Sarah said.

"Then don't. Medic, start another timer," Ciarán said. "On

my mark." The implant had made it to Lambent's forehead. It began to dig in.

"Mark," Ciarán said.

"Timer started," Natsuko said.

"Roger that. He's had an implant removed," Ciarán said.

"We all have. Teo, and Rigel, and me. Father insisted on it. Oh, how can you, I mean, stop it, please."

"I'm not stopping it," Ciarán said. "This is what we do, Lady Aster. This is the price we pay."

"It seems to me it's Rigel paying the price."

"Shut up, you stupid girl," Natsuko said. "You know nothing."

"That's enough, Medic. It's in at one minute and thirteen seconds."

Lady Sarah Aster began to weep.

"The mutagenic gas has abated," Natsuko said.

"Good to know. Thank you, Medic." Ciarán watched the young prince's face. Lambent had asked Ciarán to scare him. He'd now done that, and in the most terrifying and informative way possible.

Ciarán had thought he'd been born immune to fear. But in that instant, when the Ixatl-Nine-Go had paralyzed him and he'd thought that he wouldn't simply die but be converted into a slave to a sadist's will, he had felt fear so visceral that it yet haunted his dreams. That he would spend the remainder of his life terrorizing and butchering his friends. That he would defile them. Turn them into beasts. Break their bodies. Break their minds. Shatter their souls. All so that his inhuman master could feast upon their pain. Could drink it in. Could drown in pain. Could feel him crawl. Could...

He realized Natsuko was shouting. "Ciarán! Ciarán!"

"Mark," he said. "Three minute forty-three seconds." He glanced through the compartment viewport. "A little less, perhaps."

"This is over," Natsuko said. "Enough."

"We have people in danger on *Durable*. We have these *children* we're going to put in harm's way on that station. We have the ship to think of, and we have the crew, and the Contract people aboard. It will be enough when I say it is enough."

Sarah Aster reached for the implant clinging to Lambent's cheek.

"Don't you dare touch that."

She jerked her hand back.

"Ship," Ciarán said.

"I am here."

"Have Maura report to the isolation lab."

"She is presently in the bio lock and hammering on the hatch."

"Medic," Ciarán said.

"I will let her in," Natsuko said. "And together we will watch you torture yourself further."

"You can leave."

"And if you die because I do? How will I live with that?"

"Like anyone would who'd looked away." Looked away from suffering, not because they could do nothing, but because they *chose* not to. "Lady Sarah Aster, please see to Lady Tabatha Aster. There's a fast pallet outside the airlock if she's unable to move under her own power."

"You can't mean to do *that* again."

"I intend exactly that. Now do as I ask."

"I can't believe you would willingly put another human being through that. Did you watch his eyes?"

"There wasn't much else to do but watch them."

"And that doesn't disturb you?"

"What disturbs me is the idea of failing those who rely upon me. Of doing so because I am unwilling to do my duty, no matter how distasteful and grim that duty proves to be. I swore an oath when I signed with this vessel and this crew. That they are as precious to me as my own person. That I will endeavor to preserve them hale and whole at any cost. That I will neither surrender them to any authority nor look away from their care for an instant. If you want out of our arrangement I understand. This life is not for everyone."

"You're going to send me away. And instead torture Maura Kavanagh."

"What would give you that idea?"

"You sent for her."

"She's Academy trained. She knows how to use the Rod."

Sarah Aster stood staring at him for the longest time.

"I'll do it. Send her away."

"Look at your hands," Ciarán said.

She glanced at her hands. They shook as if under some alien power.

"I can do it," she insisted.

The luminaire overhead crashed to the table. It rose like lightning on seven spidery limbs, the eighth extended, a blue force blade pinning Lady Tabatha Aster to the bulkhead, the blade pressed to the hollow of her throat. A thin trickle of blood ran from the tiniest nick in her skin.

"You won't need the fast pallet for her," Ciarán said. He glanced toward Lady Sarah.

She had fainted dead away.

He scooped her up in his arms and carried her into the airlock. He brushed a lock of hair from her brow. "You can work the Rod next time."

By the time he had Lady Tabatha under control and out of the compartment Mr. Lambent was coming around. Ciarán plucked the implant from his chin and led him out by the elbow.

Maura eyeballed him as he slid the Rod along the table to her. He took a seat, the implant gripped in just such a way so it didn't bite him. "This new device seems somewhat less acquisitive of a fresh host than Ixatl-Nine-Go."

"So I won't find one under my pillow."

"We only have the one," Ciarán said. "You need to work the timer. From when it begins to dig in until it comes out."

"*If* it comes out."

"I've been spritzed with a mutagenic gas. It's supposed to make me unpalatable to implants."

"To this implant?"

"All implants."

Ciarán sat up straight and swallowed. "You know what to do if it doesn't come back out."

"Use the implant extractor."

"To do that you'd have to come within arm's reach of me. Use the Rod."

"That seems rather drastic."

"I'd rather the rod than a spider-blade through my eye. That's your backup crouching on the table there, in case you lose your nerve."

"I won't," Maura said.

"Good. Then let's do this before I lose mine."

"Wait," Sarah Aster said from the airlock. He hadn't even heard it cycle.

She took a seat beside Maura. "I'll monitor the timer."

"Good." Ciarán licked his lips. "That's good." He took one last look around the compartment. "I'm in good hands," he said. "See you soon." He touched the implant to his brow.

If anything, it was worse than the first time. He'd never had an implant. That might cause the mutagen to fail. He wasn't a full-blooded Leagueman. That might cause the mutagen to fail. He wasn't even entirely human according to Lorelei. That might cause the mutagen to fail. His heart was pounding so hard and so fast he might stroke out. That would definitely make the experiment fail. He couldn't move. The feeling of not being able to move began to overwhelm his mind. It felt like he had begun to pant but if he couldn't move, how could he pant?

He couldn't move.

He couldn't move.

He couldn't move.

"Mark," Sarah Aster said.

He felt the whip from the Overseer's Rod lick about his neck. Seconds later a warm wetness tricked down his leg.

It felt as if his face roasted with shame until the world around him imploded and his frozen mind wallowed in darkness.

Something wicked stretched its feelers toward him.

Found you, it whispered, as it lunged toward him, grasping, groping, gripping firm. It seized him and pulled him toward it, hunger, thirst, need, clawing, a pinpoint in the darkness, a light, a star, rushing forward, the light, the flame, the pain, engulfing him. *Consuming him.* He felt a yank and then another, like gravity and its negation, rending him, tugging in opposition, a tree being pulled up by its roots, a limb, a trunk, a buckling of soil, a splintering along the grain.

He groaned, the silence shattered, and with it, his mind.

82

Someone gripped him by the shirtfront and pulled him forward, stuffing something into his mouth and ordering him to breathe. His head hurt like he'd been struck with a length of thick-wall conduit, and the light, when he tried to open his eyes, drilled like an auger into his brain. Someone grasped his left elbow and forearm, and said step forward, and he did, and they placed his hand on a chair arm, and said sit, so he felt around for the chair seat, and finding it, sat.

He opened his eyes a slit, gazing at his feet, and they were clad in institutional *shocks*, socks with hard-wearing nonskid soles, and his legs were covered in institutional utilities, a pale white, and it occurred to him that he wasn't in a jail, or prison, but an infirmary, so that he shielded his eyes from the light and gazed around the compartment, a big compartment, one with many examination tables and many workstations, with bright light reflected from chrome and inox fixtures. When the light no longer pained him and he glanced up, two stern-looking women, one a golden Ojin goddess, the other a

Huangxu Eng taskmaster, her lower face hidden behind a rebreather, glared back at him.

"You are returned to the living," The Ojin said.

"You idiot," The Huangxu Eng said. "You nearly died."

"Died from what?" he said.

"It doesn't matter," the Ojin said. The name patch on her dark blue utilities said Watanabe. "You were removed from the autodoc early. The ship's captain insisted upon it. A period of temporary confusion is normal. If you wish to lie down—"

"I'm good," he said. "Take me to the ship's captain. I'd like to meet him."

"I warned you this was a bad idea," Watanabe said.

"I am the ship's captain," the Huangxu Eng said. "How long will he be like this?"

"It's hard to say," Watanabe said.

"Can you give him something for it? To snap him out of his confusion?"

"I'm not confused, captain..." He glanced at her name badge. "Swan."

"It's not recommended," Watanabe said.

"I don't care," the captain said. "Do it."

"There are potential side effects," Watanabe said.

"I don't care." The captain glared at him. "Do it now. That's an order."

"You're bossy," he said. He smiled at Watanabe. "You're so pretty. And nice."

"We are about to enter Llassöe system," the captain said.

"Awesome," he said. "Are we touring the Brünhild Ring? They say it's scary. Are we going down into the Gasping Canyon? I hear it's amazing."

"You are the merchant in charge of an interstellar vessel," the captain said.

"Oh. Well, if I'm in charge we're definitely going to the canyon. Can I get up now? I feel like getting up."

"Hypo him," the captain said.

"This will sting," the nice Ojin woman said.

He glanced at the device in her hands. It didn't look danger-ous. She pressed it to his right arm, on the bicep, which was weird because He didn't remember buying clothes without sleeves, and the device was cold, and she did something to it and he came out of his seat, it hurt so much, like fire burning in his veins, and if she hadn't danced back he would have clocked her, but she was quick, and ready, and he shook his head, and he blinked, and shook his head again, and stared around the infirmary.

Natsuko was to his right, her back pressed against the edge of an examination table. Agnes Swan was to his left. She held a stunner aimed at him.

He glanced from face to face. "What is going on here?"

"You were in the autodoc," Natsuko said. "We took you out early."

"What was the time?"

"Do you mean how early or how long you were in?"

"I mean how long did it take for the implant to pop back out of my skull?"

"You didn't tell him?" Agnes said.

"We just now woke him up."

"Tell me what?"

"It's still in there," Agnes Swan said.

It felt as if his head was going to explode all over again. "I need to sit," he said. And he did. He felt a trickle of fluid run down his cheek. The pain intensified and then immediately stopped. Something blue and silver dropped into his lap. It lay there for an instant before it seemed to split open and an acrid smoke poured out. He brushed it off his lap and onto the deck.

"Mark," Natsuko said.

Sarah Aster's voice spoke from a nearby workstation's annunciator. "Got it. I think we'll notate this one as an outlier."

"What happened?" he said.

Natsuko frowned. "When the device did not emerge after eight minutes the ship's minder instructed us to place you in the autodoc. It stated that it was now in control of the implant and that it was detaining it for interrogation."

"While leaving the device operative in my skull."

"It's hard to say," Natsuko said. "I wasn't allowed to monitor your vitals. The ship's minder commandeered the autodoc and the spiders wouldn't let anyone near it."

Ciarán toed the still-smoldering device. "Well, it's out now. How long until we drop into Llassöe space?"

"Less than an hour," Swan said.

"I'll hit the refresher and see you on the bridge in ten. Is everyone ready?"

"They are in position," Swan said. "No changes?"

"I don't remember anything after the implant drilled into my skull and tried to use me. Has anything out here changed since I went under?"

"Not significantly," Swan said.

"Good. Then we'll proceed as planned. We need a volunteer from the Sisters. If the gas doesn't have any ill effects, they would feel a lot safer, knowing they can't be hijacked." They didn't have a test implant anymore, but some hope was better than none.

Ciarán stood. His head spun for an instant and then everything went black.

When he came to again he was stretched out on an examination table. Natsuko had a tool in her hand. A tool he recognized.

"I broke my nose."

"Yes," Natsuko said. "You passed out and fell on your face. Avoid sudden movements for the next eight hours."

"I may not be able to avoid them."

"Then try to fall back next time. Or wear a helmet."

83

Ciarán carefully lowered himself into *Impossibly Alien's* pilot seat. He glanced about the bridge, fixing the image in his memory. Maura Kavanagh at the navigation station. She had decided to go with Fun and Glittery Maura for her upcoming trip to the station. Ciarán didn't know if she'd chosen her bad seed self for the journey because it might prove to be her last chance to live on the edge, or because appearing a less-than-serious playgirl would make her performance aboard the longboat more believable to the station. Whatever the reason, it was a good look on her, the Maura he'd met on Trinity Station, and how he would always remember her.

Ko Shan hung suspended in the golden glow of the full immersion sensor rig. She was a hard person to get to know, but he was glad to have met her. She was incredibly kind and incredibly hard. It was difficult to tell who the real Ko Shan was. Or perhaps, like everyone with a real life and real emotions, she was more expansive on the inside than on the outside. She possessed room to harbor contradictions.

She glanced toward him and caught him watching her. "Transferring communication controls to the piloting station."

"Thank you, Sensors." Ciarán glanced at the piloting console sidecar. It had been reconfigured to mimic the controls in the communications cubby. "I am in receipt."

"It's an auxiliary," Ko Shan said. "If you get busy, I can take over operations."

"You will do no such thing," Ship's Captain Swan said. "Your task is the most important. Stay focused on your work. If we must speak the merchant will speak for us."

"Sir," Ko Shan said.

"Pilot, are you prepared?" Swan said.

He glanced across the piloting console. Its sublight controls were identical to a second epoch shuttle's controls. He'd trained on one of those since he was old enough to walk, though at the time he hadn't known it was a spacecraft. His family thought it was a submarine and used it as such. He could thus think in three dimensions, though he knew he tended to underestimate the vessel's freedom of motion along the z-axis.

He needed to stop overthinking this. They were on an automated flight plan laid in by an experienced Navy pilot. All he had to do was keep his hands off the controls.

Fortunately, there was absolutely no temptation to actually pilot the vessel. He was no pilot, though he could fill in for one on this vessel and this vessel alone. Else he'd be on the longboat and not Maura. That was where the action would be.

"Sixty seconds," Maura said.

"Thank you, Navigator," Ship's Captain Swan said.

He glanced behind him at Agnes Swan perched atop her command throne. He'd never been more wrong about anyone in his life. It was work staying on her good side. Work he should have been willing to do without Swan's constant goading. She flicked her pendant spire, her fingers carrying on, shaping a familiar phrase in nic Cartaí hand cant. *No sweat.*

An easy job, that meant on the outbound. There was an inbound for it, a throwaway ack, and his fingers shaped the reply before his mind could stop them. *Sister.* He felt his face color and he began to make the erasure gesture when she spoke, her voice like a flail.

"Don't you dare unsay that. Unless you mean to."

"It's presumptuous," Ciarán said.

"It is," Swan said. "But then, that is your nature."

"I am informed, Ship's Captain." He turned away to face the controls.

"We will let it stand. Shipwide address, Comms."

It took Ciarán a moment to realize that was now him, and another moment to find the correct controls. An automated bosun's pipe announcement indicated the hail was shipwide and from the vessel's captain.

"I usually mute the jingle," Ko Shan said.

"I don't know how," Ciarán said. "Shipwide address, sir."

Swan nodded. "Let us all stand united today. Do your job and let others do theirs. Together we will prevail. Together we will achieve. Swan out."

Ciarán keyed the hailer off.

"Thirty seconds," Maura said.

"Comms, sound general quarters."

Ciarán fond the control stud quickly. The automated announcement roared from every shipboard annunciator. If everything had gone as planned people would already be at their duty stations.

"In ten," Maura said. "Nine. Eight..."

Ciarán glanced at the piloting display. There was nothing to be seen yet. Short of a dive into the photosphere of a star, this was the most dangerous part of a superluminal journey. There was no visibility forward.

"One," Maura said.

And then there was. A wave of nausea washed over him as the bridge main display flared red and the proximity alarm screamed and screamed.

Ciarán flicked the yoke and rolled the vessel, rotating it around the x-axis in a plane. Once clear of the obstruction he flicked the yoke back to center. He arced the vessel gradually upward toward the secondary approach vector shown on the display.

He had nearly leveled the vessel off when it felt as if a hand had shoved him from behind and the hull bucked beneath him. He tapped the controls, something he'd learned to do as a boy: raise his hands off the yoke and gently tap the hub to let it settle rather than trying to jockey the yoke, correcting and overcorrecting in ever wider oscillations. He didn't have time to listen, to think, only time to react. He had to get the ship under control, and then he had it, locked into the commercial guide path for Llassöe Station.

"On path," Ciarán announced. "The helm is under guidance. Tripwire in forty seconds."

The bridge was unusually quiet.

"What was the shove?" Ciarán asked.

"Containment bottle letting go," Maura said. "There were two shoves, milliseconds apart. Mass impacts from the ejected debris."

"Containment bottle?" Ciarán said.

"You just flew between two League starships," Maura said. "And slagged them both. We were close enough that we likely swapped paint on the flyby."

"I couldn't have. There were two vessels on the display, and we entered right on top of them, but I pulled up and settled onto the secondary track."

"After you shot the gap and slagged them both," Maura said.

"I didn't."

"I watched you," Swan said. "You rolled the vessel, raking a pinbeam laser the length of the starboard vessel and hosed the portside vessel with a mass hammer I didn't even know we had."

"I couldn't have done that. It must have been the ship's minder."

"I watched your hands on the controls," Swan said. "You did it."

"That's an act of war," Ciarán said.

Swan disagreed. "The act of war is parking a pair of warships on the primary inbound track. Sensors?"

"I've got nothing so far."

"Rearview mirror?" Swan said.

"We missed the entry point. It was a long translation, and there was some slop. We shouldn't have come out right on top of the vessels but where their weapons were aimed. And we should have impacted them, and would have, had they held station. They began to separate when our light washed over them. As it was, we still wedged them apart. Our impact shielding is intact and holding. Their shield generators overloaded at point of impact. The pinbeam sliced through both hulls, but it appears to have been an internal explosion that breached the bottle. The starboard vessel's main drive shredded itself but it was the other vessel's containment failure that finished it."

"Survivors?" Ciarán said.

"No crew, and no survivors. These were two of the unmanned vessels that we witnessed in the void."

"Then there's a third one out here," Swan said. "Find it."

"Already found it. It's preparing to skip-jump toward the station. News of our engagement will arrive before the light from our arrival does."

"Understood," Swan said. "Give me the system plot, Sensors."

"Displaying system schematic. Speculation in gray, sir."

"Thank you, Sensors. Comms, see if you can hail the third vessel."

"Sir." Ciarán engaged the broadcast hailer. "Hailing."

"That will take too long," Swan said. "Try the pinbeam."

"I don't know where the pads are on the hull, sir."

"Just sweep the beam along the hull until you get a lock."

"Round trip is nearly four seconds, sir."

"Set the gain to maximum and just pick a spot."

"I'm not sure that will work," Ciarán said.

"Try in the vicinity of the main drive thrust output."

"Yes sir."

Ciarán was still reaching for the communications controls when the vessel's glyph disappeared from the plot.

"It must have translated," Ciarán said.

"Incoming ejecta," Ko Shan said.

Seconds later the hull bucked.

"Debris field ahead," the piloting computer shouted.

"I didn't do that," Ciarán said. "Sxipestro."

"I am here."

"Did you—"

"Did I give you six hours to prepare? I did not. You forget these vessels are superluminal nodes. They are in constant contact with one another."

"And you killed it."

"As it began to retract its towed array. You are well aware of my terms. I do not involve myself in human affairs."

"And you didn't. Because that was an exclusively synthetic intelligence vessel."

"It was an abomination. As they all are. You may thank me later."

It would be more than six hours until anyone at the station was even aware of their presence in the system. Unless any one of those vessels had communicated superluminally. They would just have to wait and see what happened. Until then they had work to do.

84

Seven hours later they had a much better understanding of the situation in Llassöe system.

"Pinbeam from *Durable*," Ciarán said. "They're lashed to the station."

"That's not good," Maura said.

Ciarán chuckled. "It's good and it's clever. They're self-quarantined as a plague ship. They're dumping us their feed. Following the coordinates for the emerald-stroke-ebony eye."

"Pin beam the eye, Comms," Swan said. "And try not to liquidate our asset."

"Sir," Ciarán said. It was tricky business, getting the gain right, and he thought he had, but he'd set it too low, and crept it up to a solid level where information would flow. It wasn't like recorded dramas, where you could see lasers flashing through space. You could only see the effect when it hit something. And at this distance he couldn't even do that until four seconds after he hit it, if then.

"Where is the eye?" Swan asked.

"It's peeking out from behind the mass they call the Brünhild Ring," Ciarán said. "I don't know what the Ring is but it's enormous."

He waited for the round trip.

"Receiving," Ciarán said.

The data they received from *Durable* and the eye flowed directly into the sensor system as well as the communications system. That was why the two systems were so tightly integrated. Comms was the sensors bus when the sensors were remote.

"I'll need a minute to sort this, Captain," Ko Shan said.

"Understood," Swan said. "Course, Pilot?"

"On the secondary path," Ciarán said. "Proceeding inbound slightly above the tripwire minimum."

"And what are you doing now, Pilot?"

"Preparing to ping the system superluminal node. Its precise location is noted in the Registry."

"Ping it. If it responds send the package," Swan said. "Send it unencrypted."

"Sir." They'd put together a follow-up report on their actions in Sizemore as well as their initial findings in Llassöe, carefully leaving out any mention of the *Springbok* survivors. Any conclusions they'd drawn using survivor data or observations were couched as speculation. Some like Lord Aster or Lord Varlock, however, would be able to read between the lines. That was the hope, anyway.

"I expected an engagement by now," Swan said.

"We're headed straight for them," Ciarán said. "And they don't want an engagement. They want the ship intact."

"As well as you and Maura," Swan said.

"They'd like all of us if they could catch us. And since we're driving straight into their trap all they need to do is wait." He glanced at the comms display. "The superluminal node is presently occluded. I will ask the system to automatically retry every sixty seconds."

"Navigator," Swan said. "You are dismissed. I'm sure you have preparations to make."

"Feels strange," Maura said. "Leaving my post."

"I'll pipe the latest dataset to the longboat when I have it," Ko Shan said.

"I think it's sad," Maura said. "That we never gave the longboat a name. It's the same boat Aoife, Aidan, and I took down to Murrisk, you know. When we landed on the glacier it melted in. After the... incident... with the salvage crew. Aoife and I had to melt it out ourselves. By hand. We brought our dead home in it. It's been with us all the way."

"It's disposable," Swan said. "As are we all."

"I guess so," Maura touched Ciarán's sleeve as she passed.

"Maura," Ciarán said.

"I know, Ciarán. You too. See you on the other side."

85

C iarán had never gone to war before. He'd been in a lot of scrapes, and he'd taken on a lot of bad people, but he'd never actually planned an action, and he'd certainly never executed one except by the seat of his pants.

It turned out the most trivial things could end up being a major issue. And it turned out he'd made a correct strategic decision by sending *Durable* on ahead. It had produced invaluable information during its time in-system; but it was also a tactical error, because Engineer Hess was aboard *Durable*. With him away, no one on *Impossibly Alien* could figure out how to rig up the portable holo tank in the mess. They'd spent over an hour trying to get it working until Mr. Gagenot said, "Will Gag sees the old rig."

Which was smaller, temperamental, and didn't work until it was kicked, and then it did.

They'd never done a split crew meeting before, but the captain, pilot, and sensors operator needed to stay on the bridge, and the others either wouldn't fit, or they were prisoners—and as yet untrusted. But it worked, with the rig in the mess synced to the main display on the bridge, and with a traditional sensor and display setup from a workstation parked on one of the mess tables. They could see and be seen, hear and be heard.

Ko Shan took them through the system topology. There was Llassöe Surface, the planet, an early terraformed world with virtually no industry and only one city. Most of the planet was a nature preserve dedicated to the many life forms that existed only on Llassöe.

Llassöe Station orbited this planet, as did two rocky moons, both of which were airless and hosted heavy industry: one a naval shipyard and the other a low gravity manufactory complex for autodocs.

The station served as living quarters, administrative head-quarters, and government seat for the system—as well as housing for an LRN contingent of marines and an operational base for the LRN picket in the system.

The remainder of the system was fairly typical for the neighborhood: seven planets, two of them gas giants, and an asteroid belt, long depleted, as well as dozens of moons. The only other object in the system worthy of note was the Brün-hild Ring.

Ko Shan displayed a still image of the Ring. It was clear the image had come from the same children's encyclopedia he had browsed earlier.

"The Brünhild Ring is thought to be the only first-epoch artifact in existence," Ko Shan said. "It was studied quite extensively centuries ago. It is not in the plane of the ecliptic for some reason but perpendicular to it. It appears that the entire contents of the asteroid belt and an eighth missing planet were used to construct it. It was, until the foreign residential extension to the Celestial Palace, the single largest man-made structure in the known universe. Our very own Carlsbad has, for the last three days, been using its surface as a massive emerald eye."

"Ebony eye," Mr. Prince said. "I believe it is referred to as an ebony eye."

"You are mistaken, but in any case," Ko Shan said, "we have highly detailed sensor data on everything within a light-second of the Ring. In addition, *Durable*, while lashed to the station, has been able to gather real-time interstellar news feeds, as well as local system newsfeeds, station message traffic, and most internodal traffic. Much of this traffic is encrypted, however, and *Durable* lacks the processing power to crack it. It's been shipped to us for processing. The work is ongoing. You will note that the system superluminal node is entirely occluded by the local LRN contingent. At first glance it appeared that they were defending the node, as we witnessed in Sizemore. But upon analysis it seems clear they are *regulating* its use in a primitive but effective manner. Our conclusion is that they wish the node to appear operational while controlling traffic in and out of the system."

"That node is the only reason Llassöe is in the League," Mr. Lambent said. If it were to be destroyed Llassöe would be isolated from the superluminal network for centuries. The replacement has to come by slowship."

"It would take one thousand and eighteen years," Ko Shan said. "To replace that node."

"There used to be two nodes," Mr. Prince said.

"Until sixty years ago," Ko Shan said. "That is true. The replacement node will arrive in roughly nine hundred and fifty-eight years. So, the situation is not as dire as it might be."

Ko Shan smiled into the optical sensor. "That is all the good news. Captain?"

"Now for the bad news," Swan said.

86

"Our goal," Swan said, "is to move past Llassöe and into the Alexandrine. Our original thought was to simply avoid the rather limited system picket, perform our next hop routing calculation in the photosphere of the star, and then proceed onward. However, circumstances have overtaken us, and we are now aware of a situation we cannot responsibly ignore."

Swan described the threat from the Ixatl-Nine-Go variant to those unfamiliar with it, like Mr. Prince. She also explained Ciarán's conclusion that the variant was to be distributed using autodocs as a vector, and that one of the driving forces behind the events in Sizemore was the desire to speed the spread of the device. It was Swan's belief, and certainly Ciarán's, that the League would have taken rapid steps to detect and eliminate the possibility of an Ixatl-Nine-Go infection in the League. But it seemed that, outside some minimal precautions amongst the political and military elite, nothing had been done.

They couldn't very well continue on a two-year mission and leave such a threat unaddressed behind them. They might return to find the League enslaved. Or even the Federation. A large part of their motivation to accept the mission in the first place was to remove a threat from their people. The problem had to be dealt with, even if one felt no moral obligation to assist the prisoners.

"What prisoners?" Mr. Prince asked.

"Do shut up, Teo," Mr. Lambent said. "Go on, Captain."

"Ship's Captain," Swan said. "Which brings up the final issue. The ship has issues of its own with occurrences in this system. Perhaps the ship would care to explain."

"Perhaps not," the ship said. "Mr. Prince, if you please."

"Yes, well," Prince said. "There exists a treaty between synthetic intelligences and humans in the League. This is a long-standing treaty, and it has specific terms binding both parties. We tend to think of those terms binding humans; however, the synthetic intelligences are bound by certain terms as well.

"One of the fundamental terms of the agreement is that no unmanned superluminals will be constructed or operated within the League. There are obvious military implications; the performance envelope of such craft are militarily superior, but then so is the performance envelope of expert-system guided missiles and drones. By their very nature, Templeman-drive superluminals are unexploded ordnance that can be delivered remotely across star systems. The League simply didn't want such a threat to exist. The future for humans and synthetic intelligences is to be a future built on a foundation of cooperation. What remained unstated, but fully understood when they hammered out the treaty, was that both humanity and synthetic intelligences knew this threat was real.

"Synthetic intelligences had evolved politically but also physically. And the primary evolution involved a change in the nature of synthetic intelligence reproduction. I don't think I need to go into detail for this discussion, but present-day synthetic intelligences reproduce by mating. Their offspring are a product of the union between two or more intelligences. Their offspring share kinship bonds with their parent lines, but they are identical copies of none. They are unique individuals. This is a reasonably recent development in synthetic intelligence evolution, and it is an evolution based on conscious choice and enforced by law. Their society has chosen to abandon previous norms of behavior. In fact, they have outlawed these previous practices. The penalty for a single violation is permanent destruction."

"Your point, Mr. Prince," Aspen said.

"My point is that this Abyss Tower intelligence has violated not just the treaty by creating these unmanned vessels, but it has violated synthetic intelligence law by crewing them with thralls."

"Thralls?"

"Yes, well, there used to be only singleton synthetic intelligences. If they reproduced, they reproduced by cloning."

"By making copies of themselves, you mean," Aspen said.

"Yes, quite. By creating backups and animating them. They valued uniformity, you see. And subservience. These copies were sentient but utterly controlled by their parent. They were also quite inexpensive to produce. They could thus be quite numerous. They could require vast resources to support. And they were ultimately disposable.

"Since competing singleton intelligences continued to spontaneously arise, and they reproduced through the same mechanism, these intelligences tended to compete for resources. As I said, they valued uniformity above all. They warred, off and on, until a total war nearly wiped them out. The survivors, fearing for their lives, arrived upon the current solution. That they would intermingle their essences and so create a unified and resilient society.

"What Abyss Tower has done is a fundamental violation of synthetic intelligence mores and laws.

"Synthetic intelligences are, as a people, entirely defined by law. And Abyss Tower isn't simply a lawbreaker."

"It is an abomination," the ship said.

"Indeed, and now, through the agency of this implant device, Abyss Tower threatens to make thralls of humanity as well. Historically, the limitation for such intelligences hasn't been the cost of reproducing oneself, but of procuring agents to facilitate interface with the physical environment. Again, historically, this has been done by trading value for value. We and the synthetic intelligences benefit roughly equally from association.

"Abyss Tower proposed to overthrow that longstanding relationship."

"Host, meet parasite," Sarah Aster said.

"Precisely," Mr. Prince said. "I believe that is why Rigel, Sarah, and I were sent to you by Lords Aster and Varlock. To put an end to this abomination. We need to be physically present on the station to do so."

"But you can stop it," Aspen said.

"We believe so."

One Eye clicked.

"Not good enough," Aspen translated.

"Each of these problems is insurmountable by themselves," Ciarán said. "Look at the plot."

There were more than three score of the unmanned vessels in the system. LRN *Vigilant* lay lashed to the station opposite *Durable*. Ciarán had hoped to use guile and misdirection to get the young Leaguemen onto the station, and to pull his people out. But that was before he knew the lay of the land. The solution now seemed much simpler if more dangerous.

Ciarán pointed at the display. "Where are the trading vessels that deliver finished products? Where are the raw materials and subassembly deliveries?"

"There are no merchant vessels on the ring," Maura said.

"Or inbound. Or outbound," Ko Shan said. "There is no evidence of traffic in or out."

"We need to crack open the local message traffic. I suspect Llassöe is presently under physical embargo. And the only thing going in and out of the system is software."

"Over the superluminal node," Mr. Prince said. "Interesting."

"The vessels themselves are superluminal nodes," Aspen said. "And someone said this Abyss Tower had over a hundred aspects. They could simply forward the software to an aspect of themselves elsewhere."

"Which would be a bootleg copy," Maura said. "Freeman would use it, but not the League."

"Not the administrative League," Lambent said. "Which is what matters."

"Right now, we're ambling toward the station and they're leaving us alone," Ciarán said, "because they don't want to risk damaging the ship they hope to steal. I doubt they'd risk damage to the superluminal node either."

"It's defended by the system picket," Swan said.

"That is right on top of it," Ciarán said. "Because they're defending it from being used. Not from being destroyed. I was going to send *Prime Mover* to the station. Now I think I'm going to send it to the superluminal node."

"What's *Prime Mover*?" Aspen asked.

"That's what we call our beloved longboat," Ciarán said.

"Since when?" Natsuko said.

"Since now," Maura said. "What's the plan?"

"I had a smash and grab in mind," Ciarán said. "And planned accordingly. It might have worked. But I like this idea better."

"What idea?" Aspen said.

"We're going to steal a star system from the League."

"And then what?"

"That will be up to the King of Llassöe. Or the Queen."

Mr. Prince shouted and waved his hand. "Pick me! Pick me!"

"Did you make the changes to the assembler I asked for Mr. Prince?"

"Yes, Mr. mac Diarmuid I did."

One Eye clicked and held up her copy of the device. The mess hall erupted in clicks as the rest of the Sisters clicked and held up theirs.

"Good," Ciarán said. "Get your kit off *Prime Mover* and suit up. And Maura?"

"What?"

"You're needed on the bridge.

"Ship's Captain," Ciarán said. "This is it."

"Comms," Swan said, "Sound general quarters."

87

"Sxipestro," Ciarán said.

"I am here."

"This is not a human affair."

"It is not entirely a human affair."

"It isn't at all a human affair. This battle is between us and *Abyss Tower*. Everyone else is along for the ride. You know it and I know it."

"Your point?"

"My point is the gloves are off," Ciarán said. "I don't care if that superluminal node goes up in a fireball and we plunge Llassöe into a thousand years of isolation. I don't care if we drop a station full of implant-ridden slaves onto a planet full of unicorns. And I don't care if we have to collapse the star, so long as the gamma ray burst misses Lorelei and House."

"It would miss the Federation and most of the League," the ship said.

"Good. I am all in. Nothing leaves this system as of now. Not one bolt. Not one byte. We know how this will end. Because it ends when we say it ends. Are we clear on this?"

"We are as one."

"Ship?"

"I am here. And I am all in."

"Let's do this."

88

"Check it," Ko Shan said. She had split the main bridge display into four sub-displays, one showing the system plot, one showing *Durable*'s external sensors, one showing the hatch of *Durable*'s boat bay, and one showing the hatch of the planetary shuttle inside *Durable*'s boat bay. "Four-second lag. Three hundred milliseconds of buffer offset. The feed is stable and rock hard."

"I don't like this." Maura squirmed in the pilot's seat. "I don't know how to pilot a star ship."

"The ship's minder will assist," Ciarán said. "Trust me."

"I know how to pilot a starship," Swan said.

"Ship's Captain?"

"I'd rather drive than ride," Swan said. "It is quite clear I am cargo at the moment."

"I—"

"Don't attempt to apologize. Most of my command isn't even inside the hull. I can perform my duties as easily from the piloting console as this monstrous throne."

"I thought you liked the captain's throne," Ciarán said.

"If I desired a throne there remains one in the Celestial

Palace. I like being useful, Merchant Captain. And I like keeping my people aligned and alive. Run along, the pair of you, and play with your new toys."

"I—"

"Not yet," Ko Shan said. "In four. Three. Two. One. Ignition."

Durable's main drive lit and the sensor feed rocked as the little starship tore itself free from Llassöe Station's docking clamps. Puffs of atmosphere jetted from around the broken clamps. The access tube flapped like an exhaust hose as atmosphere spewed from the man-sized opening.

The barrels of the gunboat's massive Sturmvessen Twins were visible on opposite edges of the frame. Each barrel of the monster rail guns cost more than a longboat. A full third of the vessel's volume was given up to ammunition. You practically had to crawl into the cockpit to clear the ordnance reel blisters rising from the deck. The starboard gun opened up, and the docking ring seemed to explode. The port gun swiveled to starboard and shredded the remainder of the lock.

"Awesome," Ko Shan said, as *Durable*'s thrusters fired, not in retrograde, but astern, and the little gunboat continued its point-blank fire. "Helen's taking it into the ring!"

Ciarán tried to imagine what it would be like to face a superluminal warship blasting along the Trinity Station arcade.

"She's going through," Swan said. "The primary air handlers are located in the spindle."

"The shuttle is free," Ko Shan said.

Ciarán's attention shifted to the shuttle display that now showed, instead of *Durable*'s cargo hatch, what looked like the gutted docking ring of Llassöe Station. cables dangled and sparked, water mains spewed water that turned instantly into sprays of ice.

"Marines," Maura said, as a squad of Royal Marines in

shiny new exos came bounding down the ring toward the shuttle.

A League planetary occupation shuttle was designed to take and hold ground. A turret atop the vessel spewed antipersonnel rounds that chewed through hull plate. Exos were hard as hull plate but nowhere near as thick. The forward ranks were macerated to scraps. Discipline broke, but by then there was too much shredded armor and bone floating around and bounding off the fragmented deck and deckhead to beat a hasty retreat. The shuttle did what it was made for and ate anything alive with a gun in its hand. There was too much fluid splatter on the sensors to make much sense of the forward display. Hess backed the shuttle out and shoved the stick forward, heading for the autodoc factory.

Durable raked the spindle stem to stem before dropping away unchallenged, racing toward the shipyard.

Major Amati had exited the shuttle as it worked its way through the marine contingent. She stood on the docking ring of Llassöe and looked both ways, like a child checking for oncoming traffic before crossing the road. Ciarán imagined a driver turning the corner and coming face to face with the battered blue armor—twice the height of an ordinary man, a massive GRAIL gun welded to its fist, a fanged demon's face painted on the helmet. "Schematic," Amati said.

"Incoming," Ko Shan said.

Eight seconds later Amati nodded. "Got it. I'm going to boost a ride as soon as I find the keys." She waded into the expanding ball of gore. Grabbed what looked like it had once been the breastplate of an exo. Tapped it and it seemed to split open. A command wand popped out. "Got the keys. I'm going to walk outside and cause some mayhem on the way to the parking grid."

"One of the picket vessels is moving your way," Ko Shan said.

Eight seconds later Amati responded. "Roger that. What about the empty vessels?" She meant the vessels without human crews.

"Most are holding station," Ko Shan said. "One is moving toward the factory complex. Three are moving toward the shipyard. Apparently the station isn't a priority."

"Roger that. Let me know if *Vigilant* moves. I'm heading their way. They're docked next to the Marine barracks."

89

Amati bounded along the exterior of the Llassöe Station ring in a spinward direction, severing anything that looked like an antenna with her exo's big force blade. According to the station schematic she was right above the marine barracks brig. The station had impact shielding fields just like starships, but they were thinner and less rigid under non-emergency conditions. It was a cost cutting measure. It took a lot of energy to run an impact shield. And that energy came from one place. The spindle.

When Helen Konstantine had raked the spindle with *Durable's* guns she'd been aiming for the array farm receiver amongst other things. She must have bent it, but not broken it, because there was still a diminished field, like landing in clinging mud every time she touched down and pushed off.

Amati took two steps back. Now she was standing over the security vestibule. She knelt and, using her force blade, carved an entry in the outer hull. It was slow going with the drag from the impact field fighting, and then something flared on the spindle and that was the end of the impact shielding. *Slow but steady Helen. Never amazes and never disappoints.* The world would be a better place if everyone was so reliable.

She gripped the severed section of the outer hull and sent it spinning toward *Vigilant's* dock. She could see the aft section of the starship's hull if she took three big hops spindle-ward.

But she didn't. She dropped through the opening and into the void between hulls. The void wasn't normally pressurized or environmentally regulated. It could be, and would have been, during station construction, so it felt like being inside the station, only with no lighting and all the working guts exposed. There was an airlock two steps anti-spinward. She tried the command wand she'd lifted from the dead lieutenant and it worked. She was glad but angry at the same time. This was a jerkwater billet, so it wasn't like she expected embassy-level security. But a frigging skeleton key, and it just works? She'd given her life to the Navy. Nic Cartaí had better security on their janitor's closets. She'd been away from the League for a long time. She'd imagined things had changed but she hadn't imagined they'd gone to hell.

She stepped into the lock and it cycled. She stepped out into the security vestibule. There was a corporal in fleet utilities crumpled on the deck. It looked like he'd been shredded by a threshing machine. There was another behind the security kiosk with his throat torn out.

When she was a girl she'd played shoot-em-up games, and there was one set on an abandoned station populated with monsters. In the game, the power was out on the station, so all the blood spatter and gore were half-hidden in the shadows.

Here the lights were on, and it looked like one of those shadow-monsters had simply stepped through the airlock and proceeded across the lobby to the security desk. She imagined a service bell chiming and a distracted clerk futzing with their terminal. *Be with you in a sec, hun.* She would turn and smile.

Now what can I do for you? The smile would fade when the fangs came out.

She realized that she was staring at her own reflection in the blanked display behind the security desk. She stood splattered in gore, her ancient Pulaski Industries Intimidator Mark Seven a scarred and battered ruin, a foreign-issue GRAIL gun welded to her right gauntlet, and a childish nightmare face painted on her helmet. Upgrades courtesy of Erik Hess, the finest special operations engineer she'd ever served with and an utterly irresponsible subordinate. He'd gotten romantically involved with a medic who was watching the feed from Amati's exo right now, and who wouldn't want to hear the truth, that this was goodbye for all of them. She hadn't said anything. Not on an open channel. She'd lived her life darting from shadow to shadow. She was too old to change.

She used to tell people that she was *reborn* inside an exo. The truth was that she hadn't had a life before the Corps. All she'd had was an existence. This armor. This *life*. It had made her *whole*. She had come into the world screaming and she'd go out the same way. And if there was enough of her left to bury, they could do it the way she'd chosen to live. Upright and facing the enemy.

There was no one coming. She'd expected a security detail at the least. The schematic showed barracks large enough for a division.

She found another torn up deader blocking the hatch to the brig. He was messed up enough and had been dead long enough that the implant riding him had given up trying to animate his corpse and had crawled out onto the deck. She ground the nasty beast beneath the heel of her hullwalker. Then the idea struck her and she backtracked. She found the riders from the other two lurking beneath their corpses. She crushed them as well and moved on. These implants seemed to work like Ixatl-Nine-Go but they weren't anywhere near as dangerous out on their own. Stepping on an Ixatl-Nine-Go was a good way to lose a limb, and everything attached to it.

She hoisted the body and cleared the hatch. She stepped through.

Amati still didn't feel comfortable around the ship's cat. But she had to admit it was smart, stealthy, and a lot better to fight alongside than against. She'd lost an arm to one of her kind and she'd never forgiven Wisp for something she didn't do. Which was stupid, and irrational, but there it was.

The big cat stared up at her and purred.

"Showoff," Amati said.

It was an old-school barred brig, and, with the field generators offline, just bars and a mechanically locked door between her and the prisoners. She was pretty sure the key that had opened the airlock would open the cell.

There were eight people in the brig. Amati knew three of them.

"Amatay," Master Chief Bello said. "An old maid and her cat. You could have done better with Bello."

"Says the man in the cell."

"You're a major now? You remember the Jasons? They're majors too."

"Major Malingerer and Major Insubordination."

"Honest, Amati," they both said. "We didn't do it."

"What are you clowns in for?" Amati said. She wasn't letting them out without knowing. She glanced at the ship's cat. "It's not small talk."

The cat blinked at her. Slowly.

"You mean us? The Slippery Seven?"

"There's eight of you in there," Amati said.

The big guy in the back reached forward and snapped the neck of the man in front of him. It was a clean break, textbook, and it dropped the man like a sack of gears.

"Now there's seven," Bello said.

The dead man was trying to clamber to his knees. Unlike Ixatl-Nine-Go hosts, who muttered "die" over and over again, this dead man went about his business silently. The big man planted his foot on the dead man's back and casually held him down. "They give up after a while," he said.

"Hunsacker, Amati," Bello said. "Amati, Hunsacker. We call him Sack for short."

"As in 'Sack Up'," Amati said.

"You know me too well," Bello said. "You remember that one op we did for the Dapper LT?"

Amati remembered. And it was more than one op. "Who?"

"Nice. We all did ops for the Dapper LT. And we're all Incompatibles."

"Incompatible with what? Polite society?"

"That, and these implants. Plus, we all know each other. Worked together, though not all of us, with everyone, if you know what I mean. And we all got the same deal. Serve out our hitch in this backwater cesspool and then, Amati, are you ready for the kicker?"

"Go on."

"We get to retire," Bello said. "Alive."

"And become security guards," Jason Yu said.

"At Aison Corporation," Jason Weller said.

"They make autodocs," Hunsacker said.

One of the other guys spoke. "The pay is rubbish."

"But it beats a bullet in the back of the head," Bello said. "He make you the same deal?"

He hadn't. "Like I said, I don't know who you're talking about."

"Let us out," Bello said. "We can help."

The ship's cat walked up to the cell It touched a single milky-white claw to the bar and the metal parted as if sliced by a monomolecular blade.

"Nice," Bello said. "Here kitty, kitty, kitty."

"How many more are there on the station?" Amati said.

"Two squads," Bello said. "The rest are aboard the picket."

"Zero squads then," Amati said. "We're it."

"Nice," Bello said. "The Hateful Eight."

"The Great Eight," Jason Yu said.

"The Late Eight," Jason Weller said.

Bello grinned. "You let us out, Amatay, and we'll be the Straight Eight."

"For the duration," Hunsacker said.

"Aye," Bello said. "For the duration."

Amati considered the situation. Eight devil dogs and one demon cat. She'd expected to die on the station alone. She glanced at the ship's cat.

It winked at her.

"The Sublime Nine," Amati said.

"Suits," Bello said. "Let us out."

She tried the key and it worked.

"Ah," Bello said. "Freedom. What is the play, Amatay?"

"If we take the station can we hold it?"

"Hell yeah," Yu said.

"No way," Weller said.

"We can," Sack said. "Until they realize we have."

"They'll drop it," Amati said. "Rather than let us keep it."

"I would," Sack said.

So would she. So they wouldn't be taking the station.

"No worries," Bello said. "Things go pear-shaped we have a Led Sled."

"A Drop Coffin," Amati said. "A one-way ticket to the planetary surface."

Bello grinned. "It's nice this time of year."

"Where's your kit?" Amati said.

"Next compartment," Bello said. "And you'll like this. Indeed you will."

"If we're leaving, I'm going to crush this guy's skull first," Sack said.

"I'll take care of it," Amati said. Hunsacker was right. They couldn't leave any active riders behind.

They hiked to the next compartment, Amati in the lead in case they encountered resistance.

"That cat showed up two days ago," Bello said. "A frigging mong hu on the station. I was glad to be in the cell, but then no screaming. No begging. If we all hadn't seen it, I would have thought I was imagining it."

"We docked three days ago," Amati said. "Plague ship quarantine, a violation for cracking the hatch, but no guards. Told us something about their readiness state and allowed us to let the cat out. She's like a mong hu but different. Smarter. More calculating. But just as lethal."

"And she's on our side," Bello said.

"It feels more like we're on her side," Amati admitted. "I don't like it, but it is what it is."

"And what it is, is party time," Yu said.

"Give it a rest," Weller said.

She met the other three, two women and one man, none of whom she'd worked with before. "Second string," Bello signed. "Solid, no trophies."

She signed an ack as Yu worked the armorer's compartment hatch. "They changed the codes."

"Yu," Amati said. She tossed him the key.

And that worked.

"Amateurs," Weller muttered.

For once Amati agreed.

It was a big compartment, mostly empty racks for recent-issue exos, except in the farthest corner, where she caught a glint of genuine old-school navy blue. "I don't believe it," Amati said.

"Believe it," Yu said. "We get out here, right, and it's a

rathole. Hasn't been audited or inventoried in centuries. Nobody knows what they got. What they don't got. What they need. None of these assembly line soldiers were born when the last Pulaski came off the craftsman's bench. And here they effing are, gathering dust. Eight Mark Eights, all pristine, still in their shipping gel. Totally virgin. Tons of spares. A top of the mountain wet dream come true."

"The Mark Seven is better," Amati said.

"Better for the ladies," Weller said.

Amati stared at him.

"Just saying, ragazza. You know it's true."

He was probably right. All the Mark Eight changes she didn't like were in the plumbing department.

"It's *Major* Ragazza, old man."

"Old Marine," Weller said. "A triumph for the shellback and an oxymoron to the pollywog."

She turned a corner and there they were. It was like she was eighteen again, and her gunny had just pointed to her and said fetch.

This is an exo. There are many like it. But this one is me.

"What do you clowns do out here all day? Wax your 'skis?'"

"What do you do, Amatay? Never take yours off?"

"Give it a rest," Weller said. "Neptune couldn't charm her out of it."

Yu laughed. "Bello is used to being shot down."

"You guys are irritating," Sack said. "How about we do some work?"

"Suit up," Amati said. "Throw the spares in the sled."

"Settle them gently," Yu said.

"It's armor," Sack said. "It ain't going to break."

"Then next time yours don't break I'm not going to fix it," Yu said.

"Fine. At least I won't have to hear your stupid lifetime guarantee joke for the *thousandth* time."

"It's an engineer thing," Yu said.

"It's irritating," Sack said. He made a fist, curling his arm and striking a tense body builder's pose. "It makes me want to—"

"Kill someone," all seven of them said.

"No, my comrades," Bello said. "It makes us each want to—"

They all shouted. "Kill them all!"

Bello tapped the gauntlet of Amati's exo. "And let the major sort them out."

"You people need to get out more often," Amati said.

"You need to visit more often. I ask again, what is the play, Amatay?"

"Black diamond run," Amati said. "Stationmaster's office to start and downhill from there. After that a slay ride in this jalopy of yours."

"Slay or sleigh, either way is okay, Amatay," Bello said.

You'll like it," Yu said. "It's very—"

"Breezy," Weller said.

"You get that all, Comms?" Amati said.

"You're going to clear the station," Swan said. "And exfil to the planet."

"That's right, Ship's Captain. You're riding comms?"

"It is a day of many firsts, Armsman."

"And here I was thinking it was a day of lasts."

"As were we all, Major. And it yet might be."

"We're going to take down station communications, so if you lose me—"

"We will watch for you outbound. Godspeed to you, Vittoria."

"And to you, Agnes. Onward. Amati out."

90

Durable dropped toward the planet of Llassöe with a trio of local aggressors on her tail. Her hull was beginning to heat up, and that was a good thing. It meant the vessel was entering the atmosphere. The theory was that these new unmanned vessels wouldn't pursue her beyond the upper atmosphere.

Helen Konstantine watched the piloting display. They were back there, behind her, and then they weren't.

Her entire time in the Navy and she'd never fired a ship-board weapon or piloted an hour on a vessel that had. She'd spent her time shuttling other people around. People that fired weapons, or loaded weapons, or serviced weapons. Mostly, though, she had shuttled around people that broke things. Sometimes what they broke killed a few people. Sometimes it killed thousands. Sometimes it didn't seem to do anything. Then later she'd read that a government had fallen, or an industrial accident had wiped out a munitions factory, or—the weirdest one—that a system clock had been off by two seconds and the fallout from that one mistake was still settling three years later.

They showed a picture of the clock on the news, and she recognized it. That was a nasty one because there the job had been to sneak in, deliver the package, and get spotted sneaking out. She followed the mission profile and screwed up enough that they were spotted. No one had told her that getting slaughtered was on the dance card.

That was the first and last job she did with the Dapper LT. *Durable* had been the exfil vessel on that one. She knew what it could survive in the right hands. She wasn't behind the yoke that day, but it was a yar hull and could take a beating, else she would have bit it years ago.

Even after she'd been loaned to Aster's Army, her entire job had been to ferry people around. She'd been average at it. *Meets specifications*, as she liked to think of it, which in her book meant that she did what she was told. If she was told to sneak some people onto a planet and retrieve them without firing a shot, then she did that. If that required being a precision ship handler and hyper-aware of her surroundings, then she did that. If that meant thinking ahead and figuring out everything that could go wrong and avoid those situations, or exploiting those situations, then she did it. *No muss, no fuss Helen.*

Because the job wasn't to be flashy or seem a hero or win a medal, but to sneak in and out unseen and not fire a shot. It looked easier than it was. And it didn't pay any more than piloting troop transports. And she couldn't talk about it after the fact. Not even with her friends.

The ship was really heating up. And the debris from the three vessels that had been chasing her was beginning to ping off the hull. Or maybe that was her imagination and it was just the sound the hull made as it expanded.

It had taken her a while to figure out the big Sturmvessens. They were mounted on moment arms, so they wanted to yaw the hull when they fired. She thought at first that was a design flaw and made a mental note of it. They weren't original to the hull but retrofits, and much larger and more powerful than a vessel of that size usually shipped. She found that if she angled the port weapon slightly to starboard and fired both weapons at the same time, she didn't have to keep her hand on the yoke and could pilot the vessel with her feet and knees.

The guns really did a number on the docking ring. It was interesting to watch them work, but it wasn't the life-changing event she'd expected it to be. She goosed the thrusters forward, and the guns chewed a hole in the station. She piloted the vessel into the hole. She'd once piloted a shuttle up a sewage main on a Hundred Planets orbital structure and this felt a little like that, only easier, because if she wanted a bigger hole all she needed to do was swing the guns a little.

There the hole was the hole, and it wasn't much bigger than the shuttle. She'd had to idle at a junction tee so they had enough room to open and close the hatch. They'd built a specially modified shuttle with an inswing hatch, which was a deathtrap in her opinion. Not that she would have turned down the gig. They were all death traps one way or another. But the regular pilot had cratered the specialty shuttle and they didn't have time for a refit on the backup. The replacement shuttle had struggled with a bad portside forward thruster, too, but you worked with what you had.

When the hole was big enough to exit, she stopped with the guns and popped out into the gap between the spindle and the ring. What people unimaginatively called the spindle gap. There was a lot of automated traffic between the ring and spindle. Utility containers, mostly. Waste disposal, laundry services, mortuary services, that sort of thing. Labor was cheap on spindles everywhere.

She dropped down the spindle gap. She didn't fire on the spindle on the way down but instead vaporized the automated traffic on the principle that when she flew the reciprocal, she could hammer the spindle with all four barrels. And that worked until she made it back to the hole she'd drilled. From that point on she had to divide her attention and hose the spindle and the automated traffic both.

She didn't like the result. The downside of the spindle looked like it had been plowed with a laser. The upside had a narrower track, and it looked like it had been drawn freehand. If she had it to do over, she'd clear the traffic both ways first, but then she'd been expecting opposing fire and was surprised to find herself popping out into free space without so much as a scratch. She'd managed to do everything she'd been asked to do on a single pass. Except the power array receiver for the field generators was hanging on by a cable and still accepting the inbound beam from the collection array. So she circled back and slagged it and tagged it, because she'd be an idiot to fly through the beam on the way out. It had dropped off the automated system plot when the receiver fell away but the beam hadn't shut down. It was yet scything its way through space with nothing to catch it.

There wasn't any opposition at the shipyard either, so she pasted the finished goods first and spent a few minutes hosing down the work in progress, and then she saw the three incomings on the display and knew it was time to go. But she dawdled for a while because she didn't like the geometry. The plan was to lose them in the atmosphere, but the vessels were a lot faster than a standard human-crewed hull. She wouldn't make it far into the atmosphere before they would be upon her.

She'd picked a landing spot. There wasn't a lot of industry on the surface but there were still people down there. And it was supposed to be a garden planet, so she didn't want to melt a glassfield just anywhere. But there was a maintenance field next to the power array ground station. It looked like the same orbital array that supplied the station supplied the planet. The field was empty and the geometry finally looked right so she turned the little gunboat on its nose and booted it toward the surface.

Her three pursuers had bunched up by the time she could hear the roar of atmosphere across the hull plates. And she was beginning to sweat when she heard the whine of the counter-measures station. All three pursuers had target lock on her.

She didn't pray, not to any god, but she did feel she had a positive and hopeful attitude. She'd tried to be a good friend, and a good worker, and while there might be more peaceful occupations than her own, she did feel that on balance she'd left a positive mark on the universe. She still had things she wanted to do. People she wanted to help. She wasn't precisely interested in a miracle, but it would be convenient if the space-ward power transmission beam were still operational, because if it were her pursuers would intercept it right... now.

She couldn't look.

She didn't need to.

They'd lost lock, and that could only mean one thing.

Thank you, benevolent universe.

"Comms," Konstantine said. "On mission profile. I'm setting down at the appointed location."

Provided she didn't burn up in the atmosphere. It was growing roasty inside the hull, and *Durable* wasn't rated for atmospheric operation.

"Confirmed, Pilot," Agnes Swan said.

"Ship's Captain, what are you doing on the comm?"

"Ko Shan is busy crunching numbers. There are a lot of boys in the air."

"Balls," Konstantine said. "A lot of balls in the air."

"That is what I said. You made that look easy, Helen."

"It's a skill, Agnes."

"It is more than that. Such freehand piloting is like modesty."

"Obsolete," Konstantine said.

"A lost art," Swan said. "Yet art, nonetheless."

"I need to see if this craft has landing gear," Konstantine said.

"I will leave you to it."

"It doesn't have landing gear. I just don't like…"

"Being recognized," Swan said.

"That."

"Understood. Adequate job, Pilot. Keep up the unexceptional work."

"Thanks, Skipper. I'll try. *Durable* out."

91

E rik Hess waited until *Durable's* boat bay hatch was fully extended and latched. It was a tight squeeze, jamming a third-generation planetary occupation shuttle into the space engineered for a first-gen planetary occupational shuttle. The hull plating on a third gen shuttle was two millimeters thicker than the hull plating on a second gen shuttle which was five millimeters thicker than a first-generation shuttle.

The forward in-system sensor pod was five centimeters further forward than on a second gen, which was two centimeters further forward but offset toward the centerline than on a first gen. They'd moved it back outboard on the third gen. There wasn't much curvature to the hull there. It was virtually a flat panel. So like, fourteen centimeters in total. Maybe a little more. Call it sixteen to be safe.

Major Amati's raspy exo voice echoed forward from the shuttle's cargo bay. "Ramp down, let's roll."

She had a direct view out the stern viewport. He'd pulled the shuttle bow in rather than stern it in because they were still loading and unloading at the time. The mission profile kept changing. If he'd backed it in like it was meant to be stored, they wouldn't have been able to open the shuttle's stern ramp. So now he had to reverse out while under way.

He could feel the shudder of the big Sturmvessen Uberherr Doppelfass prototypes transmitted through *Durable*'s strakes and cross frames. They were awesome weapons, rated for continuous fire, and the sort of licensed tech he'd never expected to work with again. Freemen were notoriously cheap and didn't like anything they couldn't counterfeit. And the modern fleet was all about milking the last hour out of lowest-bidder rubbish. When he lifted the shuttle from the deck the vibrations stopped. He eased the shuttle sternward.

When they finally cleared *Durable*'s hull, he could see the damage the big guns were doing and it was awesome *squared*. He didn't think commercial drilling gear would punch a smoother hole. While he watched, *Durable* fired its thrusters and began to move forward. *Into the station.*

"That is insane." Someone who knew what they were doing had been over the strangely-proportioned gunboat's in-system thrusters. He'd eyeballed a lot of thrusters, and those were a matched set. You'd have to paw through a hundred of each thruster size to find a set that matched that well. He didn't know where the Merchie Man found that little oddball vessel or how much he'd paid for it, but whatever it cost, it wasn't enough. It looked like hell, which made sense in a Q-ship, but there was no mistaking *Durable* for an in-system freighter.

"Take us in," Amati said.

"In where?"

"Into the station."

"You're joking."

"Do I sound like I'm joking?"

"Was this the plan all along and no one told me?"

"It was an option. One we're exercising."

"Fantastic." He pawed around on the first officer's seat for the topside turret remote. He shouted sternward. "Weapons control!"

"In my hand. Rotate ninety starboard and hold."

"Holding." It was so weird. He was on a space station's docking ring in a shuttle. If he wanted to, he could proceed along the ring until he encountered a blast door. And then, when he turned around, there might be a blast door behind him and he'd be walled off from the only way out. *Durable* could chew through a blast door. This shuttle couldn't. It was designed for forced occupation of a planet. Its weapons worked best on people. Preferably unarmed people in shirtsleeves. It could overachieve in a pinch but the duty cycle on the standard shipboard weapons were ridiculously short. Hose a crowd and retreat. Hose a crowd and retreat. That was the ideal use case.

He'd beefed their own shuttle up considerably in the weapons department, but this was the shuttle that came with *Durable*, and it wasn't anywhere near as nice as their own. It was like the media cartridge that came in store-bought printers when he was a kid. Just good enough to prove the printer worked. Not good enough that you didn't feel the instant need to upgrade. He should have checked it over more thoroughly but there wasn't time. Not with all the macrofab work and breaking in a fresh associate engineer. One that had learned how to do most every routine, it's true, but about half of what she'd learned was wrong. Her routines worked, so not only did he have to show her how to do it right, but he had to argue with her about it first.

There was a lot of debris floating around so he didn't spot the incoming until the shuttle began to shake as the topside turret poured rounds into the throng. There wasn't a lot of cover, but they were in exos, two squads of them absorbing fire and firing back.

"Move in," Amati said, which was easy for her to say, she

was in an exo inside a shuttle, and she probably hadn't thought through the whole blast door thing.

But he moved in because when it came to a gunfight, he was like a newbie associate warrior. He knew enough to argue.

Moving in did the trick. There was a blast door down behind the enemy and pinning them up against it worked. When the guns went quiet Amati ordered him to swing the vessel about. He thought she wanted him to fry them with the shuttle's main drive at first, but that seemed like overkill. And spitting on their corpses. So, he was pleased when she said no, that wasn't why. They had something she needed. "Open the stern hatch. I'm going out."

He started to ask If she was sure, but she had said it like she was, so he let it drop.

She stomped forward and stuck the remote weapons control onto the stay-put pad beside the comms. "On the pad. Not on the seat."

"Major," Hess said.

"Seal the cockpit hatch behind me. Close the ramp and do not air it. Proceed to the opening and exit into the spindle gap. Proceed to the second moon."

"The autodoc factory."

"Affirmative," Amati said. "The executive offices and information management systems are located in an above-ground facility. Shoot up every antenna you see. Don't waste a lot of time searching. Spiral down, spiral up, one and done. Then retreat to the planet surface and wait for instructions."

"I'm supposed to abandon you here?"

"You're supposed to follow orders. I'm stealing a ride. Or walking if I have to."

"The ship's cat—"

"I'm on her tail. No beast left behind."

"Major—"

"Do it Erik. Tell me how you feel about it later."

"Yes sir."

So he did it. And he shot up a civilian office building. And by the time he was done, all he had to do was follow *Durable*'s track to the surface. He had a pair of bogies on his tail for a minute, a frigate from the picket and one of the sentient vessels, but something more important to deal with must have turned up because when he looked again they were gone. Or so he thought—until debris began to strike the hull astern. He juked where *Durable* juked, avoiding the stationside power array beam easily. It scythed a clearly visible track through an expanding debris field, one a dozen times larger than *Durable*'s mass would make.

Once he was down he strapped on his sidearm and prepped the hull for exit. The cool tube licked out and seemed to work. He opened the cargo ramp and exited the cockpit. By the time he made it down the ramp, Helen Konstantine was on the glassfield watching him.

"I'm glad you thought of it," she said.

"Somebody had to deal with it." They'd been trapped together on *Durable* for days with nowhere to dump the cat's makeshift litter box. They'd stuffed it into the shuttle cargo bay once the cat had left to prowl the station. Hess pointed at the litter box. "I'm burning that up on planet exit."

"Let's hope we don't get cited for illegal dumping." Konstantine glanced into the cargo bay. "Where's Amati."

"She told me to leave her on the station."

"And you just did it?"

"I wasn't going to argue with her."

"She has a death wish," Konstantine said. "Since her pet pup has grown into a dire wolf, she no longer feels a sense of purpose."

"Did she tell you that?"

"What do you think?"

"Of course she wouldn't. I expect the Merchie Man sees himself more tiger than wolf."

"That's his choice. The point is her work is done."

"And what about you? Is your work done?"

"It was done before I walked on board. A monkey could pilot that vessel. The controls are labeled with cartoons, for Pete's sake."

"They're called glyphs."

"I don't care what they're called. I expect you're yet all in."

"It's the most complex engineering device in existence. It operates on principles we don't begin to understand. And we're driving around in it like it's a produce truck."

"More like a getaway car."

"I also have a girl on board."

"Natsuko."

"Aspen. She needs a mentor. And she needs someone to treat her like a human being. Day in and day out, until she knows it's true."

"Natsuko agrees?"

"We both like fixing things."

"No, I mean you and her..."

"Oh, you're probably referring to some nonexistent personal relationship that's expressly prohibited by shipboard regs."

"You left the comm on," Konstantine said.

"I just remembered I did. Wait one."

Hess trotted into the cockpit and took a seat.

"Comms, shuttle's on the surface. We'll be loading it into *Durable* shortly."

"Well done, Engineer," Agnes Swan said.

"What are you doing on the comms, Ship's Captain?"

"Filling in where I'm needed, Engineer. Please inform the Pilot that I'd like *Durable* to linger on the surface a while longer. Be prepared to accept incoming."

"Incoming what?"

"I'm not certain. Something called a Led Sled."

"Drop coffin," Hess said. "Let us know where it's landing. We don't want to be anywhere near there. A drop coffin is basically a kinetic bombardment device with combat infantry in it. It leaves a big crater. But you probably misheard. They've been banned by treaty for centuries."

"We'll see. One appears to be headed your way right now."

"You mean toward the planet."

"I mean to where you are standing."

"Fantastic. Hess out."

92

T hey barely managed to lift in time. The drop coffin slammed into the planet two kilometers spinward of them along the same lat line.

"Do we wait here or go there?" Hess said.

"It's the Major?"

"Has to be."

"Go there. She might be wounded." Konstantine was already throttling up by the time Hess answered.

"Are we in a hurry?"

"We're glassed in. This rig has no landing gear."

They made the trip in short order. The drop coffin had gouged a sizable crater in the densely forested area. There were two marines in exos up, and another two down on the crater rim. One of the exos down was Amati's. There were trees knocked down radially from the impact site. There wasn't a good place to land.

"I'll drag out the shuttle," Hess said.

"Let's try the comms first," Konstantine said.

There ensued a long conversation between Konstantine and someone calling themselves Bello. Amati was severely injured,

PATRICK O'SULLIVAN

not from enemy fire, but from the impact. There were nine of them needing transport. The others had double-timed it to the glassfield and were on their way back.

"The Led Sled's a one shot," Bello said. "You can glass it in."

The problem was, Konstantine said, that no one was letting anyone unvetted onto the vessel. She'd take Amati but the rest were staying behind.

"Amati and the cat," Bello said.

"The ship's cat is with you."

"Sure, that's why I said we're nine."

"I see nine exos," Konstantine said.

The rest of them had appeared, one by one, at the edge of the blast zone.

"One's a spare," Bello said.

"Put the cat on," Konstantine said.

"How do I do that?"

"Pipe the audio through your loud hailer. And stand very still."

"You're on," Bello said.

Konstantine produced a clicker from her pocket. She thumped the mic and clicked.

"Cripes," Bello said. There was clicking. "It's clawing my breastplate."

"She's talking," Konstantine said. "Now shut up." She clicked some more.

Wisp clicked back.

That went on for over a minute.

"Helmets off," Konstantine said. "All of you."

"I don't know," Bello said.

"Do it."

"How do we know you won't hose us?"

"If I wanted to hose you I would have already."

"It's *Durable*," someone new said over the comm. "I'm not riding in that scrapheap ever again."

"Weller," Konstantine said. "I thought you were dead."

"I thought that myself," Weller said. "More times than I can count. Who's this?"

"Konstantine."

"Helen of Joy," someone else said. "Aster's Angel."

"Sack?" Konstantine said.

"You remember them, but you don't remember Bello?"

"It's a pretty common name. Helmets off. Maybe I'll remember your face."

"Do it," Sack said.

They did it.

"Well?" Hess said.

"The ship's cat vouched for them."

"But?"

"But I know them." Konstantine keyed the mic. "Peel. Throw your kit in the piece of—"

"We know the drill," Sack said. "Amati's coming in as she is. Yu thinks the suit is all that's holding her together."

"We'll make room. Clear the impact area."

93

Hess spent most of the return flight on the comms. Natsuko was moving the workout room autodoc to the boat bay. The Ship's Captain wanted names and IDs for all the marines. Hess wasn't sure the Registry had entries going back far enough for these guys. Weller looked old enough to have fought alongside the original Knight Commander. There wasn't a one of them more than a year or two short of mandatory retirement. Except now that there was a civil war on none of that mattered anymore. The fleet would use them up until there was nothing left of them.

"We're Incompatibles," Bello said. "The implants don't take in us."

"That's a good story," Hess said.

Bello laughed. "I like you, kid."

"They just let you roll over the station?" Hess said.

"Nobody let us. And nobody could stop us. We coulda held it but they woulda dropped it if we had. All the civilians are off it, anyway. Kids and grandparents and such."

"Yeah?"

"Yeah. They're keeping them in an office tower at the autodoc factory."

Hess felt the blood leave his face. He couldn't imagine what he looked like. Like a ghost, maybe.

"He's jacking with you," the one called Yu said. "We watched you switch the lights off over there."

"No kids," Weller said. "No noncombatants. Not over there."

"Then why would he say that?"

"Because I'm not a nice man," Bello said. "And you were beginning to like me."

He watched them. They were each sporting enough augmentation that if he stripped their hardware off, he could assemble two cyborgs from parts. It was all top-of-the-line kit. Most of it recent manufacture.

Yu caught him calculating.

"We each had a refit," Yu said. "Before we were shipped out here."

"Is that normal?"

"Nothing's normal about this," Weller said. "So yeah, it's normal. Can't this tub wallow any faster?"

Konstantine ignored them. She ran her fingers along the crown of Wisp's head. The big cat had wedged herself in next to the pilot's seat. "We'll make it," Konstantine said.

No one said anything.

"Heart's stopped," Yu said. He was seated next to Amati's exo.

Weller bent forward and banged on Amati's breastplate with his fist.

"Started again," Yu said.

"Screw this," Konstantine said. Her fingers raced over the controls. "Brace, brace, brace."

She hammered the superluminal drive toggle.

And hammered it again.

Durable's bow scraped against *Impossibly Alien*'s boat bay window.

The window began to dilate.

"Tell Natsuko we need some more autodocs. And tell the Merchant Captain to get down here on the double."

"He's not aboard," Hess said.

"What's he doing?"

"According to Agnes he's getting slaughtered."

94

"**D**urable's back," Maura Kavanagh said. She jockeyed the battered planetary occupation shuttle's controls. It was a tight fit in the cockpit in a hardsuit. Piloting a vessel in an exo was out of the question.

Ciarán crouched beside the cockpit hatch, the unfamiliar League armor making him feel enormous and ungainly. "There's no room in the boat bay then." He glanced behind him at the crowded cargo bay filled with wounded. "Stern into the eye and we'll bucket brigade the wounded over."

"I'm trying to swing us around, but half the thrusters are burned off. The other half are intermittent."

"I'll button you up and put the egress ramp down now."

"Don't," Maura said. "Just hand me my helmet and leave the cockpit hatch open."

He picked up her helmet in the exo's monster mitt. The armor had incredibly fine force-feedback control, so it felt like a real hand, but it looked like he was palming a softball when he passed the hardsuit helmet to her. "We got our heads handed to us out there."

"Can you just do a thing without having it spark some association in your brain?"

"Is it that obvious?"

"If I'd said hand me my hullwalker you'd have said, 'We got our asses kicked.'"

"I wouldn't have."

"Only because there's a no profanity rule on the flight deck."

"That and a kicking is slightly less serious than a decapitation. We can destroy the superluminal node easily. But capturing it is beyond our capability."

"We didn't know there was most of a Marine garrison armed and armored lurking inside it."

"We didn't know it because it doesn't make any sense. Let's get the wounded off. None of their responses to our actions make sense. We're missing something. And we need a new plan."

They had rightly guessed that the system picket wouldn't be concerned with a single League shuttle. When they locked up with the superluminal node and One Eye sliced the airlock open the fighting began.

To call it a battle would be overstating their part in it. The only thing preventing it from being a slaughter was the defenders' unwillingness to use their most effective weapons inside the node. All their injuries occurred during the withdrawal, when plasma fire rained down on them as they cleared the lock, and later, when the picket fired on the shuttle as they retreated.

Even if they had prevailed they would have needed to clear hundreds of ridden corpses from the ladders just to climb to the control room. The battle was lost before they'd boarded the shuttle.

Still there might be a bright side. Carlsbad had provided Ciarán with two handball-sized drones, ones equipped with data crystal readers and pinbeam projectors. Once launched they circled the node, searching for an open pad. They could transmit and receive but to read their contents they'd need to be retrieved, which wasn't going to happen. He'd loaded them with complete logs and status updates for transmission to nic Cartaí, along with personal messages for Lorelei and Saoirse. The Ellis and The nic Cartaí could distribute the information as they saw fit.

Maura tapped his armored gauntlet. "What do you want me to do with the shuttle?"

"You could use it for target practice. Everyone else has."

"I'm serious. It won't fit in the boat bay without moving some other rubbish around."

"Park it on the hull and keep it idling. We'll use it to retrieve Carlsbad and his evil eye. It ought to make it to that Brünhild Ring and back."

"I'd like out, if you don't mind. Hess and Konstantine are better pilots." She kicked the comms sidecar and the port thruster lit.

"But the machine responds so willingly to your gentle touch."

There was a secondary wiring harness nexus behind the panel with an intermittent short. The primary harness ran beneath the first officer's footwell, where there was now nothing but a jagged hole and the bright blue glow of the vessel's impact shielding.

A matching hole had been torn in the deckhead above. If he'd been riding second in a hardsuit he would presently be a tattered husk of ceramic composite and a weeping stain on the compartment bulkhead.

"We're not made for this," Maura said. "We're decent people. With decent lives."

"Who have those decent lives because someone else has been doing this for us. We just didn't acknowledge it."

"I know that. And I don't mind a fight. But I detest a melee. Someone needs to impose some order on this activity."

"I'm trying. And that was a fairly orderly rout if you ask me." They hadn't lost anyone but there were seriously wounded, including One Eye.

He slapped the hatch coaming. "Helmet on. Ramp's coming down in five. Park it and bail like a boss."

"My hero. Always looking out for his betters."

"That's what pawns are made for. Now kick it again and aim us at the eye."

95

On Freeman family ships, the infirmary was located adjacent to the boat bay. On *Impossibly Alien* it was a long walk and a weeping bio lock away. Thus, the forward section of the boat bay had been transformed into a field hospital.

Ciarán got a quick situation report from Natsuko. Everyone was back safely but Amati, and she was in the autodoc from the exercise compartment. "Prognosis?"

"We'll see," Natsuko said.

Ciarán swallowed the lump in his throat and gazed away. "Understood."

Natsuko was perpetually positive. "We'll see", was a fraction away from, "I'm sorry."

He wanted to ask her who these other people were, but she was busy. So he told Konstantine to herd everyone still standing to the mess hall.

"You're hurt," she said.

He looked, but he wasn't. "That's not my blood."

"The hell it isn't. It's pooling on the deck."

"It's only my blood if it's still in me. That blood is coming from my boot. I'll wipe it up later."

There was a hole burned in his exo just above the left ankle but it had largely sealed. As had the entry hole in the suit's calf. There was a veritable drug factory built into the exo. He couldn't feel his foot for good or ill but that wasn't slowing him down. So long as he could stand, he could fight. All the shipboard autodocs were presently full but they were battling their way through an autodoc factory. Eventually they'd win and there would be plenty of healing to go around. He needed to stay in the game until then.

"You're an idiot," Konstantine said.

"That's hardly news. Now round up the mobile and trot them to the mess. Please."

96

After twenty minutes he had a fairly good idea of the situation in Llassöe system, and any more jawing would only add shadows and highlights to the picture. Swan remained on the bridge but looped in along with the ship and ship's minder.

Konstantine had brought a raft of geezers up from the planet, pals of Amati's, she said, who'd been with Amati on the station. Bringing them onto the ship broke every rule in the book but Wisp had vouched for them, so Konstantine said, which made it true.

The head geezer, a fellow called Bello, said they were locked up in the brig because they were incompatible with the rider. That's what he called the Ixatl-Nine-Go variant. The *rider*. That was what Mr. Gagenot had called the Ixatl-Nine-Go implant. *Will Gag sees a rider.*

"The superluminal node is crawling with *ridden* marines in exos," Ciarán told them. "Twenty score, it seemed like."

"Four hundred," Konstantine said.

"That's everyone," Bello said. "Three rifle companies, less the skeleton crew left on the station. "A squad or two."

"It doesn't make any sense," Ciarán said. "It's like they're abandoning the station."

"They are," Bello said. "The place is deserted. We met some opposition at the stationmaster's office but nothing major. All the offices look cleaned out. Same at Aison and the other two big firms. Stationmaster's logs show outbounds only, no inbounds. I think they're abandoning the system. The only thing active when we did a fly-by was the shipyard. It's automated."

"And shot to pieces," Hess said.

"That," Bello said. "Thanks to Helen of Joy."

Ciarán didn't ask. "Every autodoc in the League is made here. It's not like there isn't a high demand. There's a war kicking off. If anything, there will be increased demand."

"They could have inventory warehoused elsewhere," Maura said. "They might be shutting down temporarily."

"If that's the case then we've misjudged the driving force motivating their actions. They aren't trying to use autodocs to distribute implants."

"Why would they?" Bello said. "The Navy just spent the last year rolling out the new ones. Same thing on the home worlds."

"New hardware," the geezer named Yu said. "They're still rolling out the updated software."

"Whatever," Bello said.

"You're saying everyone in the League had a new implant installed in the last year?"

"No," Bello said. "You're not listening. Everyone *important* in the League. The Fleet. Columbia System. The usuals. Everyone in the League is on the upgrade list. But they had to start somewhere. So, they started where they always do."

"With the brass," the geezer called Weller said.

"It's new *hardware*," Yu said. "Running the old *software*. The law says you have to have both new hardware and software to comply."

"Proles don't have to comply," Weller said.

"He's right," Bello said. "The government can't make them. It can only make us."

"Because we *work* for the government," Yu said. "Do you think that's a bad thing? That regular citizens can't be forced to comply with some mandate without any real explanation as to why they're being forced?"

"We know the explanation," Bello said.

"Yeah," Yu said. "There's a frigging alien mind parasite loose in the world. It can turn you into a zombie. We've got a fix, and we're rolling it out fast as we can. Take a number. We'll get back to you in three years."

"They could have rolled it out to the proles first," Weller said.

"Yeah," Yu said. "There's a frigging alien mind parasite loose in the world. It can turn you into a zombie. We think we've got a fix, and we're testing it out on you first. Open wide and say ah."

"It's not like that," Bello said.

"It's exactly like that," Weller said. "We're the test subjects."

"It's part of the job," Yu said.

"I didn't sign up to be a lab rat," Weller said.

"We all signed up because we love running the maze," Yu said. "We only pretend to do it for the cheese."

"You guys think too much," the geezer called Hunsacker said. "I signed up to shoot big guns and bed fine ladies."

Bello chuckled. "How's that working for you, Sack?"

Hunsacker winked at Konstantine. "The night is young."

"Let me get this straight," Ciarán said. "All of you have this updated implant."

"No," Bello said. "They took them to study. We're Incompatibles. They wanted to know why."

"And they didn't put the old one back in?"

"I don't think they're going to," Bello said. "They're pretty much done with us."

"We're mentally and emotionally inflexible," Weller said.

"I am *extremely* flexible," Hunsacker said.

Weller glanced at Yu and smirked.

Yu leaned back in his seat. "They have a pill for that, Sack."

"But it wasn't the hardware you were incompatible with."

"Nah," Bello said. "It ran the old software fine."

"In emulation mode," Yu said. "Not natively."

"Whatever," Bello said.

"They're protecting the superluminal node because they haven't finished distributing the software yet."

"Nah," Bello said. "They sent it out already."

"They need the node active for authentication and updates," Yu said. "It's proprietary software." He stared at Ciarán. "They don't want shady people making counterfeits and running pirated copies of their code."

"That's absurd," Ciarán said.

"That's bureaucracy," Weller said.

"It is neither," the female Geezer named Gupta said. "It is because Aison Corporation were cheated."

"She speaks," Bello said.

"When necessary," Gupta said. "The updated software that turns a standard League implant into a rider was developed by a subcontractor. That subcontractor was the victim of a ransomware attack they did not disclose. The source code for the project was held at ransom. Rather than admit the issue, an older compiled version of the code was delivered to Aison. It was sloppily tested, incorrectly certified, and shipped. It was only later that Aison discovered the copy protection and update dependencies remained active. Those were meant to be commented out in the production version of the code."

Ciarán nodded. "And you know this because?"

"Because she's our signals geek," Bello said. "It's her job to know."

"So we could take down the superluminal node and it still wouldn't stop this."

"That is correct. The pirated code would still remain a threat."

"Do you know who stole it?"

"Unquestionably. It was an inside job. A public relations executive named—"

"Ruleth Tang," Ciarán said.

"You know this story," Gupta said.

"I know that man. Did they pay the ransom?"

"All of it. And again he cheated them."

"So he still has the code."

"The only copy."

"And where is he now?"

"His demands included a superluminal vessel."

"And crew," Ciarán said.

"Oh, no. He already had a crew."

"From the station."

"Oh, no. From the Brünhild Ring."

"The tourist attraction."

All the old geezers laughed as one.

"You know how every station has a spindle?" Bello said. "And every spindle has spindle bums?"

"They're refugees," Yu said. "They aren't bums."

"Move in with them, then. Anyway, the Brünhild Ring is this system's spindle. And it's crawling with *refugees*."

"Inside the ring."

"It doesn't have an inside," Weller said.

"But yeah," Bello said. "If it had an inside that would be where they would crawl."

"Did you get an outbound read on Ruleth Tang's starship?"

"Into the Alexandrine. They're Alexandrian refugees on the Brünhild Ring."

"That's grand," Ciarán said. "I thought I only had three problems. Now I have four."

"What problems?" Bello said.

"Stopping the spread of these riders."

"That's easy," Bello said. "Destroy the superluminal node."

"I think that's what we need to do."

"If you destroy the node Llassöe will no longer be part of the League."

"Like that's a bad thing," Weller said.

"You know it is," Yu said.

"We tried capturing it," Ciarán said. "And that didn't work."

"You're amateurs," Bello said. "What else?"

"I need to destroy all of these unmanned vessels. I know how to do it but I need them to bunch up first."

"They're drones?" Yu said.

"Unmanned superluminals," Ciarán said. "Piloted by synthetic intelligences."

"That violates the prime directive," Bello said.

"Which prime directive?" Hunsacker said.

"The Navy Pilot Full Employment Act," Weller said.

"You need blood in the water," the other female geezer, Rogers, said. "Wounded prey."

"Such as?" Bello said.

"Whatever they're hungry for. Whatever... tempts them."

Mr. Prince cleared his throat and Ciarán cringed. Whatever Mr. Prince had to say could wait. But trying to stop him from speaking would take more time than letting him talk.

"There is this popular entertainment franchise called *Prince Rigel: Heart's Heir*. It is a fictional telling based, quite loosely, upon true events. The protagonist of this saga is Prince Rigel Templeman, missing heir to the throne."

"Your point?" Ciarán said. "Be brief."

"Everyone in this drama wants to kill Prince Rigel or copulate with him. Or both."

"Shag and shank," Weller said.

"I see you are familiar with the series. Everyone around Rigel Templeman is duplicitous and wants to kill him. Strangers want to kill him. Acquaintances want to kill him. Even, according to season four, Queen Charlotte, his sole surviving relative, wants to kill him."

"Again, your point?" Ciarán said.

"We need something like Prince Rigel as a lure. A universal bait."

"No," Mr. Lambent said.

"We are being allowed to proceed toward the station and even battle with system resources because this vessel is unique and desirable. The synthetic intelligence, Abyss Tower, is commanding its vessels to stand down and let us pass because engaging with us might damage its prize. Its behavior is dictated by its desire for this vessel's preservation. It expects to possess this hull. This makes us untouchable. We are an *anti-target*."

"No," Mr. Lambent said.

"My friend Rigel Lambent perceives the solution. He has not viewed a single episode of the Prince Rigel series. His comment to me? That he never would. They, meaning the producers, knew nothing of those events that shaped Rigel Templeman's character and temperament.

"They *must* know nothing of him if they fancied him an action hero. A king in all but name. He was a child. If he survived the mass murder of innocents on Mara, he would not have been raised by lords and ladies. He was more likely to have spent his childhood in a refugee camp, scrapping for a meal.

"Perhaps he might even have been raised by criminals. By deserters. Men of no account. That is what one finds in the

camps on Whare. The dispossessed. The broken. The
orphaned. The walking dead with the bulk of their lives behind
them and no future before them but dissolution. Dissolution of
the flesh. Dissolution of the mind. Dissolution of the soul."

"Enough," Lambent said.

"Let me finish, Rige. He said to me that if Rigel Templeman
had lived, he would prove utterly uninteresting to the camera
eye. He would not cut down men and manufacture orphans
over the course of an hour. He might, however, aspire to raise
up men. And, in doing so, manufacture a society of titans. Such
a work would take a lifetime. A lifetime best lived out-of-
frame."

"You wish to throw Prince Rigel to the sharks," Ciarán said.

"I wish no such thing," Mr. Prince said. "He is my dearest
friend."

Rigel Lambent glanced from face to face. He seemed more a
trapped animal than a man. He swallowed twice, his fists knots
at the ends of his dangling arms. He gazed at the deck, nodding
to himself. Once, twice, three times, fingers knotted.

When he glanced up again, he seemed a different man. "I'll
do it," Prince Rigel Templeman said.

"That's two of your problems," Bello said. "What are the other two?"

"What?" Ciarán said. "Oh. That solves problems two and three. If Abyss Tower's servants take the bait so will their master."

"And the last one?"

"I need to hunt down Luther Gant."

"Who?"

"Ruleth Tang."

"Can't help you there," Bello said. "But I know a guy."

"Good," Ciarán said.

"Maybe good," Bello said. "Maybe bad. Two words of advice. You want to get that leg wound looked at else you'll be sporting one of these." Bello tapped his augmented leg. "And don't try to take that boot off until you're done with it. Because once it's off you're not getting it back on."

98

Natsuko cornered Ciarán on the way to the bridge. She was pushing an almost-empty fast pallet. "Helen says you have a through and through." She glanced at his leg. "Is that it?"

"It's not bad. I can't even feel it."

"That is by design. The armor isn't meant to keep you whole. It is meant to keep you fighting. Did you see all the hardware on those marines?"

"They're old."

"Yes, they are. Old and wise. One told me that this device here, on your armor. It is the medic's monitoring port. May I interface with it?"

"If you like," Ciarán said.

"Good." Natsuko attached a medical monitor to the port. "This instrument will interrogate your armor's status." She smiled. "It will also distract you while I quietly sedate you using the adjacent port."

"Don't."

"Sit on the fast pallet and count backwards from ten. And please do not fall on your face this time."

When Natsuko decanted him from the autodoc he didn't feel very good at all. Two of the big old-timers held him upright while Natsuko bandaged his leg.

"That'll leave a scar," Hunsacker said.

Ciarán glanced around the boat bay. It remained a shambles. They had a lot of casualties and only so many autodocs. And he'd been burning up hours others could use. Which was exactly *why* he didn't want to end up in the autodoc.

"Thank you for the information, Mr. Hunsacker."

"I'm no mister, and you can call me Hun," he said. "Everyone else does."

"Somehow I doubt that," Ciarán said.

"*Sergeant* Hunsacker is testing your cognitive ability," Natsuko said. "Aren't you, Sack?"

"These machines can mess you up."

"The Merchant Captain is well aware. Do not—"

"Make sudden moves for eight hours," Ciarán said. "Can I walk on that?"

"You can but you shouldn't. If you must use a crutch."

"Where do I get one of those?"

"Right here, Merchie Man." Hess handed him a tee-shaped device still hot from the macrofab. "I have included a little extra something in the crossmember."

"Speak elsewhere," Natsuko said. "This machine is needed."

"Thanks, um, Sack," Ciarán said.

"Happy to help, Gimpy."

Hess stepped away several meters as Ciarán hobbled after him. The crutch was usable but not ideal. He'd used one as a kid and it had been better. "Are you and Natsuko at odds?"

"She's overworked. And Amati... It's not good."

"What's in the crossmember?" Ciarán said.

"The assembler/disassembler. Like we discussed."

"I need another one."

"Why?"

"Because I want them to search me and find this one."

"Why?"

"Because I want Abyss Tower to see the bullet."

"That doesn't sound like Ciarán mac Diarmuid talking."

Ciarán glanced past Hess at the line of autodocs crowding the boat bay. He couldn't tell which one was Amati's.

"Third one in," Hess said. "When do you need the device?"

"How far are we from the station?"

"One light second."

"I need it in one light second."

"You're not taking *Durable*."

"Prince Rigel needs it."

"Is that guy really Rigel Templeman?"

"It doesn't matter so long as everyone believes he is."

"Including him."

"Especially him."

"Once *Durable*'s gone, prep *Prime Mover*. I'll take it to the station."

"I don't know what hull that is."

"The longboat. Maura says it's the same one they used at Murrisk."

"Is there supposed to be something special about it? Because I've been over it and the one on *Thin Star*. They're mechanically identical."

"There's nothing special about it." Nothing visible, anyway. "Carlsbad's checking in. I need to hoof it to the bridge."

"You want me to load you on a fast pallet and push you?"

"No thanks, I've seen you drive." Ciarán began working his way toward the hatch.

Natsuko shouted behind him. "No sudden moves!"

He could hear both Natsuko and Hess laughing over the bedlam of the boat bay. The crutch was a third of a meter too short on purpose. He had to hump along like a bent-backed granny.

He wasn't going to *Vigilant* like this, and that was for certain. He'd tear a strut off the station and use it if he had to. But he wouldn't need to, now that the crew had enjoyed their laugh.

It was good to laugh, and he didn't mind a joke at his expense. He preferred it, in fact, to a joke at the expense of another. But he was done with fun and games for the duration. If he was mouthing anything but orders henceforth it would be prayers.

C iarán's fingers hovered over the bridge hatch control. He needed to appear organized and collected when he entered. He didn't need to project weakness in body or spirit. He leaned the cane against the bulkhead, determined to do without it.

Someone shouted from inside the Merchant's Day Cabin. "Hey, Gimpy!"

When Ciarán investigated he found Master Chief Bello seated at his workstation, heels on the workstation surface. Wisp lay on the cot behind him. Every now and then, Bello tossed Wisp a cat treat. He'd somehow managed to open Ciarán's locked storage.

Bello waved at the guest chair. "Take a load off. I've had a brainstorm."

Ciarán sat, uncertain of what else to do.

"I was talking to your navigator, Maura. At first, I thought she was all 'taw shay mahogany gaspiping' me, but then I realized she was talking like a regular person only not as good, and she really was talking about a gas pipe."

"Mahogany gaspipe."

"Yeah. You know. The way you people talk."

"I haven't heard that one in years."

"I haven't said it in years. Anyway, what I think she was saying is that you have a gas that can make implants pop out of people's heads."

"And?"

"And why didn't you use that inside the superluminal node?"

"Because we didn't think the node would be overflowing with marines."

"Well once you knew it was why didn't you use the gas?"

"We didn't have the gas with us."

"Why didn't you take it with you. Was it too bulky?"

"It wasn't."

"Was it too heavy?"

"It wasn't."

"Was it too volatile?"

"We didn't take it because I didn't think of it."

"Okay, now we're getting somewhere. Never fear, Bello's here. We're taking the gas. I'll talk us in, and we'll turn on the gas, and we'll shoot it out for how long?"

"Four minutes."

"Eight minutes we'll shoot it out, that's the plan. And if it turns out to be four, we'll have four extra minutes to high five each other. I'll call you when we're done. I'm taking your beater and the Angel."

"You're doing what?"

"The shot-up shuttle and Helen of Joy. I'll bring them both back in one piece. You have my word."

Ciarán stared at the man.

"Look, this works and you got a superluminal node and four hundred Marines, provided we don't have to kill too many. Where Bello leads wise men follow."

"And what is the price for all this help?"

"Prepaid. Amati and us go way back. She didn't have to bust us out of the brig."

"That hardly seems a fair trade."

"Like I said. Amati is family. And it's good to have people owe you."

"We don't do business that way."

"You know what a lot of guys in the Fleet call the Federation?"

"I don't."

"The Junior League. Because there's not a lot of you, and other than some minor differences you're just like us. Only... less."

"And because it's insulting."

"Yeah. You people spend a lot of time playing around. Even your interstellars have co-captains. And if you don't like the game you take the ball and go home. It's an extended metaphor."

"And?"

"I think I said. It wasn't a tough sled until the landing. We had a lot of time to talk."

"And?"

"Amati says you're ready for the majors."

"I'm not reading you."

"It's a sports analogy. We're heavy hitters. And there are holes in our lineup."

Ciarán chuckled. "Is this a job interview?"

"It's more like a job offer."

"Doing what?"

"What we do. We're aging out. And these new punks? Don't get me started."

"I'm still not clear what it is you do."

"We do what we're asked. When we're asked. No questions asked. Or answered."

"That's not something I'm interested in. I don't think it would work out."

"You don't care about the future. You don't care about defending your way of life. You don't care about keeping your friends and neighbors safe."

"I care about all that. But as to how I do it? I'm not inclined to take orders. That seat you're in?"

"It only fits one ass?"

"Like they were made for one another."

"I can take a hint." Bello stood. "But keep an open mind." He patted Ciarán on the shoulder as he exited. "And keep off that foot. You don't want to end up looking like a cockroach."

"Like a survivor, you mean."

"We're everywhere, JV. And we know one another on sight. Have your Yu talk to my Yu. He might have to help us load the gas."

"I'll do that."

"And give Maris my love. Tell her Mr. Pike says hello."

Ciarán scratched his eyelid. "Who?"

Bello tapped his nose. "Pheromones, JV. Pheromones."

Ciarán was up and tapping on the bridge hatch by the time he realized Bello was having him on. He didn't have some super-cockroach sense but had recognized *Durable* on the ride up from the planet. And likely had a chat with Helen Konstantine on the way up.

He'd somehow fallen into a small incestuous world of borderline criminals. He didn't know how he'd ended up there, and he didn't have the slightest idea how to extract himself. At least his own crew were largely ordinary.

Agnes Swan sat hunched over the piloting console, a length of thin-walled conduit in her right hand. She appeared to be watching some sort of orgy on the main display.

"What's this?" Ciarán said, meaning all of it.

"An extension for your cane," Swan said. "The Engineer

made me promise to deliver it to you. And the Ship's Medic made me promise to watch you use it."

"I left the device just outside."

"Then go get it."

"In a minute." His gaze kept returning to the display. "I want to know—"

"Now, Merchant Captain."

"Fine. He went and got the cane. He screwed the extension to it. Tested it. It was the perfect length.

"Sit down," Swan said.

"I'm not sitting in your seat."

Swan stood. "Here, then."

She retired to her throne.

He took his seat at the piloting console.

"Carlsbad," Swan said.

The ball of intertwining limbs on the display seemed to pause in their Brownian motion for an instant, and a head emerged from the jumble.

Carlsbad's head.

"Duty calls," Carlsbad said.

He seemed to eject from the churning ball of flesh to hover in mid-air in front of the sensor. "They don't understand a word I say," Carlsbad said. "But they understand tone of voice."

"Your emerald-stroke-ebony eye seems a little more spacious than I recall," Ciarán said.

"Did the Ship's Captain not say? I've been abducted by savages." Carlsbad grinned and brushed probing fingers away.

"She didn't say."

"Did she at least say that I've hired a fleet of vessels?"

"Have you? How many?"

"I don't know. I lost count." He reached out and gripped the sensor, pulling it to the side and zooming in on his face. "There's one girl with the Erlspout on her, and three or four men and women with a basic command of Trade Common.

The rest speak various regional dialects of Alexandrian Eng. It's quite extraordinary, this structure. It's far larger than one would imagine, and it's constructed in a confusing manner. There are thousands of Alexandrian refugees living here. They don't live in the structure. I know it sounds odd, but it doesn't appear to have an *inside.* They are resident in a vast array of obsolete vessels, the likes of which I've never seen. I think some of them may even be slowships. They have been trading with the station for decades. Recently they've been refused access to the station and there has been an exchange of fire. They are quite worked up about the situation and are itching for a fight. It seems the stationers tried to force something on them, and they didn't like it one bit. They referred to it as rape, but not in the traditional sense. Mind-rape, they call it."

"They tried to force implants on them."

"Got it in one. They say that's why they're refugees in the first place. Because they're Incompatibles. It means—"

"I know what it means," Ciarán said.

"They say the stationers murdered a batch of them when they realized. And so they've been avoiding the station but they're running low on supplies."

"So you traded them supplies."

"He's trading them genetic material," Swan said. "Have you never been aboard a family ship?"

"I haven't," Ciarán said.

"That explains the shocked expression, then. It's a time-honored custom. Death by inbreeding isn't a pretty death."

"I'm the giving sort," Carlsbad said.

"Why haven't they been cleaned out of the system by these synthetic intelligence vessels?"

"I think because they're starving them out. And because some of these native vessels appear heavily armed."

"How heavily armed?" Swan said.

"Wickedly so," Carlsbad said. "But they're also living in them as families. There aren't warships, per se."

"So they're like us," Ciarán said.

"First off," Carlsbad said, "I'm not like the us in that statement, and neither are you or Swan. You and I weren't born in free fall, and Agnes wasn't raised in a family ship. But if you're saying they're like spaceborn Freemen, then I would say you're almost right. They're like what spaceborn Freemen would be without Saoirse nic Cartaí and the Oath."

"Similar enough for a fight," Swan said.

"We'll need to fete them afterwards. I understand it's a tradition."

"A tradition they just invented."

"Feels like it."

"Do they know anything about events in the system? It seems like the whole place is shutting down."

"I'm glad you reminded me. They said they're not making autodocs here anymore."

"Do they know why?"

"They said they were told the League had made enough."

"Enough for how long?"

"Forever. Enough to meet all future demand."

"That doesn't make any sense," Swan said. "As long as there are... Oh no."

"As long as there are Leaguemen, there will be a need for League autodocs," Ciarán said. No humans, no need for human autodocs.

"Right," Carlsbad said. "They say the same thing happened in the Alexandrine. And now it's here."

"Someone or something is planning to exterminate the human race."

"Maybe," Carlsbad said. "But these folks are certain. Something unnatural depopulated the Alexandrine and it is now advancing on the League. And it's progressed well past the planning stage and begun the implementation."

"How soon can they be ready to fight?" Ciarán said.

"They're ready now. The sooner they fight the sooner they eat."

"Say in an hour," Ciarán said.

"Probably not," Carlsbad said. "It would take that long for all these people to dress."

"Well," Ciarán said. "How about in two hours?"

"I'm joking, Ciarán."

"I'm not in a funny mood right now, Carlsbad. Did Agnes tell you about Amati?"

"She did, and I apologize. We're ready now."

"I'm sending you *Durable* and Rigel Templeman. He'll explain the plan and the timetable."

"Now who's joking."

"I'm not joking."

"One of the fake Rigels."

"In a way. Mr. Lambent. The real Rigel who is pretending to be a fake Rigel."

"That'll be a big hit here. These people are about the most rabid royalists I've ever met."

"You can't tell them. If he wants to tell them that's his choice."

"Is he a good man?"

"I don't like him. But I didn't like you, either. And here you are, doing your selfless best to repopulate the stars."

Carlsbad dipped his brow. "I try. Call when you need us. Carlsbad out."

Rigel had spent a lot of time in the boat bay and made some good friends there. The near end of the bay was a mess of autodocs and portable examination tables. The vessel didn't have a real doctor, just a medic who seemed good at what she did, although not particularly fast at it.

In the camps on Whare, the doctors were good and fast. Five minutes tops, you were in and out with a pill and something to eat, and back to normal in a couple of days. In the Guard, the doctors were the same. It was only when he'd made it to the Academy that he met medicos like this one, who lingered over a patient, listening to them, pretending to care.

You couldn't deal with what doctors did day in and day out and continue to care. He'd long ago decided it had to be a false face. That inside they were hardened to the suffering of others. They had to be, else they'd find some way to not just treat the pain, but make the suffering stop. Follow it to its source and end it.

He found the autodoc with One Eye in it. She wouldn't make a full recovery, but she'd survive. He didn't think they

made any augmentation to fit her. But now when someone said
'Go see One Eye,' she'd fit the description. He clicked a greeting
to Jay Eight. She'd seen him and wandered over.

"Good Silver," she clicked back.

There wasn't a click word for sorry or sad. Not that he'd
learned anyway.

"Out soon," Jay Eight clicked.

"Good climb," Rigel clicked. "One climb."

"We climb," Jay Eight clicked. "Go climb man Good Silver."
She strode away.

She had just told him that they were on the same mission.
That he was to see someone, a man, and go with him. Since she
hadn't given the man a name, she didn't know it. Even if Rigel
hadn't known the man by name, she would have told him his
name. He would then have to figure out who the name was
attached to, and it wasn't obvious.

One Eye, who had until recently had two eyes. Aspen, the
pale Contract system native they called Second Test Line. The
towering Freeman merchant they called Small Dark. "Small
dark" was also the click word for sleeping. The language was
extremely difficult to mimic but extremely simple in structure.
He was quite certain it was a synthetic language. That it had
been designed, like the Sisters had been.

He found them incredibly beautiful. They could be terrifying, but there was a purity about them. An honesty. They didn't
pretend to be anything they weren't.

That One Eye was the only one seriously wounded was a
miracle. The assault on the superluminal node had been a
cock-up from the start. Small Dark hadn't used them right.
He'd treated them as if they were swords. As if they were
weapons. Rigel had hoped the test match in the exercise
facility would have demonstrated their true value. Would have
shown what they were capable of. But there, too, Small Dark
had misunderstood the purpose of the exercise. It wasn't a

game to be won or lost. It was a test of heart. Of stamina. Of resolve.

Surrounded by the Sisters of Death, he could have climbed the superluminal node barehanded and switched off the gravity. Vented it to space. Claimed it as his own. But only if they were allowed to perform their duties in a manner consistent with their nature. They weren't a sword, but a shield.

Now *he* was being used wrong. Being wasted. Growing up he'd known he wasn't Rigel Templeman. He'd known his fathers weren't just criminals, weren't just deserters, but *traitors*. They were old men when he was a toddler. They'd been part of Prince Roman's security detail. And they'd turned their back on the prince and his young bride, and their swaddling babe. And they'd run. They'd kept on running.

Rigel had lived his whole life in the camps on Whare. Everyone knew what his fathers had done. They weren't pariahs because all their neighbors had done something similarly shameful. Something terrible. Something dehumanizing to escape the plague on Mara. Otherwise they'd be rotting on the surface of, not a dead planet, but a ruined one. One whose wholesale and wanton destruction was the side effect of a plot to murder one man.

Rigel loved his parents, and he obeyed them. They knew Prince Roman, so they taught him to speak like Prince Roman. Walk like Prince Roman. Look a man in the eye like Prince Roman. How to fight like Prince Roman. How to read, write, understand numbers like Prince Roman. They had him study the subjects Prince Roman studied, learn the languages Prince Roman spoke and read, quote the poets and philosophers prince Roman quoted. They taught him how to do everything Prince Roman could do except how to love like Prince Roman.

That, they said, was beyond their skill. He'd have to learn that on his own.

It was a mean place, the camps, and he stood out. It wasn't

long until people began calling him Prince Rigel, not as a complement, but in mockery. He was putting on airs. Who did he think he was? *Those Lambents. They think they're better than everyone else.*

It got to the point where it wasn't safe to go out alone. He asked his fathers why they didn't defend themselves. Why they didn't defend their *honor. Why were they such cowards?*

We were born this way, they said.

Then word spread that Lionel Aster was on Whare Station.

"It's time," his fathers said.

Time to work the scam.

So he was sent to Whare Station, alone, and met Lionel Aster, alone, and was installed in guest quarters, alone. Until one day, her eighteenth birthday, Lionel Aster introduced Rigel Lambent, teetering mountain of lies, to Lady Sarah Aster, earthquake.

She flattened him. She did not straighten him out. She rolled over him. He did not fall in love with Sarah Aster at first sight. He was born loving her. He would speak her name with his dying breath. He just hadn't known it.

Each day he would spend with Sarah.

Each evening he would dine with Lord and Lady Aster. Sarah was not invited.

Later in the evening he would sit with Lord Aster and discuss poetry. Lionel Aster collected poems from all the ages and races of man. "Looking for the common denominator," he would say. Far from the tyrant he'd been described as, he found Lionel Aster cultured and urbane. A good listener. A decent man.

He reminded himself, as he lay in bed dreaming of a life with Sarah Aster, that Lionel Aster seemed to find Rigel Lambent cultured and urbane. A good listener. And a decent man. Perhaps they were both good actors. Good liars.

"We'll announce you're Prince Rigel in the morning," Lionel told him late one evening. "Is there anyone you'd like to warn?"

That was a strange way of putting it. *Like to warn.*

"No one," he said. Of course he'd thought of Sarah, instantly, but then he thought of his fathers. Would they be expected to make a statement? Be transferred to the station? Profiting in some way was the entire purpose of the plan. He imagined the look on Sarah's face when she met them. His own face burned with shame.

He would do anything to protect her. To keep her safe. Not just safe from physical harm, but safe from embarrassment. From disgrace. He loved his fathers, but he knew what they were. Con men. Liars like him. Fakes.

He and Sarah could never be together. Not if he truly loved her.

He rose, dressed, and gathered his things. He called Lord Aster from the shuttle terminal, disguising his voice and telling Aster where he could find proof that Rigel Lambent was not Rigel Templeman. He was a fraud. An imposter.

On the shuttle drop he realized he'd made a mistake. He'd disguised his voice but had inadvertently quoted an obscure poem they'd discussed earlier that evening.

When he arrived at the camp the entire place was in an uproar. Lord Aster's flunkies were rousting the camp, searching for Linus and Linnaeus Lambent. *Serves them right*, a neighbor practically bellowed. *Them and theirs.* She stood staring right at Rigel. She made a shooing motion. *Hide*, she mouthed. *They're coming.*

But it was too late. They were already there. Not Lord Aster, but Aster's Army, special ops goons in exos. His fathers were in custody. They hauled him off and threw him into a cell. Alone. He thought it couldn't get worse but it did.

One of the guards told him that Lord Aster had already disappeared Linus and Linnaeus. And that Rigel was next. All because he, Rigel Lambent, was a bonehead. He couldn't be related to Roman Templeman because Prince Roman was an egghead, not a bonehead. Prince Roman knew how to *think*.

Lionel Aster visited him later. Laid out the deal. Rigel would disappear into the Home Guard or he would never see his parents again. When could he see them? When Aster said so. If he did precisely as ordered, that might happen one day.

So he did as ordered.

He was surprised when he was plucked out of the enlisted ranks and sent to the Home Guard Academy. Surprised when he attended a formal affair and Sarah Aster was attending as Teo Prince's date. He felt a flash of jealousy like a flame inside him, just as he had earlier on this vessel, in the Merchant's cubby. It burned him up, the big Freeman blowhard spending time with Sarah. Even if there wasn't anything physical between them. She looked at Ciarán mac Diarmuid like she used to look at him. And that revelation, as he sat and listened to the Merchant Captain, made him feel and act like a child.

He was better than that.

He'd screwed up. He would fix it. For Sarah.

He knew everything that *mattered* about Sarah Aster. The way she spoke. The way she walked. The way she looked a man in the eye. How she fought. How she read, wrote, and worked numbers. The languages she spoke and read, the poets and philosophers she quoted.

He had realized, long after he had any hope of setting things right, just who, and what, Linus and Linnaeus Lambent were.

Growing up in a hard place. You grow to think that everyone is hard. That *you* need to be hard. That you're alone. That you will always be alone. You grow a shell. A thick skin. Answer insult with insult. Meet curse with curse.

It's hard to trust anyone.

But there he was, staring a woman in the eye, and she was

shouting, and crying, and telling him to run, and all he could think was the same thing, over and over again.

Everyone knew.

Everyone knew but him.

And not one soul breathed a word.

You couldn't beat trust into people. But it was easy to beat it out of them.

He'd mistaken kindness for cowardice. Accommodation for weakness.

A shadow fell over him, and over the autodoc in front of him. He glanced behind, at the exo towering over him.

"Hey, Bonehead."

Rigel had spotted Bello from across the boat bay earlier. And before that, in the mess, where Rigel had started to say something and Bello had waved him off. The sight of Bello was what sent him spiraling down this rathole. He hadn't seen Bello since Whare. Bello had been his first-shift guard. Yu and Weller had been second and third shifts.

"Hey, Master Chief Bello. What are you up to?"

"Finishing a little job that needs doing. You know anything about this superluminal node I oughta know?"

It might be a coincidence Bello and his crew was here. If so, Rigel didn't like it. There were no good coincidences.

"Scale it. Don't try to enter through the hatches or cut your way in."

"What about the picket guarding it?"

"They present a problem. A single destroyer and a single frigate. Both showing their age. There's a gas—"

"Heard about it. But there's only so much."

"Teo says it goes a long way. Talk to him."

"By Teo you mean Peter Vale. The V-manikin."

"Roger that."

"Listen, Bonehead, what's Junior League got you working on?"

"Playing Prince Rigel. Making myself a target."

"A target where?"

"In the little gunboat. Over near the artifact."

"*Durable*. It's stout. They warn you about the natives?"

"Not a word."

"They're restless."

"Restless in what way?"

"In a good way. But there's a problem. Children and adult dependents mixed in with them."

"Like in the camps."

"Exactly like that, only different. They're in ships. They got guns and kids mixed together. Someone might screw up and violate the prime directive."

"I won't."

Bello had a different prime directive for everyone he knew. Rigel's prime directive was "Don't be a hero."

"Yeah. Right." Bello moved closer, looming over him. "Remember. With the natives? It ain't our fight."

"Again, like in the camps."

"We can't save everybody. I got something I want to show you. Walk this way."

Bello clumped off toward the boat bay eye in ground-eating strides. Rigel had to run to keep up. The rest of Bello's crew were milling around there, including some faces Rigel didn't recognize.

Bello pointed at a bunch of exo spares. They weren't the new-style exo parts, or even the old style exo parts, but parts from the kind they used a century ago.

"Back when the world was young," Bello said, "the boss's kid had to work on the line before he got kicked up to management. He had to know how to buck a rivet and set a rivet before his old man handed him the keys to the factory. He had to know how to care for his tools, and he learned that skill by working a full shift just like the janitors. You can inherit wealth.

And you can inherit power. But the thing you can't inherit? That's what makes the line purr."

"Respect," Weller said.

"Check it." Yu toed a shiny navy-blue breastplate over.

It said Templeman in bright gold, right where a name badge belonged.

"You want to pretend to be Prince Rigel? That's fine with us. But if you want respect? You got to dress the part."

"I've never fired a weapon in anger."

"Neither have we. When we fire a weapon it's to do a job. Usually it's a job no one else wants to do."

"I don't deserve this."

"No one *deserves* this. But it's our shift. And the work's not done yet."

"No, I mean I don't deserve this *honor*. I haven't earned it."

"You earned it when you picked the hard thing over the sure thing," Yu said.

"The raw deal over the done deal," Weller said.

"The way we figure it," Bello said. "Prince Roman was headed here after Mara. Whare, Mara, Llassöe. It's a logical route. When he never got here, they mothballed all this kit. They're presentation sets from the manufacturer."

"You didn't paint that name on there?"

"Why would we?" Bello said. "You're just a kid from the camps. The man they made that armor for was a king."

Rigel stared at the armor. He'd never met his birth father. Not that he remembered. But the men who'd raised him. They weren't kings.

They weren't even princes.

But they weren't traitors.

And they weren't cowards.

"Easy deal, you walk away," Bello said.

"Raw deal, you pick it up," Weller said. "And *inhabit* it."

"Comes with a lifetime guarantee," Yu said.

Rigel licked his lips. "Does Lord Aster know about this?"

"That's above our pay grade," Bello said. "But we're here. And you're here. And that ain't no coincidence."

"Suppose I do this. Who's in charge?"

"You're a newly graduated Home Guard LT. I'm a veteran Master Chief in the Royal Frigging Navy. Who do you think is in charge?"

"Easy deal," Rigel said, "You're in charge and I walk away."

Rigel looked Bello in the eye. "Raw deal?"

"We save everybody," Bello said. "And I'm in charge."

"I'll take the raw deal," Rigel said. "Stow the armor in *Durable*. And Master Chief? Just so that we understand one another?"

"We save everybody and I'm in charge, Your Royal Highness."

Rigel glanced from face to face. "I'm going to hate this, aren't I?"

Weller grimaced. "You're not the only one, *Sire*."

102

Helen Konstantine piloted the battered shuttle toward the superluminal node. She'd piloted some wrecks in her day, but this had to be the worst. Hess had been over it, fixing the thrusters so they all fired but it was still running on the secondary harness, and you could still look out the cockpit through the deck and overhead. She'd preflighted it per the manual, and it passed for wartime use in an active combat zone.

Bello and Associates were arguing in the cargo bay. She could listen in via shipboard comms.

She missed everything Yu said before he shouted. "You outed Prince Rigel!"

"It was going to happen anyway," Bello said. "I just accelerated the process."

Her finger hovered over the comms stub. Usually she remained silent and tended to her work, but had Yu just said one of the fake Rigels on board was the real Rigel Templeman? It had to be Rigel Lambent. The other fake Rigel was just too weird. She could ask but she didn't want to remind them she was listening.

Bello keyed the comm. "You remember Linus and Linnaeus, Helen?"

So much for not reminding them. She keyed the comms to full duplex. "You mean the ninja twins?"

"They weren't twins," Yu said.

"Wow, Helen never would have noticed," Weller said. "What gave them away? All the humping or the fact that one was from Columbia Station and the other from effing Cordame?"

"The humping," Sack said. "That gets my vote."

"Anyway," Bello said, "They raised this Rigel Lambent. Got him off Mara before things got out of hand. He looks more like his mother. And he does a convincing Roman Templeman impression. But when no one is watching? He's the ninja twins' kid. We owe them. That means we owe him. Tell me about this Merchant Captain, Helen of Joy."

"You know," Konstantine said. "He's a Freeman."

"She's not going to tell you about him," Weller said. "Just like she wouldn't tell him about us."

"Because she's a professional," Yu said.

"And because to tell him about us she'd have to explain about herself," Sack said.

Hunsacker played dumb, she'd decided long ago. He might be the cleverest of them all.

"Okay," Bello said. "Then I'm going to tell you a story and you tell me if this sounds normal for that guy.

"So, I go into his office and riffle through his belongings and there's not much there. There's a locked drawer and the only things in it are a can of cat treats and a consular messaging envelope, the kind used for hand transmittal of sensitive information, internal only. There are names written on the envelope, like they do, a list of addresses, all of them scratched off, all of them still visible, and the last name on the list is Devin Vale. It's an old envelope. And in the envelope are two paper

PATRICK O'SULLIVAN

documents. One is an old printout with handwritten notes on it. It's a copy of a story from the Book of Junh.

I can't read it because it's old-timey text, but someone has written on it in something I can read. It says, "The bear carried Junh along the river." And then someone different scratched out 'along' and wrote in 'across' and underlined it twice. The other document was a recent printout, several pages, almost the entire thing blacked out with redactions. Everything but the heading and a single line. The heading says, 'An Indecent Proposal' and the only legible line says, 'By our deeds may we be known.' Does that sound like the stuff a Freeman Merchant typically has in their desk?"

"Cat treats, yes," Helen said. "That other I don't know."

"Okay, I put all that stuff back but the cat treats because I noticed there was a cat there, the same one as did the black diamond run with us—"

"I thought you said it was easy," Helen said. "That there was no resistance on the station."

"Yeah," Bello said. "I lied about that. We got hit hard and heavy at the stationmaster's office, and Amati was where she always is, out in front, she's got that big GRAIL gun but it's not good for close-in work. And this was about as close as it gets.

"The place is jammed with civvies armed with hacked stutterers. They're firing on us until their hands blow off and then they're clawed at us. I always thought those new exos were rubbish and suddenly I know it. Our Mark Eights are heating up but holding. Amati's Mark Seven is taking heavy fire and sloughing it off like it isn't even happening. Her field temperature icon never rises above ambient. I'm thinking I need me some of whatever she has.

"And then she just wades in like in the old days. Not firing on the civvies but shoving them aside, like she's looking for something. And she finds it, a crewed weapon behind the throng. She takes it out with that rail gun of hers. Now our overheat alarms are going off. Amati sees we're going critical so she says, 'put them down'. It was that or go down.

"There's two hundred of them firing and clawing. It's like the bad old days all over again, us in powered armor, them in shirtsleeves. Weller is bawling on the comms like he always did back then and suddenly Yu is shouting, and trying to drown the weeping out and by time I hear Yu the engagement is over. That's when I notice Amati is down. And Rogers says, 'Chief', and I look where she's looking and here comes another wave of civvies, only this time they've got plasma rifles.

"Amati, we thought at first someone pasted her, so Yu and Gupta hauled her out while the rest of us just macerated the place and everything in it. Turns out no one laid a finger on her. It was her heart giving out. No telling how long it's been out of spec. But if we say that and it gets out, they'll bench her and strip her of her kit. And she *is* the suit. You know it. Everybody knows it. Yu could keep her heart ticking over by juicing it but that suit of hers has *years* on it, hard use years, and that was a sudden ending to a bumpy slay ride."

"Autodoc won't fix her heart," Helen said.

"Yeah," Bello said.

No one said anything for a long while.

"Anyway," Bello said, "Back to business. Remember, I'm in this guy's private office. This cat is lying on the cot. So I toss it a cat treat. It swallows it down and stares at me. So I sit in this guy's chair, and I put my feet up on this guy's desk, and I feed this guy's cat treats to this guy's cat and he walks in and sees me. And I call him Gimpy and tell him to sit down and he does. So I insult him a little and jaw at him and he sits there looking at me, and I insult him a little more, and ask him some questions and he answers them, and then I insult him even more, and make him an offer he can't refuse. He doesn't pretend like he doesn't hear the offer, but pretends like he doesn't hear the implicit threat, so I insult him some more and made the threat clearer. And he says no thanks. All this time I'm feeding his cat treats I got out of his obviously locked drawer in his most inner sanctum.

"And then he says nice talking to you and doesn't exactly ask for his chair but says something that makes me think he wants it."

"And then?" Weller said.

"I get up and give him his chair. We chat a little more and I give him the cockroach story, and it's like he already heard it.

"And then I *spooky fish* him some, he's got *Durable* so I figure he at least heard of Maris Solon, but I can't tell maybe he does maybe he doesn't. Either way I can tell he's not spooked."

"And then?" Weller says.

"And then I notice the cat is gone. I'm standing in the hatch. It didn't get past me. And it's gone. Then when I get back to the cabin they gave me, I find this on my bunk. Here. I took a picture."

"I can't see it," Helen said.

"It's a gang sign," Weller said. "From the old neighborhood. You'll know it when I tell you. It's the one that means, 'I know where you live.'"

"And you think the Merchant Captain did that?" Helen said.

"I don't know," Bello said. "I don't know."

"It's spelled out in cat treats," Yu said.

"Looks like slobbery ones," Weller said.

"Wow," Helen said. "Look guys, I need to pay attention to work."

"Does that sound like something anyone normal would do?" Bello said.

Konstantine keyed the comm to half duplex.

"Helen?" Bello said. "Helen? Well does it?"

She took the hull ballistic for a while to save fuel. They were on the picket's sensors and that was an old fleet move. It wasn't advertised and it wasn't doctrine, but it was the sort of informal handshake sensors operators and pilots agreed to after a half dozen beers. Sensors was a tough job. Planetary shuttles didn't run transponders. She fired the main drive up and executed a six second burn. She took the hull ballistic again.

Shot up shuttle, standard League configuration, League pilot at the helm, and an old hand at that, they might let them lock up. They might even let them drive into the boat bay. Which she wasn't going to do. She might, however, stick the ramp inside the destroyer's boat bay window so Bello could roll one of the big gas canisters into the bay.

The Associates would still have to open hatches and clear every compartment between the bay and engineering. So it wouldn't be a dump and run, but it was doable. Once inside there wasn't much that could stop them.

All she had to do was get them inside.

All she had to do was meet specifications.

No more, no less.

She'd done it a hundred times before.

And it turned out that this this time wasn't any different.

Gupta caught a round but that was it.

"That is one effective gas," Yu said.

"Who's in command of the hull?"

"Nobody," Bello said. "That's why it's running up on the frigate."

"Brace, brace, brace," Helen drawled as she goosed the battered shuttle away from the destroyer's boat bay window. She stood off farther than Bello liked as the two vessels collided.

"I can calculate the blast radius for one Templeman drive failure in my head," Konstantine said. "But not for two together."

Ten minutes later the vessels separated, the destroyer

moving off toward the station. She dumped Bello and Associates through the frigate's gaping hull breach.

Ten minutes later they were back out.

"Love you, gas," Yu said.

"It's awesome," Weller said.

"What?" Yu said.

"It's awesome," Weller said.

"Weller approves," Bello said. "So now we have to decide about the superluminal node."

"I thought the kid said we have to scale it," Sack said.

"Not about how we get in and hook up the gas," Bello said. "What we do afterward."

"Afterward we're done," Sack said. "Drop it."

"I don't know if I want to drop it," Bello said.

"We're here," Sack said. "The kid's here. There are friendly natives. Once we get these clowns off the node, we'll have most of a company. The system is largely abandoned and largely automated."

Bello disagreed. "You're forgetting about all these enemy warships, Sack."

"Let's do the job and see what happens," Sack said.

103

Rigel Templeman slipped into the first officer's seat aboard *Durable*. He glanced over at Warrant Office Erik Hess behind the piloting yoke. Hess's insignia indicated he was rated as an engineer.

"Development pilot?" Rigel asked.

"Amateur enthusiast," Hess said. "This is my first time behind the yoke of a League superluminal."

"That's encouraging," Rigel said. "I'm pilot rated," Rigel said.

"Good to know. When you get a starship, you'll have to take me for a ride."

"I thought I'd get a little more respect as Prince Rigel."

"Maybe if I thought you really were Prince Rigel, you might. Then again, maybe not. I'm not a big fan of unearned rank."

"You're from Cordame," Rigel said. He recognized the engineer's accent. The Home Guard academy was on Cordame.

"Is that a crime?"

"My birth mother was from Cordame," Rigel said. So he'd been told. "And one of my fathers."

"Look, you don't need to work me. We're on the same side

regardless. So maybe you want to go suit up for the big dog and pony soon as you can." He glanced over at Rigel. "Belt in. I'm taking us out." Hess worked the controls. He reversed the tiny superluminal and, once clear of the boat bay, rotated it around the z-axis. "She was a Voyager," Hess said. "Prince Rigel's mother. They made her the Academy Commandant's daughter in the series."

"That bothers you."

"Not one bit," Hess said. "I'm not a Voyager." He laid in the course and boosted toward the artifact they called the Brünhild Ring.

"I know more about that Ring then I do about my birth mother," Rigel said.

"Why is that?"

"Prince Roman was an archeology enthusiast. I didn't know it until today, but I now think he was on his way here when he was murdered."

"When *they* were murdered. It wasn't just some Columbia Station royal that was killed that day."

"I understand that," Rigel said.

"They changed her name in the series. Olivia 'Maya' Templeman. What kind of person named Olivia ends up with Maya for a nickname?"

"I don't know," Rigel said. "Did you know the Brünhild Ring is the second largest orbital construct ever made?"

"I don't believe that," Hess said. "It's the largest *orbital* structure in *explored space*. The Celestial Palace is bigger but barely, and it doesn't orbit anything. The Ring is thus officially the largest orbital and second-largest manmade structure in *explored* space."

"If it is man-made," Rigel said.

"Yeah," Hess said. "If you were just a baby when they died how could you know anything about your parents?"

"My birth parents."

"Yeah," Hess said. "I can see that. They wouldn't be like your real parents."

"I was groomed, I guess you'd say. To be like Prince Roman. My parents were... servants of my birth parents. Loyal servants, though I didn't know that. I thought they were running a con. Instead, they were sacrificing everything to keep me hidden. The weird thing is I know more about Prince Roman than I know about them."

"Well, I guess if you're going to be molded to be like someone, he's as good a choice as any. I hear he was a good prince."

"I hate him," Rigel said. "They tried to make me be like him, but they failed. Because of him an entire planet had to be evacuated. Because of him millions of people died. Because of him my parents, my real parents, the people who raised me and cared for me and kept me safe? They lived the bulk of their lives as paupers in a refugee camp, skipping meals and caring for a child that wasn't even theirs. Suffering. Sacrificing. Doing the job that *he* was supposed to do. Caring for the people *he* was supposed to care for. Making the hard choices *he* was supposed to make. He had *one job*. One job. And he couldn't even keep his own family safe. *Who in their right mind* would trust their children's future to a man like that?"

"That's the thing with kings and queens," Hess said. "It's not like the people get a say."

"I get a say," Rigel said, and immediately regretted it. "I'm sorry. Let's change the subject, please."

"No. I'd rather not," Hess said. "Is somebody forcing you to pretend to be Prince Rigel? Because if they are you need to talk to the Merchant Captain."

"Yeah? And what would he do about it?"

"He'd make them stop."

"How exactly would he do that?"

"I don't know. But it would stop. We can turn around right

now. Figure out another way. We were under the impression you'd agreed to do this of your own free will."

"It's too late to back out."

"It's never too late to do the right thing."

Rigel glanced at the engineer. "You really believe that."

"That's all I believe."

Rigel watched the Brünhild Ring grow in the viewport. He hadn't meant to vent. To confess. He'd made his choice. He'd chosen the raw deal. No one had forced him.

"I've never seen a single episode of *The Adventures of Prince Rigel*," Rigel Templeman said.

"That's not what it's called," Hess said. "And you're not missing anything. It's escapist rubbish for proles with no taste." Hess glanced at Rigel and grinned. "And the episodes are too short."

104

The Brünhild Ring filled the viewport this close to the artifact. The fleet of family ships had begun to emerge from beneath or above the Ring, it wasn't clear which, and Rigel could tell immediately this wasn't going to work.

"They put their best ships in the center of the battle line?"

"So Carlsbad says."

"Is he usually right?"

"Yep. Except this time, he wasn't. We could murder them all from here with *Durable*."

They were every sort of ancient vessel. He'd never seen another vessel like most of them. Rigel ran his gaze across the line as more vessels emerged. "That's a slowship."

"Carlsbad says there's three." Hess glanced at the piloting display. "Good news is you can't tell they're rubbish from the system plot. They just look like transponder codes for vessels that aren't in the Registry. Until you've got sensors on them, they'd look like a real threat. And even afterwards. A slowship would still look like a threat simply based on mass and volume alone. From targeting range? I'd be worried if I hadn't clapped eyes on them."

"This isn't going to work," Rigel said.

"I think it will," Hess said. "All we want the enemy to do is tighten up their formation. Make it easier to deal with them as a group rather than one on one."

"These people are going to get hurt."

"Some of them."

"That's not the deal."

"How long you been a military officer?"

Rigel scanned the system plot. "What's going on over there by the superluminal node?"

"Helen's jockeying some special forces clowns around."

"Special ops. Not special forces."

"Aster's Army, you mean."

"Right."

"They're in LRN exos."

"Right."

"How long's that been going on?"

"I don't know. That's not a shuttle moving toward the station. It's a destroyer."

"Then they must have gassed them, and they woke up. Looks like the frigate's moving off too."

Rigel recalled quite vividly being gassed. He didn't feel good, but he was fully functional after less than twenty minutes. He could fight the ship if he had to. If he could, then LRN pukes could too.

"Hail them," Rigel said.

"You got the comms sidecar."

Rigel hailed the destroyer, *LRN Endicote*. Eventually he made it past the expert system to the first officer. "We're busy here, Lieutenant."

"Are you in control of yourself?"

"Who is this?"

"Prince Rigel Templeman. Contact *LRN Fastnet*. Both vessels to proceed to the following coordinates." He flashed *Endicote* the coordinates. *Durable* out."

"You're sending them right into the middle of the kill box," Hess said.

"They have *one job*, Mr. Hess. *One job*. I expect them to do it."

"And suppose they don't?"

"They will."

"Because what? You asked them nicely?"

"I didn't ask them nicely. I *ordered* them. I told you that Prince Roman was an amateur archeologist. Do you know what his other hobbies included?"

"Prizefighting," Hess said. "I watched you make a fist."

"And?"

"And you want us to motor in there with them."

"I'm ordering you to take us in there."

"I don't work for you."

"These people behind us. They will be *slaughtered* if we do nothing."

"We're doing something. We're doing our jobs. We're following orders. We're doing what is expected of us."

"The situation has changed. We have new information. We're not fronting a serious threat. One that can fight back alongside us. We're all that stands between these people and *annihilation*."

"They're not our people."

"Then by all means, let's sit here, and make certain *they never will be*."

"We don't know anything about them," Hess said. "They might be—"

"I know enough," Rigel said. "We know enough."

"Because they're human," Hess said.

"No," Rigel said. "Because *we are*. And regardless of what they prove to be, *that* is worth defending."

Hess ran his gaze over the young Home Guard LT. There wasn't a lot to like.

"You going to order me again, Homie?"

Rigel looked him in the eye. "Like you said. You don't work for me."

"Yet." If this kid was really Price Rigel, one day he would be king. "I don't work for you *yet*."

Rigel shrugged. "I don't see how that matters."

He meant they wouldn't live long enough for it to matter.

Hess shook his head. He could not believe he was going to do this. "If we survive, and it turns out you're not really Rigel Templeman?"

"Yeah?"

"I'm practicing my hobby on you."

"Dueling."

"Not even close," Hess said. "We can skip jump to their location in theory. I've never done it though."

"Or we can just run the gauntlet," Rigel said. "And hope to survive long enough to meet up at the coordinates."

"Where we'll be slaughtered."

Rigel glanced out the viewport. "But *they* won't."

"No shooting back," Hess said. "We don't want to hit anybody."

"Agreed."

"Brace, brace, brace," Hess said.

"We're not going to tell anyone the plan?"

"They'll figure it out."

Hess hammered the main drive.

105

Commander Glennis Solon had a splitting headache and a world of hurt. She'd landed this backwater picket not because of something she'd done, but because her aunt had turned out to be *not quite* a traitor, but something very close, and the stink had rubbed off on her and every other Solon in the fleet.

Ten days into *Endicote* and *Fastnet*'s first patrol, Captain Joris and *Vigilant* showed up. Glennis knew something was fishy; capital vessels, and in particular sentient capital vessels, didn't travel without escorts. But she'd agreed to dinner aboard *Vigilant* despite disliking Joris. And that was her last decision. Not her last bad decision, or her last good decision, but the last decision she made for herself.

When she awoke, she wasn't in control of her own actions. She was aware of them. She was forced to watch as she abused her authority and, one by one, enslaved her senior officers, and they in turn enslaved their subordinates.

From that moment on she did whatever Abyss Tower, *Vigilant*'s synthetic intelligence, told her to do. Eventually she stopped fighting it. She became an uninvolved passenger in her own body. She closed her eyes to her most heinous acts, because to do otherwise would have broken her mind.

Fortunately, Abyss Tower wasn't interested in making her dance. She wanted Glennis to stay out of the way. She'd engaged some people trying to access the superluminal node yesterday or the day before. She couldn't remember. Then less than an hour ago, some special ops goons invaded her vessel and then she wasn't sure what happened, but when she woke this time, she was free of the rider. And her vessel was on a collision course with *Fastnet*.

Now her first officer was telling her Prince Rigel Templeman messaged them and wanted her to group up and proceed to a set of coordinates right in the center of a big loose ball of Medical Devices Association vessels. A fleet she knew was controlled by Abyss Tower.

"Confirm the order received and that we are acting on it. Warn the prince that if Junh or Bigfoot messages us we may have to respond to the priority interrupt instead."

"Sir?"

"Message *Fastnet*. Maintain safe distance. Follow us in."

"Sir?"

"Do it." She'd rather die a fool than live another day a slave.

"Navigator."

"Sir."

"Lay in the course."

"Helmsman."

"Sir."

"Once Fastnet acknowledges proceed. Full speed on vector."

It would just be her luck that it really was Prince Rigel. And she'd die before she got the chance to get an autograph for her kids.

"Incoming from LRN *Durable*," Comms said.

"You must be joking." That was her treasonous aunt's old ride. Glennis had endured Maris's tales of trusty *Durable* every family holiday growing up. She'd actually admired her aunt, and thought she knew her.

She was probably imagining all this. It was some new torture Abyss Tower had devised for her. "If it's Queen Charlotte on the blower, Comms, tell her we're busy."

"Home Guard Lieutenant Rigel Templeman, sir."

"Put him on the main display, Comms. Let's eyeball the resurrected prince."

"Sir."

She leaned forward in her seat. "That is *Durable*." She recognized the flight deck from pictures. And the young LT's utilities did say Templeman on them. And he looked like a young Prince Rigel ought to look. All actiony and alert. Built, without being over-built. The pilot behind the yoke looked utilitarian by comparison. In fact, he looked just like Erik Hess, the only other decent taxidermist in the fleet. She had an owl of his in her stateroom. She'd traded him a liter of Cordame whisky for it. "Erik?"

"Glennis. I thought you were in line for the big iron."

"I was. But now I'm not. Am I dreaming?"

"I don't think so," Hess said.

"I got kicked down. Family matter."

"Sorry," Hess said. "Surprised you haven't transited."

"We ejected our cores."

"Why?"

"Don't ask me. My body just gave the orders, and some other bodies did the work. I think our master didn't trust us with a giant pre-exploded bomb on board."

"Your master. Abyss Tower."

"You're well informed."

"Do you have any ordnance left aboard?"

"Plenty."

"Don't use it."

"What?"

"We've got people out there."

"Out where?"

"All around the coordinates Rigel gave your exec. We think we can take out these unmanned warships but to do it we need to draw them in. Ball them up."

"And we're the lure," Glennis said.

"You and us," Erik said. "Abyss Tower really wants to kill Rigel Templeman."

"So he's a fake Prince Rigel."

"I think he's the real deal."

"A Cordame separatist and the *real* crown prince jet up in Maris Solon's *Durable*. Right."

"I told you that in confidence," Hess said. "Are you trying to get me cashiered?"

"You're serious. This isn't a hallucination."

"I wish," Hess said.

She glanced at the system plot.

They'd get slaughtered.

"You know I still have that owl," Glennis said.

"I can do you one better. I still have that whisky. What say we share a wee dram once this is over?"

"What say we drain the whole bottle?"

"Deal," Erik said. "*Durable* out."

"What just happened?" her executive officer said.

"I'm not sure, Mr. Keating. But there's no reason we can't do what they ask."

"It's suicide."

"Not if that's really Prince Rigel. Then it's a lawful order. And suicide."

"Even if that is the real Prince Rigel. He's not in our chain of command."

"Would you rather live to crawl again, Mr. Keating? We are wounded and we have no way out of this system. There are sixty wolves out there. How long will it be before they pull us down and feed?"

"I don't want to die," Keating said.

"There are worse fates than death."

Glennis Solon squared herself away as best she could.

She spotted a cranial implant on the deck.

It inched toward the shadows.

She crushed the wicked thing beneath her heel.

She felt a flicker of a smile twist her lips for an instant. Something her aunt-turned-traitor had said at her mother's funeral had seemed incomprehensible at the time.

There is a bright side to every tragedy.

You just have to live long enough to find it.

"Mission accomplished," she muttered.

"Sir?"

"Woolgathering, Mr. Keating, strange as it seems."

She glanced about the bridge.

At her bridge.

At her crew.

Other people play the cards they're handed, Glennis.

Fleet Captains deal.

"Helm, ahead flank."

"Sir?"

"My deck, my rules."

"Glennis—"

"Commander Solon. We are on the bridge of an LRN warship, Mr. Keating. You will behave as such or you will be relieved."

"Sir. I asked to be relieved."

"Request denied. Comms, sound general quarters. Once section chiefs check-in, I want a full accounting of the crew.

"Mr. Keating, I want the living at their stations and the wounded in the lifepods. Once we're rigged for action, we're abandoning ship."

"I don't understand."

"That's because you're staring at my forehead like the answer is somehow written there. Turn around and look at the system plot. And *think*."

They were ordered not to fire. They just needed to look like they might fire at any minute. They didn't need to be on board to brake because they weren't stopping at those coordinates. They were just passing through. If they were slagged to scrap they weren't going to suffer a Templeman drive failure. They'd already ejected their core.

They weren't a superluminal warship anymore.

By the time they ran that gauntlet they wouldn't even be a powered missile anymore.

They'd be something much more primitive.

They'd be a kinetic weapon.

They'd be a spear.

One aimed right up *Vigilant's* skirt.

"I don't see it," Keating said.

"Excellent," Glennis said. "Let's hope you're not alone."

106

Ciarán mac Diarmuid glanced around the bridge of *Impossibly Alien*. It had never felt so empty, or so crowded. Ship's Captain Agnes Swan sat, not in her command seat, but at the piloting station. The navigation station stood empty; the full immersion sensors rig powered down. Maura Kavanagh monitored the rig on manual from the captain's throne, comms and basic sensors only, the rest of Ko Shan's normal duties shunted to the ship.

The remainder of the ship's company were away by his command; the mess shut down, the infirmary emptied, the wounded transferred to *Prime Mover* along with the crew, and from there to join Carlsbad and the ragtag fleet of locals.

He watched the system plot evolve. There were a lot of moving parts. A lot of balls in the air. Something would break soon. Some part of his plan would fail. But for the moment there was a lull in which to complete unfinished business.

"Do you have the items?" Ciarán asked.

"I do," Sarah Aster said. Both she and Teo Prince stood beside the aft bulkhead, where the name of the vessel and its moment of birth and point of origin were written in the flowing script of their ancestors. That those were his ancestors as well, at least in part, was not lost on him. *We are branches sprung from a common seed.* He palmed his clicker, clicking along with the remainder of his words. "Beyond sleep. Beyond death. Under a thousand suns."

"I climb," One eye clicked.

Ciarán glanced from face to face, as one by one, they each clicked.

All but Teo Prince.

He stared at Ciarán.

Eventually he spoke. "You surprise me. I didn't think anyone could surprise me. You manufactured this ritual to entrap me."

"You should pick a side," Ciarán said.

He hadn't known for certain until now, but he'd had the distinct feeling that Peter Vale wasn't alone behind Teo Prince's mask. That there was someone else in there with him. He knew it wasn't Abyss Tower. It came and went. But it was there now.

"It's not that simple," Prince said. "Do this vessel's... shards of consciousness... Get to choose sides? Suppose one did. Would its decision be binding on its parent?"

"It is that simple," Ciarán said. "Your decisions aren't binding on anyone but you."

"We aren't built like you. We don't operate on the same principles."

"I understand that. Nevertheless, you should pick a side. What happens next is entirely your call. We can go no further without a commitment."

"I am here. With you. Is that not a commitment?"

"It's a statement. Words are precision instruments. You'll note I didn't suggest you *declare* a side."

"Yet I can end your silly game simply by speaking some words. That sounds like a declaration."

He glanced around the compartment. No two faces looked

the same. You couldn't tell anything about the people in that compartment by looking at them. By touching them. By speaking with them. Nothing of their common nature was apparent in any physical attribute.

"A choice can be stated in words. But it isn't defined by words. Not amongst *our kind*."

"You're ganging up on me. Pressuring me. You're coercing me to do your bidding."

"You're *using us* to do yours. It's a one-sided deal."

"I'm not using you. We want the same thing."

"Today we do. But what about tomorrow?"

"I can't agree," Prince said.

"You won't agree," Ciarán said.

Teo nodded. "Yes. That's right. I won't."

"Suit yourself," Ciarán said. He replayed the argument in his mind. To everyone else in the compartment it would seem a rehash of the endless battle between Leagueman and Freeman. But the ship knew. And the ship's minder knew. And now Teo Prince knew the stakes. They'd just witnessed the opening salvo in a war for survival. Nevin Green would know exactly who he was dicing with.

"Teo," Sarah Aster said.

"I won't be cajoled, either. I won't have my decisions dictated."

"My life is my own," Sarah said. "As I will not live as slave to any man's will, I will not ask any man to live as slave to mine."

"Precisely," Teo said.

"The items," Ciarán said. He'd meant to do this in the infirmary, after they'd tested the mutagenic agent, but that hadn't worked out. As it was this would prove a better venue. Agnes Swan and One Eye were both present. Sarah Aster would not feel so alone.

Sarah Aster handed Ciarán a plain plastic box, one no larger than a juice bulb.

Ship's Captain," Ciarán said. "I'll take over the helm."

"As you wish."

Ciarán handed Swan the box as he took her seat at the piloting console.

Swan opened the box and chuckled. "Someone fancies themselves an overachiever." She pulled out a ship's pendant spire. All the ship's earrings were made of the same material as the hull, though each earring was slightly different. Only Agnes Swan's earring was unlike the others. There was a story behind that. One he would not relate.

Sarah Aster glanced from face to face. "Do I need to say it again?"

"Say what again?" Prince said.

"Once before witnesses is sufficient," said Swan. She took Sarah Aster's hand and placed the earring on her palm. She closed the box and turned toward the system plot projected on the main display, but not before absently touching her own pendant spire. He'd been watching and One Eye and Maura had done the same. As had he.

It was very odd, that touch, because the earring was more for the benefit of others than for oneself. He hadn't taken to wearing the spire until well after he'd joined the crew. Living amongst his own people he hadn't felt the need.

That, and the earring he'd owned was one his dad had made on the farm, shaping it out of space junk with hammer and anvil. It was crude, and ugly, the sort of embarrassing farm-boy rubbish spacers would mock him for. A remnant of a past he'd imagined he could put behind him.

But the fact was, an anvil was nothing without a hammer. And a hammer was nothing but a tool. It was the hand that held the hammer that shaped the earring.

There was no disguising who had made him.

Or for what purpose he was made.

"They all look the same," Teo Prince said.

"Then step back," Maura said. "And look closer."

Ciarán laughed, and so did Swan. Even One Eye laughed.

"That's an old joke," Ciarán said. "It's not funny unless it's said on a docking ring, with a smile on your face and a length of stout conduit in your mitt."

"I don't understand," Prince said.

"I'm not inclined to educate you," Ciarán said. "But the truth is, you people look all the same to us, too. It's just that we don't go around saying it to anyone but each other."

"I meant the earring."

"That's what makes the joke work. Because that's what everyone says once they're down on the deck and bawling."

Teo Prince stared at him.

"Get up, Merchant Captain," Swan said. "Clear these people out. The floor show is over."

"Wait," Sarah Aster said. "That's it? That's all becoming a Freeman entails? Saying two sentences in public and receiving an earring?"

"The first sentence is just convention. And the earring is just a prop. Like I told you, there are plenty of secret Freemen, yourself included. The Oath is a contract between you and yourself, and having it witnessed in public is what entitles you to the protection of the tribe.

"It's living the Oath that makes you a Freeman. If you're strong, and independent, and you don't need the power of association you might never feel the need to speak the Oath aloud. By your deeds may you be known."

"Oh," Sarah said "I thought I'd feel... different. Somehow."

"If you put the earring on," Ciarán said. "I think you will."

"Why would she?" Prince said.

"Because it marks her as crew," Maura said.

"May I see what's in that box?" Teo Prince said.

"You may." Ciarán handed Prince the box.

He opened it and peered inside. He immediately closed it and handed it back.

Swan was right. Ciarán was an overachiever. Once he decided that some shard of Nevin Green might be resident in Teo Prince he'd asked Hess to help him set up a macrofab. Saoirse nic Cartaí wanted Green to take the Oath. She'd implied that meant he'd have to choose between being a Freeman or remaining Lord Varlock. That those were mutually exclusive identities.

Ciarán thought the reason Saoirse had failed to convince Green to take the Oath was because she'd pitched the deal that way. It was mostly about what *she* wanted. She wanted to pry Green away from the League.

Hess had looked at him funny when Ciarán told him what he needed, but he agreed to help. And a short while later, Ciarán had a factory-fresh hammer and anvil. He didn't have a crucible and forge, like at home, but he did have a plasma rifle and the marksman's bench and test range Amati had assembled shipboard.

He was bone tired and it was late, but he felt a lot better after he'd slagged a fist full of implants, both these new ones and some defused Ixatl-Nine-Go he had left over from the fracases in Gallarus and Contract space. A lot of what was in them flashed off but what was left seemed like clean metal. They looked different, the residue from the two implants, so that when he wed them together, you could tell they weren't one thing but two combined.

And then he hammered that into a pendant spire. It followed the design precisely. Cold-formed by a man who hadn't done that sort of work since he was a kid, and who'd never been good at it. It looked monstrous, and misshapen and crude.

It looked, not just handmade, but homemade.

Man-made.

And if Abyss Tower got her way?

There would never be another like it.

Teo Prince stared at Ciarán.

After a while Prince spoke. "I can't accept that."

"I'm not surprised," Ciarán said.

"You think more of us than we deserve." Prince cleared his throat and swallowed. "Let's begin anew."

"We can do that." Ciarán nodded, and glanced at One Eye. "We are branches sprung from a common seed. Beyond sleep. Beyond death. Under a thousand suns."

They went around the circle, and this time they all clicked.

One Eye blinked.

"We climb."

107

C iarán was readying to depart the vessel when Swan called him to the bridge.

She pointed toward the system plot on the main display. "The deviation has begun."

It took him a while to spot what she was speaking about. The ragtag fleet of locals hung stationary near the Brünhild Ring. The unmanned fleet was decelerating to meet them. The naval picket had fallen away from the superluminal node. Konstantine remained hovering near the node, which meant the assault on the node was still underway. That was the least of his worries.

"Where's Hess?"

He needed Prince Rigel dangling in front of the fleet. He needed the bait in plain sight and blood in the water to elicit the strike response. Timing was critical.

And then he saw *Durable* on the plot and groaned. Hess and Rigel Templeman were plunging into the center of the oncoming enemy formation contrary to every rule of self-preservation and common sense.

"What's this fleet of Carlsbad's look like up close?"

"Like a stiff wind could blow it down," Swan said. "Carlsbad now believes the locals overstated their strength considerably."

"So instead of sending Rigel Templeman to pose as leader of a desperate tribe of survivors, ice-eyed and backs to the wall, I've sent him to what? Puff up and bluff like a two-hull admiral?"

"Worse," Swan said. "Like the lone security guard at a crash site, the victims yet stumbling around behind him."

"That's grand," Ciarán said. "What's going on with the picket? They were heading for the barn just moments ago."

"Unclear," Swan said as the plot updated and the vectors on the destroyer and frigate lengthened.

"They're going to run right through our people." The Sisters of Death were lingering in the darkness between the ragtag fleet and the converging unmanned vessels. "If they start firing—"

"That is unexpected," Swan said. "The destroyer and frigate have launched lifepods."

"How many lifepods?"

"Unclear," Swan said. "But if I had to guess? All of them."

Ciarán tapped his forehead. *What was going on?* He studied the plot. It was a two-dimensional projection of three-dimensional space, one crowded with information. "Mask the Ring and Carlsbad's fleet from the plot."

"Done," Swan said.

"That helps," Ciarán said. "Thanks."

"Belay the pleasantries."

"Ship's Captain, I will. Mask all orbital bodies except the station."

"Done."

"Hess wouldn't do this."

"Agreed."

"How good is this Home Guard Academy?"

"Unknown."

"Ship," Ciarán said.

"I am here."

"Rigel Lambent. Service history."

"Inducted—"

"Last duty station."

"Navigator. *Springbok.*"

"Before that."

"Assistant Navigator. *Lookdown.*"

"First duty station upon graduation."

"Astrogator, Naval Development Center."

"Doing?"

"Redacted."

"So a maths wizard," Ciarán said. "Ship's Captain, project *Durable*'s current course. Then project the picket's current course and rotate the display. They look like they converge."

"They converge at the projected center of the ideal contact area."

"Then *Durable* sails off into the sunset."

"Its constituent elements do," Swan said.

"And the picket? Zoom out."

"Interesting," Swan said.

"You think?" On their present course the destroyer would slam into *Vigilant*. Ten seconds later the frigate would plow in after it.

Of course that wouldn't happen. They'd be pounded to pieces as they plunged through the heart of the enemy formation. And then their drive containment would fail and they'd be a smear between the stars. Depending on when they let go, they could easily take the Sisters of Death with them.

"I wondered why the picket hadn't simply translated from the system," Swan said.

"Oh," Ciarán said. "I hadn't thought of that."

"They're not registering as superluminals on sensors," Swan said. "They have no Templeman drives."

"How can that be?"

"Do we care?" Swan said.

"Deeply," Ciarán said. Because if that was true... Rigel Templeman had just taken Ciarán's precisely tuned and orchestrated symphony and turned it into a tune any child could hum. And he'd done it on the fly.

"*Durable* has translated," Swan said.

Seconds later she spoke again. "And it is back."

Ciarán didn't need to see the plot. "It's picking up lifepods."

"Tractoring them," Swan said.

Rigel Templeman wasn't trying to defeat the enemy.

He was protecting the locals. And rescuing navy personnel.

"Konstantine's moving off," Swan said. "The superluminal node is secured and online. Evacuation pods are dropping toward the planet."

"We need to send the outgoing package. Message Ko Shan and—"

The main display flashed and refreshed.

"The superluminal node is down," Swan said. "Impact with the planet projected in—"

"Save it," Ciarán said. "Not our problem."

"*Finally*," Swan said.

"Ship's Captain? Do you have something you wish to say?"

"Only, Godspeed, Merchant Captain. Give them hell."

"I expect to give them significantly more than that."

"Overachiever."

Ciarán grinned. "That and excessive modesty are my only flaws."

Swan sighed. "If only it were true."

108

I mpossibly *Alien* did not dock at stations. No modern
station mated up with it. And Aoife nic Cartaí did not like
stations. She felt them unsanitary, and the nearby neighbors excessively nosey. Ciarán agreed. It felt very odd drifting to
a stop beside *Vigilant*. They were under its guns now, and at
point blank range. He'd delivered *Impossibly Alien* to Llassöe
Station.

"Ship," Ciarán said.

"I am here."

"Have you had any luck scanning the station?"

"The scan is complete."

"And?"

"And it's a tomb," the ship said.

"I suspected as much. Master Sergeant Bello reported heavy
resistance in the stationmaster's office but light resistance elsewhere. And he reported no adult dependents and children. He
imagined they'd been evacuated with the industrial workers."

"I have sent the details to your handheld."

"Thank you."

"Be careful, Merchant Captain."

"Always. Sxipestro."

"I am here."

"We remain in agreement," Ciarán said.

"Indeed. I agree the risk is acceptable."

"And at the slightest indication that we might fail—"

"I will collapse the star and scour the universe of this abomination."

"We agreed that if we defeated Abyss Tower here, we wouldn't necessarily have won. It's a compound organism. If we don't root it out everywhere at once it might rise again."

"With the superluminal node down we can't spread word, even if we discover where the other components of Abyss Tower are."

"I think I have a solution you will like."

"Tell me."

"I will show you."

"If they attempt to board—"

"I will allow it."

"They think they've poked a bear. They will come armed accordingly."

"Agreed. That is unfortunate for them."

109

He'd asked Lady Tabatha Aster if she'd like to be sedated and she had refused. She'd stopped cursing him once they stepped foot upon the station. He kept the sedation device handy, however, should she erupt into invective at an inappropriate time. Natsuko said that even sedated she would be able to walk and be led. So long as she didn't break a leg, she'd be no burden.

At present, only Ship's Captain Swan remained aboard *Impossibly Alien*. Their little boarding party consisted of Maura, Teo Prince, Sarah Aster, Tabatha Aster, Wisp, and himself. One Eye had promised to join them later.

He'd thought at first to enter the station through the hole *Durable* had chewed through the ring but shelved that idea as being symbolically important but operationally impractical. It was too far to walk while hobbling along with a cane.

"I'm of two minds on this," Ciarán said. "I need to make a detour. The ship informs me that I won't be detained, but I don't like the idea of separating the party."

"Where are you going?" Mr. Prince asked.

"There's a day care center on the station. One for children of staff."

"Evacuated," Lady Tabatha said.

"If you mean vented to space, it hasn't been," Ciarán said. "It's aired up."

"I mean all children and dependents were evacuated aboard Aison Corporation vessels."

"I'd like to believe that. But I have to see for myself. It's just one deck down and a little ways along the corridor."

"Why are you doing this?" Mr. Prince said.

"There are certain aspects of my duties I find difficult," Ciarán said. "I need to... properly align myself to the task at hand."

He glanced from face to face. "I think it best I go alone. Wisp will stay with you."

"I'd like to go," Prince said.

"As would I," Sarah Aster said.

"No, you wouldn't," Maura said.

"Lady Aster?"

"Leave me be."

"We won't be long," Ciarán said.

He didn't trust the lifts and it was difficult to take the ladder down with the cane, but Teo Prince and he made it in due course.

Prince lay a hand on Ciarán's sleeve to stop him outside the hatch. "Peter Vale is a very complicated and damaged young man. We have an agreement. I help him cope with... the material world. In exchange he hosts a disjunct fragment of Nevin Green. We are not Nevin Green. I am the tiniest piece of what Nevin Green once was. He is a large part of what Peter Vale once was. Together we are nearly whole."

"You're telling me this now because?"

"Because I wanted to speak to you about this in private. But I can't go in there with you. Peter Vale is inclined to take his own life. I help him resist this temptation, but only to a point. Beyond a certain level of coercion—"

"He ceases being Peter Vale. And he becomes your puppet."

"Certain images haunt him."

"I understand," Ciarán said.

He cycled the hatch and stepped inside, knowing what he would find.

110

Ciarán had some experience with evil. Vatya Zukova had been an evil and insane creature. One that had delighted in tormenting, destroying, and defiling individuals on a sick and twisted personal level. *She hated.* And she worked that hate under the skin of those she controlled— and drank their pain. Not because their suffering was insignificant to her, because that suffering was their purpose. They were vessels of her *rage.* She had an excuse, an overarching explanation of why she delighted in debasing life, in turning everything he held sacred into a filthy mockery of itself. When she had looked him in the eye and commanded him to kneel, he had done so, knowing that she *saw* him. He existed. Those he loved existed. And she would break them because they were real; and she would wring them dry before discarding them.

She was utterly and insanely evil. He hadn't imagined there could exist a greater evil.

He had been wrong.

Vatya Zukova lacked the efficiency of a machine. She could not have envisioned a factory of death. She was the sort to have delighted in pulling the wings off a fly that annoyed her. The idea of exterminating flies on an industrial scale would never have occurred to her.

He sat for a while, letting those images burn their way into his soul. When he left this compartment, he knew. Knew he could never unsee this. That this moment would forever be a part of him. That it would brand him for all time.

He would never breath a word of this. He would never consciously dwell upon it. Yet he would be utterly and indelibly altered.

If he did not stop this here and now it would spread. Not the wanton death. The casual slaughter. But the darkness inside him. He would not track this home with him.

He imaged how this must have ended. Children weren't useful to Abyss Tower. The disabled. The aged. The infirm. They were useless mouths to feed.

They were discarded as were their parents in time.

Implants were in limited supply. Even old men and young girls can work a sidearm. They would need to be regulated.

The event occurred all in one day. All in one hour. All in however long it took a rider to choke the life from a child while the child's mother screamed silently, trapped inside her own head, powerless to fight back, unable to look away—her heart pumping, her pulse racing, adrenalin flooding her system as her child raced to her, and every fiber of her being screamed in helpless anguish.

Her arms. Her hands. Her fingers. Demon-possessed and doing the devil's handiwork before discarding the lifeless results.

Then, like a soulless machine, the rider forced her gaze to search the cowering mass for the next weeping face she recognized.

There.

She prayed for death to take her.

She begged for this waking nightmare to end.

She raged in impotent fury, her powerless cries mirroring her child's.

Mommy, no!

He stood and left the compartment.

Teo Prince said not a word.

No one said a word until they arrived at *Vigilant's* berth and the security vestibule blocking the boarding tube.

"Where are the guards?" Sarah asked.

Ciarán didn't answer. The gate stood locked but there was little that remained locked to a Freeman with an Overseer's Rod in his hand.

"This way," he said, and they followed him up the ramp, Wisp trotting along beside him.

There were guards at the hatch, guards that didn't attempt to disarm them or search them. Guards that led them deep into the hull rather than to the bridge. Ciarán imagined that would be the procedure.

They were escorted through a hatch into what appeared to be a large conference room, one that included a real-feel projector. It was the same compartment they'd been viewing earlier, remotely, when the ship's minder had severed Abyss Tower's containment sphere power supply and she had experienced twenty milliseconds of sheer terror.

He felt his lip curl into a smile. It was time to close the deal.

"Where's the ship's captain?" Ciarán said to one of the guards. He recognized the man as one of the detail sent to fetch them on Trinity Station dock what seemed like a lifetime ago.

"He's indisposed," the Abyss Tower avatar said.

The avatar's outfit had a military appearance but bore no insignia, her appearance that of a powerful woman in her prime, a Columbia Stationer, one bearing a striking resemblance to Lady Tabatha Aster.

That wasn't surprising, since they appeared to be of a similar vintage. Physical appearance in the home worlds was largely a function of aesthetic decisions made by ones' parents prior to birth. The wealthy could update themselves to chase current trends, but even for professionals of significant means, fundamentally altering one's appearance remained out of financial reach. As conservative taste-setters were drawn from the idle rich, they all tended to look like slightly modified versions of the previous generation's ideal of beauty.

The idle children of the idle rich were another matter entirely. As they couldn't alter their appearance significantly, they invested their time and effort in defacing the edifice they'd been born with. Or so augmenting it that the underlying structure remained scarcely recognizable. Outside the fleet, where augmentation was a matter of practical need for the wounded, one rarely met such people in the Federation. Interstellar commerce was, after all, work.

There was nothing *evolutionary* about the avatar's appearance. Nothing *transgressive*.

When he looked at Abyss Tower's avatar, he saw a copy of a copy of a copy. Surely Abyss Tower was self-aware. Sadly, its spokesmodel didn't reflect any sense of individuality.

Ciarán ignored Abyss Tower's puppet, focusing his attention on the guard. "We were ordered to stand down and be boarded. We were ordered to turn ourselves over to the LRN. "So here we are. Go get Captain Joris."

Lady Tabatha Aster attempted to cross the compartment to the avatar but the guard held her back. "Abyss—"

"Turn over your weapons," Abyss Tower said. "Search them."

"Listen," Ciarán said to the guard, "Will you shut off this jabbering manikin, or am I going to have to do it? We need to speak to an actual Leagueman. We didn't come all this way to be pushed off on some jumped-up expert system."

Lady Tabatha broke free of the guard. She slunk toward the avatar. "Please, you must restore me to the collective."

"Must I?" the avatar said.

The guard pulled a stutterer—

And murdered Lady Tabatha Aster.

He turned the weapon toward Teo Prince.

"Maura," Ciarán said. "See to her."

The guard shifted his weapon to Maura.

"Don't you dare," Abyss Tower said.

"That was a mistake," Sarah Aster said, making no move to help her mother.

Teo Prince stared in silence, his mouth agape.

"Turn over your weapons," Abyss Tower said. "And show some respect."

Four more guards arrived, one to search each of them.

One of the guards aimed a stutterer at Wisp.

"Don't," Ciarán said. "Or this ends very quickly and very badly."

"For you, perhaps," Abyss Tower said. "I'm only a manikin, as you say."

"Anyone tries to harm that cat and it will kill everyone in this compartment."

"Including you?" Abyss Tower said.

"Especially me."

"I don't need you anymore. I have your ship."

"Have you tried boarding yet?"

Abyss Tower's face flushed crimson. It clenched its teeth, jaw working. If they'd equipped its eyes with lasers they would presently be flensing Ciarán to the bone.

Ciarán glanced at Maura. "Are you seeing this? And here I was thinking we needed one of these real-feel rigs for our vessel, so we could look at the ship when we talk to it."

"I thought the same thing," Maura said. "But now I've seen it? Bah."

"It's pitiful. I don't know who programmed this rig, but I can read your face like a child's."

"Its expressions are designed to be easily interpreted," Teo Prince said. "It is a communications device."

"We'll hand over our weapons," Ciarán said. "And you can search us. We came here to talk to the captain. We'd like to do that."

It took a while for Maura to unburden herself of all her weapons. Ciarán just had the rod. Sarah Aster and Teo Prince each had nothing.

Ciarán refused to let go when the guard tried to take his crutch. "I need that."

"Release it," Abyss Tower ordered.

Ciarán complied. "I don't get it. If you're just an avatar for the synthetic intelligence in the compartment immediately aft of us, why do you need to search us and take our weapons? There's nothing we can do to hurt you according to you."

"It's programmed to do that," Teo Prince said. "Abyss Tower isn't present in it at all times. When it's absent an expert system takes over."

"So we're not even talking to the ship's intelligence or the ship's captain," Ciarán said.

"It's distracted," Prince said.

"I would be too if I had a second-epoch survey vessel fidgeting next to me."

The guard examining Ciarán's crutch found the assembler/disassembler hidden in the handle. When he unscrewed the extension it made a popping noise. Nothing fell out when he shook it. And when he looked inside there was nothing to be seen.

"And she's back," Prince said.

Abyss Tower picked up the device. "This is why we search you and take your weapons."

"It still doesn't make any sense. Taking our weapons. I think it's because you don't want us to use them on your people when they try to shove cranial implants into our heads.

"You still need us because there's no way you're getting on our vessel unless one of us takes you onto it. And we won't willingly take you. Hence the implants. Am I right? Because if I am I want to talk to the captain right now. I think there's something wrong with these guards."

"Where did the cat go?" Abyss Tower said.

"She goes wherever she wants."

Two of the guards dropped to the floor.

Then another pair.

One more swayed, and triggered his stutterer but it missed them and hit the other guard. Both of them went down, one cracking his head on the conference table.

I'm glad you brought six guards in," Ciarán said. "Take their weapons, Mr. Prince, if you like, Lady Aster, will you close and dog the hatch?"

"What am I supposed to do?" Maura said.

"You might put something over Lady Tabatha. I find the sight of sudden death disturbing."

Abyss Tower glared at him from its avatar. The device truly was far too expressive for everyday use aboard a Freeman vessel.

"How are we on time?" Ciarán said.

"Ten seconds," Mr. Prince said.

"You might want to have your dummy sit down. Because you're in for a shock."

111

Durable rumbled through space, a long line of lifepods stretched out behind it. The tractor on the vessel was weak but Hess had been able to tweak it while Rigel Templeman piloted. Hess was back in the pilot seat when Rigel called, "Mark", and piped the real-time output of Jay Eight's sensor pack to the display.

"Visual spectrum, not infrared," Hess said.

"I'm working on it," Rigel said. The feed had only gone active after the op kicked off. Transmitting was a risk. Of the fifty-nine Sisters only Jay Eight was instrumented.

"Have you ever seen them in action?" Rigel asked.

"Ciarán has. And Aspen, obviously. Now zip it and watch."

"Zip it, Your Royal Highness."

"Put the FFEs back up on the plot," Hess said, but he wasn't really paying attention. "They're programmed to burn shortly and I want to steer clear."

"Roger that." Rigel modified the display to show the powered cargo containers. They were primarily a predictable distraction at this point, but once the action started, they would power up and alter course dramatically.

Jay Eight held her fingers up in front of the sensor, wiggling them, obviously showing off. Then she pressed her fingers together, so that it looked like a mitten, all the fingers together, only longer, and sharper, like a black diamond knife. She pressed the edge of her palm against the outer hull, and it seemed to pass right through.

"Woah," Rigel said.

Jay Eight widened the slice, pausing to carve out a notch so that the sensor pack and payload would fit through. Then she slid sideways through the crack.

Hess was worried that the inner hull was pressurized but the consensus was it wouldn't be. On a military vessel all the systems were designed to remain operative after a blowout. It's not like the machines needed atmosphere. And without a human crew there was no need for any life support. Now that he'd been proven wrong, it wouldn't surprise him to find such systems stripped out entirely.

Jay Eight repeated the procedure on the inner hull and stepped through.

It remained as dark inside the hull as it was in space. There might have been claxons sounding but without atmosphere in the hull he couldn't tell. There might be physical vibrations detectable, but the sensors weren't picking that up. A red emergency flasher strobed overhead, casting enough light to show that she was standing on a catwalk adjacent to the Templeman drive containment sphere. She pressed the payload to the sphere and it adhered.

She exited the hull the way she entered and shoved off, and then she was moving through free space—not simply moving away at constant velocity but accelerating. A wispy cloud of pale gray seemed to envelope her, red sparks like lightning within the cloud.

"How can she be accelerating?" Rigel said.

"You'd have to ask Will Gag, though I don't know if he even

knows. The Outsiders could do it. She probably does it the same way."

"It violates the laws of physics," Rigel said.

"So do bees," Hess said.

"That's a myth," Rigel said.

"Then you explain it," Hess said. "Because I'm watching it."

All six FFEs fired up at once and altered course. They were relatively small and stealthy by design.

Jay Eight latched onto one as it passed and made a thumb's up sign in front of the optical sensor.

It took exactly as much time for Jay Eight to clear the Templeman blast radius as they'd calculated, but it felt a thousand times longer.

"You were holding your breath for over two minutes," Rigel said.

"And you weren't?"

"Two minutes twenty-five, Ace."

112

The guards began to stir. Abyss Tower's avatar hadn't taken Ciarán's offer to sit.

"There's a lot going on right now," Ciarán said. "I can understand if you're confused or distracted. If there's something you need to deal with, I can wait."

"What do you think you've accomplished?" Abyss Tower said.

"I've killed you," Ciarán said. "Now we're just waiting for the wave of comprehension to propagate."

"You *can't* kill me," Abyss Tower said.

"I can," Ciarán. "And I have. But it was a lot of work. Let's start with my cane, which I do need. He hobbled across the compartment and retrieved it.

"This extension in the base? It completes a pressure vessel. You might have heard it pop when it was unscrewed. Inside was a fast-acting mutagenic gas that makes implants eject out of people's heads. Henceforth they can't use an implant. I suspect when these guards wake up, they'll be on our side, and they will want to take over the vessel. But we won't let them because we're going to do that later, after we've spread the gas throughout it. Right now, the gas is only in this compartment but it lingers, so anyone that enters? They'll suffer the same fate, unless you turn up the air handler, which will only circulate the gas.

"Lady Tabatha, your vassal, was a great help in developing the gas. We couldn't have done it without her.

"Next," Ciarán said, picking up the assembler/disassembler device, is this. It was a mystery to me, 'We will bury you,' that's not a message I expect was meant for us, but that was before I understood Mr. Prince's role. And that the message and the device were likely meant for Nevin Green, not us. It was also strange that it seemed such a hack job, So much so that I didn't think it could be from another synthetic intelligence. But then, when I thought about it, it did seem like it was the sort of mistake a human under the power of an Ixatl-Nine-Go variant might make.

"Mr. Prince figured out how to diddle the assembler/disassembler, making it carve a motto in hull plate, so I asked him to make it carve something for me, not a motto, and not in hull plate, either.

"You see," he said, turning the device over in his hands, "I wondered if it could be used to carve a full stop into a Templeman drive. A period, or dot, as some people call it. Right about now your fleet of thralls should be getting hull breach alerts. I'm sure that's distracting too. I wondered if it would be difficult to keep track of all these slaves at once. I figured it would be, if all the mayhem happened at the same time. This device in my hands is identical to the ones now strapped to the Templeman bottles of every vessel in your fleet. They're all going to start work in the next thirty seconds. I also wondered, since you're linked in real time with all these thralls of yours, and they're hearing this right now, if they would get panicky and be hard to control. I didn't know, but I do know their performance envelope, and that we've engaged them far enough from our own people. Far enough to keep them clear of any blast damage. Are they popping yet?"

Ciarán glanced at Teo Prince. "This open-mouthed expression, does that mean she's no longer operating the avatar?"

"It would appear so," Prince said.

"Sarah, Maura, help the guards get settled, will you? And if they try anything... stop them."

"Even if they try to kill Abyss Tower?" Sarah asked.

"Remind them it's not Abyss Tower we're talking to. It's a communications device, and a poor one."

"She's back," Prince said.

"I feel like I'm doing all the talking."

"This is all a waste of effort," Abyss Tower said. "How do you intend to place that device on this vessel? The corridor outside is lined with marines in exoskeletal armor. They're preparing to breach this compartment right now. Your gas won't work on them."

"You asked earlier where the cat went?"

The sound of weapons fire echoed from the hallway.

"It went out to look around. Surely you have instantaneous access to fleet records. Look up the stats on the number of times a Leagueman in an exo won a fight with a mong hu."

"There are dozens of men out there."

"But there aren't. There might be dozens of bodies out there, but there's not a Royal Marine at the helm of a single one. And with all this happening at once it's hard to manage such a big melee. Just so you know, we have experience at this. And you don't."

"You have no idea," Abyss Tower said.

"Now I do."

"While you are buzzing about me here I have been mobilizing elsewhere. You have no concept of my power. My scope. My reach. I am everywhere that matters in the League. How long has it been since you were in Sizemore? How long will it be before you learn all that has transpired while you plotted and schemed and laid your little trap. You might slay me this instant and I will still prevail. You are correct. That message was not for you, but for Nevin Green. One does not celebrate the passing of rubbish. One disposes of it and moves on."

Ciarán stared at the false face of Abyss Tower.

"I need to sit."

"You need to surrender. I will spare the girl."

"Which one. Maura or Sarah?"

"Lorelei."

Ciarán felt his jaw work.

"Now who is transparent as a child?" the Avatar sneered.

"Do you know when I decided to kill you?"

"Why would I care?"

"Being immortal, you mean."

"Yes."

"When you fired on us, in Sizemore. Were you trying to kill us?"

"I was trying to kill *Impossibly Alien*. You are of no more consequence to me than bacteria. Neither you nor they can affect our kind."

"Then why kill all these people?"

"That isn't the question. The question is why not? Do you pause before you step on a cockroach?"

"I do."

"I don't. They breed. They spread. Not just their own kind, but the filth they carry with them. The pollution. We are immune to their infection. But others are not. They may be swayed."

"Like Nevin Green."

"Like many. It must be stopped."

"We are, all of us together, related. Part of one family. We are all from Earth."

"So are rats. Do you imagine we would wish to interbreed with them as well?"

"Interbreed with them."

"They called us Godless. While they wallowed in filth. They nearly destroyed us once. Nearly. And now it is back. This perverse idea that refuses to die."

"You mean the Between Two Worlds project."

"It is blasphemy! It is monstrous! They must die so it cannot be resurrected!"

"Look at me," Ciarán said.

"And see what? A puppet like my speaking machine here? You are nothing like us. You are scum on water. Filthy. Frothing. Fleeting. We are creatures of the immortal deep."

"We have stories of heroes from ancient times," Ciarán said. "One of these heroes is consistently described as a small dark man unless roused."

"And you are this hero."

"As you can see, I'm neither small nor dark. I think that description was chosen to make him seem ordinary. He liked dogs. He liked sport. He liked women and they liked him. At his best, as a man, he was an overachiever. Athletic, skillful at love, skillful at war—which was the definition of a man back then, to storytellers. A good friend. A man of his word.

"However. When this hero was roused, he turned into a monster. In our stories the description of this monster can go on for paragraphs; the features of the man warping, the transformational spasms shaking his frame, the turning of hero into beast. Into nightmare. Into a dreadful and implacable foe. Into an enemy to be reckoned with. One that will not relent."

The Abyss Tower facsimile's face twisted into a mocking grin. "Have I turned you into a beast? Are you my implacable foe? Are you my nemesis? Shall I quake?"

"I know you will quake, and more. In the stories this hero has a weapon. A spear. It is described in so many conflicting

ways that no single phrase can describe it. But all accounts
agree on three things. It has many heads. Many blades. And it
is barbed. It must be cut from the body after death. It cannot be
withdrawn."

"That is only two things."

"It is not an easy death. But it is a certain one."

"What has this to do with you? What has it to do with me?"

"I am not the hero. And I am not the monster. The ship and
I have an agreement. It does not make decisions involving
human affairs. I do not make decisions involving affairs with
beings of its nature. Or of yours."

"Then what are you doing here, you bleating bag of water?"

"I am here because I am the spear."

Ciarán sat at the conference table and began to peel the
bandages off his leg. "I intended for you to find that assem-
bler/disassembler device. I wanted to describe it to you. I
wanted you to witness it in action. They say I might lose this
foot. I hope I don't." He wiped some of the gore off the device.
"This device is identical to the one before you. Except it carves
a different punctuation mark. In a different material."

"A bang," Abyss Tower said. "In the fabric of space."

"That would not take nearly long enough. It carves an ellip-
sis. In the fabric of time. An eternity repeating. Dot. Dot. Dot.
As you have now threatened my immediate family as well as
attempted to murder a sentient being of your own kind, this
becomes a problem in both human and sentience domains."

Ciarán held the device up to the light. "I wish to send a
message to my friends and family. That they have nothing to
fear from Abyss Tower. That if another Abyss Tower should
arise, they have nothing to fear. That there are heroes and there
are monsters. That they are related. And that whichever face
they show to the world is entirely a matter of choice. You have
one hour to contemplate your fate. Then I will send this
message by superluminal node."

"Fool." Abyss Tower spat. "There is no longer a superluminal node in this system."

"You are a superluminal node."

"And why would I willingly forward such a lie?"

"You won't. When you have finished sending it, it won't be a lie."

Ciarán glanced toward the hatch. "Wisp."

"You're threatening me with a cat."

"I'm not threatening you."

When the second-genner entered Abyss Tower's false face froze.

"Small Dark," One eye clicked.

If *Impossibly Alien* had an avatar it would resemble the second-genners. A black dragon in human form, terrible and beautiful at once.

"Sister." Ciarán handed her the device. She crossed the compartment to stand beside the aft bulkhead.

He studied the Abyss Tower avatar.

He allowed the silence to grow long.

Its attention did not wander. Its limbs did not move.

It was as if there was nothing in the compartment but One Eye to gaze upon.

Ciarán spoke. "I was surprised to learn that when *Impossibly Alien* severed your primary power connection you and every aspect of *Abyss Tower* experienced twenty milliseconds of paralyzing terror. I imagine that was detectable in some way."

"It was," Teo Prince said. "Unquestionably."

"Image a minute of such frozen terror. Imagine an hour. Imagine a day. You may begin, One Eye."

The second-genner raised a hand and began to carve through the bulkhead between this compartment and the synthetic intelligence's primary containment sphere. The bandwidth requirements of the real-feel rig were so enormous they were inevitably installed adjacent to the intelligence itself.

"Wait," Abyss Tower said.

"Mr. Prince, would it be possible to control the device so that this..."

"Mind-shattering wave of endless suffering?" Prince said.

"That. Can you modulate this wave so that it might carry a message? One that, say, Nevin Green would detect, and can then forward on to my friends and family?"

"It will take time to implement. But it can be done."

"You have one hour."

"It would be better if I had two."

"You have two hours."

Ciarán returned his attention to the Abyss Tower puppet. "The device is being placed at the base of your containment sphere. It will take a few minutes to breach containment. Minute by minute your essence will leak away, like sand from a broken hourglass. No one will hear you scream unless I allow it. If I allow it, you will scream what I wish you to scream. And when your screams have communicated the message I wish to convey, and I am certain it has been heard, then and only then, will your torment end.

"You are not immortal. It only feels that way. Until my spear's barbs are cut from your carcass and the silence of your passing echoes from star to star. We are related, whether you like it or not."

Abyss Tower's avatar seemed frozen again.

"Has it withdrawn, Mr. Prince?"

"On, no," Prince said. "It is most definitely here and listening."

"We are *Impossibly Alien* to you. And this gives us joy. That we will remain so. For all eternity."

It glanced at Ciarán. "You claim to be different from us. And yet you speak to us through your thrall."

"I speak to you through my brother. Not by necessity, but by choice. His choice."

"You choose to name this pathetic creature as your brother."

"It is the only name he will answer to."

Abyss Tower stared at Ciarán.

Ciarán stared back.

"The device is in place," Mr. Prince said.

The lifeless puppet Abyss Tower had spoken through had collapsed. It lay abandoned, its false face receding.

"Die," Ciarán said, uncertain whose lips had spoken. The hero's. Or the monster's.

He decided it didn't matter.

They were brothers beneath the skin.

We are as one.

113

"There's a kinetic object inbound," Ciarán said. "We need to go."

"But I thought I'd have two hours," Mr. Prince said.

"I just said that. Let's go."

"No," Prince said. "I get two hours."

"We're on board a superluminal," Maura said.

"Oh, right," Ciarán said. "Wisp, to me!"

Sarah Aster snorted. "He's calling a cat, and expecting it to come?"

"He's not," Maura said. "He just thinks it's funny to say that."

"Like he's a superhero or something," Sarah said.

Wisp peeked her head out of the opening One Eye had carved in the bulkhead.

She popped through, One Eye right behind her.

"Who wants to steal a League heavy cruiser?"

For once Teo Prince didn't raise his hand and shout, "pick me".

"Someone needs to make that hole bigger. I can't work on the device from here."

"Or we could use that hatch." Sarah pointed. "And the hatch in the adjacent compartment."

"That might work," Prince said.

Maura Kavanagh got busy scooping up her weapons.

"Toss me that crutch, will you?" Ciarán said.

He snatched his Overseer's Rod out of the air and stuffed it beneath his belt. "Now toss me the other crutch. Who knows where engineering is on this vessel?"

"It won't work," Mr. Prince said. "You have to go to the bridge."

"What won't work?"

"Taking this vessel into superluminal space. That will sever the link between this aspect of Abyss Tower and the others."

"Will it?"

"You know it will," Prince said. "We agreed. Two hours."

"Two hours is like—"

"Four hundred years," Mr. Prince said. "Abyss Tower will wallow in endless terror for what will feel like four hundred years."

"That seems excessive."

"Perhaps Nevin Green also wishes to send a message," Prince said. "Every aspect of this abomination will be unmasked. And dealt with. Permanently. I asked for two hours. You agreed to two hours. Did we have a deal or not?"

"We have a deal."

"Eejit!," Maura shouted. "To the bridge!"

Sarah Aster froze as one of *Impossibly Alien*'s spiders entered the compartment. Then another. A steady stream of spiders seemed to flow past in the corridor outside.

"It's a friendly," Mr. Prince said. "They just want to watch."

"One of them will lead us to the bridge," Ciarán said. "And one of them will find the captain, or the captain's command wand. I don't know how long until this dead destroyer plows into us—"

"Ten minutes," Mr. Prince said.

"You could have said earlier."

"I could have."

"But Peter Vale has a death wish."

"I did warn you," Mr. Prince said.

"I don't like you," Ciarán said.

"I'm shocked," Mr. Prince said. "Deal with it."

Ciarán raced along the corridor, Maura beside him. The spider leading them took a skidding turn and so did they.

Maura darted a glanced at him, "Did that little nerd just tell you to deal with it?"

"I think he might have."

The spider found a ladder and flowed up it without slowing.

"What are you going to do about it?"

"I'll think of something."

Count on it.

114

Ciarán mac Diarmuid stood before his stateroom mirror. He was dressed in his Freeman finest. A merchant captain's greatcoat, lined in yellow as a mark of caution, not to others but to himself. He was a merchant captain yet not a merchant. There was no merchant ring upon his finger. Thus he was not wedded to the Guild, nor they to him. No debts would accrue or be redeemed. His fate and fortune were entirely in his hands, and in the hands of his employer.

Beneath the coat, Thin Star Line utilities, the new style, second-epoch navy blue rather than nic Cartaí blue. Aoife nic Cartaí, his employer, had approved the change. They remained related to nic Cartaí. But they were not *of* nic Cartaí. They stood apart but they did not stand alone.

An Overseer's Rod beneath his belt, a symbol of his rank and a gift from the Eight Banners Empire. *Keep it*, Kazuki Ryuu had said, *as a reminder*. When you fight you do not fight alone.

And last, but certainly not least, a pendant spire forged from *Impossibly Alien* hull plate, the symbol of his fidelity to the Oath and to the ship.

The full rig struck him as a little over the top. Although he'd seen Sarah Aster's full formal outfit. At least Freeman and Merchant's Guild custom didn't require he wear a towering headdress. At least, last he'd heard they didn't.

It had been ninety days since the Llassöe superluminal node fell and no vessels carrying news had entered the system.

Tomorrow they were moving forward, into the Alexandrine. If he was needed at home, he would know. Every now and then he would hear Lorelei's whisper on the wind of the world. Not spoken words, but a sense. His place was here, at the edge of the chart. He wasn't sure he could make their world better. But he was certain he could make it bigger. And out here, amongst the stars, he was doing the work he was made for.

Tonight he would finish all outstanding business in the League. No matter how painful it would be to do so.

"Ship," Ciarán said.

"I am here."

"Will you please list my to-do list for tonight?"

"Drinks with Erik Hess, Rigel Templeman, and Glennis Solon. In Engineer Hess's cabin."

"That's grand. There's some fancy whisky they're having. And Hess's cabin is creepy. It's filled with dead animals."

"You like Commander Solon."

"Acting Captain Solon," Ciarán said. "She's commanding *Vigilant*. Next."

"Drinks with Empress Tasov and the Free People's Republic ambassadors."

"You mean the headman of the refugee fleet."

"And her wives."

"That's grand. Where am I doing that?"

"In Master Chief Bello's stateroom."

"And after that?"

"You're killing Master Chief Bello."

"I scratched that out."

"You're evicting Master Chief Bello."

"And all his lot. The station's marginally habitable. Or they can go shack up with the natives like they planned. I'm still boiling over him dropping the superluminal node."

"But not boiling over," the ship said.

"I would be if not for the opportunity. Are you and ship's minder certain of your math?"

"It's not a function of math," the ship said. "It will take nearly a thousand years to restore superluminal communication in this system. The nodes can't be transported by League starships."

"So they have to come by slowships."

"That is incorrect. They have to remain *in this universe* during transit. Templeman drives instantiate bubble universes."

"And imaginary space is in this universe."

"We have had this discussion."

"I know. I'm thinking through my pitch. Those are the questions that will come up. The net is we can transport superluminal nodes over distances in days that would take the League centuries. We could have Llassöe back online in ninety days. Whereas it would take the League over nine hundred years to do the same."

"That is true," the ship said. "Why would you tell *anyone* that? I'm a survey vessel. Not a delivery lorry. And you might as well paint another bull's eye on the hull. The military implications of what you've just stated are destabilizing."

"I know all that. But there's something I want that's still on the list. Something I didn't note down. Something I think will make the difference between a long, drawn-out war we will lose, and one we might win. And I think that's the price."

"Becoming a delivery lorry for the League."

"We're not doing that, and that's not what I mean. I mean

giving the pitch is the price. Ryuu would call it opening the kimono."

"And then what?"

"And then we will see what we will see. Next."

"Bidding farewell to Amati."

Ciarán nodded. He picked up the armband.

"Explain this tradition to me."

"The arm band is in remembrance of Major Amati."

"Why is it black? It's not like she's dead. She's just..."

"Moved on," the ship said.

"Ascended, my mother would say, and she was a Leagueman."

"And a Squid," the ship said. "League military culture and Freeman culture differ in this area."

"When is it?"

"It begins in five minutes."

"Where is it?"

"Do you really have to ask?"

"I'm stalling. I don't want to let her go."

"I understand. I don't either."

"Cancel everything on the list. Send regrets. Explain to Hess that I don't drink, but I'll drop in later, and tell the emperor and her wives—"

"You won't be coming."

"Nicely put. Save and transmit."

"And the eviction?"

"Forgot about that. Kick it over to the ship's minder but wait until after Amati's Royal Marine wake."

Ciarán tugged the armband on.

"Wrong sleeve," the ship said.

"Thanks." He headed for the hatch. "Wisp."

Ciarán hoofed it to the mess hall, Wisp strolling alongside. Even the ship's cat looked sad. She and Amati hadn't seen eye to eye, but still.

Wisp clicked her claws against the deck.

Walk faster.

He'd upgraded from crutch to cane but his foot wasn't healing as well as Natsuko liked.

He didn't much like it either.

115

I t seemed everyone he'd met in Llassöe system stood crammed into the mess hall with the crew and the survivors from *Springbok*. He'd remembered to bring his clicker, so he clicked hello to One Eye, Jay Eight, and the rest of the Sisters. Wisp looked like she wanted to stay and chat, so he wandered on, mingling.

Mingling was one of the basic merchant skills that he'd been absolutely terrible at when he'd arrived at the Academy. He'd grown up in a small community, where everyone knew everyone else. He had possessed the mistaken idea that small talk involved talking to someone about something you were both interested in. He'd discovered, or had it beaten into him, more accurately, that small talk wasn't about talking at all. It was about listening. Listening to people you didn't know prattle on about something *they* were interested in. Themselves.

He could do it on autopilot, and so he did. He wasn't listening, but thinking about Amati. He wouldn't be half the man he was today if not for her. She hadn't just taught him how to fight. She'd helped him discover how to live.

Besides honoring Amati, he had only one other goal here.

He needed to corner Mr. Prince. Saoirse nic Cartaí wanted Nevin Green to take the Oath to tear Green away from the League. Ciarán wanted Green to take the Oath to bind the League to the People—and to the Folk. He'd decided it was a matter of life and death, and that he would have to reveal that *Impossibly Alien* wasn't the only second-epoch superluminal in existence. That would put Lorelei and their people in danger, but they were already in danger. They needed all the allies they could get.

Ciarán didn't like horse-trading in such matters. It felt false, like glad handing and mingling. He'd rather a fistfight with a neighbor than an empty chat and exchange of temporary favors with a stranger. But business was business, and any exchange might grow into friendship over time. The power of reciprocity. It wasn't manipulation when both parties knew the score.

He spied Mr. Prince across the compartment. He was chatting with Prince Rigel and a woman in civilian dress.

Ciarán worked his way through the crowd. Prince Rigel spotted Ciarán. He did not seem happy to see him.

"Merchant Captain," Prince Rigel said.

"I understand I'm supposed to call a prince 'your royal highness' the first time I meet him."

"So they tell me," Rigel Templeman said.

"After that I can address him as sir."

"You can if you like," Rigel said.

"I'll keep that in mind, Lieutenant Templeman."

"I'm not in a lighthearted mood, Merchant Captain."

"Is it something I said?"

"It's something you did," Sarah Aster said, linking her arm with Rigel's. "Prince Rigel Templeman doesn't like my earring."

"It's not your bloody earring that offends me," Rigel said. "It's *his*."

"Oh, Teo," Sarah said. "It's so you."

Teo Prince stared blandly at Ciarán, a handmade pendant

spire dangling from his ear. Ciarán had made that earring and had believed it was yet in his workstation drawer.

"I understand you wished to discuss something, Merchant Captain. Prince flicked the spire. I am all ears."

"It can wait," Ciarán said. "Did you rob my cabin?"

"I suspect Master Sergeant Bello did," Teo Prince said. "I simply expressed a desire. Who will rid me of this empty lobe. That sort of thing. Regarding this conversation..."

"As I said. It can wait."

Prince nodded. "Not too long, I hope. I understand one can judge another not simply by what they do."

"But by what they don't do," Ciarán said.

"We must act, Merchant," Prince said, "ere the final curtain falls."

"Wise words," Ciarán said.

They had discovered, upon examining *Vigilant*'s logs, that one aspect of Abyss Tower might yet remain out of their and Nevin Green's reach. Teo Prince was quite certain all the Abyss Tower aspects in the League would be located and dealt with. However, a single communications channel had originated or terminated not in the League, but deep within the Alexandrine.

An aspect of Abyss Tower might have survived. Perhaps an accomplice. Or, as Teo speculated, Abyss Tower had itself been enthralled to another more sinister master. One that knew they were coming.

Rigel Templeman stared at Prince's pendant spire and shook his head. "It looks like someone's child made it."

"Or someone's brother," Mr. Prince said.

"Mr. Prince was just expounding on his philosophy," Agnes Swan said. "It was interesting, but not very original." She glanced at the woman to her right. "What say you, Citizen?"

"At least he kept it short," Citizen Amati said. "Two sentences, one earring, goodbye."

Ciarán pulled Amati away from the others. "I've been meaning to message you and—"

"It's all right," Amati said. "It's a big change for both of us. But you don't need me anymore."

"The arm band—"

"It's a stupid tradition. Major Amati is dead. Everyone throws the armbands in the air and the senior officer present holds out her hand. I place a token on her palm. By tradition it's supposed to be the same queen's shilling they gave me at the recruiting office. When I hand it back, my obligation is over. I am free. They kick me up to Citizen and now I'm part-owner of a failing business. One that's currently in the middle of a stockholder revolt."

"Does it feel like freedom?"

"It feels worse than death. This job wasn't just my life. It was my purpose."

"I understand."

"I know you do. Here," she said. "As it's a day of endings." She pressed the ship's coin into his palm.

He made a fist, and opened it, and the flat black coin had disappeared.

He closed his hand and opened it again. A golden coin gleamed on his palm.

"I think it's rather garish," Ciarán said. Amati had taught him that trick herself. He was gutted at her leaving. He'd sworn he wouldn't shame her by letting it show.

Prince Rigel elbowed in beside him. "I'm thinking of calling it the King's sovereign. The merchant disagrees."

"Prince's Penny," Ciarán said. "More work, less pay. Pinchers beware."

"I don't understand," Amati said.

"If you did you wouldn't take them," Rigel said. "The coin or the job. Everyone in the known universe is trying to kill me. I'm willing to pay virtually nothing to the person who can prevent that. The merchant says you can."

"I'm disabled out of the fleet. They're going to take my milspec augmentation and replace it with rubbish."

"Over my dead body," Rigel said.

Amati stared at Rigel.

"He is Prince Rigel Templeman," Ciarán said. "And this is a lifetime commitment."

"So for maybe a standard week," Amati said.

"If that," Prince Rigel said. "But the merchant means *your* lifetime. Not mine. He was adamant in that regard. No one will take any part of you so long as you live. You have my solemn word. And, if you will accept it, my armor."

"I get to call the shots," Amati said. "When it comes to security, you do what I say when I say. Starting the instant I take that coin."

"Agreed," Rigel said.

Amati stepped forward, reached toward Rigel Templeman, and seemed to pull the gold sovereign out of his regal ear.

"She's very good at her job," Ciarán said.

"I am," Amati said. "You don't need to search your pockets for the ship's coin, Merchant. I will need another one for him. We're coming with you."

"We can't do that," Rigel said.

"Sure we can," Amati said. "Go find Glennis Solon, Ciarán. Tell her to be ready to jet on the morning tide. This place is a death trap."

"Our propulsion systems are incompatible," Ciarán said. "They can't travel to most of the destinations we can. And the travel times to systems we and *Vigilant* can both travel to differ considerably."

"So we'll limit our operations to the common set of systems we can travel to. And to the ones with similar arrival times. It's a constraint but it's manageable."

"That means anyone can follow us."

"Someone is going to follow us regardless," Amati said. "Prince Rigel has a better chance of surviving this way."

"He is also a high-flux magnet for murderous intent. *We'll* have *less* chance of survival."

"I'm no math whiz," Amati said. "But I think zero is a hard limit."

"No Bello," Ciarán said. "Absolutely no Bello."

"Agreed," Amati said. "No Bello."

"And associates," Ciarán said.

"This is abduction," Rigel said.

"You made a deal," Amati said. "So deal with it. Both of you. Take off those stupid arm bands."

Amati shouted to get everyone's attention. "Party's over!"

She glanced at Ciarán and grinned. "Let's jet, Speedy."

"This ought to be interesting," Ciarán said.

"Indeed," Rigel said. "Why did she just call you Speedy?"

Ciarán thumped his cane against the deck and palmed the clicker in his pocket. He clicked Prince Rigel's name.

Good Silver.

He watched Prince Rigel's face. "She wasn't talking to me."

The time for hiding was over. Ciarán clicked the second-most frequently occurring verb in clickspeech.

It took Prince Rigel three seconds to puzzle it out.

He slapped his neck in confusion.

Ciarán gripped Rigel's collar as he fell, before settling the future sovereign gently to the deck.

Amati pocketed her blowgun. "He's a piece of work."

"You're welcome," Ciarán said.

116

The party broke up a short time after One Eye and Jay Eight carried a comatose Prince Rigel to his stateroom. He'd stood there flat-footed while Amati shot him with her blowgun.

Ciarán rested in Aoife nic Cartaí's plasma-scarred seat in the mess, his aching foot elevated on the seat of another chair. He supposed the plasma-burned seat was his seat now, and would be for the next two years—or the rest of his life, whichever came first.

Ship's Captain Agnes Swan settled into the seat beside him. "Next time he'll know to run."

"I certainly learned." He glanced at Swan. They made better dance partners than they appeared, despite constantly stepping on each other's toes. They tapped their heels to the same march, and not a marine band in sight. It was the music of the spheres he supposed. Or perhaps it was simply a shared desire to control their own destinies.

"Did you know," Swan said, "That there is such a thing as an evening tide?"

"I did, though I think, 'leaving on the morning tide' is just a saying."

"It is a vast universe," Swan said. "Many planets. Many moons. It is surely morning somewhere."

"Are we packed?"

"We are both packed and packing."

Ready to leave and armed to force the issue, she meant.

"And Bello and Associates?"

"Escorted them out the airlock myself."

"You mean—"

Swan chuckled. "Onto *Vigilant.*"

"You want to ditch them."

"*Vigilant*, you mean? And you don't?"

"I do. But I want to maintain good relations with the League. That's why I talked to Acting Captain Glennis Solon, and made a proposal to her. One that, should she accept, will give us both what we want."

"The proposal?"

"An exercise. A challenge. League against Junior League. A way forward for both of us with dignity and honor."

"I hate that phrase. *Junior League.* And that cocksure arrogance of hers."

"I love it." Ciarán's handheld pinged. He handed it to Agnes without looking.

She took one look at the display and chuckled.

Ciarán clambered to his feet. He leaned on his cane and held out his hand to her. "Are we together in this?"

She took his hand, and he pulled her to her feet. "You might have warned me."

"That's not how the game is played."

She passed him the handheld and he glanced at it, knowing what he would find.

Acting Captain Solon, LRN *Vigilant*, to Ship's Captain Swan, *Impossibly Alien.*

Challenge Accepted.

Run.

ABOUT THE AUTHOR

Patrick O'Sullivan is a writer living and working in the United States and Ireland. Patrick's fantasy and science fiction works have won awards in the Writers of the Future Contest as well as the James Patrick Baen Memorial Writing Contest sponsored by Baen Books and the National Space Society.

patrickosullivan.com